O'MA

by

Ronald Ady Crouch

PUBLISHED BY:

Books We Love
192 Lakeside Greens Drive
Chestermere, Alberta, T1X 1C2
Canada

Copyright 2011 Ronald Ady Crouch

Cover art by Michelle Lee 2011

All rights reserved. Without limiting the rights under copyright reserved above, no part of this publication may be reproduced, stored in or introduced into a retrieval system, or transmitted, in any form, or by any means (electronic, mechanical, photocopying, recording, or otherwise) without the prior written permission of both the copyright owner and the above publisher of this book.

Dedication
To my wife Catherine

Forty-four years ago my fortune cookie said, "One day your dreams will be recognized and rewarded". I have held onto that piece of paper for all these years, wondering when that day would come. Thanks to Jamie Hill and Judith Pitman of Books We Love, (Judith thank you for being so patient). To Dr. Hayla Evans for reading the first manuscript and to my wife Catherine Brown, the real driving force behind the writer ... that day is here.

Chapter One

"Hey, you two, you're going to be late." Rebecca grabbed her husband's briefcase off the kitchen counter. "The school bus will be here any minute, Emma."
George carried their daughter into the kitchen, arms wrapped tightly around his neck, she was still holding on as he lowered her to the ground, her hands sliding across his brown skin. Rebecca handed him the briefcase, laughing playfully as he pulled her close into him, kissing her repeatedly on the neck, her coffee-colored cheeks taking on a delicate red glow. "Come here, my little princess," he said, lifting Emma up with one arm.
"Do I have to go to school?"
"Yes, you do, if you want to be a successful lawyer like your father." Rebecca said, as she helped her husband into his jacket.
"I love you, honey, might be late tonight." The BMW beeped when George pressed the remote. Mother and daughter waved from the doorway as he reversed out of the driveway, the shiny black sports car accelerating quickly up the tree-lined road, the school bus disappearing around the bend in the opposite direction.
"There goes the school bus, you'll never catch it now. I guess I'll have to drive you to school–again. You know Miss Parker-Brown, sometimes I think you deliberately miss the bus just so I can drive you to school."
Emma peeked at her mom through sheepishly lowered lashes. "I'm sorry, Mommy. I didn't really mean to miss the bus. I do like you driving me to school though, because I get to spend more time with you." Opening her eyes wider to sneak a look at her mother's face, she added, "I could stay home and help you today. I promise I wouldn't get in the way. I could help do the housework and make the beds."

A look of skepticism flashed across Rebecca's face. "Make the beds." She chuckled at her ten-year old. "I have a job getting you to make your own bed. Anyway, today I'm meeting my girlfriends at the gym and we're having lunch afterwards."

Emma's face dropped and Rebecca reached out and patted her hair. "When you're older I promise you can come too, how does that sound?"

"Promise?"

"Promise, now come on before we're late getting you to school." Rebecca glanced at her watch. "We've got a bit of time, why don't I do your hair all fancy for you. Not too fancy though, we don't want the boys after you."

"Ugh, they're yucky, I don't want anything to do with them."

"Well, you never know," Rebecca said, parting Emma's hair and starting to braid. "You might meet someone nice like your father one day."

"I'm going to marry him too when I grow up."

"Really?"

"Mommy how come you didn't go on to be a lawyer like Daddy? You're just as clever as he is, even more clever I think."

Rebecca paused in the act of braiding Emma's hair and sighed. "When your father and I first met, he was struggling to get through law school and I had just been accepted. We were very much in love, and we wanted to get married, so I agreed to get a job to help Daddy through law school. Eventually you, my precious, came along and now Daddy has been able to take care of us all financially, so there's no need for me to be a lawyer anymore. I decided to stay home and take care of you instead."

"Mommy when I grow up will I be as pretty as you? My friend Sarah's dad says you should be a model. Her mom says he should mind his own business."

Rebecca rested her hands on Emma's shoulders. "Emma, you are already prettier than I am; how much prettier do you want to be? Being pretty isn't everything. You know what's really important?" she said, smiling at her daughter's reflection in the mirror.

"What's that?"

"Being pretty on the inside. There are a lot of ugly people that are outstandingly beautiful on the inside, Emma, but people don't see the beauty until they get to know that person, don't you ever forget that. Remember, beauty is truly only skin deep. You on the other hand are one of the very lucky people that happens to be beautiful inside and out."

"Just like you, Mommy." Rebecca smiled, shaking her head in amusement.

"Well, I think that just about does it. What do you think young lady?"

"It looks great, Mommy, thank you."

"You're very welcome, now get your lunchbox out of the fridge while I clear up here and then I'll drive you to school." She watched her daughter skipping along the hallway towards the kitchen.

"Mommy."

"What is it, Emma?"

"Daddy's left his BlackBerry on the kitchen table."

"Okay honey, I'll drop it off at his office after I get you to school."

They walked into the triple car garage and climbed into the black Mercedes Benz SUV. Once the overhead door had closed, Rebecca activated the security alarm system and put on her sunglasses. "Put your sunglasses on, Emma, they're in the glove box, you don't want to squint and get wrinkles. That sun's bright today. Looks like it's going to be a nice day." Rebecca drove along the street past a row of other mansions like her own, before merging with the bustling Toronto traffic.

When they reached the school and pulled into the curb, Emma pointed to a car moving towards them. "Look, Mommy, there's Sarah. Her dad's dropping her off and he's staring at you again."

"That man gives me the creeps," Rebecca muttered, "ignore him, and give me a big hug."

Emma leaned across the seat and wrapped her arms around Rebecca's neck. "Okay," Rebecca laughed. "As punishment for missing the school bus this morning, I will pick you up after school."

"Thanks, Mommy, you're the best."

"Yes, and then we can go grocery shopping together."

"Oh no, do we have to? Hannah Montana will be on and I'll miss it."

"Yes, you do have to go with me, and I bet that'll help you remember not to miss the school bus next time. I suppose now I'm not the best mom anymore?"

Emma raised her eyes and smiled mischievously, "Mommy, you are always the best. Even when you're being mean you're still the best mom in the whole world. I love you, always and for ever."

"I love you too, honey, now off you go and have a great day."

"You too, Mommy."

Rebecca watched her daughter skip up the school steps and join her friend Sarah. She saw Sarah's face light up when she saw Emma. The two girls joined hands and disappeared inside the school.

As Rebecca prepared to pull away from the curb, she spotted Sarah's father coming slowly towards her Mercedes. When he came abreast he slowed down and twisted his head to leer at her through the open window. Ignoring him, she pulled quickly away from the curb and into traffic. *Asshole*, she muttered under her breath.

Rebecca merged onto Yonge Street and switched the radio to CBC so she could hear Jim Davis' traffic report.

Westbound 401 is slow due to an accident at Avenue Road, the centre lane is blocked, police, fire, and ambulance are on scene. Avoid this area if you can. Downtown Yonge Street has come to a grinding halt due to a burst water main, other than that things are moving pretty much as usual.

"This is going to be murder." Rebecca flicked off Jim's doom and gloom report and squinted at the lanes of bumper-to-bumper traffic stretching as far ahead as her eyes could see.

"That's just great," Rebecca muttered. "By the time I get there it'll be time to come home." Arriving in front of the building that housed Brown Caldwell and Associates, she discovered that as usual there was no place to park. *I'll only be a minute*, she reassured herself, pulling between the double yellow lines that warned *Loading Only* and hurrying into the imposing building.

Taking the elevator to the fifth floor, she glanced in the wall-to-wall mirror and pushed her hair back from her face. "You'll do," she told herself, straightening her skirt and blouse, and raising an eyebrow at the reflection of an attractive young woman with golden brown skin and deep chocolate eyes.

The bell rang announcing her arrival on the fifth floor and Rebecca approached the reception desk. She stood dangling her husband's BlackBerry at her side and staring at the vacant chair behind the receptionist's desk.

Okay, Suzanne, where are you? Rebecca addressed the vacant chair normally occupied by the cute young blonde who served as her husband's secretary/receptionist. After waiting for several minutes while the desk phone rang and went unanswered, Rebecca decided that enough was enough. *I'm not waiting any longer*. She turned and walked around the desk and straight up to the fancy door leading into George's office.

She reached for the doorknob, preparing to turn it open, when the sound of Suzanne's high-pitched voice, followed by an explosion of giggles reached Rebecca's ears.

"George, you are so naughty. I bet your wife doesn't let you do that to her in the shower." The voice penetrated her brain like an ice pick, and Rebecca's hand went onto automatic pilot.

She yanked the door with all her might, stomped across the floor to the front of the shower and stood directly in front of the shower.

"Not any goddam more he doesn't," she answered the little bimbo's question.

"Rebecca." George poked his head around the shower door. "Wait, please I can explain." He scrambled naked out the door, spraying Rebecca with a stream of water as he made a futile grab for her arm.

Rebecca dropped his BlackBerry and ran.

Collapsing against the wall of the elevator Rebecca sobbed out her heart. Tears streamed down her cheeks, turning her face into a streaky mess of black mascara. In the fifteen minutes it had taken her to ascend and descend in this elevator, her entire life had collapsed. Nothing was the same anymore, and to make a bad situation even worse, the elevator doors opened at the ground floor just in time for Rebecca to catch a glimpse of her Mercedes heading down the street behind a tow truck.

Rebecca raced outside–too late to stop the departing vehicle–and surrendering to the utter futility of her situation, she dropped to her knees on the sidewalk.

"I can't take anymore," she sobbed, and buried her face in her hands.

With her head down and her eyes covered, Rebecca didn't notice the Ford Interceptor police cruiser pull up to the curb and stop beside her. It wasn't until a large shadow crept across the sidewalk that she raised her head and stared up into the face of a very large and very homely police woman.

"Lady, what is your problem?" Constable Alison MacDonald bent over Rebecca and shouted into her ear.

Rebecca knew she should answer, but she couldn't get any words to come out of her mouth.

"It's a man, isn't it?" The police woman demanded. "Some no good son-of-a-bitch man. I'm right, aren't I?"

Rebecca lifted her head and still unable to form words, nodded yes.

George came running out of the building, his suit coat hanging half on his shoulders, his shirt unbuttoned and no tie."

"Darling," he cried, bending over his distraught wife.

"Get away from me." Rebecca screamed and raised her arm to shove him away.

That was enough for Constable MacDonald. With one beefy fist, she grabbed George by his collar, lifted him off the ground, and tossed him aside, discarding him like a rag doll.

"Do you have any idea who I am?" George screeched, picking himself up and rushing at the Officer.

"A jerk probably," replied Constable Alison MacDonald.

"I am a lawyer, a very well paid lawyer and you have just assaulted me. My name is George Parker-Brown. See this building? I own it. I make more in an hour than you earn in a day, probably a week." He was now nose to nose with Constable MacDonald.

Just then another officer pulled his cruiser in behind the Constable's. "Hey, Mister," the newcomer shouted through the window. "You don't wanna go there, trust me."

Constable MacDonald, turned her head and acknowledged the newcomer. "I got it, Anatolli," she said, and turned back to George. "My name is Constable Alison MacDonald," she grasped him roughly by the shoulder. "At the moment you're dealing with the Canadian side of me, and you don't want to experience the Irish side. You can take my word that it will not be pretty."

Back in the cruiser, Constable Anatolli shook his head. He knew the warning signs. The Canadian/Irish speech, followed by the dramatic reddening of the face–now in full bloom. *Too late.* shook his head and sat back to watch.

Constable Alison MacDonald bent down to Rebecca and held out her hand. Numbly Rebecca responded by placing her hand in the Officer's large palm.

"You're not taking my wife anywhere. Do you hear me?" George bent down and shouted so loud that an old vagrant who had been collecting cigarette butts off the sidewalk, stopped to watch as the tall black man clamped a hand down on Constable MacDonald's shoulder.

"Oh, he don't wanna be doing that," the vagrant said to nobody in particular.

In the split second it took George to realize he was gripping muscle and not fat, the Officer's huge fist slammed into his face in a reverse punch, sending him reeling backwards. Loose change exploded out of his pockets when his body hit the ground. The gleeful vagrant dropped to his hands and knees, scooping up the unexpected treasure.

"That's enough, Billy," Constable MacDonald said, after he'd filled his pockets.

The lucky vagrant winked at the Officer and scuttled off in the crowd heading for the nearest liquor store.

"Dispatch, it's Constable Anatolli." The second officer, spoke into his radio phone. "Send an ambulance to my location, some idiot tried to grab hold of Constable MacDonald." There was a pause before the Dispatcher replied. "No, I said an ambulance not a hearse," Constable Anatolli sputtered into the handset. "Hey, Big Mack," Anatolli addressed Constable MacDonald. "I'll clear up here, you go sort the lady out. I'll catch up with ya later."

"Thanks, Mario, I owe you," she called back.

"You don't owe me nothin', sweet cakes."

Constable MacDonald waved a hand at him, then turned to lift her briefcase off the front seat of her cruiser.

"You sit up here," she guided Rebecca to the passenger seat. "Back there ain't no place for a lady like you," she settled Rebecca into the seat. "You just sit there and we'll figure out what we're gonna do with you." Constable MacDonald squeezed herself into the driver's seat next to a still speechless Rebecca and drove off down the street while the crowd of onlookers cheered.

After driving several blocks the Officer pulled up to the curb and turned to Rebecca. "We haven't been introduced," she said giving Rebecca a toothy smile and running her hand through a mass of unkempt red hair, "time we took care of that. My name is Constable Alison MacDonald and you may call me Constable Alison MacDonald. And your name?"

"It's Rebecca. Rebecca Parker-Brown. You can call me Rebecca Brown, Constable Alison MacDonald, and thank you." Rebecca spoke for the first time since she'd lambasted George and then she burst into tears.

"Well, Rebecca Brown, you can call me Alison, and if it's okay by you I'll call you Rebecca. Now, first thing we're gonna do, if that's okay with you, is find us a coffee shop, a quiet table, a good cup of coffee and start to sort out today's mess." The Officer pulled back into traffic and headed in the direction of one of her favorite coffee shops.

"Is there anything you need to do before we get coffee?"

"Oh, yes, I forgot," sobbed again. "I only came downtown because my husband forgot his BlackBerry. When I got to his office there wasn't any parking but I was only dropping it off, so I parked in the loading zone. I rushed inside to give it to his secretary only to find that George was already giving it to her in his office shower." Rebecca's sobs increased in intensity.

"The dirty low down scum-sucking bastard. They're all the

O'Malley's Cottage
Page 12

same, brains permanently in the wrong place." Constable Alison MacDonald slammed the palm of her huge hand against the steering wheel.
 In between gasps of air Rebecca managed to say, "And when I came out my car was being towed away. Oh, my God."
 "What is it?" asked Alison.
 "I left my purse in the car. What am I going to do?"
 "You are definitely not having a good day lady. What kind of car is it?"
 "It's this year's Mercedes SUV, black, license number RPB1."
 "Hold on." The Officer keyed her mike. "Dispatch, it's Constable MacDonald. You have a black Mercedes SUV towed away this morning from outside my previous location?"
 "Wait one, I'll check," replied the Dispatcher. There was a long pause. "Yep, that's right, on its way to the pound as we speak. Marker RPB1, licensed to Rebecca Parker-Brown of Toronto."
 "Thanks, Dispatch. I'll send you a computer message regarding the matter. She looked across at Rebecca. "I don't like to type long messages on the computer when I'm driving. I want you to type in the following message after I type in where it's going, okay?"
 "Okay," replied Rebecca uncertainly.
 "Start typing this ... Phone the tow company and tell them to deliver that Mercedes SUV. Capital ASAP, to the coffee shop at Queen and Bay. Tell them I said so. Exclamation mark. Okay, press the send button. Christ, this traffic's bloody awful. Good job we got AC. You like country and western, Rebecca?"
 "Sometimes."
 "Good, let's put some on and cheer ourselves up. I haven't heard any songs about black women's husbands cheating on them and then having their Mercedes SUV's taken, it's always about

rednecks and pick-up trucks." Alison saw the pained look on Rebecca's face and changed the subject. "That smells like one expensive, but classy perfume you're wearing, lady, what's it called?"

"Dolce and Gabbana," Rebecca replied and then went back to staring blankly at the line of cars ahead.

"Smells good. Write that down for me would you, honey, I'm only used to wearing Old Spice for Men. You see I have five brothers, so growing up I had a regular choice of Old Spice or Brut. I liked the smell of both and it didn't cost me anything. I reckon I could learn a lot from you, Rebecca, about being a lady an' all, I mean."

Rebecca laughed. "And I reckon I could learn a whole lot about self-defense from you, Alison. Are your brothers in the police service?"

"Two are, one's a sergeant, the other's a CFL like me."

"CFL?" Rebecca looked at Alison, a puzzled expression on her face.

"Constable For Life," laughed Alison. "One's a firefighter here in Toronto. The other two are in the military. Infantry. Well, only one is now. My oldest brother, Mark, was killed in Afghanistan last year–blown to pieces by an IED." Alison sucked in a deep breath, exhaling quickly. "We were very close. I still have all his letters." Rebecca was now looking at the Officer, watching a tear rolling down Alison's cheek.

"I'm so sorry, Alison," Rebecca instinctively placed her hand on the Officer's arm, letting it linger there, only removing it when Alison stopped her cruiser in front of the coffee shop and expertly reversed into a parking space.

"Come on, Rebecca, my treat this morning. You never know, one day I might need your shoulder to cry on." Rebecca smiled at her new friend and together they walked inside. "What are you animals staring at?" Constable Alison MacDonald boomed.

"Two beautiful women," said a comedian with a drinker's

nose.

"Her, yes, me, no. I'm ugly enough to know I'm ugly," said Alison. "And if you think I'm beautiful, you've gotta be either, blind, drunk or just plain stupid." The place erupted into raucous laughter. "Okay, Rebecca, what'll you have?"

"A small green tea, please."

"Is that it, anything to eat?"

"No, thank you, Alison."

"Okay. Right, Miss," she said, addressing the young woman behind the counter, "large double-double, small green tea, and an apple fritter. Make that two apple fritters. Oh, and go-cups too please, just in case I get a call and I gotta go, if you know what I mean."

"Oh, I don't need a fritter," Rebecca said.

"Hell, no, they're both for me, girl. I gotta work hard to keep this figure you know."

"They didn't charge you?" Rebecca asked.

"Most places don't charge the cops for their coffee, I guess they look at it as cheap security, besides, if you noticed, the girl wrote down police on the receipt so the owner can claim it on his taxes at the end of the year. Are you going to give me an ethics lecture, Rebecca?"

"Certainly not, Constable Alison MacDonald," Rebecca gave the Officer a tiny smile.

"If I could only get the furniture stores to give out deals like that," Alison said, "then I could get my apartment furnished properly."

"If they have similar deals at Holt Renfrew, let me know. I might even join the police department myself." Feeling better in spite of the situation, Rebecca accepted the double-cupped green tea from Alison and followed her over to the cleaner of two tables set back from the crowd. Alison chose the seat facing the door, and sat down.

Rebecca took the seat facing Alison and smiled. "That confirms it," she said. "Police officers do sit with their backs against the wall, watching the entrance."

"They teach that on day one at Police College. It's an officer safety thing. The other thing you'll notice about cops when they're driving off duty, they drive down the road scanning both sides of the road and looking at the occupants of vehicles. It becomes ingrained. Do you feel like talking about what happened back there?"

"Are you going to charge my husband with assault?"

"Hell, no. To me that ain't an assault, just the price of doing business. I've got him locked up for breach of the peace at the moment. Once he calms down he'll be released, after he gets back from the hospital that is. I guess I'll wait for him to file a law suit with the department. Lord knows I've lost count of how many times I've been sued; thank God the SIU investigations haven't run into double figures yet."

"SIU?" said Rebecca.

"Special Investigations Unit."

"Oh, I see." Rebecca sat, holding her cup with two hands. Finally Alison broke the silence.

"Rebecca, if you want me to charge him with assaulting a police officer, that's no problem, just say the word. Especially if it'll help your situation."

"Oh, no, I wouldn't want to do that to him. I'm in so much shock I can't even think clearly." Rebecca set her cup on the table and looked at Alison. "Why am I telling you all this? You've got far more important things to worry about in this city, I'm sure you don't want to hear about my problems, you've got enough of your own."

"Look, Rebecca, I know one thing, everybody and their dog is going to be giving you advice about what to do, to leave the son-of-a-bitch or to stay and forgive him. But, at the end of the day you

O'Malley's Cottage
Page 16

do what you think is right in your heart. My only two cents worth is this; give yourself some time and distance from him and then, when you've made up your mind, stick to your guns and don't go back on your decision. If you want to get some things out of the house I reckon you'll have three clear hours before he's released from custody." She thought for a moment before adding, "I'll make sure of that."
    "We have a little girl too, that makes the whole thing even worse." Rebecca's eyes glistened with tears.
    "Sure it does, honey, but you'll sort it out. Just remember, much as you feel like you're dying inside, it won't kill you. The sun's still gonna keep coming up in the east and going down in the west and one day it's gonna shine for you again. Not today, not next week or even next month." Alison turned to look out the window. "Oh, and look at that, a ray of sunshine already, here's your car." Rebecca began to rise from her seat. "No, you stay right here, I'll go and sort it out."
    A heavily tattooed man with a shaved head and goatee jumped down from the tow truck, the gleaming Mercedes behind it. Rebecca watched along with the rest of the patrons as the huge man grabbed Alison by the shoulders and kissed her squarely on the lips. Rebecca was even more amazed to see Alison gently touch his cheek afterwards. He placed something in her hand and Alison strode back towards the coffee shop.
    Alison plopped down at the table and Rebecca gave her a look that had the big woman blushing.
    "What?" She sounded for all the world like a teenager caught in the act.
    Rebecca grinned. "Are all tow truck drivers that friendly?
    "That monster out there is my Brian. We've been dating for years, and no, we don't live together. Don't want to spoil a good thing."

O'Malley's Cottage
Page 17

"Not all marriages turn out like mine." Rebecca stifled a sob, Alison reached out and patted her hand.

"I know that. Hell, Brian and I have been engaged for ten years, but as sorry as I am to say this, situations like yours are the reason I'll probably still be engaged when I die. Brian doesn't mind, we both like the fact that it's still fun to go out on a date together."

"He sure seems happy."

"Sure he is. I told him if he wanted to get lucky tonight he better tear up that ticket for your Mercedes. She slid Rebecca's car keys across the table.

"Oh." A worried frown played across Rebecca's face. "I don't mind paying him Alison, I don't want to get either of you into any trouble."

"Rebecca, there were plenty of extenuating circumstances in your case and I am blessed with the power of discretion. No charge, end of story. Now, here's my business card. If you need me, you feel free to call."

"I'd like that, Constable Alison MacDonald." Rebecca stood up beside Alison and when the Constable extended her hand, Rebecca bit her lower lip to keep from crying and then flung herself into Alison's arms.

"Don't cry." Alison hugged the young woman back. "Everything's going to be fine, I promise. You're not the first lady I've met in my long career going through what you're going through, and sadly, you won't be the last."

Rebecca whispered *thank you* against Alison's neck, then like a guilty child, she raced out of the coffee shop and over to where Brian held open the door of her Mercedes.

"Thank you," she said. Brian patted her arm, closing her driver's door.

Brian watched until Rebecca pulled safely out into traffic, then he turned and entered the coffee shop where he accepted two coffees and two apple fritters from the waitress and walked over to join his sweetheart.

Chapter Two

Worried that George might call a friend and try to collect Emma, Rebecca headed straight for the school. En route she dialed her sister, Rachael.

"Hi, it's Rebecca," she choked out before bursting into tears.

"Rebecca," Rachael shouted into the phone. "What is going on for God's sake?"

"It's George. I caught him screwing his secretary in the shower."

"Where are you?"

"I'm just pulling up to Emma's school. I need to pick her up before George sends someone after her."

"You wait right there, I'm on my way."

"No, don't. Meet me at my house. I gotta go."

"Okay. I love you, sis. Don't do anything without calling me first."

Not wanting to walk into the school with all the telltale signs that she'd been crying, Rebecca picked-up her cell and dialed the school secretary.

"Mrs. McGreavy, this is Emma Parker-Brown's mom, we have a family crisis. I'm outside the school now and I need to pick-up Emma."

"All right, Mrs. Parker-Brown, I'll send her out. Just to confirm, you are in front of the school now waiting for her? I don't want to send her out if you're not there yet. Heaven forbid, that would never do. One can't be too careful, especially these days."

"Yes, I'm right out front. Thank you, Mrs. McGreavy, you're very kind."

Ten minutes later Emma emerged through swing doors clutching her lunchbox in one hand and a painting in the other.

"Hi, Mommy." Emma climbed in the front seat and gave her mother a puzzled look. "Why are you wearing those dark glasses mommy? Are you upset? Is that why you came to get me early 'cos you're sad?"

"I can't hide anything from you can I? Yes, Mommy's sad today and I need my little girl to give her a big hug."

"Why are you sad, Mommy?" asked Emma, arms around her mother's slender neck.

"Mommy and Daddy had an argument, that's all." Rebecca glanced over her shoulder and accelerated into a gap that opened up in traffic.

"We need sometime apart because we are so angry with each other at the moment." She made a right turn at the corner and continued her conversation with Emma. "Do you mind if we stay with Aunt Rachael for a little while?"

"Are you and Daddy getting divorced? Michael at school says his mom and dad are getting divorced. What does it mean when you get divorced Mommy?"

"Getting divorced means that mommies and daddies aren't married anymore and they stop living together."

"But they can still be friends though, can't they?"

"Yes, they can still be friends, if they want to."

"Are you going to divorce Daddy?"

Rebecca choked back tears as she tried her best to keep from breaking down completely. *Oh God, what am I supposed to tell her?* struggled to be as truthful as possible without giving her child false hope.

"I don't know what I'm going to do, darling."

"You and Daddy will still be friends, won't you, Mommy?"

"Yes, darling, we'll still be friends."

"And can I still see Daddy whenever I like?"

"Of course you can, baby. By the way, Aunt Rachael is going to meet us at our house to help us pack. And before you ask, I don't know how long we'll be staying with her."

When Rebecca stopped at a red light, Emma held up the picture she'd painted.

"Do you like my painting, Mommy?"

Rebecca leaned over and looked closely. The painting was a house on a hill, with yellow walls and a red roof. All around the house grew red, yellow, blue and pink flowers that were the size of sunflowers. On the grass stood three smiling figures, a man, a woman and a young girl.

"That's you, me, and Daddy."

"It's beautiful." Rebecca gave her daughter a quick hug. "Is that a big dog?" she asked pointing to a figure standing beside Emma in the picture.

"No, silly, that's my pony. I know I don't have one yet, but one day I'm going to get one and I'm going to call him Niki. It's supposed to be a happy picture. The teacher said to paint anything we liked, as long as it was a happy picture. I painted us because we were such a happy family and now it's no good anymore."

Emma burst out crying. Her tears dripped onto the figures causing the paint to smear away their smiles.

"Don't cry, darling." Rebecca rubbed her daughter's back. "We'll get through this, I promise."

They drove the rest of the way in silence. When she reached their driveway, Rebecca pulled in beside her sister's stylish blue Bentley.

Rebecca jumped out of the car and rushed into her sister's arms. "I'm so glad you're here."

"I'm so sorry." Rachael said, holding her sister's head against her shoulder. "Hang on a minute. Let me get Emma settled for you."

Walking around the car, she retrieved Rebecca's keys from the ignition and handed them over to her niece.

"Aunt Rachael is going to talk to Mommy for a few minutes. Why don't you go put your things inside. I'll come and help you in a few minutes."

O'Malley's Cottage

Emma climbed out of the car, turning her head to avoid looking at her mother and ran up the steps to the front door.

"Come on, let's sit down for a minute," Rachael said, leading Rebecca to an ornamental bench overlooking the front garden.

Allowing herself to be led Rebecca collapsed beside her sister and sobbed out the entire story, including George's ill-fated meeting with Constable Alison MacDonald.

"Oh, boy," Rachael smothered a laugh. "George is probably fit to be tied. I feel a law suit coming on."

Rebecca started sobbing again and Rachael cut short her comments. "We aren't going to talk about him anymore," she said, pulling her sister into a hug. "You go get what you need in the way of clothing, personal stuff and anything of sentimental value. Don't forget your jewelry, and your passport. Hurry up, the last thing we need is George arriving on the doorstep to either serve you with papers or blast you with a shotgun."

"Knowing George he'll be begging forgiveness."

"Well, you go get a move on. I'll go and talk to Emma, see if her favorite aunt can get a smile out of her."

Rebecca opened the impressive looking front door and walked into her palatial home, knowing it might be for the last time. Two sweeping staircases led up to the upper levels of the mansion. Rebecca wasted no time in gathering her belongings. She was struggling down the stairs with an overstuffed suitcase when Rachael entered the house hand in hand with Emma.

"Emma, sweetheart, why don't you and Aunt Rachael pack some of your favorite toys and books? I'm sure she won't mind helping you, nothing too big now."

"Can I bring Leopold, Mommy?"

"Of course you can, honey."

"Leopold, who's Leopold?"

"That's Emma's enormous stuffed lion." Emma's face lit up, she ran up to her bedroom to get her favorite stuffed toy.

"Come on, Aunt Rachael," she called back over her shoulder.

Before closing the front door behind them, Rebecca turned to her sister and asked, "Do you think I should leave a note for George?"

"Probably wouldn't be a bad idea. Don't tell him you're staying with me though, the last thing I need is to be getting harassed by your husband. He'll likely figure out you're at my place anyway and come looking. Why don't we drop your car off at Duncan's on the way to my place? He's got a garage attached to his house, you can leave it in there. He's supposed to be calling me tonight from Singapore, I'll let him know the Mercedes in his garage is not a surprise gift from me."

"Will he mind?"

"Not at all, he's like family now."

"And what am I going to drive meanwhile?"

"Don't worry, sis, you can borrow my Mini Cooper."

"Wow, Mommy, that's my favorite car."

"I'm putting you to a lot of trouble, Rachael, are you sure you're all right about this? I mean, I don't want to spoil your relationship with Duncan."

"Look Rebecca, it's not like you're arriving with two dogs, three cats and smelly cat litter. It's only you and Emma for God's sake. Besides, I could do with some company and anyway I won't be there much. Most of the time you'll have the condo to yourselves."

Rachel parked the Bentley in front of her boyfriend's house and waved Rebecca to the driveway while she lifted the garage door.

"This is going to be a tight squeeze," Rebecca said, eyeing the narrow garage interior. "Emma, you better jump out. I don't think we'll be able to open both doors once I'm parked."

"Okay, Mom." Emma jumped out of the car and went to stand by her aunt while Rebecca eased the big car into the garage.

Good job I'm slim, she muttered, as she exited the car and watched while Rachael lowered and locked the garage door.

Rachael unlocked the front door and went inside to check the plants and make sure everything was in order. Duncan's house was immaculate inside and out and his design talents were such that those who did not know him often suspected he was gay.

Rebecca followed Rachael from room to room as her sister made sure everything was in order. "What's Duncan doing in Singapore," she asked.

"He's on a business trip. He wants to get first-hand knowledge of their cuisine before opening another restaurant in Toronto. His company is sending him all over the world on these trips; they plan to open quite a few new restaurants over the next couple of years. I could have gone with him, but my work schedule is so hectic. You would not believe the amount of people sending in their manuscripts since the success of J. K. Rowling, everyone thinks they can write another Harry Potter bestseller and retire a billionaire overnight. If only that were true." Rachael took a quick breath. "Okay, ladies, hop in the Bentley and allow me to chauffeur you to my Harbor Front condo."

"I haven't got a clue what I'm going to do now," Rebecca mused, as they drove through the busy Toronto streets. "I'm going to have to find a job and about the only thing I know how to do anymore is work on the computer. I sure wish I could find something that I could do from home, that way I could still be there for Emma when she gets home from school."

"I have the perfect job for you," Rachael interrupted her sister's musing. "It won't pay a lot, but you can do it all from home and you'll be there for Emma."

"What is it?" Rebecca's interest piqued.

"You can read through some of the millions of manuscripts I receive and help me find the next Charles Dickens of the twenty-first century or the next Harry Potter wannabe."

"Really do you mean it? I love reading."

"The job's yours if you want it. No need to decide right now. Think it over, and when the time's right we'll get you started."

"Thank you so much, Rachael."

"I wouldn't thank me yet, after you get a look at some of the stuff I get you'll probably curse me." Rachael chuckled at her sister's obvious enthusiasm. "Ah, here we are," she said, turning into the entrance to an underground parking garage and stopping in front of the barrier. She lowered her window, punched in the code and waited while the overhead door opened to allow them entry. Rachael drove down the steep ramp into the underground parking lot, expertly maneuvering into her private space. Together the three of them loaded up with the cases, bags, toys and books, piled into the elevator.

"I love this condominium," Rebecca said. "I tried to get George to move here, but he wouldn't hear of it."

* * *

Rachael's condo overlooked the Toronto Harbor. The interior had been designed to focus on the unit's spectacular lake view with furnishings that mixed old and new in tasteful accord. The condo wasn't as cluttered with objects d'art and travelers mementos as Duncan's house, but everything was tastefully displayed and bespoke the fact that no expense had been spared.

"The spare room is all made up," Rachael said. "There's a queen bed with plenty of room for both of you. Why don't you both go on up and get settled. You know where the pool is, in case Emma wants to swim. I'll return a few phone calls and then we'll talk."

"Thank you." Rebecca squeezed her eyes to keep tears from

flowing. "I don't know how I'm going to repay you for this."

"Nonsense. I'm your sister. Besides, I intend to spoil my niece every chance I get."

Rachael bent down and grabbed Emma in a reassuring hug.

Rebecca's hands flew to her face and the tears started flowing in earnest. "Excuse me," she sobbed, "I need to use the bathroom."

"Don't worry, sis," Rachael called after her. "You take some time to yourself. Emma, your swimsuit is in the cupboard in my bathroom. You get changed and grab a towel. The two of us will go swimming and let Mommy have some time on her own."

Emma cast an anxious glance after her mother, and Rachael hurried to reassure the frightened girl. "Don't worry honey your mom's going to be fine. You just go get changed and we'll head out to the pool."

While Emma changed Rachael popped into the spare bedroom and gently ran her hand over her sister's back. "I love you, Rebecca. You and Emma are my family and you're not to worry about anything. Big sister will take care of you and Emma no matter how long that takes. If you want to fix yourself a stiff drink while Emma and I are swimming you just go ahead. If you want to join us you know where we'll be."

"Thank you," Rebecca sobbed rolling over and hugging her sister's neck.

"Aunt Rachael, I'm ready!" Emma sang out, and Rachael hurried out of the room to meet her niece.

"You look just like a little mermaid," she said. "Give me a minute to change and we'll be on our way." True to her word Rachael hurriedly changed into her suit, grabbed an extra towel and was back to grab Emma's hand and lead the way to the pool.

They swam for a good half an hour in an almost deserted pool, and were just about to get out when Rebecca joined them.

O'Malley's Cottage

She waved and dived into the pool to surface right next to Emma.

"Mommy," the little girl called, "watch how long I can hold my breath under water."

Rachael watched the two of them for a couple of minutes and then climbed out of the pool. "I'm sure you've got webbed feet, Miss Emma," she said. "I'll leave the two of you to enjoy the water while I take care of those phone calls."

The telephone was ringing when Rachael entered the apartment. She grabbed a towel off the rack in her bathroom, and rubbed it through her long black hair before putting the receiver to her ear. It didn't take a sixth sense to deduce the name of the caller.

"Rachael, it's George. Have you seen Rebecca?"

"No, I haven't seen her George, but she did call me, she sounded very upset."

"What did she say? I checked with the school, the secretary told me Rebecca picked Emma up from school this morning and now they've both disappeared. I don't know what's got into her lately, she's completely out to lunch. She thinks I'm having an affair with my secretary for God's sake."

"She did mention something about finding you and your secretary in the shower together." Rachael enjoyed the mental image of George squirming on the other end of the phone.

"That's a lie! She's so mistaken. I was in the shower with my secretary, but only to show her where the leak was so she could call a plumber to fix it."

"You had to get naked to find the leak?"

An awkward silence followed.

"My hair got wet when Suzanne accidentally turned the shower on, so I guess when I poked my head out of the door it looked like we were having a shower together."

"I suppose you both took your clothes off so they wouldn't get wet?" Another awkward silence.

"Do you know where she is?"

"No, George, I do not. She told me she was taking Emma

up north for a few days. If I were you I'd wait until she calls you. And another thing, George, my sister is not stupid and neither am I. Trying to play mind games with her is only going to make the situation worse. As a lawyer you should know that the case against you is not circumstantial. Your eyewitness is very reliable; unfortunately for you she just happens to be your wife. Now please don't phone me again, otherwise I'll be forced to call the police and complain that you are harassing me. Do I make myself clear?"

George slammed the receiver down so hard that Rachael had to shake her head to clear the ringing out of her ears.

Rachael sat back in a red leather chair and contemplated her next move.

After a few moments thought, she picked up the receiver and punched out another number.

"Lawton, Epstein and Williams, how can I help you?" A cheerful voice answered her ring.

"Jenny, it's Rachael Brown, could I speak to Sarah Williams please?"

"Oh, hi, Miss Brown. Miss Williams is with a client, can I get her to call you back? Oh, wait a minute, she just walked out of her office, hang on please."

Rachael heard the muffled sound of Jenny's voice, "It's Rachael Brown. She sounds upset." There was a pause and Sarah's voice was on the line. "Hi, Rachael. I haven't heard from the world's best literary agent in ages. How are you?"

"I'm fine, business is great, love life perfect. Look, I know you're busy."

"Not for you, but before we get into your call, how about a lunch date?"

"I'm tied up the first part of the week, but I've had a cancellation Thursday, does that work for you?"

"Perfect. One o'clock at the Italian Waiter, I'll make the

reservations."
"Sounds great."
"Now what's on your mind. Jenny thought you sounded upset."
"Attorney client privilege?"
"Of course, Rachael, as well as girlfriend's secrets."
"I need a good family lawyer for my sister Rebecca. She caught her husband in the shower with his secretary this morning, and I don't think she's ever going to forgive him, not if I can help it anyway."
There was a moment's silence on the other end of the phone. Sarah knew George from the legal profession as well as a few personal encounters at cocktail parties and charity events.
"Sarah?"
"Sorry, Rachael, you floored me with that one. If I was married and needed a family lawyer I'd be calling my friend Cathy Richardson, she's the best. A straight shooter and a no-nonsense woman. If you're imagining someone like Legally Blonde, forget it. She dresses in tweeds and Hush Puppies, skirts always well below the knees, even the judges fear her."
"I'm intimidated already. Thanks, Sarah, I owe you one."
"Just find me a publisher for the story I should be writing, Confessions of a Female Lawyer. Jenny has Cathy's number. I'm glad you called me. See you Thursday. Why don't you bring Rebecca along with you?"
"She has a ten-year old daughter to look after, my favorite and only niece, Emma."
"Then bring them both. See ya!"
Replacing the receiver Rachael smiled to herself. One of the things she valued almost as much as Rebecca, Emma, and Duncan, was her circle of really good girlfriends.
Now that she'd taken care of Rebecca's immediate problems she settled down to business calling her offices in Toronto and New York, and making a few decisions. Then putting

everything aside, she poured two glasses of Chardonnay and one orange juice for Emma. She added cucumber and orange slices to Emma's glass, and right on cue the two of them walked in the door giggling. Rachael handed them each a glass and smiled at the happy faces.

"Thanks, Aunt Rachael, you're the best."

"Mm, this is good, Rachael, just what the doctor ordered."

"You're very welcome. The Young and the Restless will be on in a few minutes. How about we snuggle up on the couch and watch soap operas?" Rachael placed an arm around her sister's shoulders and hugged her tightly. "I know it's hard baby. It's supposed to hurt, that's the worst of it and there's not a pill in the world that can take away the pain, only time. It's okay to hurt, don't fight it, it'll go away eventually, trust me."

"Emma's got school in the morning. I'm worried about George showing up and taking off with her. I don't know what to do."

"Simple."

"Simple. How so?"

"It's almost the end of the school year isn't it? In a week the kids break for summer holidays. What's wrong with Emma breaking a little earlier? She's a straight A student, so it won't affect her grades. Besides they won't be doing much during the final week. Tell you what, you go into my study and phone the school right now, before they all go home."

"Okay. Thanks, Rachael. I'm just not thinking clearly."

"No problem, and then tomorrow you and Emma could come over to my office and pick out a few manuscripts to read."

"Yes, that would be nice. Reading is a wonderful escape."

"While you're in there phoning, you might as well call this lady." Rachael handed over a piece of paper with a telephone number. "Her name's Cathy Richardson, she's going to be your lawyer. Just tell her that Sarah Williams recommended her to you."

Rebecca remained sitting on the couch, staring at her feet. "Rebecca, this thing won't go away, ignoring the problem won't help either. I know I'm being a real pain. I promise I'll leave you alone, once you've made those calls. You'll feel a whole lot better."

"You're right, sitting here feeling sorry for myself isn't going to do any of us any good."

"Rebecca, with regard to any finances, you are not to worry. I'll see you don't go without, and that includes having to pay for a lawyer. I have it on good authority that she's the best." Rebecca smiled warmly and closed the study door behind her.

"Okay, Emma Brown, now that I've got you all to myself." Rachael scooped up her niece in her arms and began smothering her with kisses. Emma squealed with delight. She felt safe in Rachael's arms.

Rebecca came out of Rachel's study looking more upbeat.

"Well?"

"She's a very nice lady, I like her."

"Who, the school secretary or Cathy Richardson?"

"Cathy Richardson. Actually the school secretary's a nice lady too. Anyway, I have an appointment with Cathy tomorrow morning at ten o'clock. She said the prenuptial agreement is going to hurt me; however, Emma will be okay where child support is concerned. I spoke to Emma's teacher. Mrs. Johnson told me you were the worst child in the whole school, your marks were so bad you would have to go to summer school for the whole summer holidays."

Emma opened her mouth in shock, until she saw the smile creeping across her mother's face. "Actually," Rebecca grabbed her daughter into a hug, "she said your marks were excellent and you deserved to have an extra week off school because you were a pleasure to have in the class, in fact in the whole school. I agreed with her, and I think in the whole world too."

"Amen to that," Rachael joined in with a laugh.

"Can I phone Daddy later and tell him?"

"Sure you can, honey, he'll want to say goodnight before you go to bed."

"You don't want me to say we're staying with Aunt Rachael, do you?"

"I think he already knows, sweetheart, but I'd prefer you didn't tell him just yet, in case he doesn't know. Daddy and Mommy are angry with each other at the moment, but as soon as we work a few things out you can go and stay with Daddy sometimes."

"Did Daddy do something really, really bad Mommy?"

"It's not that it was bad, honey, it's just that he broke your Mommy's heart. Broken hearts are really hard to mend. You remember when your hamster died, how your heart was broken and the pain wouldn't go away for a long time?"

"My heart is still broken over that, Mommy. It still hurts, just not so much now. If you hurt like that then that's really, really bad. I'm going to tell Daddy off for breaking your heart, but is it okay if I still love my daddy?"

"Of course it is, sweetheart, I never want you to stop loving him."

"Do you still love him, Mommy?"

"Yes, honey, I do, and that's why it hurts so much."

Rebecca, overcome with emotion, hurried into the bedroom. Emma cuddled up to her aunt and sobbed.

"I'm just going to check on your mom, sweetie, you stay on the couch and watch television." Rebecca had finally succumbed to mental exhaustion. When Rachael crept into the room she was fast asleep. Rachael gently covered her sister with a blanket.

"Okay, pumpkin, Mommy's sleeping, would you like to help your Aunt Rachael bake a cake? We'll surprise her when she wakes up."

"Yes, please, Aunt Rachael, I love baking. Mommy lets me help her too."

They went into the kitchen, closing the door behind them to cut down on the noise from the electric mixer, and together they set about baking a vanilla sponge cake, not that Rachael particularly wanted to make one, but she felt it was important to take Emma's mind off the problems that were beginning to mount.

"Mommy uses apple sauce too, she says it's better for you and cuts down on the amount of fat."

"Mommy's right, you got to eat as healthy as you can, not too much junk food. A little's okay now and then." Emma smiled up at her aunt, the tip of her nose covered in flour.

"Emma, you been stirring the bowl with your nose? Go look at your face, child, there's a mirror in the hall," laughed Rachael. Emma skipped out to the hall and came back giggling. She laughed even more when she saw that her aunt had rubbed a flour-covered hand across her own nose. Emma put her hands on her hips and looked up at her aunt.

"You been stirring the bowl with your nose? Go look at your face. No, really, Aunt Rachael, I'm not joking."

"You are so joking, look at you, you're laughing."

"You're making me laugh, Aunt Rachael. Okay then, don't believe me, you'll be the only one in the restaurant with flour on their nose."

"If you're teasing me I'm going to spank your butt, young lady." Rachael took a look at herself in the hallway mirror. "Well, I guess we've both been sticking our noses in the cake mix. We're gonna have to call this cake a vanilla nose cake, that's all."

A sleepy-eyed Rebecca stood in the kitchen doorway smiling at the two of them.

"Mm, vanilla nose cake, now that sounds really appetizing."

"Oh, hi, Mommy, we didn't really stick our noses in the cake, honest."

"I should hope not, Emma."
"Apart from the noses, Aunt Rachael and I made it just the way you like it."
"Well, why don't you and I clear up here, Emma, and then we'll all get ready to go out," said her aunt. "I'm taking you both to China Town for the best Chinese food you've ever had."
"Oh, my favorite, Aunt Rachael. That's my bestest meal ever!"
"And that's your Mommy's and your Aunt's bestest meal too, as you so aptly put it young lady, so let's get cracking."
"Can we go in the Mini, Aunt Rachael?"
"Sure, honey, if you like. I'm sure we'll all fit in going there, I'm not so sure about coming home afterwards though," she laughed.

Chapter Three

The bright yellow Mini Cooper zoomed in and out of the congested Toronto traffic, eventually pulling up in front of the Golden Mandarin restaurant in the heart of bustling China Town
"Wow, Aunt Rachael, you should be a racing driver! Even Daddy can't drive as good as you."
"Why, thank you, Emma, just goes to show that women do make the best drivers after all, and don't let anyone tell you different. Come on gang let's go eat."
The hostess recognized Rachael immediately and ushered the three of them to a quiet table tucked away in the corner of the busy restaurant.
"You can tell it's a good Chinese restaurant, Emma."
"How, Aunt Rachael?"
"It's full of Asian customers. Westerners don't know any better, but Asians only eat where the food is good."

"How do you know so much about restaurants, Aunt Rachael?"

"From Duncan, of course. If anyone knows about food, it's Duncan. What he doesn't know about the restaurant business isn't worth knowing, trust me."

"Your Aunt Rachel's right about that, Emma. Remember that time Duncan invited us to one of his restaurants, didn't we have a great meal?"

"Oh, yes, it was so good. I hope we get to go there again, Mommy."

"As soon as Duncan gets back I'll let him know how much you enjoyed yourself, and you can be sure he'll be inviting us out again. You know how much he loves his girls."

"He's a wonderful man, Rachael, you should marry him you know."

"Rebecca, are you crazy. I've got a good thing going here, I don't want to go and spoil it by marrying the man. Sister, give that head of yours a shake."

"Rachael, you and Duncan have been engaged for a long time now, if you don't know you're right for each other after ten years you're never going to know. Oh, what the hell do I know, I should be the last person giving you advice, look at the mess I'm in."

"Don't be so hard on yourself, Rebecca, and you're right, Duncan is a good man and maybe one day we will get married, but not just yet. Ah, at last the wine arrives, and a Shirley Temple for you, Emma."

"Thank you, Aunt Rachael."

"You're very welcome." I do believe this is our dinner, I can smell the king prawns from here."

"There's so much food, Rachael, we're never going to eat all this."

"No problem, what we don't eat we can take home for tomorrow's lunch. Don't forget to save a place for dessert, lychees and vanilla ice cream, that's my favorite."

During the meal Rachael sensed what was going through her sister's mind. She gently placed her hand on top of Rebecca's and gave a squeeze of reassurance. No words were spoken, but that touch told Rebecca that her sister was there for her through thick and thin, and she would be there for her along whatever pathway she took, for always.

"Those lychees were really yummy, Aunt Rachael, even better than you said. What are these things in little plastic bags?"

"Those are fortune cookies. Don't you remember having them when we went to Duncan's restaurant?"

"I forget."

"Inside the cookie is a small piece of paper with some very precious words written on it. If you don't like what your fortune cookie tells you, just screw it up and put it on the side of your plate. If you really like it, take it home with you and treasure it. Okay let's open our fortune cookies and read aloud what it says inside. Emma, which order would you like us to take?"

"You go first, Aunt Rachael, then me and the most special of all I want to save till last, Mommy."

"Okay, here goes."

They each tore open the tiny plastic wrapper and broke open their fortune cookie, pulling out the small piece of paper from inside.

Rachael read aloud, "*You are like an acorn growing into a mighty oak tree, but remember, you need more than one acorn to make a forest.* What the hell does that mean?"

"I think, dear sister, it is referring to your relationship with Duncan. It is reminding you that you and Duncan need to get together pretty quickly and have lots of acorns together, i.e. babies, and start building your forest."

"I think it means, if you're happy as a single oak tree, don't be dropping anymore acorns around your own trunk, that's what I think it means," she said laughing.

"I think Mommy's version is probably right, and I would so love to have lots of cousins to baby-sit."

"Why, Emma, child, I can't believe you of all people are ganging up me. Okay, Miss, what does your fortune cookie say?"

"Mine says, *One day your talents will be recognized and rewarded.* I'm only ten, I don't think I've got any talents yet."

Rebecca frowned at her daughter. "Now that's not true, Emma. You have many talents already, like being honest and being a good person, being beautiful on the outside as well as on the inside. And you can play the piano really well, you're good at art too. With all these talents you have already, imagine how many more you are going to have by the time you reach our age."

"Your turn, Mommy, what does yours say?" There was silence as Rebecca read her fortune to herself. She looked across the table at her sister, a shocked expression on her face.

"Well, let's hear it Rebecca, honey. I already said if you don't like it, screw it up and pick another one that suits you. You know in China they have a wall of fortunes you can pick out for a small fee. If you don't like the one you get, you simply impale it on a wire frame especially for the purpose and pick another."

Rebecca took a deep breath. "Okay. It says, *Winter is here, spring is coming. Spring will turn to summer. Do not let the ice freeze your heart.* Okay, Rachael, you had these all picked out before we even got here, I don't know how you did it, but you did it. Now don't give me that surprised look and don't deny it either."

"You know, sister, if I hadn't picked out my own scary fortune, I would agree with you, but honest to God there's no way I had anything to do with this. Okay, let's all tuck our fortunes somewhere safe and twelve months from now, on this very date, and I'm going to mark it in my diary right now, we are all coming back here to see if I've found the perfect acorn that wants to be a forest with me. We'll see if Emma has added any more talents to her collection and we'll see what season of the year you are in, sister."

They all agreed and left the restaurant arm-in-arm, laughing.

"Rebecca, seeing as you are going to be using this car for as long as you need to, you may as well drive us all back to my place, but you pay the speeding tickets. Don't forget, it's a standard."

It wasn't long before Rebecca got the hang of driving the compact car, after a while she was even double-declutching like a racing driver.

"Way to go, Rebecca, you still remember what Dad taught us when we were teenagers. You were always the rebel though." Emma's eyes were like saucers, waiting for the next snippet of juicy information about her mother's past.

"I think that's enough information, thank you, Rachael. I don't want Emma discovering too early in her young life that her mother is only human. That reminds me, I meant to phone Mom and Dad. Do you think it will be too late to call when we get home?"

"No, they'll still be up. You give them a call as soon as we get in. Tell them not to come up though, everything's been taken care of. We don't need you there with them either, so George can pester the life out of them. Mind you, old as Dad is, he could knock George into another universe if he got upset."

"No you're right, for the time being it'll be best if we keep everything as it is for a while, at least until after I've spoken with Cathy Richardson tomorrow morning. I'll have a better idea what to do after that."

As they neared the ramp that led down into the underground parking garage below Rachael's condominium, Rebecca screamed, "There's George's BMW parked by the ramp! He's been waiting for us. You know he has a violent temper when

O'Malley's Cottage

things don't go his way, what shall I do, Rachael!"
"Okay, keep calm, just drive away and head up towards 52 Division. If he wants to argue, he can argue at the police station. Who knows, maybe your new cop friend, what's her name, might be there."
"Constable Alison MacDonald," said Rebecca, accelerating quickly away.
"Yeah, Big Mack, that's what you said her nickname was, well anyway, maybe she's still at the station, George won't want to run into her again."
"His headlights have come on and he's pulling out behind us. What shall I do now?"
"Number one, remember you have a ten-year old daughter in the car and a young looking sister who wants to stay young looking, so don't do anything crazy. No jumping red lights either. Make sure all the doors are locked."
"Oh, my God, he's alongside us!" Rebecca was hysterical. The black BMW ZX kept pace with the Mini Cooper.
George began screaming through the open passenger window of his BMW, "Pull over! Pull the goddamn car over!"
"Do you still remember how to do a handbrake turn, Rebecca?"
"I thought you said nothing crazy?"
"By the look on your husband's face right now I'd say crazy is okay by me."
"Okay, hold tight everyone, here we go. Rebecca checked the rear view mirror. The traffic that had been following was now stopped at the red traffic light behind her. She eased the steering wheel to the right, eased off the gas pedal and at the same time yanked up the handbrake. The car turned on a dime, and as it spun around practically on the spot, Rebecca eased off the handbrake and gradually depressed the gas pedal. The Mini Cooper shot off back down the way it had come and turned sharply up a side street. George was stuck in the traffic that had filled the void where the

Mini had been. Within a few minutes Rebecca's cell phone rang.

"Don't you answer the phone, you just concentrate on driving. I'll answer it, it's probably him anyway."

Rachael took the cell phone from Rebecca.

"No, you listen to me. Now you're playing with fire. You want a restraining order on you, you just got yourself one. No you listen! Don't you ever, and I mean ever, pull that stunt on me or my family again, you understand? If I so much as see a hair of your head on my street again I'm calling the cops and I'll make sure it's Constable MacDonald I'll be calling, cos she's gonna kick your sorry ass all the way down the street again. You hear me. Now you hear this too, you want to start playing like a thug then two can play at that game. You upset my day one more time and I promise you, you'll wish it was the police coming to see you because the thugs I'll be sending to your door will not be playing by the rules. Yeah, your damn right you're sorry. Hold on I'll ask. He wants to talk to Emma."

"As soon as he leaves us alone and we can go back to your place safely I'll get her to call him from there. Emma, honey, are you okay? I'm sorry baby, but your father is really mad at your mom and I don't want to talk to him when he's that angry."

Emma nodded her head. She'd been sitting motionless in the back seat, her eyes round and her mind obviously trying to make sense of everything that had gone wrong in her world.

"Okay she'll call you from my place, now you stay away. I'll be making a couple of calls myself to ensure you start playing by the rules." Rachael hung up and made another call.

"Winston ... Yeah, I know I only call you when I got a problem ... I love you too, baby. George Parker-Brown ... Yeah, the lawyer, he's starting to be a nuisance ... No, I don't need anything heavy, he needs to be told not to bother me again or my sister that's all. Meet me at the ramp to my condo, he's sure to be there again in about ten minutes, he's driving a Black BMW ZX ... Thanks, honey." She looked over her shoulder at her niece. "You know, Emma, I'm real sorry about all this, but your dad is mad as hell at the moment and he needs to cool down and start thinking straight. He's going to get a visit from a friend of mine who's a doctor, well not a real doctor, he's just very good at making pains go away, that's why they call him, *The Doctor*. Because he's black some people call him, *The Witch Doctor*. When you have a painful problem he makes it go away."

"That's very nice of you, Aunt Rachael. Mommy, your driving was awesome!"

Rachael's condominium came into view.

"What do you want me to do, Rachael?"

"Just pull up to the ramp, but do not open your window to press the code."

As soon as Rebecca stopped the Mini Cooper, George appeared out of nowhere and began pulling on the driver's door and slapping the window with his hand, while mouthing obscenities at Rebecca.

Frantically, Rebecca tried to get the Mini into gear, only to stall it. Rachael remained calm. She could see the tall dark, powerful looking figure emerging from the shadows.

The shouting and hammering on the Mini's window suddenly stopped.

"Oh, my God, is that *The Doctor*?" Rebecca whispered as she watched a huge black man grab her husband up in a chokehold.

Rachael began exiting the car as though this was all part of an evening out.

"What are you doing, Rachael!"

"Just press the code and make your way up to my place, I'll be there in a minute. As soon as you arrive, telephone George on his cell phone so he can speak to Emma. Go on be quick before *The Doctor* administers too much medicine to the patient."

Rebecca did as she was told, as soon as the overhead door

opened she squealed off down the ramp.

Rachael walked slowly towards Winston, who looked as though he was strangling a manikin. George was no longer struggling.

"George you are no longer acting rationally and quite frankly neither am I anymore. This stupid behavior of yours stops right here, right now, do you understand. You chose your secretary over your wife. From now on, everything will be handled by lawyers. There will be absolutely no problem regarding access to Emma at all, unless you make it an issue. Now let's get one thing straight, you spoil my day one more time and I'm going to spoil yours permanently. *The Doctor*here has a team of surgeons that would be only too happy to operate on you if you upset me again. Do I make myself clear?"

The cell phone in George's pocket began ringing. "That will be Emma wanting to talk to you. This is between you and Rebecca. Emma is not there as a pawn to be played by either of you, and furthermore, as her godmother I will not allow either you or my sister to upset my niece. Is that clear?" George tried to nod his head in agreement. Rachael gave *The Doctor*a nod and he released his grip, but did not let down his guard. "Answer the phone George."

"Hi, baby, it's Daddy." George was struggling with his emotions. "How are you? ... Yeah, I'm sorry about that, I was really upset that's all. I did some dumb things today that one day we'll talk about ... Yes, I still love you and Mommy lots ... No nothing bad happened at the hospital. My nose wasn't broken. I just had a concussion ... Yes, a concussion. I walked into something this morning at work. It was my own fault ... Yes, I'm crying, I'm trying not to though, I'm mad at myself for being such an idiot. Can I call you tomorrow? ... Okay sweetheart, I love you too."

George put the phone back in his pocket and turned to

Rachael. "I truly am sorry for everything. I don't know where my head was today. I used to defend idiot husbands that terrorized their wives and never truly understood the pain they were going through or the emotional upset they were causing their wives and children. I think the good Doctor here gave me the very medicine I needed to bring me back to reality. You won't have any more problems from me, Rachael, I promise."

George moved in to give Rachael a hug, *The Doctor* was between them in a flash, surprising George at how quickly the big man moved.

"It's okay, I think a hug is called for."

"I'm sorry, Rachael." George sobbed against her shoulder. "Thank you for being there for my family."

As he walked back to his BMW Rachael felt just a little sorry for him, but not sorry enough to want to see Rebecca back in his life again.

"I'll walk you back to your apartment," Winston said, moving up beside Rachael.

"Thanks, Winston, but I'll be fine. I really appreciate you," she said, handing him an envelope.

"What's this?"

"It's five hundred dollars. We're friends, but I don't expect you to help me for nothing."

Winston shook his head and pushed the envelope back into her hand.

"Tonight was a freebie, princess. You've helped me a lot with my writing. Thanks to you I've won a couple of competitions already and I'm going to be sending you my first novel. I know you'll give me an honest opinion. How about that for a fair exchange of services?"

"It's a deal then, and thanks, Winston, for bringing George to his senses."

"You have any more problems with Mister Parker-Brown, you call me, day or night. You got that?"

"I got it." Rachael grasped his neck and kissed him on the lips. They smiled at each other for a few seconds and then Winston melted away into the shadows.

As she re-entered her apartment Rachael smiled at the thought of Winston bent over the keyboard, his huge fingers pecking out the words to his latest novel. Never in a million years would anyone guess that *The Doctor* wrote romance stories.

"You didn't hurt him did you?" Rebecca was waiting right inside the apartment doorway and Rachael could tell that she was close to hysterics.

"No, honey. George was not hurt–at least not physically."

"What do you mean?"

"It means that he has finally come to terms with the situation that he created, and he now realizes what an ass he's been. He is sorry, and if he could turn back the clock I know he would. But don't you go feeling sorry for him. What happened this morning wasn't a dream or a figment of your imagination. You caught him with another woman, and you need to remember that when he sends you flowers and sets you up for that second honeymoon bullshit."

"I know, I know."

"I hope you do, because you're one of the prettiest women in the whole of Toronto and I bet you've had plenty of opportunities to break your marriage vows. Haven't you?"

Yes, I have, but I'd never be unfaithful to George."

"Exactly, and you know as well as I do that a leopard doesn't change his spots. That's what you need to remember when you consider what you're going to do about George."

"I know." Rebecca's voice threatened to break and Rachael changed the subject.

"How was Emma after speaking to her dad?"

"She was a bit upset, but I sat down and explained that she

would get to see him a lot and could call him often. She seemed a little better after that. Poor little mite was worn out. She fell asleep as I was talking. That reminds me, I haven't phoned Mom and Dad yet."

"Do you want me to phone them for you, you look pretty beat yourself?"

"No, that's okay. Can I use the phone in your study?"

"Of course you can. My house is yours, now go make your call and be sure to give them my love."

Rebecca went into the study and picked up the phone to call New York. While she waited for an answer Rachael slipped into the room with a glass of Drambuie and set it down on the desk. Rebecca smiled her thanks and Rachael left the room.

"Hi, Mom." Her mother answered the phone and Rebecca steeled herself to tell them without falling apart.

"I'm fine, Emma's fine too. How's Dad? That's good. Did George phone you by any chance? He didn't?"

Up until this point Rebecca had managed to stay in control, but the strain of asking about George proved too much. Rachael heard the sound of her sister sobbing and rushed back into the room. Gently she eased the receiver out of Rebecca's hand and placed a comforting arm around her waist.

"Mom, it's Rachael. Has Rebecca told you yet? No, Emma's fine. George is okay, but the fact is, Rebecca caught him in the shower with his secretary this morning. No, Mom, they were not fooling around, they were having sex. I said they were having sex. Rebecca and Emma are staying with me. No, there's no sense you and Dad coming here. Dad will only be out looking to give George a good hiding."

Rachael tucked the phone tighter under her chin and softened her voice. "You're right, Mom, don't tell him about the secretary in the shower part. You'll think of something. Now don't worry, I'll look after Rebecca and Emma. Yes, I've already arranged a lawyer. Rebecca has an appointment in the morning. Of course I will, she'll call you tomorrow evening, and you and Dad can have a chat with Emma."

Rachael nodded at Rebecca to reassure her that things were fine. "Okay, Mom, I will. I love you too. Love to Dad. Yes, work is good. Duncan's in Singapore at the moment. Love you. Bye."

"Mom says you're not to worry about anything. She says you can move in with them anytime you want. She says she loves you very much and I'm to give you a big hug and kiss from her."

Rachael caught her sister in a hug and squeezed her tighter, then kissed her soundly on both cheeks.

"What do you say we both get ready for bed. We've got a busy day ahead of us tomorrow."

Rebecca wrapped her arms around Rachael and snuggled up to her neck. "Thank you, sis. "You've always been there for me no matter what."

"You've always been there for me too little sister. Whenever I've needed you, you've dropped everything to help me through my troubles. I love you, sis. Now let's get some sleep."

Rebecca tossed and turned for several hours, unable to stop her mind from playing and replaying the events of the past couple of days.

At three a.m. she gave up and went to the kitchen. There she fixed a cup of coffee and sat staring at the clock. She didn't hear Rachael until her sister's comforting arm wrapped around her shoulders.

"Couldn't sleep, sis?"

"No, I've been tossing and turning for hours."

"That coffee won't help, but you don't need me to tell you that." Rachael poured herself a cup and sat down at the table.

"Life was so simple when we were kids." Rebecca held her cup in both hands as she reminisced about their childhood. "Don't you sometimes wish we could go back?"

O'Malley's Cottage

"Sure I do, we were lucky kids. We had the best parents any child could wish for, and we had each other."

"Yes, and we still do."

"Even when we were kids we hardly ever fought, except maybe a few arguments when we were teenagers."

"I know. I was always borrowing your makeup and sometimes your clothes without asking. You used to get pretty mad about that. Dad fixed the problem though, by installing a lock on your bedroom door. That really made life challenging for me until one of the boys at school showed me how to pick the lock."

"I knew it! One of the Brett twins I bet. It was, wasn't it?"

"Malcolm actually. I'm sure I told you that?"

"No, you did not! What a little smarty pants you were. You turned from thief to burglar overnight and Mom and Dad still thought you were Miss Goody Two Shoes. I can't wait to put them right on that one."

The two sisters laughed at the memories and when they had finished their coffee Rachael had a suggestion.

"Let's go sit on the couch like when we were kids and watch some meaningless TV. If we find a boring enough show we might fall asleep."

"Okay, maybe they'll have, Today in Parliament. Five minutes of that and I'll be out like a light."

Chapter Four

Rebecca got up, had a quick shower and forced herself to eat a small breakfast. At eight-thirty a sleepy-eyed Emma wandered into the kitchen.

"Good morning, my little princess. Did you sleep okay, honey?"

"Uh huh. You look really beautiful this morning Mommy, are you going out?"

"For a little while, sweetheart. I have some things I have to take care of this morning, but I shouldn't be too long."

"Can I come with you?"

"I'm sorry, honey, this is big girls' stuff I have to take care of. Aunt Rachael is going to take care of you while I'm gone, okay?"

"You bet I am," said Rachael, appearing at the kitchen door. "I was going to take you swimming, afterwards I thought we'd go into the games room and have some fun there too if you'd like."

"Can we?"

"You bet we can."

"Thanks, Aunt Rachael."

"Rebecca, make sure you take your cell phone with you. Take the Mini, hopefully you'll find a parking space outside Cathy's office."

"Who's Cathy, Mommy?"

"She's a friend of Aunt Rachael's. Okay, I better get going if I'm going to get there by ten o'clock." Rebecca gave Emma a big hug.

"Good luck, sis. Make sure you phone me when you get there and when you leave. Please, I'll only be worrying about you.

I feel I should be coming too."

"No, you stay home and take care of Emma. Bye now, see you later. Oh, and Emma, don't forget your manners and help your auntie out, okay? Love you."

Rachael closed the apartment door behind her sister.

After driving around the block three times, Rebecca finally found a parking space within easy walking distance of the rather dull looking office building that contained Cathy Richardson's law practice. She walked briskly towards the building carrying a small black leather attaché case. Heads turned to look at the beautiful, slim black woman, elegantly dressed in a black thigh hugging skirt, hemmed just above her knee, and crisp white blouse. Her stiletto heels made that unmistakable sound on the sidewalk that told the well-tuned male ear that the likelihood of an attractive woman coming their way was imminent.

She walked over to a large directory that gave the names, floor numbers and room numbers of the various businesses located within the building. Cathy Richardson's building was clean and well maintained, despite its age, but nothing like her husband's law firm, with its imposing glass tower block and tinted blue windows.

Rebecca followed the sign to Cathy Richardson's office and stood in front of the door with her eyes closed. *Do it, Rebecca, open the door and go in. Go on, you can do it. No I can't. I just need more time to think about this. I'll give it another week. No, Rebecca! Do it.* The images of George in the shower with his secretary filled her mind. She opened the door and walked boldly inside.

"Good morning, how may I help you" asked a pleasant looking middle-aged woman in her early fifties. She was sitting behind a highly polished black desk, with neatly arranged files, in and out trays, a computer and a complicated looking telephone. She stood up to greet Rebecca. "I'm Nancy, Cathy Richardson's secretary."

"Good morning," smiled Rebecca. "I'm Rebecca Brown. I

have a ten o'clock appointment with Cathy this morning."
"Please take a seat. I'll let Cathy know you're here."
"Thank you."
While Nancy was in Cathy Richardson's office, Rebecca sat down in a comfortable black leather chair and began to thumb through the magazines that were neatly set out on a side table near her chair. There were the usual ubiquitous copies of Readers Digest, only unlike most reception areas, these copies were still actually quite current. There were copies of Vogue, Cosmopolitan, Oprah, Canadian Living, Time and MacLeans.
"Judging by the obvious lack of auto and sports magazines, I'd say most of your clients are women," mused Rebecca under her breath.
Suddenly the office door burst open and out strode a tall, stocky looking woman in her late fifties, with grey hair, tied back in a bun. She was wearing a pair of large tortoiseshell spectacles, a dark brown jacket with matching skirt, cut well below the knee and a pair of dark brown, soft leather shoes that some women refer to as, *sensible shoes*.
"Rebecca. May I call you Rebecca?"
"Please." Rebecca winced in the vice-like grip of her lawyer's handshake.
"Come on into my office and let's get down to business, shall we?"
Cathy led the way into her office. Immediately on entering the room Rebecca was taken aback by the large round oak table, topped in dark green leather, which stood in the centre of the room, with six matching chairs spread well apart around the table
Rebecca took a large brown envelope from her attaché case. "I brought a copy of the prenup agreement with me as you asked."
"Oh, yes, the dreaded prenup. Let me take a look at it

O'Malley's Cottage
Page 51

please, Rebecca. My word, it's quite the document isn't it, my dear? It's more like a short story than an agreement. Just let me read through it will you?"

Cathy sat back in her chair and studied the document very carefully. About halfway through, the lawyer remarked quite casually, "Ah, how blind love is," and continued reading. After twenty minutes Cathy laid the document back down on the table in front of her. "I'll need to make a copy of this agreement, if I may, Rebecca?"

"Yes, of course." Cathy pressed a buzzer under the table and Nancy appeared in the office almost immediately.

"Nancy, run off a copy of this for our files would you, please? Thank you, dear." Nancy left the office, clutching the prenuptial agreement.

"I'd be completely lost without her, one of a kind is our Nancy. Hardworking, as honest as the day is long, always on time, and very dependable." Cathy sat back and considered the notes she had made. "We could fight this, but with the research Nancy's done on your husband already, he could have us tied up in court bureaucracy for years. You know, I really think all high school students should spend a few days in family court. After they get a glimpse of love turning to hate and greedy lawyers and pompous judges feeding off their suffering like sharks in a feeding frenzy, it would make them think more seriously about getting into a relationship and having children. Well, Rebecca, plain and simple. What do you want?"

"I want to ensure that I get full custody of Emma, above everything else, I want that. And to have everything settled as quickly as possible so I can get on with my life."

"If we fought this and won, you'd be entitled to some very generous spousal support payments based on George's income."

"I don't want his money. The last thing I need is him telling my own daughter that it's his money that's still keeping us, and rubbing it in my face every time he speaks to friends. That may sound rather stupid to you, Cathy, but the thing is, my sister has offered me a job in her literary agency business, it won't be paying me a fortune, but it will at least make me feel independent."

"I understand, Rebecca, and that's very commendable, but don't be foolish my dear. Please don't take offence, when you and I have finished, I want to be sure, as your lawyer, that when the ink is dry and the tears too, that you felt you made the right choices and that you were more than happy with my services. I never want my clients to feel I let them down; ever. Now, having said all that, how about money for Emma? He has a responsibility to provide for her. At least in the prenup he's agreeable to that."

"That's fine, but I don't want to be greedy."

"He certainly isn't being exactly charitable in this document, Rebecca. I don't think there's any danger of anyone calling you greedy based on what I've been reading so far. Quite frankly, Rebecca, at the moment I feel like I'm acting for him more than I am for you, my dear. Okay, how about access?"

"As much as possible. I'd rather not have that carved in stone at the moment, unless it becomes a real issue down the road."

"Okay, assets. We could go for half the house, pensions, RSP's, that sort of thing."

"He'll fight that tooth and nail. I agreed just before we got married, that in the event of a separation I would get full custody of the children, he would assist with them financially while they were in fulltime education and he could keep the house and his financial assets. I must sound so dumb and stupid to you, Cathy." Rebecca burst into tears. "I'm sorry," she gasped between sobs.

Cathy leant over and put her arm around Rebecca, with her other hand she grabbed a box of tissues.

"Please don't apologize. You sound just like I did when my marriage went sour many moons ago. I made the very same mistakes you did Rebecca, being blinded by love, signing a prenup and believing my marriage was going to be the best marriage in the world. It was after that tragedy that I went into family law. I guess I'm still inflicting my revenge on as many males as I can, not very professional I know, and I would prefer it if you never told a soul I just said that."

"I take it you don't get many male clients?"

"Not too many. Is there anything else you think I should know? For instance, is he having serious mood swings, reasonable one minute and aggressive the next, that sort of thing?" Rebecca did not answer immediately. "Your hesitation betrays you, Rebecca, my dear. Come on, out with it."

"I'm sure he's fine now, but there was an incident last night I didn't tell you about. My sister intervened and I think everything is okay now."

"Do enlighten me, my dear, this may be important." Rebecca explained what had taken place the previous evening. "Well, I don't know who should have been calling the police first, you or George. Poor Emma, this is something children should not be subjected to. I feel very strongly about that Rebecca."

"I agree with you, it wasn't something I wanted to happen either, believe me. I just wanted to be allowed to get on with my life without being harassed, or stalked by an angry ex-husband. This wasn't something I actually planned for."

"I think we should consider asking the judge for a restraining order today. Based on what you've told me so far, there'd be no problem getting one I assure you. I'll rephrase that. There wouldn't have been a problem had the mystery man not intervened and no doubt threatened your husband."

"Cathy, I don't think getting a restraining order is going to be necessary, not after my sister's friend spoke to George."

"You know, Rebecca, I think you're absolutely right. Before you leave give me the name of this enforcer, I could give him enough work to see him into retirement. Just a phone call, eh? Beats all that paperwork and standing in front of a judge who can't wait to get out of the courtroom because he's teeing off at three o'clock. All right, but you be very careful. Love and hate are the same primeval feelings."

"That's why you were recommended to me I'm sure, and I'm grateful that there are people out there like you who are so passionate, Cathy."

"Thank you, my dear. Okay, any idea who George will be using to represent him?"

"I'm not sure, it won't be anyone in his firm, they're all corporate lawyers into billion dollar mergers."

"In that case I'll fire off a letter to him today to get the ball rolling and we'll go from there. I'm going to give you my cell phone number as well, I don't give it out as a rule, but as Sarah recommended me to you, I'll make an exception. You can call me anytime, Rebecca, and I do mean anytime if you have a problem. If George continues to harass you and it's two o'clock in the morning, phone me, I won't mind. I like to keep my clients alive and well."

"Thank you, Cathy, that's very kind of you."

"Kind, my ass. It's hard to get money from a dead client. It's hard enough getting money from a live one too sometimes." Cathy laughed and Rebecca smiled back at her, amused by her sense of humor.

"Rebecca, before we go any further. Now that we've met each other, would you like me to represent you or would you like a few days to think about it? I shan't be offended if you decide to shop around for another lawyer."

"Cathy, I already knew I was going to be in good hands before I met you, and now that I have met you I'm even more sure than ever, and thank you."

"No, my dear, thank you. It has been a pleasure meeting you. I know it's hard to accept at the present time, but this too shall pass. I hope when it's all settled and you've finally got on with your life that you will give me a call and let me know how you are doing. I always like to hear from my former clients down the road. Most of them tell me that they are happier than they've ever been, and just hearing that makes what I do worthwhile. Well, go and enjoy the rest of your day and try not to worry about anything, you're in good hands." The two women shook hands warmly.

Rebecca walked along the sidewalk back to the Mini with a spring in her step. A construction crew had arrived outside the building and were busy digging up the road. The men stopped work as Rebecca walked by them on the other side of the street, one of the men made a loud wolf whistle. On any other day Rebecca might have been offended by this sexist male act, but today it made her smile. *Yes, this morning I feel good.*

Rebecca unlocked the Mini's door and climbed into the driver's seat. She pulled her cell phone out of her purse and called Rachael.

"Hello?"

"Rachael, it's Rebecca, how's Emma?"

"She's fine. We've been in the pool for so long we've both grown webbed feet. Well, how did it go?"

"It went very well, she's a real sweetie and providing George doesn't go ballistic when he gets her letter, things should move ahead pretty smoothly I think."

"Were you satisfied with Cathy; I mean did she give you good advice?"

"I liked her, she gave me good advice."

"Well, that's just what you need at the moment. Are you on your way back now?"

"I'm on my way as we speak and I simply love your car. Oh, by the way, no kidding aside. Is that job offer still open?"

"Job offer?"

"Yes, Rachael, don't you remember? You offered me a job reading manuscripts. Have you changed your mind already?"

"No way, of course not. When do you want to start, sis?"

"Right now. Get those manuscripts lined up, I mean business!"

"In that case, meet me at my office instead, and I'll introduce you to the staff and we'll get you started."

"What about Emma, I can't just ignore her?"

"She may as well see where her mom will be working. With Emma on holiday, just take it easy for a while. You can do most of the work at my place part-time until we get you settled. You'll hardly need to come to the office at all anyway. Once you've got your own place I can have work couriered out to you no problem. With e-mail it's even easier. Enough chit-chat, see you at my office in say half an hour, make that forty minutes and we'll have a girls' lunch out."

"Thanks, Rachael, I love you."

"Yeah, yeah, whatever. See you soon."

Rachael's office was located in downtown Toronto just off Yonge Street in a modern office building, shared by other successful companies. Her office was on the top floor with magnificent views over the city. This was not Rebecca's first visit to her sister's plush offices, but it was the first time as an employee of the firm.

Rachael's receptionist, Jean Carter was there to greet Rebecca, and she in turn handed Rebecca over to Rachael's personal assistant, John Adams, a short, slim man in his early thirties. He was impeccably dressed in a light tan suit with crisp white shirt, open at the collar, complimented by a pink cravat. His brown leather shoes shone like a highly polished mahogany table. He was obviously gay, his effeminate mannerisms and voice confirmed Rebecca's suspicions. Whatever grey clouds there might have been hanging over Toronto, or over John's personal life, he was always smiling and always in a pleasant mood. He was absolutely delighted to meet Rebecca again and she naturally warmed to him as she had done the first time she met him.

"Oh, Rebecca, how simply wonderful to see you again," he said with genuine warmth and sincerity. "I've just heard the news. Congratulations and welcome to our humble abode. Allow me to show you around, and may I say, and not just because Rachael is your sister, and if I recall I told you the very same thing the first time I met you, Rachael has to be the most wonderful boss anyone could possibly wish for. This really is one happy ship I must say, and having you aboard is the icing on the cake or the fairy on top of the Christmas tree." John clapped his hands once in a very unmanly fashion. "As I'm sure you know, Rachael has another office in New York and tries too hard sometimes to be in both places at the same time. Not that I should be telling tales out of school Rebecca. She works so hard, I think it will be good for her to have you around to keep an eye on her, lord knows I've tried." John fluttered his eyes and looked up at the ceiling as if awaiting an acknowledgement from the heavens.

"The one thing I won't be doing, John, is interfering in the way my sister runs her business. I don't want to find myself fired in the first week. It's very good of her to even offer me a job here. No, I intend to keep a low profile, I don't want to upset any members of staff by getting preferential treatment."

"We're not like that here, Rebecca, we're one small, but very happy family. Rachael was telling me over the phone that you'll be doing much of the work from home, that sounds like a marvelous idea."

"Hi, Mommy."

Rebecca turned to see her daughter walking hand in hand down the corridor with Rachael, her new boss.

"Hi, sweetheart, have you had a good day?"

"Yes, we had lots of fun. We went swimming for hours. Aunt Rachael was teaching me to dive off the diving board, not the springy one at the end, but those high ones. I can dive off the first level now, you should see me, Mommy."

"I can't wait, it sounds very exciting. You didn't hurt yourself, did you?"

"Aunt Rachael said you'd ask me that. She told me that now she had me to herself we were going to live dangerously."

"Oh, she did, did she?"

"She only made one belly flop and the tears didn't last long," said Rachael entering John's office. "Well, John, what do you think of our new employee?"

"I think she is definitely going to be an asset to this company, Miss Rachael."

"I know how backlogged you are, John, with all the mountains of paperwork flying through our letterbox. Okay then. John perhaps you could show Rebecca the tons of letters we get from aspiring authors and sort out a ton of them for her to take home. Hopefully somewhere among the million letters is a possible bestseller."

"Absolutely. The good news is Rebecca, that if you happen to be the one who spots that budding bestseller, the office shuts down and we all go out for lunch at the Company's expense, and you get a bonus."

"What's the bad news?"

"Tell her, John."

"The bad news is that you will have to wade through every type of personality that you could possibly think of on paper. There will be begging letters, pleading letters, threatening letters. Spelling the likes of which you've never seen before. And after you have read through page after page after page of garbage, you will read through page after page of mediocre literature. Your eyesight will suffer and your head will constantly ache. Your dreams will be filled with words circling overhead in a constant stream, but suddenly, there amongst all those billions of words you will spot it. It will be like a bright jewel shining up at you from the bottom of a muddy pool, and then you will know you have found it."

"Don't you dare put her off, John, you know how hard it is to keep staff," joked Rachael. "Okay, sis, welcome aboard, now let's go and introduce you to all the members of the work force and give you a handle on how things work around here. If you have any problems, don't come to me, go through John, he's the kingpin here. The wheels of this company turn silky smooth because John keeps them oiled. Very rarely does one fall off, but if it does and it's your fault, look out! Working for me and being my sister is going to be more of a curse than a blessing I can tell you." Rachael led the way out of her office, as she did so John took hold of Rebecca's arm.

"She's really a pussycat, don't take any notice of her," he whispered.

"Don't give her false hope, John. Do you have plans for lunch?"

"No, Miss Rachael."

"In that case I'd like you to join us for lunch, we can go over a few things and you can bring me up to speed on our latest project."

"Yes, Miss Rachael, it will be a pleasure."

At the end of the day Rachael popped her head into John's office.

"Well, Emma, what do you think about your mommy working in the book business?"

"I think it's great, all those new stories to read before anyone else gets to read them."

On the way back to Rachael's condo, Rebecca was deep in thought.

"Penny for them," said Rachael.

"I was just thinking about how life can take a fork in the road that you didn't even know existed. There I was in my blissful life with George, when suddenly wham! I get blindsided, derailed, and now I'm on a different path. I wonder where this one's going to lead. You sure you don't mind me working for you, Rachael? I won't get in the way or interfere I promise."

"Rebecca, I know that, in fact I was going to ask you if you'd like to work for me from home anyway. I had this idea ages ago. I knew you didn't need the money, I just thought it would be interesting for you, you know, stimulate the mind. I just thought you would vegetate being stuck at home. You got brains, girl. Under George's regime you never had a chance to use them, now you do. The sky's the limit girl, believe me."

"Thanks again, Rachael. As soon as I know where I stand with George I'd like to start looking for a place for Emma and I. I know you don't mind us being with you, but I don't want to spoil my relationship with you. No matter how much we may love each other, eventually you are going to want your place back and your routine."

"We'll cross that bridge when the time comes. I'd be delighted to help you find a place eventually, but in the mean time, I don't want you rushing into something because you're worried about overstaying your welcome. That's not going to happen. This is like a mini break for me, you know I rarely take a break from work. To spend it with two of my favorite people, what more could I ask for."

"Mommy, when we move, can we move to the country and buy a house with lots of fields and a barn and keep horses and chickens and then we could get a dog and a cat."

"Where on earth did you come up with that idea, Emma? I thought you were a city girl."

"Well, I am kind of a city girl, but I really think I'd like to live in the country now and have riding stables."

"I see. And what am I going to do all day living in the middle of nowhere, especially when you've gone to school. I'm a city girl. There are no street lights out in the country you know. It'll be pitch black when the sun goes down, and the winters are real winters, not like here in Toronto. When it snows out in the sticks you can get snowed in and some days the school buses don't run so you get the day off school. They call them snow days."

"Wow, that's even better Mommy. I've never had a snow day in Toronto, that sounds really cool."

"I'm surprised we never bought a family cottage ourselves, but then George hated the countryside."

"I thought about buying one on Stony Lake once, nearly bought it too."

"You never told me that before, Rachael."

"You know me, Rebecca. I never like to tell anyone I'm thinking of doing something. The world is full of people who are always going to do something, but never actually do it. I don't like to say anything until I've done it, otherwise it's just a lot of hot air."

"Ah, but it's nice to dream sometimes, Rachael. You have my interest piqued. So why didn't you buy it?"

"I'd just opened up the New York office and I knew I couldn't spare the time to get away, not even for a weekend. I kind of regret it now. It was a beautiful place with magnificent views across the lake, as one would expect. A million dollar view with a million dollar price tag."

"That much? It must have been gorgeous."

"It was."

The lull in the conversation was broken by Rachael announcing, "Why don't we all take a drive into the countryside. Let's go the day after tomorrow. I'd like to go and look at some real estate again up at Stony Lake, afterwards we could drive up to Algonquin Park. I've never been there, but always wanted to go."

"That sounds like fun." Rebecca's voice was full of excitement. "Let's take a picnic with us. I've never been to Algonquin either, what do you say, Emma?"

"Count me in too. I'm so excited already I can't wait to go."

"We could take a look at the old cottage too, while we're up in that area, and see what changes the new owners have made," suggested Rebecca. "I haven't been back since Mom and Dad sold it."

"Yes let's do that, I haven't been back there myself either. Okay then, that's settled, so let's start planning our first trip out together. It's going to be an all day affair and if we're too tired to come home the same day, we'll find a motel somewhere and stay overnight. This trip will either destroy any thoughts of moving out of the city for good, or Miss Emma, it might be just the thing for you and your mom."

"Why do you want to look at Stony Lake again, Rachael? You're not thinking of buying a place there again are you?"

"If I don't take some time off I'm going to burn myself out. I just seem to be working all the time. I know it's my choice, but since you and Emma have been with me, it's made me think about life differently. If I do buy a place, I'd want you and Emma to use it as often as you can."

"What about Duncan?"

"Duncan actually hates the city. In fact if he knew I was looking for a place out in the Kawarthas, he'd be over the moon about it. He lives in the city because that's where his work is, that's where the real money is and because that's where I am too, not that he'd admit that."

"Why don't you marry him, Aunt Rachael, he's such a nice man?"

"Emma, that's not a polite question for a little girl to ask a grownup."

"Sorry, Mommy, sorry, Aunt Rachael, I didn't mean to be rude." Rachael looked in the rear view mirror and saw the crushed expression on her niece's face.

"That's okay, honey. You're right, Duncan really is a nice man and if we ever do get married I want you to be a bridesmaid."

O'Malley's Cottage

"Oh, thank you, Aunt Rachael, I'd really like that."
Rachael caught her sister staring at her. "What?"
"I do believe the thought is in your mind. Can I be a bridesmaid too?"
"I don't know what forces are at work here, but since you two came on the scene, my life seems to have been turned upside down."
"Can I ask one more question please, Aunt Rachael?"
"Sure, honey, can't guarantee you'll get an answer though, Emma."
"Has Duncan ever asked you to marry him?"
"Why, yes, he has."
"What did you say? Look at me. I'm as bad as you, Emma."
"He's still waiting for an answer. It was years ago since he asked the question. Guess it's about time I gave him an answer."
"Oh, please say yes, Aunt Rachael, please," squealed Emma.
"When I do tell him, I promise you two will be the first to know, and that's all I'm saying. Now let's change the subject, please."
When they got back to the condo, Rebecca spread the road maps over the dining room table, all three of them gathered around the table excitedly.
Together they planned their route up to Bobcaygeon, deciding to take Highway 36 east to Tates Bay Road, where their cottage had been, then on through Buckhorn to Burleigh Falls and Stony Lake. From there they would head north up to Bancroft and on up to Huntsville and finally Algonquin Provincial Park.
"We got ourselves a whole lot of driving ahead of us, Rebecca. That settles it, we're staying overnight somewhere up there. Everyone in agreement?" Rebecca and Emma smiled and nodded their heads in complete agreement as they looked up from studying the maps. "Okay. You two keep planning the route up there and home again, I'm going on the internet to find us a place

to stay."

"Tomorrow we'll have to go shopping for our supplies. Emma, why don't we make a list now of the things we'll need to take with us and what we'd all like to eat and drink for our picnic?"

"It's a shame Daddy can't come with us, Mommy."

"I know, honey."

"Perhaps Daddy will arrange a picnic and I could go with him too. That would be okay wouldn't it, that would be fair."

"Of course it would, Emma. When you phone him this evening why don't you ask him, I'm sure he'd like to do that with you too."

"You wouldn't be mad at me?"

"No, of course not, silly, why on earth would I be mad at you? Your father and I may be mad at each other, but that has nothing to do with you seeing your father. I think the time you spend with him now will be very precious for the two of you, and it's important that the two of you maintain a good relationship. As long as he's understanding, as I'm sure he will be, there won't be a problem. It's not like you're never going to see him again, Emma. It's up to him to make the time for you and that will be his choice. There's nothing for you to worry about, everything will be fine, you wait and see."

Rachael walked back into the room. "It's all arranged. By good fortune there was a last minute cancellation and I have secured us a room right on the lake for the day after tomorrow, so make sure you ladies bring your swimsuits with you. Look out Algonquin here we come!"

"Why don't I prepare a celebratory dinner for us all?" suggested Rebecca.

"Better still, why don't we all prepare dinner together? We'll just get it ready and before we eat, I suggest we all go down to the gym for a ladies workout before dinner. Come on troops, no slackers, you're gonna have to be in shape for all that hiking and swimming we're gonna be doing, and I'm not taking no for an answer."

"Come on, Emma, let's get changed. This reminds me of growing up with your aunt, she wouldn't take no for an answer then either. The reason I'm so skinny is because of her, she had me hiking, swimming and climbing almost every day at the cottage."

"Yeah, but you loved it and don't say you didn't. Emma, go choose a CD to take down with us, something lively to work out to."

"The Black-Eyed Peas okay, Aunt Rachael?"

"Mm, good choice. Let's get our swimsuits, we can go for a quick swim afterwards."

"I knew you were going to say that, Rachael. I just knew it, just like after we got back from hiking at the cottage and we were all exhausted. Let's go swimming now, you would say. You haven't changed a bit, Rachael Brown."

"And neither have you, Rebecca Brown, you're still whining," laughed Rachael.

Emma had never been to a gym before and was excited to try out all the equipment.

"Emma, let your Aunt Rachael and I supervise you, I don't want you lifting weights that are too heavy for you, especially at your age. It's not about lifting heavy weights anyway, smaller weights are better for you, just more repetitions. You'll see what I mean. Just don't overdo it."

"I won't, Mommy, I promise."

"Okay, we'll start off with a few stretches first to warm up."

By the time they had finished, with the Black-Eyed Peas still ringing in their ears, they were hot and sweaty.

"That swimming pool looks inviting, Rachael."

"Told you."

"Rebecca, Emma, let's change into our pajamas and eat dinner on our laps. I'll order a movie."

"Can we watch The Pink Panther please, Aunt Rachael?"
"Great idea, I just love Steve Martin, he's hilarious."

* * *

The following morning, Rachael was the first one up followed by Rebecca and then Emma. By the time they all sat around the kitchen table for breakfast, it was already ten o'clock. At eleven o'clock the phone rang.
"Good morning, Miss Rachael."
"Good morning, John. Everything okay this morning?"
"Oh, absolutely, everything is just wonderful. I thought I'd give you a call just to let you know that I stayed a little later last night and this morning I have sorted out enough work to keep Miss Rebecca busy. It's all here bundled up ready to go whenever you like. If you wish I can bring it over."
"No, that won't be necessary, thank you, John. By the sounds of it you have been busy, I appreciate this very much, especially as this gives me a good excuse to call in at the office today and saves me from going food shopping, which you know I hate. We'll come by before lunch, that'll give me the afternoon to catch-up on a few things. Rebecca and Emma can take off shopping. Thanks again, John, see you soon."
"You're most welcome."
"Well, Miss Rebecca, that was John. He really must be delighted that you've come to join the workforce, he worked late last night and all this morning getting you some manuscripts to read. They're ready and waiting at the office. I'll bring them home in the Bentley. I hope you don't mind, but I have a few things to sort out at the office, so I thought you and Emma could take my Mini and go shopping. You don't mind do you?"
"No, of course not. I know how much you hate food

O'Malley's Cottage

shopping." Rachael looked embarrassed. "Believe me, Emma, if we were going shopping for clothes, your Aunt Rachael would be coming with us and would be the first one out of the car and into the boutique."

"Oh, don't be like that, sis, now you make me feel guilty."

"I'm only joking Rachael, that sounds like a good idea to me."

When Rebecca saw all the manuscripts neatly packaged ready for her she was so excited she threw her arms around John and kissed him on the cheek. He stood there quite shocked, but delighted. Rachael smiled at her sister.

"Miss Rebecca, as one of my employees, may I remind you of the laws regarding workplace harassment. We do not kiss each other in the workplace."

"Oh, I'm so sorry!"

"Miss Rachael, I assure you I wasn't in the least bit offended."

"Oh, for Pete's sake, lighten up you two, I was only joking." Rachael walked into her office shaking her head in disbelief. "Okay, fun's over, back to work everybody, there are people queuing up for your jobs."

"Thank you, John, for going to all this trouble."

"It's a pleasure, Miss Rebecca. We're so glad to have you with us. Any problems, any problems at all, I am only a phone call away. Here's my card, it has my cell phone number on it. As you are now part of the team I'll write my home number on the back."

"Oh, I wouldn't call you at home, John."

"Not at all. Think of me as your support service. By the way, have fun tomorrow, I hear you're off to Algonquin. You'll absolutely love it there. My partner, Bradley, and I spend a week up there every fall, the colors are simply gorgeous. You should visit Algonquin in the fall if you can, I know a delightful place to stay, positively enchanting. Well, better get back to work."

Rebecca and Emma bustled off to the mall to go grocery

shopping for the next day's excursion. They decided to make a huge chicken salad for their picnic.

That evening Rachael's kitchen was a hive of activity filled with rich, pleasing aromatic smells that wafted throughout her condo, courtesy of Rebecca's cooking.

"We should have done this ages ago, Rebecca. I can't believe we waited all this time to do this."

"I know. Isn't it fun? I've packed my camera, binoculars, bug spray, sun hats, sunglasses, sun lotion, tissues, maps, note pad and pen."

"Are we going for good, Rachael? Look at all the stuff we're bringing with us. Good job you've got a big car, we'd never get half this stuff in your Mini."

"You know, sis, I'm having so much fun I can't wait to get going. I'd like to be on the road by seven thirty, if that's okay by you. I know you need more beauty sleep than I do."

"I don't think so, Miss Rachael Brown, about the beauty sleep I mean. Seven thirty's fine by me. I guess an early night is in order for us all, Emma's already tucked up in bed reading her book like an old lady."

"There's nothing better than snuggling up in a warm bed with a good book or a magazine at any age."

"I might just start reading one of those manuscripts in bed tonight. That way I can mix business with pleasure, and to think I'm getting paid to do it."

"Fill your boots, Rebecca, don't burn yourself out though. One thing's for sure, you'll never run out of reading material again." Rachael held her sister's gaze. "You don't fool me, Rebecca Brown. I know you're hurting big time inside and just putting a brave face on things for Emma's sake. I admire you for it, but remember, it's okay to hurt, just don't start bottling it all up inside. That's not good. You know what I'm saying?"

"I hear you, Rachael. Do you think Emma's okay? I mean, am I doing the right thing?"

"Rebecca, only one person knows the answer to that and it isn't you or me. He's up there looking down on you, and you be guided by His wisdom. Girl, you're a good person and it'll turn out all right in the end, you'll see. For what it's worth, I know you're doing the right thing and Emma's gonna be fine too."

"I sure hope so, Rachael. Anyway enough of that, I'm going to turn in, getting up at six in the morning is not my idea of fun, and no more wisecracks about beauty sleep either."

Chapter Five

Rebecca swung her feet out of bed. It was 6 a.m. Today was going to be a special day, and she was excited about it. She awoke early to be sure of getting her shower first. Rachael rose with the same thought in mind. The two met at the bathroom door.

"Well, Rebecca, I think we're going to have to draw straws for the bathroom this morning. Ordinarily, as my guest I would let you go first." She turned to see a sleepy headed child dragging a stuffed toy along the hall. "Good morning, Emma." She bent down to hug her niece. The bathroom door shut behind her. "Rebecca! You two had this planned. Don't be too long in there."

"I won't," came a muffled reply.

"It was like this when your mom and I were kids," Rachael smiled at Emma. "That's the kind of sneaky thing she would have done back then too. Let's go and start breakfast, I'm dying for a cup of coffee. How did you sleep?"

"I had a dream about horses."

"Was it a nice dream?"

"Yes, I got to save all these horses."

"How many horses were there?"

"Over a hundred. And every one had their own stable with lots of straw and fresh hay."

"That does sound like a nice dream."

* * *

They made good time leaving Toronto and were soon heading east on the 115 towards Peterborough.

"The air feels so much fresher," Rebecca leaned her head against the window and breathed deeply.

O'Malley's Cottage

"If you think this is fresh, wait until we get up north, it's almost pure oxygen." Rachael laughed and turned briefly to glance at Emma. "Would you pass the clipboard up to your mom, it's tucked behind her seat."

Emma pulled the clipboard out and handed it over the seat.

"Thanks," Rebecca said. "What am I supposed to be looking for?"

"After you went to bed last night I did some checking on the online real estate site. There are a couple of properties on Stony Lake that are worth investigating."

"Look at this one," Rebecca pointed her finger at an impressive lakeshore estate. "It's gorgeous. Emma and I will definitely be coming to this cottage if you buy it."

* * *

After a couple more hours of driving they arrived in the small town of Bobcaygeon.

"Look how built-up it is now," Rachael commented. "It's nothing like I remember. I hope they don't spoil it by over development."

"Let's see if the Kawartha Dairy's still open."

"That was our favorite place to go," Rachael explained to Emma. "Your grandpa and grandma would bring us here for the best ice cream. I wonder if they still have all those flavors?" They turned off the main road. "I'm sure it's around here somewhere. Any ideas, Rebecca?"

"I seem to recall it being around here too. Take the next left."

"Hey, what a memory," Rachael pulled up in front of the building and high-fived her sister, "and even better, it's open. Come on, Emma, you're in for a real treat."

They stood in front of a large chalkboard menu and studied the choices.

"And what can I get you ladies this morning," asked the cheerful teenage girl from the window.

"A small butterscotch, a small praline and cream, and a medium bear claw, thank you." Rachael handed across the money, and they all moved to the window to her right, where a lanky teenage boy handed out their ice cream

They piled back into the car and headed across the swing bridge and into the old part of town.

"At least this part of town hasn't changed much. Remember that restaurant?" Rebecca pointed across the street. "When we were at the cottage, Grandma and Grandpa used to take us there every week," she said turning to face Emma. "Why are you stopping, Rachael?"

"Bigleys!" Rebecca caught on an instant after she asked, and shouted the name in unison with her sister.

"Come on, Emma." Rachael grasped her niece's hand. "We're going shopping for shoes and purses."

It was almost an hour before they left the store carrying two large bags each.

"You didn't have to buy me all these expensive shoes and a new purse," Rebecca said, "but thank you. They are gorgeous."

"It's no fun shopping on your own. Having you along is what makes it fun. And don't keep thanking me, you're my sister and I love you. Spoiling you and Emma gives me great pleasure. Come on, let's tour the town."

"That used to be Mabel's candy store," Rebecca explained as they drove by a boarded up store. "When we were kids, Aunt Rachael and I would walk all the way from our cottage to buy candy at Mabel's store."

"That was a long walk, sis. No wonder we were skinny."

At Tates Bay Road, Rachael turned onto a very narrow tree-lined road and followed it a short distance to where their old cottage used to be. Memories flooded back to Rebecca and Rachael as they listened to the sounds of children laughing and screaming with delight.

"Does it make you sad, Mommy?" Emma asked, noting Rebecca's expression.

"A little, but I'm happy that a bunch of other children are having fun just like we did."

"Me too," said Rachael, her eyes watering with emotion. "I can see you and me, sis, playing among those kids."

* * *

Leaving the lakeside scene, they drove towards the Lovesick Lake Restaurant at Burleigh Falls.

"I forgot to tell you," Rachael turned to Emma. "I was thinking about it last night when we were watching, *The Pink Panther*. They filmed, *Cheaper by the Dozen Two* at Burleigh Falls. To think Steve Martin was right here, fancy that."

"Really, Aunt Rachael? Mommy, we have to rent that movie now that we've actually been here."

"It's the next one on our list," Rebecca laughed. "Are we ready to go see those falls?"

"You bet. Last one up there's a rotten egg." Emma raced out the door and headed up the path.

"Emma, wait for us!" Rachael streaked after her niece.

"Not so close to the edge," Rebecca called after her daughter. "If you slip and fall that will be the end of you."

"And if you fall in your mom and I will get your share of the picnic basket," Rachael called after her feisty niece.

"No way!" Emma backed away from the magnificent, but lethal falls and both women breathed a sigh of relief.

They stood on a huge rock, transfixed by the beauty and power of Mother Nature, in awe of the cascading rapids, watching the foaming water roaring over the limestone rocks and out into

Stony Lake.

"Can we have our picnic here?" Emma danced on her toes and looked hopefully at both her aunt and her mother.

"It's too early to eat," Rebecca said.

"I wish we could live here, Mommy."

"Wouldn't you miss Toronto and all your friends?"

"I'd miss my friends and I'd miss Toronto a bit."

"I hate to interrupt," Rachael said, "but I told the real estate agent to meet us at Lovesick Restaurant at midday, I expect he'll be there by now."

"Are we actually going to look at that estate?"

"You don't think we drove all this way just to ooh and ah at this waterfall do you? Lovely as it is. Come on, let's not keep the man waiting."

They returned to the restaurant just as another vehicle drove into the parking lot.

"That's got to be him," Rachael nudged her sister. "Look at that fake smile."

Rebecca nodded agreement and they shared a chuckle when he headed in their direction.

"Ms. Brown?" The agent extended a limp hand.

"I'm Rachael Brown. This is my sister Rebecca and my niece Emma. We thought we'd all come for the grand tour." She gave the agent a firm handshake.

"Splendid. You chose a beautiful day to come. Sun shining and not a cloud in the sky. As you will no doubt appreciate, a property like this doesn't come on the market very often, and when it does, it's soon snapped up."

"Mr. Williams," Rachael interjected.

"Please, call me Ben."

"Ben, I don't need the sales pitch. At the price your asking, this house isn't going anywhere in a hurry. However, I would like to see it."

Williams blushed and quickly changed his approach. "Why don't I just show you where the house is and give you the key. I'll wait outside. Take all the time you like. If you have any questions, I'll be more than happy to answer them for you."

"That would be perfect, Ben." Rachael smiled in her most disarming way.

They drove up to a large estate home overlooking the lake with carefully manicured lawns and a priceless view. The lake frontage was long and the entire estate was surrounded by mature trees. It was a very private setting.

As soon as they started up the drive Rachael gave a gasp of delight. Ben would have been salivating had he seen her reaction. Neither Rebecca, nor Emma spoke, all that could be heard from the two of them was the occasional gasp of surprise.

When they pulled into the circular drive and parked behind Ben, they all got out and he handed Rachael the keys.

"Take as much time as you like!" he called after them. Holding hands they walked up to the huge front door.

Rachael unlocked it and let the solid oak door swing open.

"Wow!" Rebecca let out her breath. "It's huge. I love the cathedral ceiling, and look at that view of the lake through the dining room window! Look at all the wood. Oh, Rachael, it's beautiful."

"Are you on Mr. Williams' payroll?" Rachael chuckled. "If not, you certainly ought to be. I think real estate might just be the business for you."

"Oh, stop, it is beautiful you have to admit it. I love the design of that window overlooking the lake. This view makes me want to take up my paint brushes again."

Emma dashed from room to room exhibiting that special excitement that only a child feels when looking around the inside of a large house.

Rachael and Rebecca strolled through the house together,

secretly wishing they could run through it with as much delight and naivety as Emma.
    "You know, Rachael, this house has a nice atmosphere."
    "It does, doesn't it?"
    "Do you like it?"
    "No, I wouldn't say, I like it."
    Rebecca looked at her sister in surprise.
    "I'd say it's more like I love it! But don't you let old Benny know that. It does seem to be in fantastic condition, but I won't make any decisions until I've had a full inspection done."
    "Of course you won't."
    "That's a lot of money to have tied up in real estate, when it could be earning me money on the stock exchange."
    "But you really are considering buying this house?"
    "I've always liked this area. I don't have to get a plane to get here and it's just far enough away from Toronto to make me feel I've really left the office behind me."
    "Yes, but knowing you, you'll bring work along anyhow."
    "Not as much as I might have. You'll be taking a lot off my shoulders; I didn't just hire you for your pretty face you know."
    "Even with the extra beauty sleep I need?" Rebecca placed an arm around her sister's waist. "I'm so glad that I'm going to be working for you."
    "Me too. Now, let's get that child and go stroll around the grounds."
    "Emma! Come on, honey, we're going to take a look outside."
    "Coming, Mommy! I found the perfect room for me. It's right at the top of the house. It's already painted in my favorite color, pink. I can see for miles from up there too, right across the lake."
    "Well, that's you organized then," Rachael laughed. "What

O'Malley's Cottage
Page 77

do you think about this house? Do you think we should buy it?"

"Oh yes, Aunt Rachael. If I had the money I'd buy it today."

"Well, that's an important endorsement," Rebecca hugged her daughter. "Come on, let's take a look outside. Mr. Williams is probably regretting giving us the key; we've been looking around for ages."

"He won't be regretting the wait if I end up buying the place." Rachael snorted. "He'd be camped out there in a tent in the pouring rain if he so much as had an inkling I might buy this house."

"Are you still going to keep your condo in Florida?"

"Damn right I am. No way I'm freezing to death all winter. Ah, Mr. Williams," Rachael winced because he'd been standing just outside the front door and no doubt heard her comments.

"Ben," interrupted the grinning real estate agent. "Please call me Ben. Would you like to look around the grounds?" If it meant making a sale, he'd have stretched out across a puddle, so Rachael could walk across his back to avoid getting her feet wet.

"Yes, we would, and please join us, Ben, I have a few questions."

As they strolled about the grounds Rachael made a series of notes on her iPad. When she told Ben that she'd be sending someone to make a detailed examination of the house, he could hardly contain his excitement.

"I am at your disposal. Feel free to call me anytime, day or night. Here's my card."

"And here's mine. And, Ben."

"Yes, Ms. Brown?"

"Please don't pester me. If I make a decision, you will be amongst the first to know, I assure you. Based on my surveyor's findings, I will book another viewing with you sometime next week. If the matter requires more urgent attention, phone me, but remember I will not be cajoled into buying anything."

* * *

After leaving Ben Williams, the little party continued northwards up Highway 28 towards Bancroft.

"Look at that," Rachel pointed straight ahead, "this place even has a Tim Hortons, I guess it's civilized after all. Let's use the washrooms and grab a coffee to go."

They piled out of the car and walked into the restaurant.

A very good-looking man stood up as they entered and both women tilted their heads to get a better look. Tall and slim, dressed in a crisp white T-shirt, clean blue denim jeans and brown leather cowboy boots, he definitely rated a second look. His T-shirt sported a picture of two draught horses hauling logs and the words, *If you can't pull with the big boys, stay out of the barn*, in bold black letters.

The cowboy walked towards them and Emma ducked behind her mother.

"No offence ladies," the cowboy flashed a big grin, showing off a set of perfect white teeth.

"Good dental plan," Rachael muttered.

"I can't speak for the others here. I apologize, I was only staring because I've never seen two more beautiful women, and if that's a crime I'm sorry."

Rebecca's eyes widened in surprise and Rachael chuckled loudly.

"Chuck Rivers at your service ladies," he said, politely raising his Stetson.

"Rachael," Rebecca whispered to her sister. "He looks like Alan Jackson."

"That's kind of you to say so," the cowboy smiled at Rebecca. "I like his music too. I do play a little guitar and sing around the campfire sometimes, if the mood is right and the company's good. You should come on over to my place sometime, you'd all be very welcome."

"Chuck Rivers?" Rachael didn't look convinced.

The cowboy rummaged through his wallet, pulled out his driver's license, and handed it to Rachael.

"The one thing I learned to do at school was to read real well, and if I'm not mistaken that says, Charles Rivers. Chuck to you ladies and my friends."

Rachael looked at the driver's license closely. She was surprised to see a Toronto address, a very nice neighborhood too.

"Let me buy you ladies a coffee and a drink for the princess here." The word, *princess* hurtful, suppressed emotions. Chuck immediately recognized it on Emma's face. "I'm sorry, did I say something wrong?"

"No, it's okay," replied Rebecca, looking flustered. "Princess is what my ex-husband calls our daughter. We appreciate the offer of coffee, but we have to get going. Thank you anyway." She smiled at the stranger, locking eyes with his, the stare a little too long to be called, *a casual glance.*

"My pleasure. I'm up here at my cottage, if you have any problems, here's my card, give me a call. Have a good day and enjoy yourselves." He returned to his chair and picked up his coffee, but his eyes followed Rebecca as the women left the restaurant.

Without thinking, Rebecca smiled back at him before stepping outside.

"Rebecca, I do believe you're flirting."

"What does flirting mean, Aunt Rachael?"

"It can mean a whole lotta trouble, that's what flirting means."

"Was I flirting, Aunt Rachael?"

"At your age, I sure hope not." She glanced at Rebecca. "Had to let him know you were single didn't you, I'm surprised you didn't give him you're phone number too."

"As a matter of fact I did. I wrote it on a napkin and gave it to him as we were leaving."

"You did not! Tell me you didn't."

"You're so easy, Rachael," Rebecca burst out laughing. "Of course I didn't."

"All right, all right. I'll admit, he was kind of cute, probably a serial killer though."

As they drove along the road, Rebecca pulled the business card out of her purse.

"He's a crown attorney."

"He's a what? A crown attorney, no way. Him a lawyer, well I'll be. According to the address on his driver's license he lives in a neighborhood similar to your home in Toronto. Must have money."

"That's what it says on the card. Works for the Toronto Crown Attorney's Office. And that's not my home anymore."

"The last thing you need is another lawyer. Throw that card out the window right now."

"I am not going to deposit garbage on this pristine landscape. At the next available garbage can I'll drop it in, how's that?"

"Perfect. Okay let's get moving, I'm starving, it's time we found a place for our picnic."

Rebecca placed the business card back inside her purse. This time she carefully tucked it between her driver's license and credit cards.

They stopped at a gas station on the outskirts of Bancroft. Emma insisted on helping her aunt pump the gas.

"Don't spill any, Emma, that stuff's almost the price of gold these days."

"I won't, Aunt Rachael, I'll be careful I promise."

O'Malley's Cottage
Page 81

"Mind the paintwork with the end of that nozzle. Don't squeeze the trigger until you got the nozzle in the gas tank. That's right, you got it you little gas pump attendant you."

"It took a lot of gas, Aunt Rachael, I think you almost emptied the pump."

"I think you're right. Next time we'll either bring the Mini or cycle up."

When Emma got back in the car Rebecca smiled and ruffled her daughter's hair. "That was nice of you to help your aunt pump gas."

"It sure cost a lot of money."

"I bet it did. When we get home I'm going to sell the Mercedes and buy a smaller car. We don't need a four-wheel drive in the city anyway."

"Okay, off we go." Rachael climbed into the driver's seat and started the car.

"You throw that lawyer's business card out like you said you would? Rebecca, are you listening?"

"Sorry, Rachael, I was daydreaming."

"I bet you were. I said, did you throw that lawyer's card out"

"Of course. Don't give it another thought, I'm certainly not."

"Mmm ... And that's coming from a girl who burgled her own sister's bedroom. Let's change the subject. The countryside sure is pretty up here." After a lull in the conversation Rachael asked, "Where are we now, navigator?"

"Judging by that sign we just passed, not where we're supposed to be. I think we're on the right road, but we're going the wrong way."

"Oh, how very Irish. You hear that, Emma? We're on the right road, but we're going the wrong way." Rachael put on her best Gaelic accent.

"I think we're somewhere near Kingscote Lake." Rebecca

O'Malley's Cottage

pointed to a road sign. "Yes, we're on Kingscote Lake Road. Look, I see water, over there to the right. Let's go there and have our picnic, it looks a nice spot."

"Fine by me."

Rachael drove a bit further and then stopped and put the car into reverse.

"Why are we backing up?" Rebecca asked. Rachael pointed across the road.

Set back off the road a short distance was a small house. It was old looking, but appeared to be well maintained, with newly painted white clapboard exterior and dark green wooden shutters. The front door and eaves were also painted green and the roof looked to have been recently shingled. The place looked inviting and very cozy.

In the centre of the crossbeam over the front door was a decorative ceramic nameplate. The name of the cottage stood out in old English black lettering from amongst the brightly painted wild flowers; *O'Malley's Cottage.* sign in the front garden said, *For Rent.*

An old couple, busy gardening, looked up over the hedge and waved at them from the front garden of the cottage.

"Lovely day!" said the old man, who looked to be in his eighties. He was baked a deep brown by the sun from working outdoors most of his life. He had on green coveralls and an old straw hat. Straightening himself up with obvious discomfort, he walked towards the car. He was a short little man without an ounce of fat, and by the time he had eased out the kinks in his back, he wasn't that much taller.

"Good day to you," said the old man. "Can I help you good folk?" The Irish lilt to his long forgotten accent was still present, mixed-up somewhere in mid Atlantic.

"We stopped to admire your cottage!" Rachael smiled and

pointed her hand at the small house.

"It's for rent you know."

The old lady wandered over to join her husband. She was as sun ripened as he was and just as small and skinny. She too looked to be in her eighties.

"Pay no attention to him," she said, "he's as deaf as our barn door. Have you come to look at the cottage? Well, come on in and take a look."

"Well, I ..." Rachael hadn't expected anyone to be in the garden. The old couple had been hidden by the low hedge that grew haphazardly around the front garden.

"Oh, please let's take a look inside," pleaded Emma.

"What on earth for, Emma?" Rebecca interrupted. "We're not going to be renting it."

"Oh, come on, just for a bit of fun," Rachael jumped out and opened the door for her niece. "You can stay in the car if you want. Coming, Emma?"

Emma didn't need to be asked twice. Rebecca reluctantly got out of the car and followed them across the road to the cottage.

"Do you own this cottage?" Rachael walked along beside the old woman.

"Yes, we do." The old lady proudly claimed ownership.

"Where do you live?" asked Emma.

"We live on that farm right there." The woman pointed to a red brick farmhouse that was just visible in the distance. Not far from the farmhouse was a big barn, and one grain silo, its steel roof brown with rust, the brass weathervane still attached on top.

"I don't see any animals. Don't you have animals on your farm?" Emma quizzed the woman anxiously.

"We used to have lots of animals when we were younger, but we're retired now. We keep a few pigs, a few chickens, ah, that's the cockerel calling out to his hens now. Did you hear him?"

"Yes. He's loud. Do you have any other animals?"

"Yes, we do." The old man spoke up. "We've got two

Belgians, two Quarter horses, a Shetland pony, a few cattle and Robby our Border Collie, and lots of barn cats," added the old man, whose hearing was not quite as bad as his wife maintained.

"What are Belgians? Do the cats have any kittens?"

"Belgians are draught horses, we used to use them for plowing, but now they help draw in the wood for us. And do the cats have kittens? You bet they do, would you like to see them?"

"Yes, please. Is that okay Mommy?"

"I guess so."

"What are Quarter horses?"

"It's just a name for another breed of horse. They make good riding horses, very sturdy and strong, fast too. Good for rounding up cattle and barrel racing," replied the old man.

"Barrel racing. That sounds funny."

"You race the horse from one barrel across the paddock to another barrel, round that barrel and back to the first one, as fast as you can go. If you're up here long enough I'll take you to see a race."

"Did you ever enter your horses in any races?"

"Nope. Never made the time to do that. My horses have won enough competitions around this farm to make me happy. I thought you wanted to see inside the cottage?"

"That's right," said the old lady, "come on in and take a look around."

The old couple led the way up the path to the front door and stood back proudly as Rachael, Rebecca, and Emma walked inside.

"It's very clean." Rebecca looked around, warming to the cozy rooms in spite of herself. "I love all the antique furniture. How many bedrooms does it have?"

"Three," replied the woman. "The third bedroom is really tiny though, you couldn't swing a cat around in it. We'll leave you to it, if you need us we'll be out in the front garden. Come on, Roger, let them look around on their own."

"All right Donna. She's a slave driver you know. I'm actually only in my forties, but she's worked me so hard that I look like I'm in my eighties." The old man scuttled laughingly out of the house after his wife.

"Nice old couple." Rachael said when the door closed behind Roger and Donna.

"Yes, they are. He's quite the comedian too. I don't know why we're here though. It's a cute little cottage but not what we're looking for certainly. All the same, it would be a very nice place to spend the summer."

"Summer's only just started, Mommy. Perhaps we could rent it for the rest of the summer and if we really like it, we could stay longer. I could work on the farm to help pay for the rent."

"You'd spend all day playing with the kittens and never get any work done. And I don't think you'd like cleaning out the pigs, besides, what about school in the fall?"

"I could go to school here, they must have a school somewhere nearby."

"I don't think there's a school for miles around and anyway, you'd have to take the school bus, and I don't think you'd like that. It wouldn't be like in Toronto where you're only on the bus for ten minutes; up here you're more likely to be on it for an hour. I tell you what, let's finish looking around the house and we'll think about renting it for the summer. No promises though. I guess it would be a nice place to unwind for a while and a really great place to sit back and read all those manuscripts. What do you think, Rachael?"

"I think it's a splendid idea, not that I want to get rid of you or anything. Let's see the rest of the cottage and then we'll go and see those kittens. I'd think on it overnight, Rebecca, no need to make any decisions just yet. It is peaceful up here though, might be what you need, and if you do decide to take it, I might even come and stay a few days myself."

After they'd looked it over and Emma had excitedly approved every room in the place, they rejoined Donna in the garden.

"What do you think?" she asked.

"It's very nice. I don't want to make any snap decisions though. I'd like to think about it overnight at least."

"Of course you would. I tell you what, you think about it overnight, and if anyone comes between now and tomorrow afternoon I'll wait until I hear from you. Roger's already quite taken with your daughter and it would be nice to have a young one about the place again."

"That's really very kind of you, Mrs.?"

"Donna, call me Donna and this is my husband Roger."

"I'm Rebecca, this is my sister Rachael and my daughter Emma. She'd like to move in today if she could and has already told me that she'll help with the farm chores to help pay the rent. By the way, and I know this is not what you were wanting I'm sure, but if we decided to rent, could we try it until the end of the summer to see if we like it? Coming from Toronto all the way out here would take some adjustment."

"What do you think, Roger? The lady would like to rent it till the end of the summer to see if she likes living out here."

"Oh, that's fine, good idea. Be a devil to rent in the winter months though if she don't take it. Ah, what the heck, they seem like nice folk. Sure they can have it just for the summer if they like."

The old couple climbed into their battered red Ford F150 pick-up truck that looked as ancient as its owners, and drove off towards their farm, followed by the Bentley.

The rusty old Ford bounced up the rutted driveway, drawing up alongside the farmhouse. Rachael pulled in behind.

Rachael and Rebecca were dressed casually, but immaculately like any self-respecting Toronto woman would be, even if they were out visiting a farm.

"I'll go and put the kettle on. Roger, you go and show our guests around the farm," said Donna walking towards the farmhouse.

"Donna, don't go to any trouble on account of us."

"It's no trouble, Rebecca."

"We actually brought a picnic with us, we just haven't found the ideal spot to have it yet. At this rate we'll be having it for our supper."

"Well, just have a quick look around, a quick cup of tea and off you go. I'll draw a plan to show you a favorite spot that Roger and I occasionally visit. We used to picnic there all the time."

"Why don't you join us?"

"Oh, I don't know, you don't want a couple of old fuddy-duddies like us with you."

"Oh, come on, it would be fun," interjected Rachael. "We've got enough here for all of us."

"Okay then. On one condition, that I bring our own food and drinks. I'm not going to impose on you, and before you leave I'll give you one of my home baked apple pies and a jar of homemade raspberry jam. Agreed?"

"Agreed," replied Rebecca.

Roger took them for a guided tour of the farm, followed by Robby, his faithful Border Collie. Emma was enthralled with the animals and decided that as well as a writer and horse breeder, she was now going to be a vet. When Roger showed them the two Belgian horses, Maxwell and Minnie, Emma was shocked at the size of them. She thought Star and Blazer, the two Quarter horses looked big when she first saw them, but they now looked small compared to the Belgians. But when Emma's eyes fell upon Toby, the Shetland pony, it was love at first sight.

"Oh, he's so cute!" she kept saying over and over. Roger

put a small halter on the pony and led him out of the field through the sturdy steel gate. He had to slap the huge Belgians on their chests to move them back, they too wanted to be a part of the action, while Star and Blazer galloped around the field in excitement.

"Don't mind them," Roger said, referring to the Belgians. "They're both very gentle, they wouldn't hurt a fly. The trouble is they don't know their own strength and can be a bit playful at times. You don't want one of them treading on your foot believe me. Okay, Emma, why don't you take Toby for a walk. Here, hold the lead rope like this, he's a bit boisterous and inclined to play up like a naughty boy for five minutes and then he'll calm down. He'll be good for you to practice on before you take the Belgians out." He winked at Rebecca. "You never wrap the rope around your hand, ever; especially with a large horse. If they take off on you, you'll be dragged along the ground and trampled to death under their hooves. Toby's strong enough to pull you off your feet too, but I see you've already got the measure of him."

"Okay," said Emma completely undaunted and fearless. "Come on, Toby, you and me are going to be best friends." Toby began to buck. "No, Toby." Emma remained calm, but spoke firmly. "I know you're excited to be out here, but you have to behave or you'll go straight back in the field again and no walks. I am not going to let go of this rope, do you understand?"

Roger kept an experienced eye on the situation and could see that Emma had passed the test he had given her with flying colors. Toby quietly walked off with Emma, rubbing his head and shaggy mane over her arm.

"Join up between Emma and Toby has occurred," Roger announced proudly. "Will you look at that, we have the makings of a horsewoman. You have a fine girl there, Rebecca, a grand lass indeed."

O'Malley's Cottage

Emma, who was in seventh heaven was reluctant to bring Toby back.

"Come on, Emma, if you want to see the kittens, and thank, Mister?" Rebecca looked at Roger awaiting his surname.

"It's O'Malley."

"Emma, thank Mr. O'Malley."

"Thank you, Mr. O'Malley."

"It's O'Malley," he said again. "Next time you come, Emma, I'll teach you how to ride Toby, unless you know how to ride already that is."

"No, I've never been on a horse, Mr. O'Malley, I mean, O'Malley."

"Well, I must congratulate you on the way you handled that spirited animal young, Emma. I thought you were masterful. I can see that you have all the makings of a horse whisperer in you. Monty Roberts would be proud of you."

They didn't have a clue what Roger was talking about, let alone who Monty Roberts was.

As they drifted over towards the barn where the kittens were huddled in the straw with their mother, Emma discovered for the first time, the joy of love between a human being and an animal. She glanced over her shoulder to look at Toby peering through the gate.

For a feral cat, the mother was quite tame and didn't seem to mind Roger picking up one of her furry kittens and handing the little bundle to Emma. The kittens had their eyes open and were almost weaned, and all covered in the same coarse fur. There were four of them, a black, a ginger and two calico, all actively climbing over their mother. Emma held the ginger in her arms like a baby, cradling and cooing how cute he was.

"Oh, Mommy, can I take him home, please?" Emma pleaded.

"I don't think Aunt Rachael needs a cat in her apartment and I'm sure she would disown us if we stunk out her apartment

with cat litter."
"You got that right!" said Rachael pointedly.
"I'd keep the kitty litter box clean, I promise."
Realizing that an awkward situation was developing, O'Malley intervened.
"Well, Emma, this kitten is a country kitten and he'd be heartbroken to be brought up in a big city. Not only that, he'd miss his mom and his brothers and sisters. Tell you what I'll take care of him here for you. He can be yours whenever you're here, in fact you can even give him a name if you like."
"Marmalade. I'll call him Marmalade, because he's just the color of orange marmalade."
"Then Marmalade it will be."
Rebecca raised her eyebrows, demanding the appropriate response to such a gift. "Thank you, O'Malley."
"You're very welcome, Emma."
"If we do rent the cottage, Mommy, we'd need a cat to keep away the mice and I just know Marmalade would be a great mouser, so he should stay with us at the cottage. That's if we rent it I mean."
Rachael had been busy snapping photographs of the farm for her scrapbook.
"Come on, Emma, let's get another photo of you with the kitten. I'll get this one blown up for your bedroom wall."
Emma posed, beaming like a mother would with her newborn baby.
Rachael and Rebecca didn't want to linger around the pigpen for too long, but Emma insisted on having her photograph taken next to a huge sow that was nursing more piglets than you could count in one breath. At the chicken coup, Roger let Emma collect a dozen fresh farm eggs for them to take home.
"I guarantee these eggs will be the best you've ever tasted.

You won't get a dozen brown eggs better than these. That reminds me, I forgot to show you the beef cattle. We always keep a couple for ourselves, you can't beat homegrown beef. We'll be driving by their field on our way to the lake."

When they arrived back at the farmhouse, Donna had packed a small picnic for her and her husband.

"I don't know how you two can call yourselves retired," remarked Rachael. "It looks like you've both got a full time job just looking after all these animals, let alone the farm and the cottage. I don't know where you get the time or the energy."

"It's a labor of love, my dear," replied Donna. "We certainly don't do it for the money, we could never have got by just farming. I used to be a schoolteacher and Roger worked for the Township driving the grader in the summer and plowing the snow in the winter. It's been hard work. We've got three hundred acres to look after, but I wouldn't have changed a thing, well perhaps Roger maybe. Only joking, my love. Right, I suggest you all give your hands a good wash and we set off."

"We might as well go in my car," suggested Rachael. "No sense taking two vehicles is there?"

"That would be very nice. It's been a long time since I rode in such a posh looking vehicle, I almost feel as though I should get dressed up for the occasion. Roger, we're going in style this afternoon, so go put a clean pair of pants on and clean shoes too."

* * *

Driving down the road past the field with the cattle, so Emma could at least say she saw them, Rebecca made an observation about the cottage.

"It looks very rugged behind the cottage. Once you leave the back garden it looks as though you're heading into the wilderness."

"You are," replied Donna. "That's something we should

O'Malley's Cottage

discuss if you rent the cottage. You wouldn't want to wander in there unless you knew the ways of the backcountry. In seconds you could be completely lost, swallowed up by the sheer vastness of it. You'd soon become disorientated and think you were heading back towards the cottage, when in fact you were going in completely the wrong direction. You don't fool around like that up here, I mean that sincerely. Many people have found themselves lost in those woods. Most of them, thankfully, have either found their way out again or been rescued, but not all of them. It's no fun being lost in the woods I can tell you. Roger and I got lost a couple of times when we first moved up here. We were lucky to find our way out again, before the sun went down. You might get away with it in the summer, but certainly not in the middle of winter, not up here anyway."

"What kind of animals are in there, Mrs. O'Malley?"

"Moose, deer, black bears, wolves, cougars to name just a few. Generally speaking the bears don't bother you, just don't leave food in your car overnight, bears have an excellent sense of smell. They'll rip your car door off its hinges just to get at that chocolate bar you forgot to bring in."

"There's no danger of leaving a chocolate bar in the car with Emma around," Rebecca joked and Emma blushed, but said nothing.

"Here's a tip when walking around in unfamiliar country," said Roger. "Always stop and turn around when you reach a fork in the trail. Look back down the trail you're on, so what you see sticks in your mind and looks familiar when you're heading back. That way you've got a better chance of remembering which way to go. Golden rule though, never step off the trail, or you'll get into some serious trouble. Best thing to do if you get lost, Emma, is to stay put and let the rescuers come to you. Find a tree you like, a friendly tree and give it a big hug. The tree will watch over you

O'Malley's Cottage

until we come and find you. I'll show you how to find north using the sun, a stick in the ground and three small stones. Remind me about that when we get to the lake. Turn right here, Rachael. It's a bit bumpy, but not too bad this time of year."

They followed a narrow winding dirt road with steep hills you couldn't see over, not until the hood of the car began to come down on the other side. With the Bentley's long hood, it felt like they were on a boat at sea, cresting up and down large waves.

"I guess you don't drive down here in the winter?" Rachael said.

"Not even in a four-by-four. You might risk it on a snowmobile, but even then you'd be cautious. It's a long walk back out, and that can be exhausting in deep snow, believe me. You look up at the sky tonight, Emma, and you'll see things you can't even see in the sky in Toronto, like stars for instance."

"Now don't get him started. Roger likes to talk only he doesn't have an off button, do you dear?"

"What's that, precious?"

"Nothing, dear. My, this is a comfy ride. You ought to trade that old truck of yours in, Roger, and buy one of these. A girl could get used to this."

"I'd have to take the back seats out so I could take the pigs to market, apart from that I think it would be fine. Needs a few dents in it, some scratches and rust. I like a vehicle that looks like it's being used."

"By the time we get to where we're going I think this vehicle is going to fit that description to a tee," muttered Rachael. "If I'd known we were going off road I'd have bought a Hummer. Maybe that's what I need, one of those big old army style Hummers."

"You'll be fine, it doesn't get any worse than this. When we get there you're gonna thank me."

"And when we get there we're going to thank Rachael for taking us there," added Donna.

Cresting the next hill the lake came into view, surrounded by rocks and trees that stretched for miles. Roger and Donna smiled, listening to the gasps of appreciation from their visitors. The view was spectacular.

Approaching the deserted lake, even the talkative O'Malley was silent, staring ahead through the windshield. Emma noticed tears rolling down his cheeks and nudged her mother. Donna caught the movement and whispered to her.

"Don't pay any attention to him, dear. He gets like this sometimes, remembering the past. It's been a tough life. He's not long for this world and doesn't want to leave it. In his mind he hasn't finished all his chores and climbed all those mountains he wanted to climb. And now he's just too old to climb them. He thinks he's still a young man, but his body is failing him. He'll come out of it soon and won't even know he left us."

Rebecca felt sad for the old man and wondered how she would feel when her time was coming to an end. She hoped she would be as much at peace with herself as Donna was with herself.

"Are you okay, dear?"

"Yes, I'm fine, I must have drifted off."

Rachael slowed the car and brought it to a stop at the end of the road. Roger got out and guided her across an area of grassland adjoining the lake, making sure that she didn't hit any of the rocks hidden in the long grass. With great care, mindful of the rocks, those visible and those hidden, Rachael turned the car around to face back up the road.

They found an old, but still serviceable wooden picnic table down by the lakeshore. There was still enough decent wood left among the rotting parts to keep it together, however it creaked and shifted position when they sat on it, but its rusted bolts held firm.

Rachael brought out a sun umbrella. Roger secured the pointed end into the ground and lashed the pole securely against the table using a piece of orange baler twine he always carried in his pocket. Within ten minutes the table was set, covered in a red and white checkered plastic tablecloth with overflowing hampers on top, full of food and drink.

"Mommy, can I go swimming before I have my lunch, otherwise I'll have to wait ages afterwards? Please."

"Is it safe to swim in the lake?" Rebecca asked Donna.

"Oh, yes, she'll be fine. We'll keep an eye on her."

"Okay, honey, but don't go too far out, we'll keep your lunch here for you. I'll come up to the car with you while you change into your swimsuit and get you a towel. You know the rules, be safe and have lots of fun. Come on while I get you organized."

"Thanks, Mommy."

Emma hugged her mother clinging to her waist as they walked across the rough grass together. She soon emerged from the back of the car in a bright pink swimsuit and dashed off down to the lake. Before anyone thought to tell her that the water was freezing, Emma ran full speed into the lake. As fast as she had run in, she was even faster running out, screaming in shock and giggling with delight.

"Aunt Rachael, you should come for a swim, it's lovely and warm, you'd love it! It's much warmer than the swimming pool I promise." The huge smile across Emma's face coupled with her mischievous look was not convincing.

"Well, I'm going to have to test that out, Emma. I'm going to dip my toes in the lake and if you're lying to me I'm going to tickle you to death." Rachael got up and walked down to the lake. The closer she got, the more Emma coaxed her on.

"Just run in like I did, you'll love it," she giggled.

Rachael, always a good sport jogged across the sandy beach into the lake.

"Yikes! This water's freezing, you little minx," she turned and raced barefoot across the sand after her niece. Emma ran screaming along the beach with her aunt in hot pursuit. She couldn't believe how fast her aunt could run. Rachael scooped Emma up in her arms and began tickling her. Emma's screams became even louder, pleading with her aunt to stop. Amid fits of laughter the two of them collapsed onto the sand.

"All right, just to prove I'm no scaredy cat, I'll come swimming with you. I'll be back in a minute."

Rachael walked back down to the beach in a pair of flip flops, wearing a black one-piece swimsuit, carrying a striped towel over her arm.

Donna turned to Roger, "Shut your eyes, Roger, otherwise you'll give yourself a coronary." Rebecca smiled in amusement.

"Well, am I ever glad I came for a picnic, everything looks so delicious," replied Roger, a big smirk across his weather-beaten face.

"I'm sorry, Roger, she's already taken," joked Rebecca.

"Pity. I figured a good-looking young chap like meself would have a chance. Ah, well."

"In your dreams, my dear. Are you going swimming, Rebecca?"

"No, I'd rather sit and watch those two, besides I really don't like the cold. I'm quite content to sit here and chat. Shall we start our picnic? Who knows when they'll be out of the water, they could be there all day."

While Rachael and Emma swam, Rebecca, Donna, and Roger fell into conversation. It was as though they had known each other for years instead of only just having met. Rebecca found the two of them very easy to talk to. She opened up to them, telling them about her recent separation. Despite the sunshine, she began to cry. Donna placed a comforting arm around her shoulders.

Rebecca asked them if they had children. She saw the anguish clearly visible in their eyes. Neither of them spoke. Roger looked down at the ground in sorrow as if still mourning something from the past.

"I'm sorry," said Rebecca. She felt awkward and busied herself arranging the table again. After a long silence Donna spoke in short, stilted sentences. Images appeared in her mind as if a slide projector was showing each image one frame at a time. She was staring far off into the distance to a place that only she could see.

"We had a daughter, Rowena. She would have been about Emma's age. At that time we lived on the outskirts of Toronto. As you can imagine it was pretty rural then, not like it is now. It was a day much like today, sunny and hot with a nice breeze. I still remember it. It was a Sunday afternoon. Roger was working in the basement of our house, building a laundry room for me. I was in the kitchen preparing dinner. I had a small piece of roast beef in the oven already. I was standing at the kitchen sink peeling carrots and had forgotten to bring some potatoes up from the basement. I could see Rowena happily riding her bicycle up and down the lane in front of the kitchen window." Rebecca sat riveted to every word.

"It had a little wicker basket on the front, stuffed with her dolls and teddy bears. She told me she was taking them for a ride. I told her not to go too far, to stay in front of the house where I could see her. I went down to the basement to fetch the potatoes. Roger asked me to hold up one end of a two-by-four, while he nailed it into position. I wasn't down there long at all. When I got back upstairs and looked out the kitchen window again, Rowena's shiny red bicycle was lying on the ground in the middle of the lane. I could see the front wheel still spinning and her dolls and teddy bears strewn across the ground. Rowena was nowhere in sight. I looked up the lane and saw a cloud of dust. I could just make out a dark colored car speeding away in the distance. The police never found our daughter."

"I'm so sorry," said Rebecca, now crying. She realized her troubles were nothing compared with Donna's and felt embarrassed about having said anything.

"After I spoke with the detectives, I never spoke about it again to anyone. In over fifty years you're the first person I've ever told. Roger and I used to come out here before Rowena was born. After she disappeared we sold everything and moved here to start a new life. We've carried a sense of guilt with us ever since. We felt we didn't deserve to have any more children, and so we didn't. A decision we have both regretted. There wasn't such a thing as grief counseling in those days. You really just had to get on with your lives, and that's what we've tried to do. We used to rent the cottage. After we lost Rowena we were lucky enough to buy it. Then the farm came on the market and the rest is history. Roger is not ready to leave the earth yet, he still hopes for an answer to what happened."

"What about you, Donna?"

"When a mother loses her child, there is no greater pain you can inflict upon her. For many years I fell into a deep depression. Roger had his own grief to deal with, but somehow he found the strength to help me with mine. The whole ordeal nearly killed us. Roger's Catholic faith gave him a crutch to support him. As for me, I lost my faith the day I looked out that kitchen window, for the last time."

Roger got up from the table when he saw Emma running out of the lake. He picked up a huge beach towel and enveloped the little girl in the towel. For a moment he was with his Rowena again. Rebecca looked puzzled and a little uncomfortable. Rachael looked furious. Before Rachael could say anything she would regret, Rebecca stood up quickly, placed a finger against her sister's lips and led her away towards the beach. By the water's edge she related the story of Rowena.

Rachael let out a sigh. "My God, Rebecca, that's awful. It's a good job you told me."

Donna dried her tears, but it was obvious she had been

crying. Like the good schoolteacher she had been, she had everyone organized around the table. Rebecca let Emma sit between the old couple, both she and Rachael were confident that after what the O'Malleys had been through, they would never let anything bad happen to Emma.

Emma was enthralled by all the different birds she saw. Roger and Donna being avid ornithologists, took pleasure in naming all the birds that Emma pointed out to them. She thought they were joking when Roger told her that the large black birds flying in a circle overhead were turkey vultures.

"We have vultures in Canada? I thought they only lived in Africa."

"They live in lots of countries all over the world, Rowena," replied Roger.

"Rowena, who's Rowena? My name's Emma, silly."

"Emma, don't be rude," Rebecca shot Emma a warning look.

"Yes, but Mr. O'Malley called me Rowena and my name's Emma, not Rowena." Emma saw the look on her mother's face and knew she was about to cross the line if she said anymore.

"I'm sorry, Emma," O'Malley spoke up. "Of course you're not Rowena."

Rebecca sighed. The floodgates were open now, and any second the curious questions were going to pour out through her daughter's lips.

"Who's Rowena, O'Malley?" Emma saw the look of exasperation on her mother's face, but she forged ahead anyway. She wanted to know who Rowena was, and she meant to find out come hell or high water.

"Rowena is my daughter." Roger O'Malley could never bring himself to use the past tense when he spoke her name.

"Where is she, O'Malley?"

"I don't know, Emma, I think she's probably in heaven with the angels, but I'm not sure."

"That's enough questions, Emma."
"What happened to her, O'Malley?" Emma defiantly tuned her mother out.
"Emma, that's enough!"
"It's okay," said the old man looking across the picnic table and smiling at Rebecca.
Rachael spoke quickly. "She had an accident on her bicycle when she was a little girl like you, Emma, and sometimes Mr. O'Malley thinks you're his lost daughter."
"She couldn't be brown like me, Aunt Rachael, the O'Malleys are white people."
Oh my God. Rebecca gulped.
"You're quite right, Emma," O'Malley nodded happily. "She was a little white girl, but I don't notice the color of people's skin, I only see their beauty and feel their love, whatever color their skin is."
"Well, the day's getting on," Rachael spoke up, "and we should be getting along. We plan to spend some time at Algonquin Provincial Park, I've rented a room up there for the night in one of the lakeside motels. If we really enjoy ourselves it wouldn't hurt to stay an extra night. Would that be okay with you, Rebecca?"
"That would be fine by me, but I might send Emma back in a taxi for her cheek."
"I'm really sorry, Mommy, I promise to behave and I'm sorry, O'Malley, that I asked you all those questions about Rowena, I really am." Emma burst into tears and ran through the long grass to the privacy of the car, and climbed in the back. It was stifling hot, but she didn't care, she had upset her mother.
"I don't like to see a child cry," said Donna. "Would you mind, Rebecca, if I went to her? I'll explain things so she's not so confused."
"Not at all Donna, I think that's probably a good idea."

"You must be sorry you came across us now."

"Nonsense, Donna. We've all really enjoyed your company. Emma obviously thinks the world of you two. I'm glad that we were able to open up our hearts to each other, it helped me tremendously and I hope it helped you too."

"Rebecca, more than you know."

Donna walked up to the Bentley and gently persuaded Emma to leave the sanctuary of the car and to go for a walk along the beach with her. They held hands as they walked, Donna talking to the child in a soothing voice. Feeling that her faith had been restored, she vowed next Sunday both she and Roger would attend mass together, instead of him going on his own, something he had been doing for years.

When they arrived back at the farm, Rachael took a photograph of Emma cuddled between the O'Malleys.

"I almost forgot, your apple pie and pot of jam and your eggs. Wait while I run in and get them." Donna hurried inside the house emerging shortly afterwards with a large pie, a jar of homemade jam and the dozen eggs Emma had collected. Rachael and Rebecca hugged the old couple, feeling the frailness of their bodies against their own.

"I forgot to say goodbye to Toby." Emma gave her mother a pleading look.

"Come on," Roger interceded, "but be quick, don't keep your mother waiting."

The two of them headed off to the field, Emma skipping along in front of the old man with Robby trotting along at her heels.

"Thank you, Donna, for showing us your secret picnic spot. We really enjoyed ourselves."

"Don't be so silly, Rebecca. I should be thanking you for letting Roger and I join you. Meeting you has helped restore my faith, something that had been lost for the past fifty years. You have no idea how grateful I am to you both for introducing that

lovely child to us. Thank you." Donna clutched Rebecca and Rachael's hands. "And please, don't be strangers. You can come anytime."
"Donna, that's very kind of you. What is the rent by the way, I never did ask?"
"It's what you can afford, Rebecca. You're a single mom now and it will take a while before any money starts flowing your way from your ex-husband. If ten dollars a week is all you can afford, then ten dollars it is."
"I can afford a lot more than that, Donna. I've already made up my mind about the cottage. I'll take it for the whole summer and beyond if Emma and I are both happy here. I'll phone you tonight and we can discuss finances over the phone, if that's all right with you?"
"It's a prayer answered, my dear." Donna hugged Rebecca. Over her shoulder she saw Roger and Emma walking back towards the farmhouse hand in hand. Roger appeared to have taken on a new lease on life, and even had a spring in his step.
"This is a hard place to break away from," joked Rachael. "Emma, did you tell Toby that you'll be back to see him again?"
"I did, and I told him I loved him and I was going to miss him and I know he was thinking the same about me too."
"Well, Emma, I have some news that will make you very happy." Emma looked up at her mother, mouth open in anticipation.
"I've managed to get you a place in summer school." Emma's mouth fell open even wider, this time in horror.
"Oh, Rebecca, that's cruel," Rachael chastised her sister. "Now tell her the real news."
"I'm sorry, darling," Rebecca laughed and hugged her daughter. "I just couldn't resist. The news is, you and I are going to rent O'Malley's Cottage for the whole summer!"

O'Malley's Cottage
Page 103

Emma inhaled a giant breath and screamed with excitement, leaping into the air, and jumping up and down like a jack-in-the-box. "Yippee! You're the best mom in the whole world."

"Robby, you and me are going to be neighbors," she dropped to her knees and wrapped her arms around the dog's neck, "and I'll come over every day to take you for a walk, but you have to be a good boy. I want you to tell all the animals I'm coming back for the whole of the summer holidays, especially Toby."

Robby hadn't had so much fuss made of him in years. He wagged his tail like a puppy. Roger stood there grinning from ear to ear.

"Tis like a prayer answered," he said, his eyes glistening with tears.

Where have I heard that before? Rachael murmured.

"Come on, away with you all now. Rachael's right, it's hard to get away from here," said Donna finally.

They all piled back in the car, now a muddy brown on the outside, smelling distinctly of horse manure on the inside. They honked and waved as they drove away. Rachael stopped in front of the cottage for one last look.

"Goodbye O'Malley's Cottage, we'll see you again soon," said Emma, waving furiously out of the window.

"Okay, Miss Emma, fingers inside the car please, I'm going to close the windows and put the air on now," said her aunt.

* * *

"Mommy, Aunt Rachael, thank you for a lovely day, and Mommy, I'm sorry I made you angry. Mrs. O'Malley told me what happened to Rowena and that made me sad for them."

"That's okay, honey. It's behind us now, let's look forward to the fun we're going to have at Algonquin Park."

At the East Gate of Algonquin Provincial Park, Rachael

stopped at the park wardens' office and they went inside. Rebecca paid the visitors' fee, while Rachael and Emma looked through the brochures, selecting those that interested them along with some maps of the park.

"Okay, here's my suggestion," Rachael said. "Since we've got two nights, how about we take a slow drive through the park to our motel, which is just outside the West Gate? We can have dinner and an early night, because to be honest I'm beat. Then in the morning we can go exploring after breakfast."

"That sounds great," Rebecca agreed. "Why don't you let me drive us through the park so you can enjoy the scenery?"

"Thanks, I like that idea." Rachael handed over the keys.

"This car is really easy to handle," Rebecca commented as they wound slowly through the park. "I wouldn't mind driving back to Toronto and giving you a break."

"That would be great. That way I can sit back and enjoy the view. From here on the driver's seat is yours. Which brings up a point, I wouldn't be in too big a hurry to sell that Mercedes of yours."

"Why not?"

"Well, for one thing it's almost new so you shouldn't have too many problems with it, plus you'll only lose money on it and, who knows, you might just love it up here and stay on into the winter. If you do that you'll need a reliable four-wheel drive vehicle. I'd keep it at least until the end of summer before you make a decision."

"I'm sure I won't make it until the end of the summer locked up in that cottage, I'll get cabin fever in no time. I'll be heading back down to civilization within the first week, believe me."

"I would hardly call Toronto civilized these days. With all the shootings and gang warfare going on, I'm more likely to be heading up to you."

"I didn't realize this was such a popular place," Rebecca commented as she noticed all the cars with trailers, motor homes and other people, like themselves, out for a drive.

"According to the map there are hiking trails that go way inside the park. You can hike for days or canoe if you want to. Duncan and I keep meaning to do that, and now that I'm here I think I'll look into it."

"Somehow, Miss City Girl, I don't see you with your backpack, khaki shorts and hiking boots taking off into the wilderness. Besides, where would you plug in your hairdryer, a tree?"

"I wasn't planning on a week. Maybe two nights, just to see how I like it."

"Well, the nearest thing to a camping holiday you'll see me on is staying at O'Malley's Cottage. What do you think, Emma?"

"I think a hiking holiday sounds like a lot of fun, Mommy. We could all go, that would be great."

"And what about the bears? You know there are black bears in the park."

"Uncle Duncan would protect us, he wouldn't let anything bad happen. Aunt Rachael, let's look at the map and start planning."

"Emma, you are turning into a real tomboy and I thought you liked to wear pretty dresses."

"I do, Mommy, but that's in the city. I'm going to wear jeans up here and dress like a cowgirl. You'd look good in jeans too, Mommy."

"Okay," Rebecca laughed, "we'll both dress like cowgirls when we get to the cottage. Blue jeans, gingham blouses."

"Straw hats and a piece of grass hanging from your mouths," chimed in Rachael.

"Ha ha. That goes for you too, sis, when you come to stay with us, you're going to have to dress like a cowgirl too. Oh, sorry

I forgot, you'll be dressed up like an explorer. Dr. Livingstone, I presume?"
"Who's Dr. Livingstone, Mommy?"
"A famous African explorer many years ago. He was also an anti-slavery campaigner as I recall."
"Back up will you, Rebecca. We just passed a small hiking trail on our right." Rachael looked up from studying the map. "It looks to be a fairly short trail. What do you say we go for a hike before supper?"
"I thought you said you were tired?"
"I was, but I've perked up again. Come on, let's do a bit of exploring."
After backing up to the spot, Rebecca pulled over to the side of the road and the three of them piled out of the car.
Bouncing with excitement, Emma dashed ahead of them on the path minding Rebecca's admonition not to get out of sight. She raced back and forth, climbing to the top of huge boulders and stopping to investigate the wild flowers growing along the path. There were other families hiking on the trail, accompanied by children Emma's age. It wasn't long before the group of children, boys and girls, banded together and began playing as though they had been friends for years.
Eventually they reached a cliff edge with panoramic views across the park. Anxious parents, including Rebecca, kept a sharp eye on their children. They wanted them to have a sense of adventure, but did not want their offspring disappearing over the cliff edge, like lemmings hurtling to their deaths.
"Not too close to the edge! That's close enough! Get away from the edge!" were frequently heard shouts from parents, including Rebecca.
On the way back to the car, Emma and another girl, who looked to be about the same age and height, walked side by side,

their heads close together in animated conversation. By the time the girls had reached the parking lot they were hand in hand. Emma and her new friend walked straight up to Rebecca.

"Mommy, this is Lindsay. She's on holiday from England for the whole summer. She's given me her e-mail address, is it okay if I give her mine?"

"Sure, honey. Hi, Lindsay, is this your first trip to Canada?"

"Yes it is." The little girl smiled up at Rebecca.

"And what do you think, do you like Canada?" Rebecca looked over at a group of adults standing outside a huge and very sleek looking motor home. She assumed Lindsay's parents were amongst the group. They looked across and waved, Rebecca waved back.

"I wish I could live here, but I don't like the bugs." Lindsay shook her shoulder length auburn hair to discourage the flying insects. "I hate the smell of skunks," she wrinkled her nose accentuating a splatter of freckles, "and I miss my friends, but other than that I love it here."

Rebecca warmed to the child with her big eyes, one hazel and one dark blue. She found her accent enchanting.

"Could Lindsay come and stay with us at O'Malley's Cottage? She doesn't have any friends here and she's lonely."

A tall, slender woman walked over to where Rebecca and the two girls were standing by the car. She looked like a grown-up version of Lindsay. The two women smiled at each other. Rebecca caught herself checking the mother's eyes, they were both a piercing blue.

"Lindsay, I hope you're not making a nuisance of yourself?" said the woman, in her crisp British accent.

Rebecca spoke up before Lindsay had a chance to reply. "No, not at all, Lindsay and my daughter seem to have become great friends already. I'm Rebecca Brown." She extended her hand.

"How do you do, I'm Jacqueline Brooks." The two women shook hands warmly. "We're over here on a month's holiday, a sort of fact finding mission. We've got the go-ahead to immigrate, but decided we really ought to see this wonderful country of yours–well, as much as we can in the time we have."

"That'll cover some of Ontario." Rebecca smiled and the woman nodded her head.

"I know, we're discovering that Canada is a vast country."

"Where are you staying?"

"We've made our base in Peterborough. And of course we're spending most of our time traveling around in this motor home. My husband, Richard's fallen in love with this place, he'd be quite content to spend the rest of the holiday right here. Do you live around here?"

"No, we are from Toronto. This is my sister Rachael." Rachael and Jacqueline shook hands.

"That's one of the places we plan to visit."

"I wouldn't take that monster into the city if I were you." Rachael warned. "If you take the Go-Train from Whitby, you'll be glad you did."

"Okay, how do we get to the Whitby Go-Train? Let me get the map." Jacqueline walked back to the motor home, returning with a tall, slender man wearing John Lennon glasses.

"This is my husband, Richard."

"This place is breathtaking," he gushed. "I can't get over the magnificence."

Jacqueline sighed. "See what I mean?"

"Your wife says you're immigrating to Canada," Rachael addressed Richard. "Will you be working in the area?"

"We're both professors. We'll be teaching at Trent University in Peterborough. I teach computer science and Jackie teaches chemical engineering. I know, it sounds boring."

"On the contrary, it sounds fascinating. See what hard work at school can do for you," Rebecca said and smiled at her daughter.

Emma and Lindsay looked at each other and rolled their eyes.

"Will you be living in Peterborough?" Rebecca ignored the youthful eye-rolling.

"We have our eye on a house in Lakefield," Jacqueline replied. "It reminds us of an English village, which makes us feel at home, and it's close to the university. I'm hoping we close on it soon. The motor home is lovely, but I'm beginning to suffer from cabin fever. Look, we're having a barbeque tonight, why don't you join us?"

Rebecca looked at Rachael who nodded. "We don't want to impose," Rebecca turned back to Jacqueline.

"You won't be imposing," Richard piped up. "We'd be delighted to have your company."

"Well, thank you. We have a few things to sort out first then we'll be back."

* * *

Back at their motel Rebecca telephoned Donna and they settled on a rental for the cottage. The arrangement suited both of them and when they'd agreed, Donna called across to Roger and his excited shout easily carried to Rebecca's ears. After she hung up with Donna, she called her daughter over and held out the phone.

"Honey, I think you should call Daddy and tell him about your day. I'm sure he'll be thrilled to hear from you."

Rebecca dialed the number and handed the receiver to Emma. When she heard the child speak into the phone, she crossed the room to join Rachael at the table of their kitchenette. In the background they could hear Emma bubbling with excitement as she told her father about the trip to Burleigh Falls. The house on Stoney Lake had been forgotten. Only the farm, its animals, Donna and Roger and O'Malley's Cottage were important enough to discuss, and her new friend Lindsay. "And Daddy, I have my very own kitten, I've called him Marmalade. And guess what else... I took a Shetland pony for a walk. His name's Toby, he's so cute. I might even get to ride him!"

Rebecca was relieved to note that Emma did not mention the fact that they'd rented the cottage, much as she hated doing it, Rebecca had asked her daughter not to tell George that they had rented the cottage. She didn't want him stalking her, especially in such an isolated place.

"Love you too, Daddy," Emma said, replacing the receiver. That ended the telephoning for the night and an hour later they were back at Lake of Two Rivers enjoying a barbeque with their new friends.

"I'm so glad we met," Jacqueline said. "I don't know anyone here. Richard, of course, is in his glory with the wilderness, but I confess to feeling the lack of feminine companionship. I hope we can keep in touch, especially for the girls, it would mean so much to Lindsay."

"We will, Jacqueline. Once we're settled in O'Malley's Cottage I hope you'll come and visit us."

"Count on it."

The evening was a great success and when they said their goodbyes, the women promised to keep in touch. "Phone me anytime," Rebecca invited, "especially if you get lonely."

"Thank you, Rebecca, I will."

They hugged each other and parted company with the warm assurance that they'd be seeing each other real soon.

It was nearly midnight when they reached the motel. Emma had fallen asleep on the back seat and didn't even stir when the car stopped. Rebecca and Rachael each took one of her arms and guided her to her bed. She was back asleep the minute her head hit the pillow.

"Remember those days, sis?"

Rebecca laughed. "Do I ever? Oh, to have that innocence back when everyday was like a cone full of ice cream."

"Yeah, then we grew up and discovered boys and everything got ruined."

"Look at you and Duncan. If ever there was a success story it's you two."

"That might be because we hardly ever see each other. I don't mind getting married to the guy, as long as we can continue living separately, you know, keep things as they are and just be married."

"Rachael, you're awful, he's head over heels in love with you. He's not controlling or possessive, he's generous, kind and loving."

"And he's a fabulous cook too, not bad in bed either."

"T.M.I., Rachael."

"Those were real nice people weren't they?" Rachael changed the subject.

"At the barbeque you mean?"

"Yeah. You and Jacqueline really hit it off, and Emma and Lindsay were inseparable. I hope I'm up at O'Malley's Cottage when they drop by. If she gives you notice of their arrival date, let me know will you, I'd like to come."

"I'd like you to come too. Have you had a nice day?"

"I have had one of the best days I've had in years. I'm glad we did this together, sis."

"Me too. Let's hit the sack, I'm so tired. It's the fresh air I'm sure."

* * *

It was almost 10 a.m. before anyone stirred. Rachael was the first up. Rebecca could not endure her sister's cheerful singing any longer so she and Emma finally climbed out of bed. It was agreed, they would go out for breakfast before spending the rest of the day exploring the park. Rebecca took another one of her famous wrong turns that led down a long winding rugged trail, at the end of which they discovered a rustic looking hotel deep inside the park. The hotel was by a lake, and judging by the number of people already there, it was a very popular place. They decided this would be the perfect spot to have their last dinner together before returning to Toronto.

Chapter Six

Rebecca was surprised with her thoughts. The closer they got to Toronto, the more she missed Algonquin. *You be nice to us O'Malley's Cottage if you want us to come back after the summer.*

It was late when they arrived in the city. Rachael awoke to neon lights and traffic noise. "Let's drop by a fast-food restaurant. I'm too tired to even think of cooking and I really don't feel like sitting in a restaurant."

"I'm all for that, I'm beat."

Rebecca parked the car in the underground parking lot. The weary trio carried up their belongings to the condo.

Rebecca and Emma sorted things out so that Rachael could have some peace in her study. She needed to know that everything was still running smoothly in the world of publishing, during her short absence.

The office had long since closed. Rachael telephoned John at home and he brought her up to speed. Rebecca entered the study with a glass of red wine for her sister. Rachael looked up with the phone to her ear and smiled. Rebecca bent down and gently kissed her on the cheek before leaving.

"Emma, I'm glad I made the decision to rent the cottage. Much as your aunt and I adore one another, Aunt Rachael is used to being on her own and we must respect that. I don't ever want to strain my relationship by overstaying our welcome."

"Mommy?"

"Yes, darling."

"I wish I had a sister."

"Oh, sweetie, come here." Rebecca hugged her daughter into her arms.

* * *

Over the next week, Rachael busied herself at the office, while Rebecca and Emma made arrangements to stay at the cottage. George had become more accommodating, allowing Rebecca to return to the house to get some things she would need. The animosity between them softened. Rachael would not hear of Rebecca returning to the house alone and insisted on being there with her, on the understanding that George remained at his office. He agreed to do that, and kept to his word. Emma stayed overnight with her father for two nights over the weekend and met Suzanne, her father's secretary for the first time.

* * *

"This is our last night together, Rachael. Tomorrow morning Emma and I are heading north." Rebecca squeezed her sister's hand. "I'm feeling scared and now I wish I'd never agreed to rent O'Malley's Cottage. It seemed a good idea at the time, but it doesn't feel such a good idea now. I could kick myself for being so stupid renting a place out in the middle of nowhere. I should have got something closer."
"Rebecca, calm down. You don't have to go, you can stay here. I'll phone Donna and tell her how you're feeling, she'll understand. We can find you a nice apartment around here."
"Emma would be so disappointed if I backed out. She's been through so much already and she's so looking forward to this. I can't do it to her. If it was just me I'd back out right now, but then I wouldn't have done it in the first place."
"It's only for the summer; you'll be back in Toronto before you know it."
"You better believe it. You will come up and see me, won't

you?"

"Of course I will. Duncan is already making plans. Now, let's not spoil our last evening together. I thought we'd go over to Duncan's house and get your Mercedes, so we don't have to do it in the morning. Besides, you won't have time to feel depressed with all the work I've got lined up for you." Rachael pulled Rebecca into a hug, cradling her head like a child. "It'll be fine. Give it a week. If you still hate it out there, come back. Never mind what Emma wants, you have feelings too."

Later they drove over to Duncan's house in the Bentley. When they reached the door, Rachael fumbled in her purse for the house keys.

Before she could get them out, the door burst open and Duncan barreled out.

"Surprise!"

Rebecca and Emma stood on the doorstep, speechless, until Duncan stepped forward and hugged them.

"Come on in, you guys, it's lovely to see you again. Rebecca, as gorgeous as ever and you, Emma, my, how you've grown!"

Rebecca sniffed the air. "What a delicious smell."

Duncan beamed. "That, my dear, is dinner for three of the most important people in my life."

"When did you get back?"

"Yesterday. Rachael's kept me up to speed with developments. Now look, Rebecca, if you end up needing a place of your own for a couple of months or a couple of years you can use this place. I'm hardly ever here anyway. I'm either visiting the restaurants, traveling abroad or over at Rachael's. We've discussed this already, so it's not an issue. I don't want you to think you've got nowhere to go, after all, we're family."

"Thanks, Duncan, you're always so generous."

"Only to those I love. Now let's get the party rolling. Let me fix you ladies a drink." He turned and kissed Rachael tenderly

on the lips.
"I think you've already looked after yourself in that direction, Mr. Dashwood," Rachael chuckled, licking the taste of wine from her lips.
"As the head chef, I'm entitled to a little slurp of nectar during the cooking phase." Duncan disappeared into the kitchen emerging shortly afterwards carrying a tray of drinks and hors d'oeuvres. "Okay, ladies, here we are. I have a Shirley Temple for you, Emma."
"Thank you, Uncle Duncan."
"My pleasure. Oh, before I forget. A small gift from overseas for you both." He returned from the bedroom with two elegantly wrapped boxes.
"Duncan, I tell you this every time, just bring yourself back. You're far too kind."
"I shouldn't say that until you see what it is, Rebecca."
"It's beautiful, Duncan thank you so much." Rebecca held up a gold bracelet, delicately handcrafted, surrounded by tiny orchids. She got up from the couch and threw her arms around his neck, kissing him on the cheek.
Emma bounced over to Duncan, reaching up to hug him. She was holding a small silver bracelet, not unlike her mother's, but this one was surrounded by doves.
"Thank you Uncle Duncan." She squeezed him for all she was worth.
"It's my pleasure, I hope you like them. You make yourselves comfortable while I add the finishing touches to this gourmet meal. Dinner will be served in ten minutes."
They trooped into the dining room with their glasses. The table was set beautifully, as though Nik Manojlovich from the television show, Savoire Faire had attended to it personally.
"Dinner by candlelight, how romantic. Rachael, I don't

know how he manages to create the perfect atmosphere, cook a delicious meal and do it all without the slightest hint of stress."

"Over twenty years of experience, a love for the art of cooking and a real love for those who genuinely appreciate my creations," replied Duncan, waltzing into the dining room carrying steaming plates of king prawns cooked in coconut, garlic, ginger and garnished with fresh vegetables and jasmine rice. "Bon appetite!"

"Well, Emma, I hear you've got some new friends already at O'Malley's Cottage. Do tell me all about them."

"My best friend is Toby, he's a Shetland pony and Mr. O'Malley, we call him O'Malley, is going to teach me how to ride him. Then there's Robby. He's a Border Collie, he's old, but still likes to play like a puppy. Um, oh yes, four kittens, I've already named one Marmalade because he's like a jar of marmalade, the color, not the taste."

"I should hope so," interjected Duncan. "I don't think O'Malley would like you eating his cats."

Emma looked indignant. "No silly, we don't eat cats."

Duncan decided it would not be prudent to correct Emma on the subject of cats as a culinary delight in some of the countries he had visited. For one thing, Rachael would be furious if he so much as hinted at it. He smiled pleasantly instead, aware that Rachael was staring at him with that, *You dare,* look of hers.

"Um, there are two humungous Belgian horses. They're kind of like the size of an elephant, only they're horses; one's called Maxwell, the other one's called Minnie. O'Malley said he's going to teach me all about them too, after I've learned all about Toby. He's got two Quarter horses, Star and Blazer. When I've learned how to ride Toby, O'Malley is going to teach me how to ride them. Then I'm going to learn how to harness the Belgians to the hay wagon and take everybody for a ride around the farm. Oh, yes, he's got pigs and chickens and a rooster and some cows as well. I think that's about it. Mommy and I are going to learn how to be cowgirls."

Duncan raised his eyes toward Rebecca and smiled in amusement. "This I have got to see. You I can see as a cowgirl, but your mother, now that's something I'll have to see to believe. My image of your mother is one of the lady in Green Acres, high heels, fancy dresses, makeup and her hair beautifully coiffed."

"Well, thank you very much, Duncan Dashwood."

"I'm only teasing, Rebecca. I bet the two of you will adapt to this new way of life very well. My worry is that you might not want to come back."

"Trust me, I'll be back, make no mistake about that. I'm a city girl through and through. You can take the girl out of the city, but you can't take the city out of the girl."

"I think that should be the country not the city."

"I know, sis, I'm just adapting it to suit my situation. Emma, did you tell Uncle Duncan that you made another friend and she's coming to visit us at the cottage?"

"Oh, yes, I almost forgot. My friend, Lindsay, she's from England. She and her parents are going to immigrate to Canada."

"That sounds great. I hope I can stay at the cottage too sometime."

"You may be going there sooner than you think if you don't stay on your best behavior, Mr. Dashwood."

"Rachael, I'm serious, I'd love to see the cottage I really would."

"Duncan, you and Rachael would be welcome anytime. You and O'Malley are kindred spirits. I think somewhere down the line you must be related."

"Well, all I can say is that this Mr. O'Malley must be a damn fine looking fella."

"I'm not so sure, Rebecca, that it would be a good idea to introduce the two of them, what do you think?"

"I couldn't agree more. Two O'Malley's in the same Province, God help us."

"Duncan, you haven't told us about your trip to Singapore. Did you enjoy it?"

"I most certainly did. The people were so helpful and friendly. Mind you, the authorities are pretty strict over there."

The conversation around the dining table was both lively and entertaining. Duncan had his audience captivated as he regaled them with stories about his travels around the world.

"Emma, would you mind giving me a hand to clear the table and then you and I can get the dessert? As a reward you can have the largest portion."

"Sure, Uncle Duncan."

"I thought something refreshing and light would be in order for dessert, I hope that's okay with everyone. There's some cream if you'd like it, I have to confess that I did pour a little liqueur in the fruit salad. Enjoy."

"Mmm, it's delicious. Do you like it, Emma?"

"It tastes really good, Mommy. Could I have some more please, Uncle Duncan?"

"Thank you, Duncan, for turning my ten-year old niece into a lush."

"Oh, there's not enough in there to have her dancing on the table, but she might start singing a few raucous sea shanties."

Rebecca and Rachael gave him disapproving glares.

"Only joking."

"All right, Emma, just a little more, but not too much."

Ignoring Duncan's protestations, Rachael and Rebecca transformed the kitchen back to its original pristine state. Afterwards they relaxed in the living room with their coffee. All too soon it was time for Rebecca and Emma to return to Rachael's condominium.

"Rebecca, I'm going to stay the night at Duncan's." Rachael hugged them both. "I don't want to say goodbye in the morning and then rush off to work. I'll say goodbye now, and that way you can take your time getting ready to leave in the morning. Call me as soon as you arrive."

"I will, promise," Rebecca hugged her sister and swiped at her eyes with a tissue.

"As soon as you arrive," Rachael sobbed. "Get your computer hooked up, that way we can e-mail each other."

"I will, and don't you work too hard. Duncan, make sure she takes some time to relax."

"You bet I will, and you take care of yourself too, Rebecca."

"Bye, sweetie, take care of your mom." Rachael hugged Emma tightly. "And look after all those animals. Give my love to Toby and Robby and those kittens and all the other animals up there at O'Malley's Farm."

"I will, Aunt Rachael. Bye, Uncle Duncan, thank you for a wonderful dinner and for my present."

Duncan bent down to embrace the little girl. "You're very welcome. You're not to worry about anything, your Aunt Rachael and I are only a phone call away. If you or your mom have any problems we'll be up there in a flash, even if we have to hire a helicopter to get there."

"Thanks again for a lovely evening, Duncan, for a wonderful dinner and a beautiful present." Rebecca hugged Duncan tightly. He was like the big brother she had always wanted. "Okay, let's hit the road, Emma. Thanks for looking after the Mercedes, Duncan."

"It looked after itself. Shame I didn't have more time for a test drive."

"Duncan, you only buy cars with carburetors, rust holes and worn seats. The day you buy yourself a decent car, we'll have discovered life on another planet," piped in Rachael.

"I like the old cars, they just don't make them like that anymore. Besides, my old Caprice Classic still runs like a charm, can't afford the gas to put in it mind you."

Rebecca carefully reversed the Mercedes out of the garage. Emma waited outside on the driveway standing between Rachael and Duncan, holding their hands. She got in next to her mother and they drove out of the driveway and up the street amidst frantic waving, blown kisses and honking horn.

"Emma, honey, I'm so tired, I think tonight we'll just go straight to bed. We'll load up the car in the morning. Hopefully we'll be on the road by nine, stopping for breakfast on the way. Now that we know exactly where we're going we should be at O'Malley's Cottage within three hours. Okay?"

"I love you, Mommy; that sounds like a good idea."

"I love you too, sweetheart."

"Daddy still loves you, you know." Emma was looking out of the passenger window, trying to make the statement sound casual.

"Emma, honey, sometimes love is just not enough anymore, especially when someone you love has hurt you so much, when the trust you had between you has been betrayed. I still love your father, but not as much as I used to. I know it hurts you, but Mommy has feelings too and right at this moment I really don't want to talk about it. Maybe down the road we'll sit down and talk about it some more, when I'm feeling a little stronger and when I think it's the right time for you to listen."

"What was Daddy doing in the shower with his secretary, Mommy?"

"Who told you that!" Rebecca turned to look at her daughter, a furious expression on her face.

The sound of her mother's angry and unexpected retort made Emma jump. "I kind of heard you and Aunt Rachael talking about it," she said hurriedly. "And Daddy was telling someone on the phone about it too when I stayed overnight. I wasn't trying to listen, but he was talking so loud I couldn't help hearing it."

"Okay, Emma. As I said, I really don't want to talk about it right now. I'm sorry that you heard any of it, and yes, I'm really mad about it!"

Both of them fell silent. Emma shrank into her seat and watched her mother. Finally, the dam broke and she burst into floods of tears.

This brought Rebecca immediately back to reality. Without even checking her rearview mirror, Rebecca pulled over to the side of the road, released her seatbelt and leaned across to release Emma's. Almost in the same motion she grabbed Emma and hugged her to her, her own tears dropping down on top of her daughter's head.

"I'm sorry, Mommy," Emma sobbed.

After a very long embrace, Rebecca lifter her daughter's chin and smiled. "Don't cry sweetheart. You have absolutely nothing to be sorry for, you haven't done anything wrong. I'm so sorry I lost my temper, I wasn't angry at you."

Rebecca was so ashamed for being angry with her daughter. Emma was just an innocent child caught up in an adult problem. She wished she could take back that moment. She had handled the situation terribly and felt lousy and less than a good mother. What made her feel worse was having broken a sense of intimate trust that they both shared. She hoped Emma would understand in time and forgive her. In Emma's eyes, her mother was a goddess, but tonight she appeared more darkly human.

Back in Rachael's apartment the two of them snuggled up in bed together. They talked about how they were going to spend their summer holidays at O'Malley's Cottage. They were so excited as they discussed all the things they were going to do. They couldn't wait to go down to the secret picnic spot by themselves and this time Rebecca promised her daughter she would go swimming with her.

"I suppose we should ask the O'Malley's if they mind us going down to their picnic spot on our own, after all, it is their special place."

"I don't think they would mind, Mommy, but I am going to ask them if it would be all right to take Lindsay down there. If too many people got to know about it, it wouldn't be special anymore. It would get crowded and we'd have to find another secret place."

"That's right, Emma. Once too many people got to know about it they'd all want to go there and in no time they'd spoil it. They'd leave all their garbage behind, ruin the peace and quiet by bringing radios with them and leave broken beer bottles all over the beach."

"I know. Everyone we take there will have to be sworn to secrecy. We could blindfold them when we take them there," she was serious too.

"Lindsay might go along with that, but somehow I don't think her parents would," laughed Rebecca. "Maybe we should keep that beach a secret just between us and the O'Malley's, what do you think?"

"I agree, but Aunt Rachael and Uncle Duncan can come anytime they like because they're family."

"Agreed. Now come here, I need to give you some more smooches."

They cuddled up and eventually fell fast asleep in each other's arms. The unpleasant incident in the Mercedes was forgotten by Emma, but Rebecca hadn't yet allowed herself to forgive her actions and still felt guilty.

Chapter Seven

By 7 a.m. they were both up and out of bed, wide-awake and excited to be on their way. The Mercedes was packed in no time. Before leaving they stopped off at a florists. A thank you card and a huge vase of Black-eyed Susans would be waiting when Rachael got home.

It was a beautiful day to be leaving the city. The sun was shining, and already starting to get hot. Rebecca gave thanks for the air conditioned vehicle that made their journey pleasant. About an hour later, well outside the city, she stopped at a small roadside restaurant.

"This place must have good food."

"How do you know, Mommy?"

"Look at all the cars in the parking lot. Let's have a nice sit-down breakfast to start what is really day one of our holiday."

The two of them walked hand in hand towards, *Josie's Roadside Restaurant*. Rebecca pulled the door open, a bell jingled above their heads, lace curtains fluttered on the window.

The restaurant was busy, all eyes looked up at the new arrivals. There were other families sitting together having breakfast, alongside truck drivers, bikers and even a couple of OPP officers. Their eyes seemed to linger on Rebecca a little longer than was polite. A buxom woman in her fifties with long bleached blonde hair greeted them with a big smile. She was wearing a red cotton blouse with one too many buttons open, revealing a black lacy bra. Her blue jeans a little on the tight side.

"Come on in, ladies, let me find you a table. Is it just the two of you?"

"Yes," replied Rebecca, smiling.

"I've got just the table for you, tucked away in the corner."

O'Malley's Cottage

"That'll be fine, thank you."

Rebecca and Emma sat down on either side of a table, covered with the ubiquitous red and white checkered vinyl tablecloth.

"Beautiful day, thank heavens for the air conditioning though," smiled the waitress. "You on holiday, I've not seen you folks here before?"

"Yes, my daughter and I are having some girl time together."

"My name's Josie. Can I get you something to drink while you look through the menu?"

"Yes, thank you. I'd like a green tea if you have it and a white milk for my daughter please."

"Hey, Josie, the coffee's run dry here!" shouted a middle-aged man in a gruff, but friendly voice. He had on green coveralls and a green and yellow baseball cap with the words, *John Deere* the peak. Seated around him were three other similarly dressed men with the same weather beaten faces, typical of farmers.

"Marie!" shouted Josie. "More coffee for Arnold's table and a jug of water to cool him down. The regulars get out of hand sometimes," joked Josie to Rebecca. "Pay no attention to them. I'll be right back with your tea and milk."

Josie was soon back with their beverages. "Have you decided what you'd like for breakfast?"

"We'd both like scrambled eggs and pea meal bacon with brown toast." Rebecca was surprised to see Josie staring at her.

"Ma'am I don't mean to be rude, but you sure look like Halle Berry."

"Why, thank you, what a compliment. I just wish I had her money and her looks," chuckled Rebecca.

"Ma'am, I don't know about her money, but you've certainly got her looks. You sure you're not her?"

"Quite sure."

Josie, unconvinced walked over to the kitchen to place their order. Rebecca looked past Emma, watching Josie in conversation with Marie, as she served Arnold's table with their coffee refills. Marie glanced quickly in Rebecca's direction and then back at Josie, nodding her head in agreement with whatever Josie had just said to her. Emma caught her mother smiling to herself.

"What's so funny, Mommy?"

"The waitress thinks I'm that beautiful looking actress, Halle Berry. She must be very short sighted."

"I don't think so, Mommy. She's right, you do look like her. All my friends say so too."

Josie arrived with their breakfasts, smiling more than ever, obviously convinced that Rebecca was Halle Berry. Marie made a point of walking by Rebecca's table a number of times. Even the cook came out to ask if everything was all right with their breakfast.

"Emma, sweetheart, I think it's time we ate our breakfast and got the hell out of here."

Emma's eyes nearly popped out of their sockets, it wasn't like her mother to say, *hell*.Rebecca asked Josie for the bill, rummaging through her purse for a pen. On the back, in blue ink she wrote, *Thank you, Josie, for a lovely breakfast, all the best to you and the staff.* She then signed it, *Halle Berry* and made sure to leave a good tip.

"Mommy, why are you laughing," Emma asked as they drove out of the restaurant parking lot.

"I'm laughing, Emma, because I gave Josie my autograph, well, Halle Berry's autograph actually. She's convinced I'm her so I made her happy by signing her name on the back of the bill. We'll be the talk of these parts for generations to come."

"Mommy, that's naughty, we won't be able to go back there now." Emma began to laugh too. "That's just what Aunt Rachael would have done, I can't wait to tell her what you did, she won't believe it."

"Oh, yes she will. You can see why being famous isn't as much fun as it's cracked up to be. Imagine every time you go out, people are coming up to you wanting your autograph and pestering you. I wouldn't like that at all, would you?"

"No I wouldn't, I'm never going to be that famous."

"Oh, we're only going to be just a bit famous, are we?"

"Maybe just a tiny bit, Mommy, then I can earn lots of money and buy you your own house. Daddy's already got a house so I'd buy him a new car. I'd buy lots of houses all over the world and fill them with poor people with fridges full of food."

"That's very generous of you, Emma, but what would you buy for yourself?"

"A huge farm, with lots of barns so I could look after lots and lots of animals that need a good home, where nobody could hurt them. Perhaps O'Malley will let me do that on his farm, I'll have to ask him once we've settled in."

* * *

They made a quick stop in Bancroft for gas and groceries, and it seemed like no time at all before they were turning up the drive to O'Malley's Cottage.

Rebecca reached across the seat and squeezed her daughter's hand. They looked at each other and shared happy smiles.

Rebecca stopped the Mercedes in front of the garage door. It was a single garage with an overhead aluminum door painted dark green to match the shutters on the windows.

The O'Malleys had told Rebecca to settle themselves into the cottage first and phone them later. They would come over briefly to show Rebecca and Emma the little idiosyncrasies of the cottage.

Rebecca and Emma squealed with delight when they

walked up to the front door and spotted the oval plaque screwed onto the front door. It was painted a creamy yellow, bordered in dark green, with the words, *The Browns*, painted in gloss black. To the right of the lettering a green shamrock had been lovingly painted.

"It's official, Emma, the cottage is now ours!"

"It's beautiful, Mommy, I bet the O'Malley's made it themselves."

"I bet they did too. Now let me find the key, O'Malley said he would leave it in the window box to the left of the front door."

The window box was ablaze with petunias, lobelia, pansies, geraniums, impatiens and sweet alyssum. Rebecca parted the flowers and spotted the key attached by a string to a wine bottle cork that had been dipped in bright orange paint.

"Here we are, Emma, the key, right where O'Malley said it would be. Let's unlock the front door together, and just before we open it we'll make a wish."

Rebecca inserted the key into the lock and together they unlocked the door. Both mother and daughter clasped a hand on the brass doorknob. Before opening the door they stood on the threshold with their eyes tightly shut, both making a secret wish. They opened their eyes and looked at each other before turning the knob and swinging open the door.

Emma walked into the hallway, stood on the granite-tiled floor and removed her sandals. The grey tiles felt pleasantly cool beneath her bare feet. She remained silent, looking down the short hallway into the kitchen. Rebecca removed her own sandals, enjoying the same feeling of coolness beneath her own bare feet.

Together mother and daughter walked around the cottage, exploring every room and every nook and cranny. They walked up the wooden staircase to the three bedrooms. The master bedroom had an en suite bathroom. This would be Rebecca's bedroom.

Emma opened a small wooden door at the end of the hallway revealing a short wooden staircase. She climbed the stairs up into a small bedroom built into the loft space. A single window looked out over the endless forest behind the house. Everything was immaculately clean and fresh. Despite being a hot day, the cottage was surprisingly cool. A breeze blew fresh air through the open windows.

"Mommy, Mrs. O'Malley put a vase of wild flowers in my bedroom, they look so beautiful."

"She did the same thing in my bathroom. There's a vase of wild flowers on the vanity unit beside my sink. Well, my darling, I think it's time to unload the car, put everything away and then I'll let you phone the O'Malley's to let them know we've arrived."

Rebecca decided to use the spare bedroom as her office. She was pleased to find it already contained a phone jack. A comfortable La-Z-Boy wingback chair, covered in a dark plaid material was positioned in the corner of the room. Rebecca couldn't resist the temptation to sit in the chair and try it out. As soon as she did, she knew this was going to be the place where she would sit and read the manuscripts.

"The O'Malleys will be here in a jiffy." Emma poked her head in the doorway.

Give her a week and she'll be sounding exactly like O'Malley. Rebecca muttered to herself. "Okay, let's go greet them." She rose reluctantly from the La-Z-Boy and took her daughter's hand.

They waited outside, with Emma dancing up and down, until the O'Malleys chugged into the yard. After hugs all around, they trudged inside the cottage. Rebecca thanked Donna for the flowers and then they all quieted down while Roger went into detail about the location of the fuse box and the cut-off switch for the well pump and how to reset it. He explained how the oil furnace worked, where the exterior oil filler pipe was located, where the phone number was for the oil company, which switch did what and which switches not to touch. Rebecca wrote everything down, certain she would forget it all in no time if she didn't. Roger pointed out all the smoke detectors and proudly informed Rebecca that he had installed new batteries in each one only a week ago. Behind the pantry door he proudly displayed a new carbon dioxide fire extinguisher. But his pride and joy was the new airtight woodstove he'd had installed before the last winter. It occupied a position of prominence in the corner of the kitchen.

"Don't reckon you'll be needing that for a while, but the evenings can get a little cool towards the fall. If you're still here then, and I hope you will be, I'll show you how to use it. I've left you a few nice dry logs if you need them." He pointed to a small pile of split maple logs piled near the woodstove. "There's plenty more where they came from and don't worry, I won't charge you for them, that's because Donna and I feel you and Emma aren't really renters, we feel you're more like family."

The lecture over, Donna had to coax Roger away from the cottage. True to form, he just wouldn't stop talking.

"Roger, they're not going anywhere, let them settle in. They'll be over for supper this evening and you can talk some more then. And you won't have to tell them everything at the supper table all in one go either, they're staying for the whole summer; you've got plenty of time."

Roger smiled cheerfully as he followed his wife back out to the pick-up truck.

"What a lovely old couple, don't you think so, Emma?"

"Yes, Mommy. You know something?"

"What's that, honey?"

"I hope one day you meet someone just like O'Malley and then we'll all live happily ever after."

"I hope he's a lot younger than O'Malley," Rebecca laughed.

"I wouldn't mind, Mommy, I like O'Malley, he's funny and he's good with animals."

"Oh, Emma, you're funny too." Rebecca took Emma's head in her hands and kissed the top of her head. "Now let's get some unpacking done and then we'll go exploring!"

It was such a lovely evening they decided to walk to O'Malley's Farm. From front door to front door was a pleasant twenty minutes. The smell of fresh cut hay in the fields and wildflowers growing along the fence filled their nostrils. Not one car passed them in either direction as they strolled hand in hand along the gravel road.

Emma pulled the flowering head from a shoot of Timothy grass and sucked on the other end.

"Now you really do look like a country bumpkin." Rebecca laughed and squeezed her daughter's hand.

Robby, the black and white Border Collie was lying under the shade of the veranda when Rebecca and Emma strolled up the long driveway to the farmhouse. They were almost upon him when he finally heard their approach and stood up, tail wagging and started barking.

O'Malley greeted his guests at the front door, ushering them inside the farmhouse, where the delicious aroma of country cooking wafted down the hallway.

Donna had a hug for both of them.

"I wasn't sure what to bring you," Rebecca said, "I hope this bottle of sherry is okay."

"Beautiful!" O'Malley beamed with delight.

"It's Harveys Bristol Cream, our favorite. Unfortunately it won't last long in this house."

O'Malley took the bottle, disappeared into the dining room and selected three sherry glasses. Emma watched as he poured a glass of sherry, downed it in a few gulps and then refilled the glass. "Just testing," he winked at Emma.

Gathering in the kitchen, Emma asked innocently, "What

were you testing the sherry for, O'Malley?" Rebecca looked at her daughter quizzically.
"To see if it still tasted as delicious as I remember."
Donna shot her husband a stern look. "How many times did he have to test it?"
"Just the once I think."
"Oh, I hope so, or we'll be forced to hear O'Malley singing like an old tom cat, and if we're really unlucky he'll bring out his harmonica and he and Robby will start howling together."
Rebecca and Emma burst into laughter.
"Okay, let's have everyone seated around the table. I hope you and Emma like pork chops, homegrown potatoes, carrots and peas."
"We do, Donna, it's so kind of you to go to all this trouble for us, thank you."
"No trouble at all. Roger and I are delighted to have you as our neighbors."
Sitting at the antique harvest table, Donna and Roger bowed their heads, placing their hands together. Emma looked across at her mother for guidance. Rebecca nodded and they too prepared for grace.
"Keep it short, Roger. The Lord knows you'll talk ten times longer after a glass of sherry, with two glasses in you, we'll be here for breakfast."
In response Roger giggled. This delighted Emma. Rebecca opened an eye to see Emma's shoulders heaving as she tried to suppress a fit of giggles, her hands in angelic prayer, fingers pressed tightly against her lips, unsuccessfully stifling the burst of laughter that was about to erupt.
Rebecca whispered, "Emma, let it go before you burst."
Emma did, falling across the long trestle seat, crying with laughter. The moment was infectious. Rebecca and Donna began

laughing. O'Malley had tears running down his face.

"Right, that will do!" Donna spoke like a schoolteacher, admonishing an unruly class. Slowly the sputters and giggles subsided. With hands still clasped in prayer, Donna continued. "I think the Lord would appreciate an explosion of spontaneous merriment in lieu of grace this evening. I can't recall the last time I heard such laughter in this house ... Amen." She looked up, fixing her gaze on her husband at the other end of the table. "Roger O'Malley, you are an incorrigible rogue, make that glass of sherry last, it's the last one for you tonight!"

Rebecca lowered her eyes and a guilty expression settled on her face. "I'm sorry, Donna. I don't know what came over me, I apologize."

Donna broke into a smile. "Nothing of the sort, Rebecca. Laughter is a wonderful tonic. In Emma's case it's like champagne, simply beautiful and bubbling over with joy, as life should be for any child. Reminds me of my teaching days."

"What time is chores?" Emma asked O'Malley.

"I'm normally up by six o'clock, but this time of year they don't take so long. Not like in the winter when the animals need hay. I give the cattle grain and the horses a little sweet feed, but not too much, I don't want them to founder.

"What's founder, O'Malley?"

"Founder, it's basically overfeeding the horses. Their bodies can't handle it, causes all sorts of problems especially for their hooves. There's a lot to know about horses, Emma."

Donna returned with dessert. "O'Malley will teach you all about animal husbandry. When you own a horse farm, Emma, you'll know all there is to know about horses."

"Donna, I think tomorrow morning, I'll take the opportunity to have a lie in and sort things out in the cottage. I'll walk over later on in the morning to see how Emma's doing."

"Excellent idea, I'll have coffee and apple pie ready for you."

"I've eaten enough apple pie this evening to last me a year. After this delicious meal I don't think I'll need to eat for a week. We'll walk it off. Looks like the stars are already starting to come out."

"Well, it is a pleasant walk I must say, but do keep an eye out for the skunks, the last thing you want is to get sprayed on your first day here."

"I don't want to get sprayed by a skunk either," Emma piped up.

Standing on the porch, the idea of walking back to the cottage no longer seemed such a good one. A full moon bathed the landscape in an eerie glow. Rebecca almost took Roger up on his offer of a lift, but decided she might as well get used to living in the country. Thoughts of being eaten by a marauding black bear or a pack of hungry wolves made her shiver. Taking Emma's hand in hers, she stepped off the porch into the moonlight and began walking down the lane, her heart racing.

It was an exhilarating walk. The air was fresh, the sky cloudless. Emma marveled at all the stars she could see. When a shooting star streaked across the sky they stopped to watch it.

"Emma, quick make a wish. You're supposed to make a wish when you see a shooting star."

"Okay, Mommy, I made one."

"Don't tell me what it is, that'll spoil the wish."

They heard a rustling sound in the grass and froze, hearts pounding.

A skunk shuffled out of the long grass and ambled down the road towards them. They stood dead still, unsure what to do. Twenty-feet from where they were standing it wandered off into the field on the other side of the road.

"Oh, Mommy, isn't this fun? It's so exciting!"

"I don't know about fun, but it's certainly exciting."

Rebecca was glad that Emma couldn't see how scared she really was.

Arriving at the laneway to O'Malley's Cottage, they heard a rustling sound to their left. Judging by the sound, the animal was big. Suddenly a large dark shape hurtled across the road in front of them.

They screamed, clutching each other tightly as a huge buck, raced off into the field, the moonlight glistening off his antlers. Rebecca and Emma laughed out loud in relief, breathing heavily, every nerve ending tingling from the shock. When a pack of coyotes began howling in the distance, Rebecca grabbed Emma's hand and they ran for their lives.

With the front door closed behind them they clutched each other and laughed at their own fright. Tonight's episode was definitely one for the diary Rebecca had decided to keep.

"Emma, you have an early start tomorrow. Are you sure you still want to go?"

"Yes, Mommy, I can't wait to help O'Malley and to see Toby again. I'm going to learn everything I can while I'm here. This is going to be the best holiday ever." She threw her arms around her mother's neck and hugged her tightly.

"Okay, young lady, bed for you. Go wash your face and clean your teeth while I sort out some clothes for you for tomorrow. I guess you'll be wearing your jeans?"

"Yes, please, Mommy. I want to go looking like a cow girl."

With Emma fast asleep in her room, Rebecca poured herself a glass of red wine and phoned Rachael. Both sisters were soon laughing hysterically as Rebecca recounted the exploits of their first day at O'Malley's Cottage.

Chapter Eight

It was a beautiful sunny morning, hardly a cloud in the sky. Emma stood on the porch with her mother anxiously awaiting O'Malley's arrival. She heard the distinctive sound of his truck, long before she saw it. Dead on seven o'clock, O'Malley drove into the driveway of the cottage
"Good morning!" shouted Rebecca from the doorway, her arm around Emma's shoulder. She was still in her pajamas.
"Good morning, Rebecca! I see you have my hired help ready for a day's work on the farm."
Rebecca kissed Emma goodbye as the child jumped off the porch, almost tripping over her feet in her excitement to climb aboard the truck. Roger waved to Rebecca then reversed out of the driveway, then headed off up the road towards the farm.
Rebecca, sleepy-eyed, crawled back into bed, luxuriating in the comfort of the king-size bed.

* * *

Donna was standing on the veranda when Emma and O'Malley drove up, Robby crouched next to her wagging his tail.
"The household chores can wait, I'm going to accompany you and Emma this morning," Donna announced, removing her apron and tossing it onto an old rocking chair.
Emma walked between Roger and Donna as they made their way over to the barn. They glanced across at each other, smiling as they each held her hand.
The pigs were squealing with anticipation. Donna tossed a bucket of kitchen scraps into their trough while Roger topped up their water. Emma clumsily carried a heavy bucket of grain. Donna

helped her lift it onto the wall and together they poured the ground corn into the trough.

"O'Malley grew this corn then harvested it himself. You can help me grind some more another day."

"Oh, can I really?" Emma was thrilled. "When do the piglets go to market, O'Malley?"

"When they reach two hundred pounds, Emma. Okay, we need a little sweet feed for the horses, one big scoop each for Maxwell and Minnie, a medium scoop each for Star and Blazer and a small scoop for Toby. Never give them anymore, especially Toby. If you do, you'll be killing them with kindness. That's the sort of thing city folk would do, but not you, you're a country girl now." Emma's eyes lit up. "Their buckets are in the corner with their names on."

They walked over to the field, Emma carrying Toby's bucket. She was so happy she was fit to burst. *O'Malley called me a country girl.*

"Watch out when we enter the field, they'll go crazy, bucking and kicking with excitement. Let me go in first, then follow behind with Donna. You feed Toby while I feed the horses."

"Okay, O'Malley."

"Mind you watch out for their hooves. One kick from one of the Belgians and your skull will be crushed like an egg. Farming isn't playtime, Emma, don't for one minute think that it is. As soon as you do that, that's when accidents happen. That's not to say it isn't fun. If it wasn't, I wouldn't be doing it. It's a lot of fun, gets into your blood and once it does it will never let you go, you'll always hanker after it. In time you'll come to understand what I mean. Okay, let's go see your best friend."

The horses galloped across the field at the sight of them approaching with buckets in their hands. It sounded like a stampede, their hooves pounding across the dry ground. O'Malley undid the steel gate, shouting, "Get back!" as they danced around him wildly, turning and kicking playfully at each other.

"Go on, get out of it you brutes!" O'Malley carried four buckets, two in each hand, waving the horses off with the buckets if they got too close. The two Belgians tried to thrust their huge heads into the buckets, but Roger wasn't having any of it. He placed one bucket on the ground and then walked a few paces to place the other one down. He did the same with the other two buckets. As quickly as he put one down, a horse's head was in the bucket gobbling up the grain. Toby displayed the same bad manners, chewing his grain with an anxious eye on the other horses. Emma showed no fear when the horses galloped across the field towards her.

"Get out of it!" she shouted, slapping the Belgians' chests to move them out of the way. She picked up Toby's empty bucket. The two horses looked at Emma with as much surprise as Roger and Donna, then nuzzled their massive heads against her tiny body, almost knocking her off her feet. She reached up and patted them on their necks then headed back towards the gate, the huge horses trotting along behind her.

"Emma, wait for me!" shouted O'Malley.

They returned to the barn filling more buckets with grain for the cattle. "They like the taste of grain," O'Malley said, "which in turn makes them taste good too."

"You mean you eat them?"

"What do you think we do with them, keep them as pets? Of course we eat them. Don't you go all vegetarian on me, Emma. My cattle are free range. They have the run of this huge field. They can shelter in that pole barn if the weather turns yucky. They have fresh grass, good hay in the winter, good grain and plenty of fresh water. They are well taken care of, they don't get abused and are a lot better off than many others who never see a green field, let alone walk on one. And here's something else to remember. After you've come to respect these animals you will never leave a piece of meat on your plate again. Store bought meat doesn't taste anywhere near as good as the meat from this farm. I'm going to send you home with two steaks for you and your mom for your supper."

Donna placed an arm around Emma's shoulder. "Let's go see those kittens."

Emma couldn't believe how big they'd grown, especially Marmalade. She could have stayed in the barn playing with them all day.

"Okay, Emma, are you coming? We've got the chickens to do. After that it will be your first horse riding lesson."

"You're really going to teach me how to ride?" Emma began jumping off the ground with excitement.

The rooster was crowing loudly, dancing a jig around the bustling hens. Emma collected twenty-three brown eggs, carefully placing them in her basket.

"What are those hens doing in those boxes, Mrs. O'Malley?"

"They're setting on their eggs dear. In about twenty-one days they'll hatch out little chicks, that's why I've separated them from the others. Mind you take a dozen of those fresh eggs home with you. Roger, before Emma's riding lesson, I suggest we take a break. The poor girl must be exhausted."

They went into the kitchen and washed their hands vigorously. Emma sat on the bench at the harvest table, O'Malley at the head of the table. Donna poured Emma a large glass of milk and gave her a generous slice of homemade peach pie with cream. She joined them at the table with a slice of pie for herself and Roger and waited for the coffee to brew.

"How do you like farming so far, Emma?"

"I love it, Mrs. O'Malley."

"Mrs. O'Malley sounds a little formal these days. Why don't you call me Donna?"

O'Malley's Cottage

"You might not like it tomorrow," added O'Malley, pie crumbs sticking to the stubble on his upper lip. "Tomorrow I'm cleaning out the pigs and chickens. If you survive that, you've definitely got the makings of a farmer. There are no fancy gadgets on this farm, we use a wheel barrow, pitch fork, shovel and a wooden peg."

"A wooden peg?"

"To put on your nose because of the smell." O'Malley laughed at his own joke.

"Take no notice of him, Emma. We use a mask because of the dust, you don't want that getting in your lungs."

"How come your chickens don't lay any white eggs, Donna?"

"That's because they're Rhodesian Reds, they only lay brown eggs. Now the rooster, he's a Plymouth Rock and Plymouth Rock hens lay white eggs."

"My mom says brown eggs taste the best."

"Actually, my dear, they say there's no difference, but I do prefer brown eggs."

"Do you have a tractor, O'Malley?"

"I do. It's an old Case. Runs as sweet as the day I got it, rather like Mrs. O'Malley here," he chuckled.

"You old sweet talker you, Roger O'Malley, just wish I could say the same about you." Donna burst into good-humored laughter.

Emma sat and smiled at them, feeling relaxed in their company. She was surprised she hadn't thought about her mother, she was having so much fun.

"All right, the big moment has arrived. Time to tame the wild beast, Toby the incredible Shetland pony!" O'Malley rose from the table, pie crumbs sputtering from his mouth as he mouthed the words, *Shetland pony.*

He entered the tack room, emerging shortly afterwards with a bridle in his hand.

"Okay, Emma, this is Toby's bridle. As soon as he sees it he'll take off across the field and play hard to catch. They're not like dogs, fetch the lead and they're all over you. Horses like to be difficult, kind of like a woman."

"Roger! That's enough of that talk," reprimanded Donna. "She's a farm girl, not a farm boy and a nice young lady too, just you remember that."

"You're right, that was uncalled for." *True just the same though*, he muttered under his breath.

O'Malley opened the gate and they trooped into the field. The horses galloped towards them, then veered off at the last minute.

Turning to Emma, O'Malley announced, "Time for a little animal psychology. Turn your back on them, pretend we're not interested, and wait patiently."

They turned and waited. Emma felt a tingle buzzing through her whole body, sensing the horses approaching. She could hear the occasional snort from them, but their hooves were silent. Suddenly she felt the breath from one of the Belgians on the back of her neck, and nearly jumped out of her skin. Finally Toby came up behind her and placed his head over her shoulder. Emma gently raised her hand and stroked the side of his head. The four horses encircled O'Malley and nuzzled him, he in turn patted their huge necks affectionately.

"Bring your hand under his chin and over his nose. That's it, hold him there, don't let him get away on you. That's good. Now, bring the reins up over his head nice and gently, that's it, good girl. If he gets away on you don't try holding him with the reins. Okay, I'll show you how to get the bit in his mouth, over his tongue, not under it. Good boy, Toby. I know, it's been a while since you had someone take you for a ride. Okay, Emma, now his chin strap, not too tight, slacken that off another notch, that's it,

perfect. Bring the reins back over his head nice and gently, you got it. Now you're ready to lead him back to the gate."
"Am I doing okay, O'Malley?" Emma looked at O'Malley with big brown eyes, searching the horse whisperer's face for reassurance.
"Excellent job, Emma. You remembered not to wind the reins around your hand, good girl."
Emma led Toby into a small paddock followed by O'Malley. Donna stood at the gate watching them. She knew Emma was in good hands.
O'Malley attached a lunge line to Toby's bridle and showed Emma how to control the pony in a tight circle. The pony began bucking and kicking like a rodeo horse.
"Got to get the kinks out first, Emma. You wouldn't want to get on his back when he's like that. He's a little devil is that one. Right, your turn. Remember to keep your feet out of the line and don't let it get wrapped around your neck. Toby responds quite well to voice commands, so just do what I did and you'll be fine."
Initially Emma's performance was faultless, however the pony sensed she was unsure of herself. It purposely let the line slacken and then bolted off across the paddock. Emma panicked, gripped the line tighter and was pulled off her feet.
Instead of letting go, she clung on. Toby dragged her across the dry earth, arms stretched out in front of her, dust flying up behind her boots. Now she was mad. The pony made a circuit of the paddock, dragging the child behind him, both enveloped in a cloud of dust.
"O'Malley! Aren't you going to do something?"
"I'm not going to intervene just yet, Donna. She'll survive the cuts and bruises; the humiliation I'm not so sure about." The two of them looked at each other in surprise. "I know I'm going deaf, but did I just hear her shout, *Wowa you son-of-bitch!*"

O'Malley's Cottage

"It certainly sounded like it, dear. How unladylike of her."

After a full lap of the paddock, Toby slowed down to a casual walk. Tears in her eyes, Emma scrambled to her feet and reined in the wayward pony. By the time she brought him in close, she lost the urge to punch him in the mouth, instead she looked him square in the eyes and gave him one of her most severe verbal scoldings.

"Don't you ever do that to me again, do you understand! We're supposed to be friends, what kind of a friend are you?"

Without so much as a backward glance, Emma led Toby back into the centre of the paddock once more and continued the lesson as if nothing had happened. She didn't even bother to brush herself off. Her blue jeans and red gingham blouse were streaked with dirt and dried horse manure. This time, however, Toby behaved himself, his little initiation ceremony was over. Emma had him going around one way and then the other as if she had been working with horses all her life. She reined him in once more, removed the lunge line and walked back to the gate, coiling the line neatly between her hands. Toby walked behind her, his head down as though in disgrace.

"I know you feel the urge to rush in there and give her a hug, Donna. Don't, you'll ruin everything and she won't thank you for it later."

Without a word Roger took the lunge line from Emma and handed her an old riding hat that fit perfectly. Emma was not in the mood for conversation anyway. Her mud-covered cheeks were streaked in dry tears. Her bare arms grazed and sore. Her new blouse was torn, her brand-new jeans now had holes in the knees, with two very sore looking knees poking through.

"I ride bareback," said O'Malley. "I don't like saddles. If you want one I'll get you one."

"I ride bareback too!"

O'Malley looked taken aback, then smiled at his spirited protégé. He gave Emma a leg up onto Toby's back. Before giving

Emma the reins, O'Malley whispered a few words into Toby's ear.

O'Malley explained how to hold the reins between her fingers, how to steer the horse using the reins and her knees and how to make him speed up and slow down.

"Walk on, Toby!" Toby began walking around the paddock. "Okay, Emma, the worst part is coming, just try and get your rhythm with the pony. Put him into a trot."

Emma gently stuck her heels into Toby's flanks and he broke into a trot. She bobbed up and down all over Toby's back and began sliding off, quickly grabbing a handful of his mane. She was totally out of rhythm. Finally she slid off into the dirt, still clutching the reins. Toby stopped instantly.

Jumping to her feet she vaulted back onto the pony like an Indian warrior. She gave too much of a spring, disappearing over the back of the pony and into the dirt on the other side. O'Malley put a hand over his mouth to stifle his laughter.

Emma was so focused, she didn't see her mother leaning over the fence talking to Donna.

"How's she doing?"

"We'll know soon enough if she's got what it takes or not. At the moment she's battered and bruised, in need of a hot bath, some ointment for her abrasions, clean clothes and some tender loving care for her crushed ego. Apart from that she's fine. My God, she's a spirited young thing, and stubborn too. I think that's why she and Roger get on so well."

"Kindred spirits I think, Donna."

Emma leaped up again and this time she lay stuck across Toby's back. He broke into a trot. Quickly she dropped to the ground, then leapt back up, judging it just right. She swung her leg over his back and together they cantered around the paddock.

Emma saw her mother and waved, a huge grin across her dirty face. Rebecca waved back, an anxious look on her face. She dismounted, hugged Toby and forgave him for being so naughty initially.

"Well done, Emma, that was a superb bit of riding!" exclaimed O'Malley.

Emma stood proudly in front of her mother beaming from ear to ear. "My God, Emma, look at you! Are you okay, sweetheart?"

"Don't fuss, Mommy, please. I'm a cowgirl now, and sometimes these things happen to cowgirls." Emma was trying hard not to cry, the stinging pain in her arms and knees a painful reminder of her first riding lesson.

"Oh, honey, you look like you've been in a fight with Toby instead of riding him."

"He won the first fight, I won the second. Now we're even and we don't have to fight anymore. I'm just going to walk him for a bit to cool him down. After I've brushed him down could I have a cold drink please, Donna?"

"Of course you can, dear. Well done, you were a champion out there. Bring Toby over to the farmhouse, you can brush him on the lawn under the shade of the old maple tree."

O'Malley showed Emma how to brush Toby and how to pick his hooves clean. Donna insisted that he take Toby back to the field, while Emma immersed herself in a hot bath before lunch. She gave Rebecca some ointment for her abrasions.

When Emma stepped out of the bath, Rebecca enveloped her in a large white fluffy towel.

"Emma, look at you! You're covered from head to toe in abrasions and bruises. I'm of a mind not to let you back on the farm without my supervision."

"Mommy, it's okay. If I'm ever going to learn how to ride those Quarter horses, I might as well learn how to fall off Toby and be dragged around by him first."

"Emma, if this is what a little pony can do to you, I don't think you'll be going anywhere near those horses or those other two monsters. How about I take you somewhere for riding lessons, so you can learn how to ride properly without falling off and getting hurt? I'm sure that doesn't happen at a proper riding school."

"O'Malley told me I passed the *O'Malley School of Riding* in one day. He said, what I learned today would take months at a riding school. And yes, you do fall off at riding schools too." She was doing her best to protect her allegiance to her unorthodox Irish riding instructor. "Tomorrow I get to gallop Toby."

"All right, on one condition. No more of this nonsense. If your father could see the state you're in, he would be filing a lawsuit against the O'Malleys and taking me to court as an unfit mother."

"I love you Mom." She threw her arms around her mother and kissed her.

"Mom? You've never called me mom before. Is this all part of being a cowgirl?"

Emma wrinkled her nose, touching her own on her mother's.

Once the initial stinging sensation had gone away, the ointment felt good on her abrasions. Rebecca drove back to the cottage to get some fresh clothes for her, while Emma sat at the harvest table wrapped in one of Donna's housecoats, drinking a glass of orange juice. Rebecca returned with Emma's change of clothes wrapped inside a plastic shopping bag.

"You know Mr. O'Malley," a hint of annoyance in her voice, "my daughter is only ten-years old, she is not a teenage boy. I'm sure you mean well, but I would like Emma to return to school with all her limbs still attached."

Emma was upstairs getting dressed, conscious that her mother was likely to say something about the incident and wanting to be downstairs as fast as she could to support her beloved

O'Malley.

"Ah, you're right," replied O'Malley, looking down at his feet a little sheepishly. "I apologize, but the worst is over now. Trust me, in a couple of days Emma will be riding that pony as though she was born on its back and loving every minute. She's a fine spirited young girl and a credit to you. I'll understand if you don't want her to come back again."

"I'm as much to blame. I should have intervened sooner." Donna was upset.

"Well, O'Malley, when are we going riding again?" Emma bounced into the kitchen, looking like a new pin, aware of the atmosphere in the room. The adults looked at each other waiting for someone to speak first. O'Malley broke the awkward silence.

"Are you sure after your initiation this morning Emma, that you want to continue riding?"

"Damn right I do, O'Malley! Oops, that didn't come out right. I'm sorry I mean as long as you think I'm good enough."

"You're better than good enough, Emma, you'll make a fine horsewoman. Come to think of it, I have a couple of books on caring for your horse. I'd like you to take them home with you and read them at your leisure. You'll find them very interesting, especially as you want to own your own horses one day."

O'Malley walked over to the bookcase and pulled out a couple of ancient looking books, handing them to Emma.

"Well, Rebecca, am I keeping my best student?"

"Are you sure you want to continue, Emma? I don't want you coming home with broken bones or worse."

"Mom, I'll be fine. You have to expect to fall off at least seven times before you can ride properly, and I've practically done that already. And besides, this is all good experience for when I buy my horse farm."

"Okay," said Rebecca, taking a sip of her coffee. "Make sure you wear that riding hat. Maybe I should look out for a suit of armor for you, perhaps I can get one on eBay."

O'Malley's Cottage

Rebecca and Emma returned to the cottage laden with more fresh produce. O'Malley proudly handed Emma two large sirloin steaks, carefully wrapped in brown paper.
"Barbeque these tonight for your dinner Rebecca, compliments of the farm. Did you give Rebecca the fresh eggs, Donna?"
"I did, Roger. It's a nice afternoon, why don't you two go down to the lake for a swim."
"That's a good idea, let's do that, Emma."
After a light lunch Rebecca and Emma drove down to the lake, the first time they had been on their own since O'Malley showed them the secret picnic spot. Apart from a young couple who had cycled down on their mountain bikes, the beach was deserted.
To avoid catching the Mercedes on a boulder hidden in the long grass, Rebecca parked farther away from the lake. The couple were playing Frisbee in the lake, and waved to Rebecca and Emma as they too splashed into the cool water. They introduced themselves as Brad and Julia, university students on summer break. Rebecca and Emma joined in the game of Frisbee; afterwards they swam lengths up and down the small bay.
When it was time to leave, the couple was still playing on the beach. Rebecca invited them back to the cottage for a barbeque, an offer that was readily accepted. Brad and Julia insisted on cycling up to the cottage once they had pitched their tent on the lakeshore.
Rebecca had the barbeque all fired up by the time Brad and Julia cycled into the driveway. They leaned their expensive mountain bikes against the garage, hooking sleek cycling helmets onto the handlebars.
Brad set his glass of red wine on a tree stump in the garden, then he and Emma played Frisbee. Julia helped Rebecca prepare a

salad while the potatoes baked on the barbeque.

The two women fell into easy conversation, both glad of female company. Julia explained that her boyfriend had grown up on a farm in Zimbabwe. It had been in his family for generations, until Robert Mugabwe decided to return the land to the blacks and kicked the white farmers off their land.

"Brad doesn't talk about it much, he still harbors a deep resentment about what happened."

"Hey, Julia, why don't you come and join us? I'm getting whipped by Emma, I need some help."

"I'm glad someone found a way to beat you at something. Way to go Emma!" Julia raised her glass in approval. "Shall I put the steaks on now?"

"Yes, please."

"Would you mind if Brad looked after the steaks, he's just amazing with the barby."

"No, that's a great idea."

"Hey, Brad, the steaks are ready to go on, we'd like your expert touch!"

"You got it, coming right up. Hey, Emma, want to give me a hand? I'll show you how to make a great piece of steak into the best in the universe."

"Sure. Those steaks came from Mr. O'Malley, he owns the farm next door. This morning he taught me how to ride a horse, well, a pony actually."

"Wow, that's great, Emma. I grew up on a farm and that's where I learned to ride too. Does Mr. O'Malley have any other horses?"

"He's got two Belgians and two horses he calls Quarter horses."

"Do you ride Western or English style? My, these steaks look great."

"I'm sorry, I don't know what that means."

"Don't apologize, there are lots of things I don't know

either. It refers to the type of saddle you're using. Mr. O'Malley likely has Western saddles for the Quarter horses, but not necessarily."

"I'm learning to ride bare back, O'Malley says he doesn't like using a saddle, he says the Indians didn't use saddles and they were good riders."

"Emma, that's great. I'm impressed. It's hard learning to ride bare back, even harder than with a saddle, that's very good. Perhaps Julia and I could come and watch you ride. Do you think he'd let us ride his horses?"

"If he likes you I think he would, and I'm sure he'll like you and Julia. You'll know if he likes you."

"And how will I know that?"

"If he says you can call him O'Malley then you know he likes you. If you don't get to call him O'Malley you can forget about riding his horses."

"That's good to know, Emma. I'll be very disappointed if I don't get to call him O'Malley then."

"I think you'll be fine."

Rebecca glanced up from the kitchen counter and looked out the window at Brad and Emma.

"I think Brad would make a great dad, Julia. He and Emma are getting on famously."

"That's enough of that talk, thank you, Rebecca!"

"Okay, these steaks are ready. Medium rare like you asked. I'll leave yours on another few minutes, Emma."

The bugs were just too annoying to sit outside, so dinner was served in the small, but cozy dining room.

"Great place you've got here, Rebecca, Julia and I would love this."

"I wish it was ours, we're only renting it for the summer. If you're interested in renting it, the owners live at the farm next

O'Malley's Cottage

door. The O'Malley's, they're a wonderful old couple, I'm sure they'd have no problem renting it to you. At the moment I'm not sure if I'm going to be renting it after the summer or not, I haven't made up my mind yet."

"Emma told me all about them, the old guy sounds like quite the character. Hey, Julia, fancy horse riding tomorrow?"

"I'd love to, did you sneak in a couple of horses in your backpack without me seeing?"

"Not exactly. I am reliably informed that the O'Malley's have a couple of horses that don't get ridden as much as they should. It just so happens that Emma is going for another famous O'Malley riding lesson tomorrow morning. From what I hear they're legendary. She had her first lesson this morning, and the way she described it to me, it reminded me of my first riding lesson when my grandfather taught me how to ride back in Zimbabwe."

"Emma, why don't you telephone O'Malley and ask him if you can bring a couple of friends over tomorrow, I'll come too of course. Let Brad speak to him afterwards so he can ask about riding the horses."

Emma excused herself from the table and went into the kitchen to phone the O'Malleys. After a short conversation with O'Malley himself, Emma hung up the phone and returned to the dining table.

"O'Malley says that Brad and Julia can come over to watch me ride Toby in the morning. I asked him about them riding Star and Blazer, he said he'd want to take a look at them first before he'd trust them with his horses. He said he didn't need to talk to Brad on the phone, he'd make his mind up when he saw him in the flesh tomorrow morning."

"Sensible fellow. I'd have said the same thing myself."

Julia sat back in her chair. "That was a wonderful meal, thank you, Rebecca. I hope we can do this again sometime. We must keep in touch."

"And thank you to the O'Malleys for the steaks, they were great," added Brad.

"You two did a great job on the barbeque. Julia I'll give you my e-mail address before you go."

After the dinner things were cleared away the sun was already hanging low over the horizon.

"Let me drive you back to your campsite. I can fold the rear seats down and put your bikes in the back."

"No, that's okay, Rebecca, thanks anyway. Brad and I have been looking forward to cycling back to the lake. Look at the sky, it's ablaze in a fiery red and orange glow."

"It is beautiful."

"Emma, we'll meet you at the farm at nine o'clock in the morning. Julia and I don't want to miss your riding lesson."

O'Malley's Cottage
Page 153

Chapter Nine

When O'Malley arrived early the following morning to collect Emma, Rebecca was dressed and ready to come with them. She was curious to know what farm chores were all about.
After the chores were done, they set off to check the fence line, not that it needed checking, but Emma insisted they do it again because her mother had missed it the day before. By the time they got back to the farmhouse Rebecca was dying for a coffee. Donna stayed behind to sort out her own farmhouse chores and when the hungry trio arrived, breakfast was all ready for them.
Brad and Julia arrived on their mountain bikes and joined the new farm workers for breakfast. O'Malley was thrilled to talk about farming to another farmer, warming to Brad immediately. When he told Brad to call him O'Malley, Emma looked across the table and gave him the thumbs up, Brad winked back across the table at her, smiling.
"Care to share the secret you two?" asked Rebecca.
"No," giggled Emma.
After breakfast O'Malley rummaged around in the basement and found two old riding hats belonging to him and Donna. He had never worn his, preferring to let the wind blow through his hair. Dusting them off, he handed one each to Brad and Julia.
They watched Emma enter the field on her own with bridle in hand. Toby trotted over to her. She placed the reins over his head, gently eased the bit into his mouth, secured the chin strap and led him back out through the gate to the outside arena, the scene of yesterday's near disaster. She trotted Toby around in a circle at the end of the lunge line, this time without any mishaps.
O'Malley gave her the thumbs up. Emma removed the lunge line, handing it to him. In one fluid motion she mounted Toby and began trotting around the paddock. She dug her heels in

gently spurring him into a canter and then trotted back over to O'Malley, who was now holding open the gate.

"Okay, Emma, ride Toby out through the gate and follow me."

At the stable O'Malley handed the young couple the tack for the Quarter horses. "Don't put the saddle on Blazer just yet, I'm going to ride him alongside Emma to see how she does. After I'm done, Brad, saddle him up and you and Julia can take off riding. You'll find them a real pleasure to ride."

Brad gave O'Malley a leg up onto the horse. He turned and rode over to where Emma was waiting, mounted on the Shetland pony. The old man raised his hand high in the air and said in a loud voice, "Move 'em out!"

They trotted along the grassy track that led alongside the stable then cantered down the trail and out onto a large open field. When O'Malley was satisfied that Blazer had warmed up enough, like a runner stretching before a race, he led Emma over to the edge of the field. Beyond them was a vast expanse of grassland.

"Okay, Emma, give Toby his head. Kick your heels in and race that sucker right across the field, wheel him around before you hit the fence on the other side and gallop him back here. Bring him to a gentle stop, dismount and walk him around the edge of the field to cool him down. I'll be right beside you. If you come off, let go of the reins and just roll clear. You ready?" Emma nodded. "Okay then. Get on there! Ha!"

Away they raced, side by side across the field. Emma bent low across Toby's back, the pony bolting across the grassland, giving it everything he had. O'Malley had to rein in Blazer, otherwise he would have been there and back before the pony had reached the other side. Toby galloped, head down, nostrils flaring. Emma looked down to see the ground rushing by below her. When she saw how fast they were covering the ground, she made up her mind she wasn't coming off, she knew it was going to hurt if she did.

As the ancient cedar rail fence drew closer, Emma brought Toby around in a wide arc, turning him to the right. Instinctively she raised her right knee high, tucking it in hard against Toby's neck, made the turn and galloped back across the field. O'Malley gave Blazer his head on the return trip. The horse shot ahead of Toby, sending up clods of turf in its wake. O'Malley's thin grey hair was swept back across his head, ruffled like the black mane of his charging steed. Rebecca, Brad and Julia stood at the edge of the field thrilled at the spectacle of the old man riding like a demon and Emma in full control of Toby, galloping fast towards them.

Donna watched, praying O'Malley wouldn't come off, knowing if he did, his next ride would be to his Maker. Finally O'Malley turned just before the spectators, as though whipping around a barrel and headed back across the field to join Emma. Together they rode in, this time O'Malley let Emma take the lead, grim determination on her face, as though she was riding Secretariat in the Kentucky Derby.

Emma's face was flushed with pride. Rebecca snapped photograph after photograph. The two riders dismounted and gave each other a high five. Emma stood panting, full of emotion and exhilaration. She hugged Toby before leading the sweating pony around the field to cool him down, with O'Malley and Blazer walking alongside.

"Emma, I'm so proud of you. You rode that pony like a pro, well done." O'Malley was so happy he had tears in his eyes.

The old man handed the reins over to Brad and watched as Brad and Julia saddled up the two horses, glad to see they both knew what they were doing. The horses responded well to them, always a good sign in O'Malley's book.

"If you bring them back in as good a shape as you're leaving, you can borrow them again."

"I haven't asked how much you charge, O'Malley, we'll pay

you of course."

"You could never pay me enough to be allowed to ride those priceless beasts. And anyway, I should be the one paying you for exercising them. Be off with you, have fun and stick to the trails, that way you can't go wrong. If you get lost, don't worry, they know their way home, just be sure you don't part company from them that's all."

They turned the horses around and trotted back across the field to where the trail began, stopping to congratulate Emma on an excellent ride.

Rebecca was so overcome with emotion she was crying. She'd never seen Emma so happy. She and Donna walked back to the farmhouse to prepare lunch. Rebecca envied her daughter, who was now receiving a horse grooming lesson from O'Malley.

Rebecca was slicing a loaf of freshly baked whole wheat bread. "Donna, do you think O'Malley would teach me how to ride?"

"I'm sure he would, Rebecca, as long as you don't mind falling off a time or two. He's taught many people to ride, old and young alike."

"Emma's having so much fun, I would love for the two of us to go riding together."

"My guess is, he'll want you to get more comfortable working around the horses before he puts you on one of them. When they get back ask him, and watch his face light up. Emma will be even more thrilled."

* * *

"Rebecca, I would be delighted. Tell you what, after lunch why don't we bring Maxwell and Minnie into the stable and give them a good grooming. If you can work around those gentle giants, you'll be fine with anything, except maybe a stallion that's spied a mare in heat. Emma, you can help your mom can't you? I think you two are ready to handle 'em."

Rebecca looked surprised. "Ready to handle them? That implies I've already done some work around horses in the first place."

"Nothing like diving straight in. At the end of the day you'll know in your heart if you and horses belong together. What do you think, Emma?"

"Mom, you'll be fine. Don't look so worried, it'll be fun."

"Donna, you still have that old pair of work boots. Maybe they'll fit Rebecca?"

"I think they're in the scullery, at least that's where I last saw them. Hold on, I'll take a look." Donna could be heard rummaging around shelves and muttering to herself.

"Ah, here we are, these should fit you, Rebecca, you might need a pair of thick socks though." She carried out a pair of dusty looking tan colored work boots that looked stiff and uncomfortable.

"We don't want to leave Toby in the field feeling lonely, Emma, why don't you take him for a gentle ride around the field we were in this morning. You know what to do. Don't gallop him up and down the field though, it's too hot for that, just a nice walk will do. Mind you keep to the field, don't go wandering off up the trail after Brad and Julia, that'll take you into the middle of the wilderness. There's nothing up there except trees, more trees, rocks and more rocks, lakes and old hunting camps. You could ride for a week through there and you'd still only be halfway in. Okay, have fun. We'll know if you've fallen off, Toby will come back and tell us. If you see any people, not that you're likely to, come straight back."

O'Malley saw the concerned look on Rebecca's face. "She'll be fine. If I didn't think so, there's no way I'd let her off on her own, especially after what happened to my own daughter. Emma has a wonderful spirit, let's not kill it because of one misfit in the world. Okay then, Rebecca, let's go catch us a couple of big horses. Donna, will show you how to put the halter on Minnie, while I get Maxwell."

Rebecca was in an emotional state somewhere between nervous and terrified when the two Belgians trotted over to see what was going on. They were pleased to see Donna and O'Malley, but took turns at pushing their huge heads against Rebecca, almost knocking her over.

O'Malley saw the panic rising in Rebecca. "Push 'em back Rebecca. Speak firmly to them. They need to know you're the boss, not them. At the moment they're trying to dominate you. If you let that happen all is lost and it'll be a hard job getting back their respect. You don't need to be harsh nor cruel though, just firm."

Rebecca stuck her shoulder into Minnie's chest and pushed hard against her, slapping the mare's muscular chest. Minnie stood her ground and began to push back, enjoying the game.

"Get back, Minnie!" shouted Donna firmly. The giant horse took a pace back. "Good girl, now stand easy. Stand easy I tell you! That's a good girl. Okay, Rebecca, get the halter on like we practiced in the barn. Other way up, that's it. Okay, buckle up the chin strap, not too tight. Take a firm hold of the halter and clip on the lead rope. Remember, don't wrap it around your hand. Okay, let's head over to the gate."

Minnie didn't budge. Rebecca pulled on the lead rope with two hands. Still Minnie didn't budge, she merely lifted up her huge head pulling Rebecca into her chest.

"Okay, Rebecca, stand to the side of her, she'll go now. Walk on, Minnie! Walk on. Good girl."

Rebecca nervously held onto the lead rope, not sure if she was actually contributing anything to the exercise at all. Minnie calmly walked towards the gate. Donna swung it open to allow the horses through.

"Stand easy!" Rebecca said firmly, once she was clear of the gate. Minnie paid no attention and continued to walk on. Rebecca pulled back on the rope, this had as much effect as a mouse trying to pull back a supertanker. "Stand easy, Minnie, whoa, stand easy there, girl!" The horse stopped. "Good girl." She patted the horse's neck appreciatively. Standing together, Rebecca felt a bond between herself and the monstrous horse. Minnie cast a huge brown eye back at her.

Rebecca began to feel comfortable working around the horses, especially under the expert guidance of Roger and Donna. It was pleasurable grooming Minnie, talking calmly to her.

In the aisle ahead stood Maxwell, being groomed by O'Malley. Even when the horses passed wind thunderously and dropped a huge pile behind them, Rebecca maintained her composure. O'Malley shoveled away the pile behind Maxwell, reassuring the horse all the time, letting him know what he was doing. He passed the shovel over to Rebecca for her to do the same with Minnie. Like a trooper, Rebecca rose to the challenge and shoveled the steaming mess over to the side of the aisle.

"Good ride, Emma?"

"The best, O'Malley, Toby was really good. We walked all around the edge of the field like you said, cantered a little, but no galloping. I'll get his halter and clean him up out here if that's okay."

"Whatever you like, young lady."

"How's Mom doing?"

"Really well."

The afternoon drifted by pleasantly. They led the horses back to the field and removed their halters. It didn't take them long to roll in the dirt.

"They're just like naughty children," remarked Rebecca. "And to think we spent all afternoon cleaning them up."

Brad and Julia returned with Star and Blazer. Both riders and horses looked hot and exhausted. They enjoyed themselves so much they decided to camp for a few more days.

O'Malley offered to drive Rebecca and Emma home, they looked so exhausted. They didn't argue.

Chapter Ten

The following morning Rebecca awoke tingling with excitement at the prospect of riding a horse for the first time in her life. Right on cue, O'Malley drove into the driveway in his pick-up truck. This morning's chores included cleaning out the pigs and the chickens. Rebecca didn't mind cleaning out the horse stalls. Pushing the overloaded wheelbarrow to the manure pile took some practice; she only lost one load, spilling the contents halfway between the stables and the manure pile.

The pig stalls were another story, Rebecca almost quit on the spot. The smell was awful, she ran outside gagging, bent over at the waist, hands on knees, sucking in air. The chicken coup was no better. It was hot and dusty work and at times smelly, the dust mask didn't help her disposition much either, making breathing more difficult.

All she wanted was a long hot shower. Her back itched where the occasional piece of straw found its way down the back of her blouse. If it hadn't been for the sheer joy of seeing her daughter so happy in this awful environment, Rebecca would have stabbed the pitchfork into the dirt and stormed off back to Toronto.

By the time the chores were done, Rebecca was starving. The three of them walked back towards the farmhouse, Emma and O'Malley engaged in lively conversation, Rebecca dragging herself behind in silence. She felt irritated and angry. O'Malley sensed this and decided not to make any wisecracks.

Donna was waiting for them at the kitchen door, smiling; until she saw O'Malley's raised eyes and the exasperated look on Rebecca's face. Emma looked up, all smiles, exuding happiness from every pore. Donna walked down the steps, took hold of Rebecca's hand and gently led her upstairs to the bathroom.

"Take as long as you like in the shower, Rebecca. I have a T-shirt that should fit you." Donna placed a gentle hand on

Rebecca's cheek, aware that she was on the verge of crying. "See how you feel when you come down for breakfast dear, I'll have a large mug of coffee waiting for you. And don't worry, you don't have to do this ever again. I am not letting O'Malley drive my new best friend away."

Donna returned to the kitchen, leaving Rebecca in the bathroom. She placed a glass of milk in front of Emma, turned to her husband, crooked her finger at him and together they walked outside. Donna was furious. If Rebecca left, Emma would be gone too. She knew his heart was in the right place, but he was old fashioned in his ways and infuriatingly stubborn.

Rebecca came downstairs, drying her hair with a towel, almost feeling human again. Her smile returned. The smell of bacon and eggs, toast and coffee filled the kitchen.

"I guess farming chores are something like climbing a mountain. The idea seems so romantic in the planning, but the act of actually doing it, is horrendous. It's not until the ordeal is over and you're sitting in the kitchen drinking a cup of coffee that you can say; that was a wonderful experience! I have no desire to repeat it, thank you very much."

O'Malley was subdued after Donna's reprimand. Sheepishly he commented, "Nice T-shirt Rebecca." The words, *If you've eaten today, thank a farmer*, emblazoned across the front. "Still want to go riding?" He half expected to be told where to shove his pitchfork.

"To coin one of Emma's new phrases; damn right I do, Mister!"

* * *

O'Malley carried a bareback blanket out of the tack room. "You'll like this. It has a handle to hold on to if you find yourself losing your balance, and it stops the sweat from the horse's back ruining your jeans. If you look at Emma's backside you'll see what I mean. She's got more confidence riding Toby, so I didn't bother with the bareback blanket for her." Emma's jeans were a greasy brown between her thighs from the oil off the pony's back.

"These are my best jeans now, Mom."

"Don't you want a new pair, honey?"

"No way!"

"Star's very well behaved, you won't need to lunge her."

O'Malley helped Rebecca put the bridle on the horse and let her lead the mare out through the gate. He placed the bareback blanket on Star's back, securing the single strap under her belly.

"No time like the present, up you go, Rebecca." He gave Rebecca a leg up onto the horse. "Don't be nervous. I'm not going to let anything bad happen to you and neither is Star, she's got more sense than me anyway."

Donna reached up and squeezed Rebecca's hand. "I'll second that. You're in good hands, I mean with the horse, not O'Malley."

Even though the horse was only walking, Rebecca felt electrified. By the time they reached the paddock where Emma had learned to ride, Rebecca was beginning to feel more confident.

O'Malley swung open the gate, Star followed him in, leaving Rebecca alone inside the paddock nervously astride the horse.

"Aren't you coming in to help me?"

"No need for that. I can give you all the help you need from here. Just remember everything we talked about this morning at breakfast, okay?"

"Okay, if you say so. I'm trusting you, Roger O'Malley, but this could be the last time."

"Good luck, Mom!"

"Okay, Rebecca, here we go. Walk on, Star, good girl. Slowly now, not too fast."

Star began to walk around the paddock, steered by Rebecca to commands from O'Malley. This went on for a good fifteen minutes.

"Whoa, stand easy, Star! That's my girl. Right, Rebecca, you try it on your own. When you're comfortable dig your heels in gently and put her into a trot. At first you'll hate it. If you find yourself slipping, grab the handle or a handful of mane, whichever you like. Once you've learned how to trot the rest is a piece of cake, trust me."

"O'Malley's right, Mom. Cantering and galloping are easy, just like walking, but faster."

Rebecca reluctantly dug in her heels and Star broke into a gentle trot. "I don't like this!" Rebecca clung onto the handle of the bareback blanket for dear life. She was at the point of giving up, when she got into the rhythm. She and Star began to trot around the paddock in sync with one another.

O'Malley turned to Emma and winked. "Natural born rider just like you."

"Well done, Rebecca!" shouted Donna encouragingly.

"Edge her up another notch, Rebecca, into a canter, but not a full gallop!" shouted O'Malley.

"Are you sure I'm ready for that?"

"You're ready; in your own time. That's it, perfect. Now isn't that much more comfortable. Ride her around the paddock a couple of times one way, then diagonally across the paddock and round the other way. Do that about ten times."

Rebecca cantered Star around and across the paddock as O'Malley had instructed without mishap, her confidence growing all the time.

"Okay, bring her back down to a gentle trot. Take your time, Rebecca, get that rhythm going again. Come on, you can do it. Okay, very good, now walk her, practice turning her one way

O'Malley's Cottage
Page 165

and then the other, use your knees as well as the reins. That's it, keep talking to her, she likes lots of praise. All right, that'll do, let's head over to the field."

"O'Malley, I don't think I'm ready for that. What if she takes off on me?"

"She won't, she's a good horse. Just get her into a gentle canter across the field and back. Remember to slide your knee up her neck when she makes the turn like I told you. You'll do it instinctively anyway, so you won't have to think about which knee to use. This is the O'Malley One-Day School of Riding, you'll either succeed or die in the process. Only joking."

"If this is day one, O'Malley, what is day two of the O'Malley School of Riding?"

"Steeple chasing. And day three you'll be racing at Woodbine," he chuckled.

Rebecca cantered across the same field that O'Malley and Emma had galloped across the day before. She made a wide right turn, raising her right knee against Star's neck to keep her balance and began to canter back to where O'Malley, Donna, and Emma were waiting for her. As O'Malley knew she would, Star broke into a gallop, leaving it to Rebecca to decide to go with it or rein the horse in.

Rebecca was exhilarated by the sudden increase in speed and let Star fly. The horse's mane almost in her mouth as she crouched low, shouting encouragement to the horse, knees in tight against the horse's flanks, hands low and close over the mare's mane. As long as there was nothing to startle the horse, Rebecca was staying on its back. If she came off, what the hell, she'd roll out of the way and get back up with a few cuts and bruises, hopefully nothing worse. Closing in on her spectators she gently reined in the horse. O'Malley looked on proudly. Nobody noticed his hands behind his back, fingers tightly crossed.

Rebecca's eyes were streaming from the wind blowing in her face, her excitement clear for all to see.

O'Malley's Cottage

"Good ride, Rebecca! May as well ride her back to the stable and get her cleaned up. You sure you haven't ridden before," asked O'Malley, incredulous at how well Rebecca had ridden on her first attempt. "What you just did there would have taken you months at a posh riding establishment. You just saved yourself a fortune girl!"

"Beginners luck I guess." Rebecca couldn't stop smiling.

"Mom, you were terrific! I'm so proud of you, now we can go riding together."

"You've both gone through the fundamentals, obviously there's a lot more to riding a horse than I've shown you. The rest comes with practice and time. This afternoon, why don't all three of us take a gentle ride down to the lake, we'll take our time, no racing. The horses haven't splashed through the water in ages, it'll do them good."

"What about Donna?"

"She doesn't ride anymore. Her bones are too fragile, one fall and that would be the end of her. Even experienced riders come off sometimes. The difference between a great ride and a tragic ride is pretty academic, you'll get to appreciate that the more you ride."

"I think I have already. Emma and I would like to invite the two of you over for lunch today, and we will not take no for answer."

"Now that sounds like a lovely idea, don't you think, Donna? When was the last time we got invited out for lunch?"

"About forty years ago. I remember it well. You attacked the host because you didn't like the way he was treating his horses. You beat him with the same stick he was beating the horses with, if I remember correctly. I don't think we ever did sit down to lunch. You got yourself arrested for assault with a weapon."

"I know, but the judge threw the case out when he heard the

facts. And he told the police they should have charged him with cruelty to animals, which is what I said in the first place. Did you have to bring that up?"
"We'd be delighted to come, Rebecca."
"We're going to walk back to the cottage, I need another shower anyway after this morning. Thank you, O'Malley, your teaching methods I'm sure are very unorthodox and likely frowned upon by riding schools, but they work."
"You're welcome. Sure you don't want a ride home?"
"No, the walk will do us good, thanks anyway. Come on over whenever you're ready."
The walk home was hot, but pleasant. The deer flies hardly bothered them as they walked along the road. They carried a short leafy branch to swat away those flies that wouldn't give up their relentless dive-bombing. There were a few butterflies, but not as many as they had expected to see. Now and again a small rodent scurried away through the tall grass at the side of the road, just a patch of brown fur disappearing beneath the stalks. The hedgerows were ablaze with wild flowers. They stopped to pick some for the cottage.
After a long shower Rebecca told Emma she was so exhausted, she was going to put her feet up for half an hour. When Emma had showered she went and lay down beside her mother on the bed. Rebecca turned and smiled at her daughter, the two of them held hands and drifted off to sleep.

* * *

"Anyone home!" shouted O'Malley entering through the back door. "They must be out back, Donna."
"Oh my God, Emma! We overslept, the O'Malleys are here already. Coming! We'll be right down. Make yourselves at home."
Rebecca rushed over to the mirror, adjusting her hair with her hands, conscious that both she and Emma looked as though

O'Malley's Cottage

they had just woken up, their hair, their eyes and the lines on the sides of their faces were a dead giveaway.
"Ha ha! Caught you both out, napping." O'Malley sounded delighted, a broad grin across his face. "Figures, you city folk can't take the pace."
"It's all the fresh air up here, I don't think my lungs have adjusted to it yet."
"Not to worry. Roger and I brought over a few things to go with lunch. Roger, why don't you play a game of dominoes with Emma while I help Rebecca?"
"Sounds good to me. There should be an old wooden box in that drawer over there Emma. That's the one. I'll show you how to play if you don't already know."
"O'Malley, there really isn't any need to pick us up in the mornings, we can drive over or walk you know, save you some time and gas."
"Nonsense, Rebecca, besides I like doing it, makes me feel useful. We wouldn't mind a couple of glasses of that cold apple cider over here if you don't mind. The game is fierce and I'm afraid I'm getting beat."
"Coming right up you two, just as well you're not playing for money."
"Oh, yes, we are, Mommy!" squealed with delight. "And O'Malley owes me fifty cents already." Rebecca shook her head, thoroughly amused by the pair of them.
"You've turned my daughter into a country bumpkin, O'Malley. I don't think I'll ever be able to turn her back into a city girl again. When her father discovers that she's become a gambler, he's going to be furious. Oh, by the way, Emma, I took the camera and downloaded the pictures of you riding Toby yesterday and e-mailed them to Aunt Rachael and to your father. Rachael was tickled pink. She says she's going to frame her favorite ones and

O'Malley's Cottage

keep one by her bedside and one on her desk at the office. She sends you hugs and kisses."

"Which one did she like the best, Mom?"

"She didn't say, honey, I think she liked them all. She said she would have liked to have got a picture of Toby taking you for a ride around the paddock on your tummy, I told her that happened just before I got there, which was just as well." Emma pretended not to hear that last comment. "We should take the camera with us this afternoon when we go riding again. Tonight I'll download some more pictures and send them to her. You can send some to your father too, I'm sure he'd be impressed."

"Thanks, Mom, I'd like that. O'Malley owes me seventy-five cents now!"

"Don't tell your father you were playing dominoes for money, I don't think he'd be impressed."

"I won't."

During lunch, O'Malley brought up the subject of hay. He had a huge field to cut soon and would need a hand loading the hay wagon with the square bales. He'd drive the tractor, but needed someone to drive the team, Maxwell and Minnie, drawing the hay wagon. That left loading the square bales onto the wagon. The higher up they had to be tossed, the harder it got. Donna couldn't do it anymore, Emma wasn't strong enough, so that left only Rebecca and she'd be okay for the first row.

"You got any ideas, Rebecca? It's hard to get help these days. Seems the young folk don't want anything to do with farm life anymore, everything revolves around those damn computer games; well computer games don't grow food! Five percent of the population feeding the other ninety-five. Soon it'll be one percent feeding ninety-nine percent the way things are going, what with those damn developers building subdivisions on valuable farmland!" He banged the table with his fist. "Damn city folk!"

All eyes were suddenly on O'Malley. He was clutching his chest in obvious pain, his face now an ashen grey. Rebecca rushed

to his side and put a comforting arm around the old man.
"I'm fine, I'm fine." He was anything but fine, wincing in pain, agitated at being pampered and embarrassed at the situation he found himself in. "I'll be all right, just give me a minute," he wheezed, his lips turning blue.
"O'Malley, I'm calling an ambulance and don't argue with me!" Rebecca snatched up the phone.
"I'm not going in any bloody ambulance! The only way I'm leaving this farm is in a wooden box."
"No-one's going to force you to do anything, O'Malley," said Rebecca dialing 9-1-1. "Ambulance please."
Twenty minutes later they heard sirens coming up the road. Two paramedics rushed up the driveway followed by four members of the fire department and an OPP officer, their vehicles parked haphazardly outside the cottage, emergency lights still flashing.
Brad and Julia had been planning to go riding that afternoon and were about to cycle into the driveway of the farm, when they saw the emergency vehicles pulling up outside the cottage. They pedaled furiously up the road.
O'Malley was unconscious on the floor, an oxygen mask over his blue lips. The paramedics applied a defibrillator to the old man's chest and administered an electrical shock.
"Got a pulse!" shouted the young raven-haired female paramedic.
The OPP Officer, a pretty young brunette, hovered nearby. Both she and the paramedic often visited the farm to go riding.
Roger O'Malley no longer had any say in whether or not he was going to hospital, he remained unconscious. The paramedics, assisted by members of the volunteer fire department loaded the stricken O'Malley into the back of the ambulance as Brad and Julia cycled up.

O'Malley's Cottage
Page 171

Donna was in a state of shock and looked as though she would collapse at any moment. Rebecca sat her down in an armchair and tried her best to comfort her. Emma ran up to her bedroom burying her face in her pillow, unable to control the flood of tears that overwhelmed her. Julia went upstairs after her.

"Donna, there's no need to worry about the farm. We'll all pitch in, whatever it takes. O'Malley's a fighter he'll pull through I just know it." Rebecca knelt in front of the armchair, holding Donna's hands.

"He always made a point of checking on the animals before going to bed every night. I'll be lost without him, I'll have to sell the farm."

"Don't jump the gun yet, Donna, we don't know anything at the moment." She realized no one had gone with O'Malley. "Someone should be with him."

"Would you and Emma go please, dear? If he knows you're there, especially Emma, it'll make him so happy if he wakes up."

"When he wakes up, Donna, not if. Are you sure you don't want to come with us?"

"If he sees me fussing over him instead of looking after the farm, he'll be even more upset."

"Julia and I can stay over a little longer, Donna, and give you a hand around the farm until O'Malley's well again," suggested Brad. "It's beautiful down by the lake, another week or two won't be a problem."

"No, don't do that, Brad, there's plenty of room over at the farm. To tell you the truth I'd quite like your company."

"Julia and I would be delighted, we'll be glad to help in any way we can. Our time is our own at the moment."

The Police Officer's radio broke the silence. "Great, that's all I need now, a fatal accident. I'll be glad when this day is over. I'll phone you later, Donna, to see how things are. At some point I'll pop into the hospital, if I ever get the chance." She turned to Rebecca and Brad, "Nice meeting you both."

When Julia and Emma walked into the kitchen, Emma was holding Julia's hand, in the other she clutched Leopold, her cuddly lion.

"Is he going to die, Mommy?" she said running across the kitchen floor, burying her head in her mother's chest.

"He's in God's hands now, honey." Rebecca gently stroked the back of her daughter's head. "He might be allowed to stay with us a bit longer if we're lucky. Donna would like you and I to go and be with him at the hospital. Are you up to that?" Emma nodded her head, but wouldn't look up. "Okay, it could be a long night for us. Let's bring a couple of blankets and pillows and something to eat and drink. You are going to have to be brave, Emma, I know that's asking a lot of a little girl. Mommy's going to have to be brave too. Come on, let's get some things packed."

"What about the animals, Mommy?"

"Don't worry, Julia and I are going to take care of them until O'Malley's better. You can still come over and help; we're going to need you to show us the ropes for a while until we get the hang of it. That's okay isn't it, Julia?"

"Absolutely."

"You may as well make use of the truck, Brad." Donna rose from her chair and gave him a hug. "Roger always felt it was better for a vehicle to be used regularly than lying idle for weeks. It doesn't look like much, but it drives like it was still new, well maybe that's a bit of an exaggeration. Do you know how to get to the hospital, Rebecca?"

"Yes, I do. Before Rachael left, she insisted on giving me a map of how to get to the local hospital in case of an emergency, among other bits of information she thought Emma and I might need up here in the wilderness. Okay, we're ready. Donna, I'll call you the minute I have any news."

"Don't pretend he's still alive if he's gone. I don't want you trying to spare my feelings until you can tell me in person. I'd rather know up front, please."

"All right, I promise."

Rebecca hugged her tightly then left with Emma for the long drive to the cottage hospital.

* * *

"Well, Emma, it must have been divine intervention. Lucky we met Brad and Julia, especially with Brad having been brought up on a farm. At least we know Donna's in good hands"

"I hope God doesn't take him from us yet, Mommy. I know O'Malley was so looking forward to riding down to the lake with us. I've been praying that he's still alive, and if he isn't, I'm never going to believe in God again!"

"It doesn't work like that, sweetie. Maybe God needs O'Malley to take care of his horses. He couldn't find anyone better than O'Malley, you know that. Besides, we don't know yet what God has decided, so don't give up hope. And if he has taken him, don't be mad, just think how lucky we both are to have met someone as wonderful as Roger O'Malley. Our job now is to help Donna through this terrible time in her life, so we have to keep our spirits up for her."

With mounting dread, Rebecca parked the Mercedes in the visitors' parking lot at the hospital. She held Emma's hand and together they walked into emerge. The ward sister was pleasant, but businesslike.

"They're still working on him, but it doesn't look good. He's had a massive heart attack, it's a wonder he's still alive at all. There's a comfortable waiting room just down the end of the hall on your right, why don't you wait in there. As soon as I have any news I'll tell you." She smiled, turned and got back to the business of healing the sick and comforting the dying.

Rebecca immediately telephoned the farmhouse. Julia

picked up the phone on the first ring. Rebecca told her the news, it wasn't good, but it wasn't all bad either. There was still hope. She'd phone again when she had more news.

Donna was busying herself baking. Brad had gone to check on the animals. Robby was still lying at the foot of O'Malley's favorite chair. When Donna got back to the farm, the dog hadn't moved, as if he knew something was wrong with his master. She tempted the old dog with his favorite tidbit, a piece of cheese; Robby ignored it.

Rebecca and Emma were both mentally and physically exhausted. They fell asleep on a small couch, Emma cuddled into her mother.

Rebecca was aware of the presence of someone in the room and opened her eyes to see a young doctor dressed in a long white coat standing in the doorway.

"How is he?"

"Well, the good news is we have him stabilized."

"The bad news?"

"He won't be farming anymore. His heart is damaged. Though it's still too early to tell, he won't be able to engage in anything strenuous or stressful. This is going to be life altering for him."

"When he finds that out, that'll kill him for sure; the farm's his whole life."

"Well, he's going to need a lot of help around the farm, and from what I understand it's just himself and his elderly wife trying to cope with it. That's correct isn't it?"

"Yes, it is. Can we see him?"

"Of course you can. I should let him sleep for a while though, but I'm sure your presence in the room will be a comfort. He's going to be with us for about a week, then we'll see about letting him go home. He'll be on some pretty strong medication

O'Malley's Cottage
Page 175

and if he's like most old farmers I've met, he'll be as stubborn as a mule. You're going to have to see that he takes his medication as prescribed and leaves the farm work to someone else."

"Will he be able to ride a horse, he wants to take us riding down to the lake?" Emma awoke groggily. Rebecca wrapped a comforting arm around her.

"As long as you help him on and off the horse and he doesn't go any faster than a walk, I think that'll be all right. If he falls off though, I'm afraid that will definitely be the end of him. My name's Doctor O'Connell by the way."

"I'm Rebecca, this is my daughter Emma. We're friends of the O'Malleys, we're renting a cottage from them for the summer, that's how we met. We all adore him. He taught my daughter and I how to ride." Tears welled up in Rebecca's eyes as she shook the doctor's hand and mouthed the words, "Thank you," almost silently in her grief.

"Rebecca, he's not in good shape, if we can get him back to the farm and he sees the summer out with you, that's more than I could hope for. Every day after that will be a bonus. Emma, you let me know if you get to make that ride down to the lake with him. That would be wonderful."

Rebecca telephoned the farm and gave Julia the news, exactly as Dr. O'Connell had given it to her. She didn't stay long on the phone because she and Emma were going to sit with O'Malley.

Late in the evening O'Malley stirred. Emma was asleep, wrapped in a blanket on an armchair next to her mother. Rebecca had been dozing on and off.

"Where am I?" His voice was weak.

"You're in hospital, O'Malley. You've suffered a heart attack." Rebecca spoke softly, rising from her chair.

"Rebecca, is that you?"

"Yes, I'm here, so is Emma, she's asleep next to me. We're going to stay with you."

"What about the animals? I must get back to the farm.

O'Malley's Cottage

Donna can't do it on her own."

"That's all been taken care of. Brad and Julia are there with Donna and they're going to look after things until you're well enough to come home. You have to rest and get your strength back, if you don't, you won't be coming home."

"I've got to get the hay in, Rebecca, otherwise I'll have nothing to feed the horses and the cattle in the winter."

"Don't worry, somehow we'll find a way to do it. Brad's a farmer, he'll know what to do. The main thing is to get you well again. Emma and I want you to get better so we can ride down to the lake with you."

"Yes, I promised her that. Don't want to break a promise, that would never do. I feel so tired and my chest feels like Maxwell hoofed me. How's Donna?"

"She's fine, worrying about you of course, as we all are. She said you'd be mad if she left the farm to sit with you." O'Malley smiled.

"You don't need to sit here with me all night Rebecca. I'm in good hands. You take that little princess home with you and get some sleep. I'm gonna make it home I promise you that, and if it's the last thing I do, we're going on that ride down to the lake."

The nurse entered the room and began to check the monitors hooked up to O'Malley. Rebecca woke Emma. When she saw that O'Malley was still alive her eyes lit up, as did his when he saw her. Mother and daughter tenderly kissed the old man on his stubbly cheeks and left the room.

Rebecca telephoned the farm again. This time Brad answered the phone. She gave him the latest update and told him they were on their way home, but would be back to see O'Malley again in the morning after they'd helped with the chores.

It was late when Rebecca drove into the driveway of O'Malley's Cottage. That night Emma cuddled up in bed with her mother.

Chapter Eleven

At a quarter to seven in the morning Rebecca's alarm clock pierced the silence of the morning with the sound of Up! Up! Up! sung by Shania Twain. "Not this morning, Shania, sorry," groaned Rebecca as she rolled over, searching for the off button.

By seven ten, Rebecca and Emma were out the front door, driving up to the farm to help Brad and Julia with the chores, yawning and wiping sleep from their eyes as they made their way along the road in the Mercedes.

"I'd like to get the hay cut and baled before O'Malley gets home." Brad looked up from buttering his toast. "I can drive the tractor and I know how to hitch the team to the hay wagon. Thing is, we don't have enough help. I reckon there's probably going to be about a thousand square bales to load and then unload in the barn. Got any ideas anyone?"

The telephone rang in the kitchen. They all stopped and looked at each other, fearing the worst.

"It's your sister." Julia handed the phone to Rebecca.

"I e-mailed her last night about the hay problem, she said she'd get back to me. Looks like she has."

Rebecca updated Rachael, then listened intently to her sister. "That's great news, Rachael, that's really nice of Winston. Hold on I'll ask him." She turned to Brad. "Rachael has six strapping young men ready to help with the hay at a moment's notice. She wants to know when you want them."

"That is great news. Okay, I'll cut the hay today, give it a couple of days to dry, if the weather holds like it's supposed to. Tell them to be here Wednesday morning nine o'clock and we'll start baling, unless the weather breaks that is."

"The other good news is, they come free, just feed them she says." Rebecca hung up the phone.

O'Malley's Cottage

"That's real nice of this Winston guy. I'm impressed." Brad began making notes on a paper napkin. "Where are they coming from?"

"From Scarborough."

"The other good news is; Robby's eating again. His master must be doing okay."

Julia placed a cup of coffee in front of Donna. "That is good news."

"I'm going to make a start on the hay field this morning and check out the rest of the machinery. Why don't you ladies head into town, check on O'Malley and have a day in town together. I'll manage here no problem, it'll be like old times for me. I can't wait to get on a tractor again, even one as ancient as O'Malley's."

When they arrived at the hospital, O'Malley was sitting up in bed and though frail looking, he wasn't as grey as he had looked the day before and his lips were not so blue. He was thrilled to see them all, especially his beloved Donna, thankful that the farm was in good hands while he was laid up.

After their visit they did some shopping and had lunch out. Later in the afternoon they returned to look in on O'Malley. Even he accepted the reality that he was too weak at the moment to return to the farm, and agreed that he had to get himself stronger before he could do that.

By the time they all returned to the farm, Brad had just about finished cutting the hay. Donna looked worn out. Rebecca and Julia insisted they would prepare supper, while Emma went out with Robby to check on the animals.

"Don't spend too long with those kittens, Emma, supper will be ready soon."

"I won't, Mommy."

"Isn't that funny, Julia? Only last week she stopped calling me Mommy and began calling me Mom. Now I'm Mommy again. I guess she felt grown up around O'Malley and the horses, now she's back to being a little girl again."

"She needs her mom even more now. She really loves that old man doesn't she?"
"Yes, she does. I don't know how I would have handled it if anything had happened to him when we arrived at the hospital yesterday."
Donna fell asleep in the reclining chair, looking frail and drawn.

* * *

When they went in to see O'Malley the next day, they told him they wouldn't be able to come in on Wednesday because they were going to be baling hay. O'Malley said that was okay, because the pretty young policewoman and her paramedic friend were coming to see him on Wednesday anyway.
"Well, that'll be enough to give you another heart attack," laughed Donna. "I don't think that's such a good idea after all."
Brad came with them and received instructions on the operation of the temperamental baler. O'Malley gave Brad an oral examination on hitching up the team of Belgians to the hay wagon, adding that Emma should take the reins as he had already given her some instruction on how to drive them. If he forgot anything about hitching up the team, Emma knew how to do it blindfolded, which wasn't far from the truth.
Before they all left the hospital, O'Malley insisted that Rebecca and Emma were to continue with their riding, and not to stop just because he wasn't around. He told them it was time for them to learn by their own mistakes anyhow.

Chapter Twelve

At 9 a.m. sharp on Wednesday morning a shiny black Cadillac Escalade pulled into the driveway of the farm. Out stepped a huge man in black track pants and matching T-shirt, wearing mirrored sunglasses. He was built like the Rock. A black ball cap protected his bald head from the sun, peak backwards.

Winston walked up to the doorway of the farmhouse as six black boys in their late teens clambered out of the Cadillac behind him. They were all dressed as though they were about to go on stage to sing a rap song, with their ball caps askew on their heads, wearing baggy pants and baggy shirts, thick gold chains around their necks.

"Yo, man, what kinda shit you got us into!" said one of the boys, addressing Winston. "We ain't looking to pick no cotton for no white folks, you know what I'm saying."

"Leroy, you ain't picking no cotton!" said Winston angrily. "You be baling hay, that's what you be doing. All day till the sun goes down. You ain't up here to rob the place and tie up the little old white farm lady, you's baling hay, my man, or I'm gonna kick your ass. I don't wanna hear no more complaining. You got that!"

"You lied man! You said you had a job for us!" whined Leroy.

"I didn't lie to you! Yes, I said I gotta a job for you and this is the job, so let's get started! Your folks told me to help clean up your act, well it starts right here. Welcome to O'Malley's Work Camp, brothers!" Winston said this with a huge smile.

"Yo, that be Methuselah coming out the front door!" exclaimed Leroy rudely.

"Hi, boys, thank you so much for coming," said Donna. "Now come on in and have a hearty breakfast before you get started. And you, sir, must be Winston, how lovely to see you."

"Ma'am, it's a pleasure. Hard work is good for the body and

soul."

"It looks like you've got a lot of both already." Donna had never seen such a huge man before.

They all trooped inside the farmhouse and made themselves comfortable around the harvest table. Leroy, who acted as spokesperson for his teenage gang had never been treated so well in his life.

"Lady, you make a mean breakfast. You can come back with us and cook for my gang anytime!"

"Well, young man, if you enjoyed breakfast, you'll really enjoy dinner after an honest, hard day's work."

Rebecca walked into the kitchen and immediately the teenage boys all looked up; Leroy gave a loud wolf whistle.

"You boys show some respect, this here woman is a personal friend of mine." Winston was both angry and embarrassed.

The boys saw the look of anger on Winston's face, bowed their heads and got on with their breakfast.

"Hi, Winston, thank you so much for coming. You have no idea how much we appreciate it, especially Donna."

Winston rose gracefully from the table and gave Rebecca a gentle hug. It was brief, but long in terms of the electrical explosion that occurred between them when their bodies touched.

"Glad we could be of service." Winston was genuinely shocked at how awkward he felt, something that just didn't happen to him in the presence of women; ever.

Brad, Julia, and Emma walked into the kitchen to meet the new helpers.

"Wow, a rap group!" said Brad, jokingly. His introduction was not well received, except by Winston who roared with laughter. His deep voice sounding like Barry White, the sound of his laughter reverberating off the kitchen windows. Brad

O'Malley's Cottage

introduced himself as the group of teenagers scowled back at him.

"Great, Brad," Julia whispered in his ear. "We have a near mutiny on our hands and we haven't even finished breakfast."

"Granny," said Leroy. "On behalf of me and the gang, thank you for a delicious breakfast and we hope your husband gets better soon."

"Thank you, Leroy, that's very kind of you. I guess you all belong to a church group?"

This time Winston nearly brought the house down with his laughter. He laughed so long and loud that tears began streaming down his cheeks. He had to leave the kitchen for the porch outside. Those inside the house could still hear him laughing as though he was still inside the room with them.

"Did I just say something funny?" Donna was looking at Rebecca who was trying not to laugh, but the expression on Rebecca's face and the tears running down her own cheeks made it obvious that she had said something hilarious.

Rebecca daren't tell her the kitchen was full of hardened criminals, not until the hay was baled and inside the hay barn and the young hooligans were on their way back to Scarborough that is. The mental image of Donna grabbing O'Malley's shotgun, rushing into the kitchen shouting, "Git!" was not one that Rebecca cared to imagine.

Breakfast over, the motley crew stepped outside to see the two Belgians harnessed to a huge empty hay wagon, patiently waiting to get to work.

"Wo!" said Leroy. "Them horses gotta be on steroids man! You mean that little girl's gonna drive the team. I'm sittin' up there with her. This is so cool, I wanna see how this is done."

Leroy sat next to Emma as she drove the team out to the hayfield, a band of workers, willing and unwilling riding on the wagon behind them.

For the first ten minutes the boys halfheartedly lifted the hay bales onto the wagon, preferring to watch Julia and Rebecca's backsides as they bent over to lift the hay bales in their tight blue jeans.

"Are you assholes gonna spend the whole day watching my ass or are you gonna do any work!" shouted Rebecca in exasperation, her hands on her hips.

Emma put her hand over her mouth and burst into a fit of the giggles. She reminded herself to definitely add this one to her diary before she went to bed. She would entitle it, *The worst word I heard Mom say so far*.

Winston smiled, he had been just as guilty, taking advantage of the pleasant view of two beautiful women bent over a hay bale, only he had been more discreet and hadn't apparently been caught.

Already the two women and Winston had loaded twice as many bales on the wagon as the six boys, the youngest of whom was fifteen. The strength of the women embarrassed all of them. Having been shamed they set to work with a vengeance. Emma slowly walked the horses forward as the hay bales were loaded on. To everyone's surprise, Winston knew how to stack the bales, preventing them from toppling off the wagon.

"I worked on a farm when I was down in the States one time. The difference there was, they had prison guards with shotguns looking after us. You don't wanna be committing no crime down in the US of A, no sir." The big man continued to load bales, two at a time, not even out of breath as he spoke.

Brad drove the tractor, hauling the baler around the field. It scooped up the loose hay and dropped the tightly packed square bales behind it, secured with polypropylene orange baler twine.

Every time the wagon was loaded to capacity, the crew climbed to the top of the hay bales loaded on the back, and Emma drove the team across the fields to the big hay barn, where everyone lent a hand to stack the dry bales inside the barn, including Emma.

Brad continued baling the hay relentlessly. Winston tried to persuade Rebecca and Julia to take a break under the shade of the trees while they were gone, but the two women wouldn't hear of it, they were not going to allow themselves to be shown up by a group of teenage boys.

The more he was around Rebecca, the more Winston found himself attracted to her. She still looked gorgeous, even after working all morning, hot and sweaty under a blazing sun. He didn't want to spoil his publishing prospects by having designs on Rebecca, that would really upset his relationship with Rachael. He knew in the long run that it wouldn't be a good thing for Rebecca to become entangled with him. The unlicensed Glock 40 caliber semiautomatic pistol concealed inside the Escalade, was testimony to that.

Rebecca met his gaze and smiled, wiping her forearm across her brow. Unbeknown to Winston, Rebecca was feeling the same mutual attraction.

At one o'clock, Donna arrived in the pick-up truck, laden with cold drinks, sandwiches and her famous homemade apple pie for the hungry workers. Brad continued to drive the baler; he wanted to get the field cleared by nightfall and wouldn't stop for lunch, he'd eat his on the tractor. They had to get the hay off the ground before the dew set in. Once the field was baled he would help with the loading and unloading of the hay wagon.

Emma drove the wagon over to the shade of some trees, more for the comfort of the horses than the workers, who rode on top of the hay bales, ravenous for food. Donna brought some water with her in the truck for the two horses. Emma allowed them to have a refreshing drink and a large scoop of sweet feed. Nobody was permitted to lie under the wagon, on the off chance the horses had a change of plan themselves and decided to take off, crushing some unfortunate who happened to be lying near a wheel.

They toiled on late into the evening, taking dinner in two

exhausted shifts. Donna would drive down in the truck, collect one group, feed them, return them to the field and collect the second weary group. To get the bales into the barn and off the ground before the dew came, they worked like demons, eventually just throwing the bales loosely into the dry barn, stacking them when the last bale was thrown inside.

By midnight they had the last of the bales stacked neatly inside the barn. Donna was so happy she stood in the kitchen crying, hugging each of the exhausted workers as they trooped into the house for a light supper before heading home.

"Yo, before we go, I gotta get something from the car. How 'bout you folks move that kitchen table over by the wall, go on, this is our goodbye to y'all."

When Leroy returned, he was carrying a large and what turned out to be, a very loud ghetto blaster. To the sound of loud rap music, Leroy began break-dancing, twisting and turning and flipping his agile body across the kitchen floor. His gang members clapped and cheered him on.

The fact that Leroy had any energy left after a strenuous day of work lugging hay bales around, was a big surprise to everyone. Before leaving, Leroy led Emma onto the dance floor and showed her how to break-dance like him. Everyone cheered as Emma demonstrated her agility on the kitchen dance floor, and much to Rebecca's surprise, her little girl was a natural born dancer. When they had finished, Leroy presented Emma with the CD. O'Malley's Cottage had just experienced rap music for the first time in its history.

Winston was the only one who took up the offer of having a shower before heading home. Rebecca led the hulking figure upstairs to the bathroom, a little quick on the uptake to show him where everything was, before Donna did. Rebecca felt embarrassed as everyone stopped to look at her in surprise.

"I mean, you must be worn out, Donna," she said lamely.

Rebecca opened the bathroom door and ushered Winston inside, she was breathing heavily as she handed him a clean bath towel. The big man towered above her as he pulled off his sweat-soaked T-shirt, revealing a muscled chest and a six-pack from long workouts in the gym and a good diet. Feeling foolish, Rebecca turned to leave, but not really wanting to. Winston grabbed her wrist and instantly pulled her to him and kissed her long and hard. Rebecca pulled him tightly to her, wishing somehow that she could persuade him to stay the night.

"Some things aren't meant to be Rebecca. If I stay the night, as I know you want me to, and believe me I want to just as much as you do, it will spoil something precious to me, like my relationship with you and Rachael."

He placed his enormous hands against her cheeks and kissed her on her forehead. Rebecca left the bathroom, her heart and body aching for him. She knew Winston was staring at the back of the bathroom door, his mind in turmoil. She heard the shower running. *I bet he's taking a cold shower.* She was right.

As the black Cadillac Escalade drove away, with those at the farm waving goodbye to those in the SUV, Leroy's voice could be heard shouting out of the vehicle window into the darkness, "You sure do have a nice ass, Miss Rebecca!"

This was followed by raucous laughter from among the wayward teenage boys accompanying Leroy back to Toronto. Winston was really pleased with the way the six of them had worked and behaved, he decided to let that one go.

"Well!" Donna sounded shocked. "That young man should have his mouth washed out with carbolic soap."

"You fancy Rebecca don't you, Winston?"

"She's a friend, that's all, Leroy."

"Better gets some miles between you, Boss, otherwise I can see us turning around and heading right back."

"Shut up, Leroy!" But Winston knew he was right.

O'Malley's Cottage

Chapter Thirteen

At the end of the week, Rebecca drove to the hospital with Julia and Emma to bring O'Malley home. He was delighted to see them and anxious to get back to the farm. Julia wheeled him out to the car in a hospital wheelchair. Together they sat him in the front passenger seat of the Mercedes, because there was more leg room. The nurse explained to Rebecca the medication he was on and the importance of taking it easy at the farm.

O'Malley said little on the drive home. He was quite content to look out at the countryside. When Rebecca finally drove up the laneway to the farm, Robby ran down to meet them, wagging his tail excitedly as though he knew O'Malley was inside the vehicle. Donna and Brad came out of the house to meet them.

Brad strode over to the front passenger door to give O'Malley a helping hand. He didn't want to offend O'Malley, but they had all agreed that he would be his own worst enemy if they didn't intervene. If they let him have his own way, they didn't think he'd survive the first day at home, however, they were all surprised to see O'Malley grateful for the assistance. He was too weak to walk into the farmhouse on his own. He gave a sigh of relief when he finally sat down in his comfortable reclining chair. Rebecca and Julia helped position the chair so that his feet were elevated.

"A man could get used to this." But they all knew he would give anything to walk on his own down to the barn to see the horses. "I owe you all a big thank you for getting the hay in for me, you have no idea how much I appreciate it."

"Brad brought the bed down into the dining room for us, Roger; before you get upset I asked him to do it. Until you feel well enough to climb the stairs again that is. We'll be able to watch television in bed." Donna tried to sound cheerful as she bent down and kissed his forehead. "It's lovely to have you home again where you belong." She began to tremble, then burst into tears. O'Malley gently patted her hand and fell asleep.

O'Malley's Cottage

Rebecca and Emma returned to the farm to join them for dinner. O'Malley sat at the head of the table looking very frail and grey, finding it an effort to feed himself. Emma insisted on sitting next to him. From time to time she squeezed his hand, he smiled at her with blue eyes that no longer sparkled and seemed sunken further into his head.

"Tomorrow, if you like, O'Malley, I'll ride Toby past the window so you can see him. I know he's missed you. I told all the animals that you were coming home. Me and the animals all prayed for you, you know."

O'Malley raised his hand and ran his fingers through Emma's hair. His, "Thank you, Emma," was barely audible.

"Julia and I decided to stay on a little longer, if that's okay. We figure we can stay another week before we have to get back to university, but don't worry, we plan on coming up on our days off to lend a hand."

"You've done more than enough, Brad." O'Malley spoke quietly. "I can't expect you to live your lives around my problems. I'd appreciate you staying one more week, but after that you must go on home, you've got your own lives to lead. Donna and I will be pleased to see you at any time. You're more than welcome to stay with us."

Rebecca tried to sound cheerful. "Emma and I have an announcement to make. Haven't we Emma."

"Yes. And we think you'll like it, O'Malley."

"We'd like to continue renting the cottage. We've decided to stay on for another year. Emma will go to school here in September and between us we will come over every morning to feed the animals and ride the horses." She saw the look on O'Malley's face. "O'Malley, don't argue with me, you're in no fit shape to do it yourself. I've already discussed it with Donna and it's a done deal. It's not charity; we expect to ride the horses for free."

O'Malley's Cottage
Page 191

O'Malley smiled, then looked down embarrassed, tears running down his stubbly cheeks. Rebecca got up from the table and went to him, putting her arms around the frail old man, holding him close to her. "We'll get through this together, O'Malley," she said rocking him gently.

At the end of the week it was time for Brad and Julia to return to Peterborough. They agreed to let Rebecca and Emma drive them back. The long cycle ride home and camping overnight on the way had lost its appeal, it would save them a lot of time too. Rebecca promised to e-mail them regularly to keep them up to date with O'Malley's progress. She told them not to be strangers, there was always a spare room for them at O'Malley's Cottage. As an afterthought, she told them to keep an eye out for the two new professors from England that were going to be teaching at Trent University.

When they arrived back in Peterborough, Brad and Julia wished Emma all the very best for the up and coming new school term. They hugged each other then Brad and Julia wheeled their mountain bikes up to their apartment door, turning to wave as Rebecca and Emma drove away, waving back at them frantically from the Mercedes. They parted company with heavy hearts, having become so close at the farm.

Chapter Fourteen

It was three weeks before O'Malley found the strength to walk to the stable with Rebecca and Emma. He didn't have the energy to do much. The horses picked up O'Malley's scent and trotted into the barn, more spirited than they had been since his heart attack. O'Malley buried his face into the neck of each horse.

"They really missed you, O'Malley."

"And I really missed them too, Emma. When I get my strength back, we'll all ride down to the lake together."

"It's okay if you don't feel well enough to go. I don't mind. We can always drive down and have a picnic like we did with Aunt Rachael."

"I'll see how I feel. By the way young lady, it's about time you took your kitten home. Today would be as good a day as any."

"Can I really?"

"Sure, let's get him out of the barn. That's okay isn't it, Rebecca?"

"Sure it is." She placed a hand under his arm and guided him towards the barn.

"But I don't have anything for him, Mom. I don't have any food or litter."

"Yes, you do. While you were waiting in the car, Donna and I got everything you'll need, including something for fleas."

"Thanks, Mom, you're the best. I'm so excited. Daddy would never let us have any pets."

"I'm excited too. Marmalade is going to be your very own kitten. It will be your responsibility to take care of him."

"Yes, Mom, I already help on the farm, looking after Marmalade will be easy."

Another three weeks passed before O'Malley's health began to improve. His skin retained the same grey pallor and his lips had that bluish tinge, something they didn't have before his heart attack.

O'Malley and Donna had been talking about the farm and decided the best thing they could do now was to sell it. Without constant attention it would start to look neglected. O'Malley finally accepted that he could no longer take care of it on his own.

One evening O'Malley and Rebecca sat on the front porch chatting. Emma was in the kitchen helping Donna.

"I'm going to have to sell the farm, Rebecca. I'll make sure whoever buys it understands that Toby belongs to Emma. I'll make that part of the agreement. A gentleman has already put an offer in, which we're considering. They're a couple from Toronto looking to buy something in the country away from the bustle of city life."

"I understand, O'Malley. It must be very hard for you; I'll break the news to Emma."

"I know this sounds terrible, but sometimes I think if I didn't have Donna to worry about, I'd walk into the barn, sit down on a straw bale with my shotgun between my knees and decorate the interior of the barn with my brains."

Rebecca let out a gasp. "Don't even think such a thing. Emma and I would be devastated."

"I guess it wouldn't be a fitting end to my life's story."

"And what if Emma found you? I'd never forgive you. Besides, if you took your own life you might go to hell and never get to see Rowena."

" Ah, who knows, I might go to hell anyway. Donna certainly can't manage the farm on her own and I'm in no condition to help her. We've decided it wouldn't be fair to take Robby to a seniors' home, he's too old. We're going to have him put down."

"Oh, no you're not, I won't let you. Emma and I will take him."

"I was hoping you'd say that," smiled O'Malley.

"You're obviously going to sell the cottage, and I'm certainly not holding you to renting it to me for the year. Emma and I can be out within a week, we'll find something else and Robby can come with us. He may be old, but he's still healthy. Let him see out his last few days among friends. If he starts to suffer you know I'll have him put down humanely."

"Actually, we have no plans to sell the cottage. Donna and I would like to hold on to it, it'll give us a little extra income, so there's no need for you to worry about that."

"Without you and Donna as our neighbors, I'm not sure how much longer I'd want to stay there."

"I'm sure you'll like the new people, whoever moves in I'll make sure it'll be for the best in the long run. The farm needs a younger couple to keep it going."

"So, do Emma and I get to keep Robby?"

"Bless your hearts, you bet you do, and thank you, Rebecca. Thank you for everything. After lunch tomorrow afternoon, if I feel up to it, I want to take you and Emma on that ride down to the lake. I'd like you to ride Blazer this time, I'll ride Star, she's better behaved, but don't say anything to Emma, just in case I have a bad turn. I don't want to disappoint her."

"Are you sure you're up to it?"

"Look, if I fall dying on the ground right now and I have breath left in me to tell you what my biggest regret in life was, apart from Rowena that is. I would tell you it was not having my last ride on my own horse among friends, so don't you deny me that, Rebecca Brown."

"I won't, O'Malley, I promise. And I won't say anything to Emma yet."

"And before you ask, Donna knows."

* * *

The following afternoon the telephone rang at the cottage.

O'Malley's Cottage

"Answer the phone would you, Emma, my hands are caked in flour."

"Hello?"

"Emma, it's O'Malley. You and your mother get your riding hats and come on over right away. Meet me in the stable; we're riding down to the lake." Click, the phone went dead.

"Mommy, O'Malley says to come over right now with our riding hats, we're riding down to the lake."

"Typical man, not even a minute's notice. Okay, honey, let's quickly tidy up here, and I mean quickly."

Rebecca stopped off at the farmhouse to speak to Donna.

"I can't say I'm happy about it, Rebecca. I'm just glad you're going to be there, otherwise there's no doubt in my mind he would have taken off on his own anyway. You'll find him down by the stable getting the tack ready. Here, take these granola bars with you, I made them this morning, just in case you get hungry."

"Thanks, Donna, that's kind of you. Don't worry, Emma and I will keep an eye on him."

"He's letting Emma ride Star, so don't be surprised if he sits her on the horse when you get to the lake. Don't tell her though, he wants to surprise her. Don't worry, he's not going to make you ride Toby back."

"Actually I'm riding Blazer this afternoon. I guess we're all getting a higher grade today."

"When you get back I'll have supper ready for you. I'm being selfish really, I want to spend as much time with you and Emma as I can before we sell the farm."

"Donna, no matter how far away you move, we'll still come to see you."

Emma was standing on the veranda looking over the farm, deep in thought when her mother came out of the house.

"A penny for them, Emma."

"I was just thinking how much I love it here, Mom, and how I wish we could buy the farm."

"Sometimes I feel that way, Emma." She put an arm around her daughter. "Come on, let's go and give O'Malley a hand with the horses."
"Here's Blazer's bridle. Did you want the bareback blanket, Rebecca?"
"No, thanks."
"Okay then, let's go get us some horses."
Outside the gate, O'Malley accepted a leg up from Rebecca onto the back of Star. Emma hopped onto the back of Toby effortlessly. Rebecca leapt up in one agile motion and swung her leg confidently over the back of Blazer, Indian style.
"Very impressive, Rebecca. We'll head out across the field and take the trail into the woods. It's a more scenic route to the lake, especially on horseback."
They set off at a gentle trot across the field, O'Malley upped the pace into a canter. Rebecca decided it was useless arguing with him, she thought the best thing she could do was keep up with him and try to remember the way back, worried that O'Malley would die on her somewhere along the unknown trail.
When they reached the trail, they slowed the horses to a walk. O'Malley led the way onto the narrow trail followed by Emma and then Rebecca.
In places the trail was steep and rocky, twisting in all directions, in the narrowest of stretches, the vegetation brushed against their legs. Sometimes they had to duck low under branches hanging across the trail. The trees shaded most of the path, periodically they would reach large swaths of open grassland, where deer came to feed. They crossed a couple of shallow creeks that would become impassable raging torrents during the spring run-off.
O'Malley kept an eye out for bears. He did not want to come across one by surprise. *Better to see them before they sense*

you, was his motto.

Entering another meadow, O'Malley raised his hand. Rebecca and Emma drew up alongside him and stopped. On the other side of the meadow, two hundred yards away, was a mother bear, playing with her two cubs. Her sight wasn't good enough to see the intruders clearly, but she caught a whiff of their scent on the gentle breeze. She looked in their direction, rising up onto her hind legs, sniffing the air before dropping down on all fours. She ambled away into the cover of the nearby trees, her cubs scampering after her.

"In all the years I've lived here, I've never lost that feeling of excitement at seeing something so beautiful in its natural environment." Rebecca and Emma remained speechless; this was their first encounter with black bears.

"See those?" O'Malley pointed towards the ground. In the mud were large paw prints ringed with five claws. "Bear tracks, those round ones are the front paws, the longer ones the back paws."

"They're huge aren't they, Emma?"

"Wow, they're massive."

Off to their right a huge marshland opened up. O'Malley raised his hand. Rebecca and Emma stopped alongside him. He pointed far off into the distance, to the other side of the marsh to where a bull moose was feeding, head down in the water. Rebecca and Emma were spellbound.

Rebecca realized she had completely lost her way and her sense of direction. If anything happened to O'Malley now she would be totally lost. The best she could hope for was that O'Malley was right; the horses knew their way home. She could not always rely on seeing the horses' hoof marks on the ground, because there were areas where the ground had been dried rock hard by the summer sun and left no tracks.

A rising sense of panic welled up inside her, a feeling that she did not like and that scared her. The thought of being lost out here in the wilderness with Emma began to terrify her. She made up her mind that she was not taking this route back, beautiful as it was; she and Emma would take the road back to the farm. The incessant bombardment by deerflies was driving her mad.

Eventually they emerged from the forest. A magnificent, panoramic view of the lake stretched before them, even more beautiful having reached it on horseback. A trail led to the left and right, following the edge of the lake.

"If we get separated, don't take the right fork, that'll take you farther northward into the wilderness, away from the lake."

They branched off the trail taking the left fork. In the distance they saw the sandy beach, recognizing the spot where they had picnicked with Rachael. O'Malley led them into the shallow water near the bank, letting the horses cool themselves as they trotted along the beach. He coaxed them into a gentle canter, the spray from the horses' hooves splashing up behind them, and then into a full gallop.

Rebecca was furious. *He's going to drop dead right in front of us; that's just great.*

They galloped around the edge of the lake at full speed, horses and riders soaked from the spray. It was a flat-out race. Rebecca, head down low, urged her horse alongside O'Malley and spurred Blazer on into overdrive.

Blazer spurted ahead of Star, leaving O'Malley in his wake, reaching the other side of the bay before him. She brought Blazer to a gentle walk, just as O'Malley caught up to her. They waited for Emma and Toby to catch up.

"Don't be mad at me," O'Malley said, catching the angry look in Rebecca's eyes. "I feel fine. That ride did me the world of good." He was lying and she knew it.

"And what would have happened if you'd collapsed back on the trail. I could never have found my way out with Emma. That

O'Malley's Cottage
Page 199

was very irresponsible of you, and yes, I'm ticked."
"Don't be worrying yourself, as I told you before, the horses know their way home, just be sure to stay on their backs that's all. And by the way, that was a fantastic bit of riding, my dear, you should be very proud of yourself, I know I am. Emma, would you be so kind as to ride Star gently back down the beach for me? Let her get her wind first and then gallop her back up the beach. I'll wait here, just give me Toby's reins." Emma's face lit up.
"Sure, O'Malley, if you want me to."
O'Malley, in obvious discomfort lowered himself down from his horse, taking the reins from Emma. He gave her a gentle leg up onto the back of Star, before Rebecca could stop him.
"A lot different to Toby, isn't she?" he said wincing. "It's like going from a small car to a bigger one, the principal of riding them is just the same. Whatever you were doing on Toby you do on Star. I suggest your mom rides alongside you, but don't get too close together, just in case one of you dismounts accidentally at a gallop. I'll be watching the two of you to see if you pass your final exam in the *O'Malley School of Riding*, now off you go and good luck."
Rebecca swung Blazer around. She and Emma rode the horses at a trot all the way across to the other side of the sandy lake. At the far side, near where they had come out of the trees earlier, they turned the horses around and stopped. O'Malley and Toby looked tiny, standing together in the distance.
"Emma, we won't make this into a race, we'll ride side by side at a full gallop, we both know Blazer is faster than Star. Let's finish together as a team. Are you ready?"
Emma nodded. Rebecca mouthed, "Three, two, one, go!"
They dug in their heels and shouted to the horses to, *Get on.* They were like two jockeys on racehorses under starter's orders, released from the starting gate. The horses tore across the beach, their heads rising and falling, manes flying in the wind, hooves pounding the surf.

O'Malley's Cottage

Rebecca reined Blazer in slightly to keep neck and neck with Star. Emma crouched low over the horse. They shot past O'Malley and Toby, drenching them both in spray before wheeling the horses around together and trotting back to where O'Malley was standing, water still dripping from his face.

Rebecca and Emma drew their horses together and gave each other a high five. O'Malley was so happy. His whole face was ablaze with sheer joy and tremendous pride at the riding skills of his two students.

"Both passed with flying colors. Let's walk home back along the road in the sunshine and get ourselves dried off. Emma can you give me a leg up onto Star please; I'm afraid I'm just a little too heavy for Toby. Did you enjoy that?"

"It was fabulous, thank you, O'Malley, I still love Toby of course, he'll always be my favorite."

"You and your mother galloping across the beach together, 'twas a beautiful sight to behold, indeed it was. The horses' nostrils flaring red as you raced by me, oh, this is one of me best days ever. I can't wait to get home to celebrate the graduation of me finest students."

Before heading back along the road to the farm, Rebecca handed out the granola bars Donna had given her.

"Truthfully, O'Malley, how are you feeling?"

"Rebecca, to tell the truth, if I died now I would go to heaven with the biggest smile on me face. I'd be the happiest man dead."

On the ride back to the farmhouse, Rebecca kept a close eye on him. She saw him wincing in obvious pain, trying his best to hide his discomfort. When he lent forward, his head almost touching Star's withers, Rebecca edged Blazer closer to him, taking hold of Star's reins.

"O'Malley, that's as far as you're going on horseback this

evening. Come on, I'll help you down. You can sit on the grass and rest your back against that rock."

She realized he was too weak to answer and in too much pain. Together they helped the old man down from his horse, gently sitting him on the grass, easing him against the rock. Rebecca went through his pockets, found his pills and inserted one under his tongue.

"Is he going to be all right, Mommy?"

"Emma, one of us has to stay with him. I'd feel better if you rode back to the farmhouse on Star. Get Donna to come back in the truck with you. I was going to bring my cell phone, but the reception's useless up here. There's no need to go at a full gallop, a canter will do. O'Malley will be fine once his medication kicks in so don't go crazy. Make sure you tell Donna that he's okay, but he can't make the ride home. Put Star in the field and when you get back here with Donna, you can ride Toby home alongside me on Blazer. We'll put O'Malley in the back of the truck. Donna can drive him home with us following. Tell her to bring some cushions to prop him up. Okay?"

"Okay, Mom, I'll be careful, I promise."

"Don't take any chances, we need you to get there in one piece and don't stop for anyone."

Emma handed Toby's reins to her mother. They embraced then Rebecca gave her daughter a leg up onto Star.

"Emma, don't forget to come back with your riding hat, in fact don't take it off when you get there so you won't forget it. I love you, sweetheart, and do be careful, honey."

"I will, Mommy," she shouted back as she cantered away down the gravel road, aware that the success of the mission depended on her good riding skills.

She didn't feel lonely or scared because she had Star with her. All the way she whispered words of love and encouragement to the horse. She took a short cut across the wide-open field and spurred Star into a gallop. She didn't bother to slow down when

O'Malley's Cottage

she reached the path behind the barn and went flat out all the way up to the farmhouse. Leaping off the horse she ran into the farmhouse to tell Donna what had happened.

Donna was adding the finishing touches to dinner and threw off her apron, grabbing cushions off the couch. Emma put Star back in the field and jumped into the truck beside Donna. Donna took the shortcut too, and gunned the motor on the old truck as they raced across the field, the cushions bouncing all over the place in the rear of the truck, almost tossed overboard by the bumpy ride. Donna turned and smiled at Emma. "I haven't driven like this since I was a teenager."

They sped onto the gravel road, making a sharp right turn that sent the back of the truck skidding across the road in a shower of dust and flying gravel. Donna steered into the skid as skillfully as any rally driver would have done and roared off down the road towards the lake.

"Donna, you should be a rally driver. That's going in my diary." The old lady never ceased to amaze her. Age had not dulled her spirit one iota.

Emma spotted the horses eating grass along the hedgerow, their reins tied to a couple of saplings. The horses looked up to see the approaching truck. Donna slowed down, so as not to startle them. O'Malley lay propped up against the rock, Rebecca kneeling beside him.

Rebecca and Emma helped O'Malley to his feet, while Donna reversed the truck closer to her husband. Emma, still wearing her riding hat, pulled down the tailgate. All three of them helped O'Malley onto the tailgate then gently eased him into the back of the truck. There wasn't much of the old man to lift in the first place, so it wasn't difficult. Rebecca and Emma climbed into the back, sliding him up against the cab, a cushion behind him and one on either side.

O'Malley's Cottage

"I don't know whether to take you home or straight to the hospital," said Rebecca, adjusting the cushions to make him as comfortable as possible.

"Just take me home. I'm not going back into any bloody hospital again, I don't care how pretty the nurses are," croaked O'Malley, still managing to grin mischievously.

Donna got back in behind the wheel and drove slowly back to the farmhouse, Rebecca and Emma trotting along behind on Blazer and Toby.

Donna decided against the shortcut across the field, driving down to the end of the road instead, taking the long way back to the farmhouse. Rebecca and Emma galloped across the field. When they arrived at the farmhouse, Donna was reversing the truck up against the veranda, close to the front door.

They slid O'Malley easily along the corrugated metal surface of the truck bed and onto the tailgate. Together all three of them carefully eased him onto the ground. Ordinarily O'Malley would have kicked up a ruckus because of all the fuss the women were making, but not this time; this time he was really beat.

Emma ran ahead, holding the front door open. Rebecca and Donna practically carried O'Malley inside the farmhouse. Emma stayed outside with the horses.

"You don't need to say anything, Rebecca, I can guess what went on. I'm not mad at you, I knew he would misbehave the moment he got the chance. All right, Roger, let's get you out of these wet clothes."

"I'm not letting any other woman see me with me clothes off."

"You see, I knew it, O'Malley, you're all talk," laughed Rebecca. "I promise I'll close my eyes, how's that?"

"You mind that you do. And no peeking neither."

Having undressed O'Malley, they gave him a quick wash and dressed him in a warm pair of pajamas and a thick housecoat. Seated in his reclining chair he was soon fast asleep.

O'Malley's Cottage

Rebecca and Emma took care of the horses, aware that O'Malley would be furious if they put them back in the field without first grooming them after a hard ride.

"Dinner's not quite ready yet."

"That's okay, Donna. I think it might be a good idea if we spent the night with you." Donna smiled. "Emma and I will zip back to the cottage and freshen up. Marmalade needs to be attended to anyway. We won't be long."

O'Malley was still sleeping when they returned. Robby met them at the backdoor. The aroma of a delicious meal filled their nostrils.

"Good timing. Come and sit down the pair of you, lord knows you must be famished."

"How's he doing?" whispered Rebecca.

"Hasn't stirred since we sat him down. I'll make a tray up for him, he can have his supper sitting in his chair. Roger?" She gently shook his shoulder. "Supper's ready." O'Malley opened his eyes wearily. "Supper's ready. I've made a tray up for you, just stay where you are."

"Bless you, Donna." He clasped a hand over hers.

After supper, Rebecca helped Donna put O'Malley to bed. Rebecca slept on the couch nearby. She wanted to be near at hand if O'Malley took a turn for the worse.

Emma slept upstairs in the spare room. Robby crept upstairs unnoticed, curling up at her bedside.

Before falling asleep O'Malley looked across at the two women, a big smile spreading across his whiskery face. "First time I've slept with two beautiful women."

"In your dreams, dear," remarked Donna. Rebecca chuckled.

* * *

At 7 a.m. Rebecca was wide-awake. Donna was already up. O'Malley was still sleeping. The two women sat at the harvest table drinking coffee, talking in whispers, not wanting to wake either O'Malley or Emma.

At 8 a.m. Rebecca phoned the doctor's office for Donna. They agreed O'Malley shouldn't be told the doctor was dropping by to take a look at him.

Rebecca made her way down to the barn to make a start on the farm chores, allowing Emma to sleep in. She knew her daughter was a lot more upset about O'Malley's condition than she was letting on.

At 1 p.m. Dr. Chalmers arrived at the farmhouse, wearing a dark green tweed sports jacket with brown leather elbow patches, giving him the appearance of a schoolteacher from the 1950's. He was a short, stocky man with a weather-beaten face. Now in his seventies he had been the O'Malley's family practitioner for many years. His hair, though now thinning, still had a red tinge to it from a time when he'd had a head of bright ginger hair.

He banged on the backdoor then strode into the house, not waiting for a reply. Donna was in the kitchen when he walked in. He eyed her through his thick bifocal spectacles. It was obvious he was making a mental diagnosis of her condition, before giving her a hug.

"Where's the patient?" He wasn't a man to waste time on idle chatter.

"He's still in bed, Doctor."

"Then the man must be sick, that's not like O'Malley to be malingering in bed when there's work to be done. Let's take a look at him."

Rebecca and Emma entered the house, having just cleaned out the pigs and the chickens. Donna introduced them, suggesting they might want to become his patients. Dr. Chalmers removed his stethoscope from his ubiquitous black doctors' bag and began a thorough examination of his patient.

Rebecca explained what had taken place the previous day with a sense of embarrassment, feeling somehow that she was responsible for O'Malley's decline in health and angry with herself for not being more insistent. She expected a reproachful look from Dr. Chalmers, instead he looked up at her and smiled.

"Now don't go blaming yourself, Rebecca. There's not a damn thing you could have done. If you and Emma hadn't gone with him, the old fool would have gone on his own anyway. It's just as well you went with him, otherwise you'd have been bringing back a corpse. To be honest with you, O'Malley, you should be in the hospital, that's where you should be."

"I'm not going back into no bloody hospital."

"You really are a cantankerous old bugger. You can't expect Donna to take care of you man. The poor woman looks worn out as it is, and I'm sure Rebecca and Emma have lives of their own."

"We really don't mind helping out, Doctor. We're only next door and I work from home anyway."

"Rebecca, that's very good of you. Okay, I'll be perfectly frank. It'll kill O'Malley for sure if he goes back into hospital. Knowing him as I do, he'll just give up." Dr. Chalmers was momentarily lost in thought. "All right then, he can stay at home. Meanwhile I'll have a nurse drop by everyday to help out. I'll make the arrangements. Long term? Well, to be honest I don't think there is any long term. O'Malley, old friend, savor that last ride of yours, if you try that again I guarantee it will be your last. Emma, would you mind running my bag out to my car please? Thank you, dear." Emma took the bag without question.

"Emma's not going to want to hear this." There was a long pause before Dr. Chalmers spoke again. "O'Malley, I'll be blunt, I know that's what you'd prefer. I've already spoken to the hospital, and their diagnosis coupled with my own examination this afternoon tells me you're not long for this world old boy. Donna let him do what the hell he likes within reason, he won't have the strength to do much anyway. Let him enjoy what life he has left. Here's my cell phone number and my home number. Call me at any time of the day or night if his condition deteriorates and I'll come straight over. We've been friends a long time."

Dr. Chalmers took O'Malley's hand in his and gently squeezed it. "Goodbye, old boy." There was a sense of finality in the way he spoke those three words.

Before leaving, Dr. Chalmers gave Donna a hug, passing Emma on her way back in. In his other hand he carried a dozen fresh farm eggs.

Chapter Fifteen

Out of the blue one evening, Rebecca received a telephone call from Jacqueline Brooks. She was thrilled when Jacqueline asked if they could come up to the cottage one weekend. Lindsay hadn't stopped talking about Emma since they met at Algonquin Provincial Park. After the phone call, Rebecca telephoned Rachael.
"That's great news. Duncan and I will drive up the same weekend. I'm really looking forward to seeing you and Emma. I miss you so much. How's O'Malley doing?"
"According to Dr. Chalmers, if he makes the New Year, it'll be a miracle. Donna seems to be coping. I think she's resigned to the inevitable. Sometimes Emma and I drive them down to see the horses. Can you believe it? he's had me teaching Emma how to drive that old truck of his around the farm."
"How's she doing?"
"She'll be wanting to take her license next."
"I mean, with O'Malley."
"Not good. She hides it a lot. I don't know how I'm going to console her when he passes. Let alone myself. He's become such a huge part of our lives." Rebecca started to cry.
"Rebecca, would you like me to come up sooner?"
"No, I'm okay. Thanks anyway. Sometimes I find him quietly sobbing. It's not that he's feeling sorry for himself, not at all. It's like he still has dreams and ambitions; mountains he still has to climb and now his body has let him down. He told me he's been praying to God, asking to give him another day, and then another day, but he knows eventually the Almighty isn't going to give him that, one last day. He loves those horses of his. He told me their scent is more beautiful than any woman's perfume. Before I came here I would have thought he was nuts, now I agree with

him."

"I think you need to come back to the city, girl. You've been in the country too long."

* * *

Friday afternoon, the Brooks arrived. Rebecca was as thrilled to see Jacqueline, as Emma was to see Lindsay. It was agreed Lindsay could sleep with Emma in her bedroom. The two girls squealed with delight then raced off upstairs.

Rebecca showed her visitors around the cottage and then sat them all down in the kitchen for a cup of tea, aware that the British liked their afternoon tea. They sat and caught up on the news. Finally Rebecca excused herself to go and attend to O'Malley's livestock. Emma insisted on bringing Lindsay along with her, she wanted to introduce her to Toby, once Lindsay could be persuaded to leave Marmalade behind.

When Rebecca returned to O'Malley's Cottage, Rachael and Duncan were sitting in the kitchen engaged in lively conversation with Jacqueline and her husband.

"Wow, sister, just look at you. Even dressed as a cowgirl you look gorgeous. This working on the farm is obviously good for one's figure. I think I better come up next year and help bring in the hay."

Rebecca looked a little uncomfortable, mentally associating hay with Winston. Rachael caught a glimpse of something in her sister's face; a woman's intuition told her it had something to do with Winston. The two sisters hugged each other tightly, thrilled to see one another again. This time Rachael looked directly into Rebecca's face.

"Well, how did you and Winston get along, sis?"

There it was again, that fleeting downward shift of the eyes.

"Fine, why do you ask?" *Damn. What a stupid answer.*

"No reason. You look so well, I can't get over how good

you look, doesn't she, Duncan?"
"I agree. You look great, Rebecca. And from what Rachael tells me, you are doing a first class job in the literary world."
"No best sellers yet, but definitely some hopefuls. There really are a lot of good writers out there, but there sure is a lot of garbage too." She was relieved that the subject of hay and Winston had been diverted.
"How's O'Malley?"
"Looking forward to seeing you, Rachael. I think the sight of you walking out of the lake in your bathing suit has been indelibly etched in his memory forever. Tomorrow Donna wants us over at the farm for breakfast." She noticed the look on the adults' faces. "Don't worry, she's making an exception, we don't have to be there at the crack of dawn, nine o'clock on the dot will be fine."
Lindsay and Emma giggled throughout the night. It was well past midnight before the two of them dropped off to sleep. Not long after that the adults finally went to bed. Rebecca was exhausted, but excited at the same time to see her family and friends.

* * *

At 7 a.m. Rebecca stole out of the house, a now familiar routine, and drove over to O'Malley's Farm to attend to the chores. She never once regretted doing them, enjoying her time alone with the animals, especially the horses. Even the pigs she found enchanting, they were so much fun and very smart too.
It was just after 9 a.m. when they finally sat down to breakfast with the O'Malleys. Rachael was visibly shocked when she saw O'Malley; he had lost so much weight and his eyes were sunken in. He looked like a man waiting for the final call to the grave. When he saw Rachael his eyes lit up. She tried her best not

to look upset.

It was a pleasant weekend that came and went all too soon. Before Rachael and Duncan returned to Toronto, Rachael handed Rebecca a cardboard box full of manuscripts.

"I'm really pleased with the way you've been working, Rebecca. You definitely have an eye for a good story. Based on your recommendation I'm going to take a look at that children's story."

"I've been reading it to Emma and now it's one of her favorites."

"Duncan has no problem with you bringing Marmalade and Robby to the house. He's just sorry he doesn't have the space for Toby."

"He's such a good man."

"Yes, he is. Let's take a walk."

"Sure."

"Now we're away from everyone, Rebecca, there's a question that's been bugging me. What happened between you and Winston, the truth please?"

There was a long silence before Rebecca answered. Rachael took her sister's hand, they stopped walking. She looked at Rebecca; Rebecca reacted by looking at the ground.

"It was my fault, it wasn't Winston's. I don't know, I guess I came on to him." She looked at her sister. "I wanted him so bad. We just kissed that's all. I wanted him to stay the night, but he wouldn't, he said he didn't want to ruin his friendship between us, especially his friendship between the two of you. If it hadn't been for you he would have stayed and we would have made love. That's it, now I feel like a slut. Why are you smiling?"

"Winston is one terrific guy, I'm almost sorry he didn't stay the night, but don't you ever tell him that. The thing is, Rebecca, Winston has a very dark side, believe me. He knows he wouldn't be good for you. It took a real gentleman to walk away from you, and I know Winston, that wasn't easy for him. He and I used to be

lovers."
"You never told me that."
"Do you tell me everything, Rebecca?"
"As a matter of fact I do. Okay, I probably wouldn't have said anything about Winston."
"When my business became very successful, Winston walked away from me. He saw how well I was doing and he didn't want to ruin my life. He told me he loved me that much he had to let me go; broke my heart."
"Do you still have feelings for him?"
"Of course I do. Duncan doesn't know and I don't ever want him to know. I should have told Emma never to mention him, especially in front of Duncan."
"Don't worry, I'll talk to Emma about it, she won't say anything."
"Rebecca, honey, don't pursue it or that kiss will become the kiss of death. It's not that I'm jealous, you do what you want, but it won't be good for you and it certainly wouldn't be good for Emma. Do you want to be involved in gangs, drugs and violence?"
"No, of course not."
"Then Winston did you a big favor. If he had stayed the night, I guarantee you would have been hooked on him and you would have sold your soul for him, just like I nearly did. He's a friend now and always will be, and that's how it's going to stay. Keep him as a friend, don't turn him into a lover, and besides and here's the kicker. Winston is definitely not a one-woman man, trust me on that. You would have ended up as part of his stable of beautiful woman, that's all. You would never be, *The One*, because there never is. I came the closest, at least I like to think I did."

They walked back to the cottage more upbeat, the air between them cleared. After supper it was time for everyone to say goodbye.

O'Malley's Cottage

Rebecca and Emma waved to the procession of vehicles as they drove out of sight around the bend, leaving them both alone in the driveway with a feeling not unlike grief at the temporary loss of loved ones.

"Well, Emma, it's just you and me again kiddo."

"And Marmalade."

"Did you have a nice visit with Lindsay?"

"Uh ha."

"Once Lindsay and her parents have settled into their new house, they've invited us to come down and visit them, would you like that?"

"Yes, please. How long do you think that will be?"

"We'll try and get down to see them before Christmas, I'm sure they'll be feeling a bit lost in a new country, don't you?"

"I think so and Lindsay has to go to a new school in a new country. I thought it was going to be bad enough for me starting a new school up here, but I don't think I've got anything to worry about compared with Lindsay. I hope she'll be all right."

"I'm sure the both of you will be just fine. I guess we're very lucky to live in such a beautiful country, Emma, everyone seems to want to come here."

Chapter Sixteen

It was 6 a.m. Rebecca was dreaming the telephone was ringing. When she finally opened her eyes, the telephone was still ringing; it was not a dream. She turned on the bedside lamp, recoiling at the bright light and wearily stumbled out of bed, making her way over to the small telephone table on the other side of the room, anxious to answer it before it woke Emma.

"Hello," her voice sounded tired and croaky. She was so tired she did not immediately recognize the voice on the other end of the phone, or comprehend what was being said, and then suddenly it hit her.

"He's gone," said Donna, crying into the phone.

"I'll be right over." Rebecca was immediately awake, replacing the receiver without another word and rushing into Emma's bedroom. It was going to be a long day and she didn't want to leave her daughter alone in the cottage, Emma would have to come too. She had to shake Emma several times to rouse her.

"Emma, honey, get dressed quickly. I have some very sad news. Donna just phoned me, O'Malley passed away. We have to go over and help her. Don't cry, honey, we have to help Donna, we have to be strong for her. Would you prefer to stay here in the cottage, I'll only be a phone call away?"

"No, Mommy, I want to come, I'll take care of the animals while you look after Donna. I'll have to tell them what's happened. They'll be so upset."

The child was suddenly overcome by grief and burst into tears. Rebecca hugged her tightly, rocking her back and forth, feeling her daughter's tears dampening her nightshirt, her own tears falling silently onto Emma's hair.

Within minutes the two of them were dressed and out the

door, jumping into the cold Mercedes and roaring up the road to the farm. They bounced up the driveway at a speed that would have made O'Malley cross, stopping abruptly in front of the farmhouse.

"Okay, honey, you go and attend to the animals. Don't come straight into the farmhouse, knock on the door first and wait for me to answer it, okay? There's nothing to be afraid of, I just want to be sure that O'Malley is in a dignified position. You know, if he died in his underwear he'd be mad at me for letting you see him like that and we don't want that do we?" Emma smiled at the thought, it almost struck her as funny had the occasion not been so sad.

"I don't have to see him dead do I, Mommy?"

"No, honey, of course not, not if you don't want to."

"If he is." Emma hesitated, choking back the tears. "If he is, dignified, I might want to say goodbye to him, would that be okay?"

"Sure, honey, give my love to all the animals. Oh, don't be alarmed, the police and ambulance will be arriving soon, that's normally what happens, honey, so don't worry, okay?"

They embraced and Emma ran off to feed the animals, her tears streaming across her face as she raced towards the barn. Donna was waiting at the backdoor. Robby seized the opportunity to run by her legs after Emma. Rebecca entered the warmth of the farmhouse and hugged a very distraught, frail old lady.

"Where is he?"

"Sitting in his favorite chair. He insisted on getting up with me this morning. I sat him in his chair while I made him his coffee. I heard him gasp and that was it, he was gone." She began sobbing again. Rebecca held her close, the two women now crying together, united in their grief.

Rebecca reluctantly walked into the kitchen. O'Malley was sitting in his chair, his head tilted back against the headrest. At first glance it looked as though O'Malley was asleep. His mouth was open, but no sound came from his lips. His eyes were open, the sparkle they once had, now gone, replaced by a thin, milky film. They stared lifelessly ahead at everything and nothing. The texture of his skin had begun to tighten, especially around his face and forehead; he now looked more like a waxworks figure than the proud human being he had once been. O'Malley was wearing his blue-striped flannel pajamas and his thick old brown and dark green moth-eaten housecoat, which he refused to throw out, his threadbare brown suede slippers were on his feet.

    Rebecca placed two fingers against his neck, feeling for the faintest sign of a pulse from the carotid artery. She felt nothing. She reached into her pocket and pulled out a tissue, tearing it into a small strip and then separated the strip into two halves, placing one half against O'Malley's mouth and then his nostrils. The small piece of white tissue paper betrayed her forlorn hope, remaining motionless, save for her own trembling hand. Rigor mortis had not yet set in. She placed her hand over O'Malley's eyes and gently closed them and then gently closed his mouth. Then she placed O'Malley's hands in his lap and lent over his lifeless body, her own body now trembling in grief, and tenderly kissed his forehead.

    "Goodbye and God bless. I love you, O'Malley. Thank you for everything." Her tears fell upon his lifeless hands.

    Phoning 9-1-1 was not going to bring O'Malley back to life. Rebecca recalled seeing the young policewoman's business card stuck on the fridge with a magnet that said, *If you ate today, thank a farmer*. She took Mandy's card and dialed the main police station number. The phone rang and rang; she was just about to dial 9-1-1 in frustration, when finally the phone was answered. Without fuss, Rebecca calmly explained what had happened at the farm to the sympathetic dispatcher on the other end of the phone line. Having made the call Rebecca gave all her attention to Donna

    All Donna could say was, "Bless you, bless you. God sent

you to me I know he did. I don't know how I would have coped without you and Emma."

Having been married to a lawyer, who had practiced criminal law, Rebecca had a pretty good idea of the questions the police officer would ask when he or she arrived. Donna got O'Malley's drivers license out of his wallet and placed it on the kitchen table at Rebecca's suggestion, along with the bottles of pills that O'Malley had been prescribed; the police officer would need the information for the police report.

Rebecca was beginning to worry about Emma, she hadn't attended to the animals on her own before, there had always been an adult nearby, either herself or in the past, O'Malley. She was about to go down to the barn and check on her daughter, when she heard the faint sound of someone knocking on the back door. Emma stood on the doorstep, eyes red with tears, Robby at her side.

"It's okay, sweetheart. O'Malley has gone to heaven. He looks like he's fast asleep. Do you want to say goodbye to him before the ambulance arrives? It should be here any minute, it's okay if you don't want to, O'Malley won't mind." Emma nodded her head, unable to speak.

Rebecca took her daughter's hand in her own and together they walked into the kitchen. The first rays of the morning's sunlight began to shine in through the kitchen window. O'Malley looked so peaceful sitting in that worn old chair of his, the dark shadows of the room quickly disappearing with the rising sun, making the sight of the beloved old man, no longer a sinister, haunting memory that would plague a child's sleep for months to come.

Rebecca could feel Emma's hand slip from hers. She stayed back letting her daughter approach the lifeless O'Malley. Emma had never seen a dead body before and Rebecca wasn't sure if she was doing the right thing.

As if sensing that Emma needed some extra comfort,

O'Malley's Cottage

Robby moved forward alongside the child. Emma stood in front of the chair for a while without moving, staring at her old friend. Slowly she moved closer, being careful not to tread on O'Malley's toes, not wanting to hurt him on his journey to heaven. She gently lifted his hands, holding them in her own, initially surprised at how cold and stiff they felt. Robby stood at her side, whining pitifully. The child stood in silent prayer while Rebecca and Donna looked on. She moved to the side of the chair and tenderly kissed O'Malley on his right cheek.

"Thank you for everything, O'Malley. I'm going to miss you terribly. I told all the animals this morning that you had gone to heaven and they were all very sad, especially the horses. I know there will be lots of horses in heaven for you to take care of. I hope one day I'll see you in heaven, but I don't want to go there for a longtime if that's okay. Mommy and I will look after Donna for you so don't worry and I promise to take care of all the animals, especially the horses and especially Toby. Say hi to Rowena. For the rest of my life I'm going to say a prayer every night before I go to bed so I can talk to you."

"The ambulance is here, honey, why don't you go upstairs to the spare room with Robby and I'll bring you up something to eat and drink."

"Robby's not really allowed upstairs, Mommy." Donna gave Emma a cuddle.

"Sweetheart, today he is. He's going to need lots of comforting too. The two of you are going to need each other. In fact, O'Malley told me he wanted you to take care of Robby for him when he died, and when I have to leave the farm I'd like you to take Robby home with you to live."

It was all too much for Emma, she didn't know what to say, burying her face in the comforting arms of the old woman. "Come on, I'll come upstairs with you. You tuck yourself into bed and let

Robby cuddle up next to you on the floor."

As they disappeared up the stairs, Rebecca opened the backdoor for the paramedics. She was relieved to see Lucy and her partner and showed them into the kitchen. Rebecca explained to them what she had found and what she had done as they examined O'Malley for signs of life; they were not expecting to find any, but experience told them that life was full of surprises; but not today. It wasn't a crime scene and nobody was going to chastise Rebecca for touching the body.

"Well," said Lucy standing next to O'Malley, one hand resting on his shoulder, "the old boy is probably riding Pegasus across the sky right this minute on his way to heaven. I'm going to miss him."

"So am I." Mandy stepped into the kitchen. "At least he got his wish to die at home on the farm instead of in the hospital. Hi Rebecca, where's Donna?"

"She's upstairs with Emma."

Donna entered the kitchen. Everyone gave her a hug, offering their condolences. While O'Malley sat dead in his chair in the kitchen, Donna prepared breakfast for everybody. Rebecca poured the coffee. Soon they were all seated around the harvest table, laughing and joking about some comical, but fond personal memory of O'Malley.

"Well, this is a first for me," said Mandy, "having our own private wake while on duty. I almost forgot, better call the coroner. Do you mind if I use your phone, Donna, the radio reception here is never very good at the best of times?"

"Help yourself, Mandy, you know where it is."

Having made the call, Mandy sat down at the table again. Rebecca went upstairs to check on Emma. When she peeked into the bedroom, Emma was fast asleep in bed lying on her tummy, with her right hand resting on Robby's back. He lay sound asleep on the floor next to her, his hearing not what it used to be.

An hour later, Dr. Chalmers walked in through the back

O'Malley's Cottage

door. Lucy, her partner, and Mandy looked embarrassed as though sitting down to breakfast with the corpse was not very professional of them.

"Don't get up on account of me," said Dr. Chalmers gruffly. "The Coroner, Doc Morgan is over at a suspicious suicide. As I used to be a coroner myself, he asked me to look in. I'm sorry for your loss, Donna, O'Malley was a good man, a bloody good man. Well, let's take a look at the old fella, shall we?"

"Can I get you anything, Dr. Chalmers?"

"Ah, you can indeed Donna. Fetch me a glass, a large one at that of O'Malley's favorite Irish whiskey and let me drink a toast to my old friend. God speed him on his way." He shook his head sorrowfully. "You can call the funeral home, Officer. Windleshams all right, Donna?" Donna nodded in agreement as he came over to her and gave her a hug. "And how are you doing, my dear?"

"I'm okay, Doctor," she whispered weakly.

"Any problems, Donna, you call me, day or night, okay?" Donna nodded appreciatively.

"Will you have some breakfast with us, Dr. Chalmers?"

"Donna, that would be very kind of you." His face was even more ruddy now that the whiskey had reached the spot.

When Windleshams arrived, Rebecca took Donna into the dining room. They brought in a collapsible stretcher on wheels and carefully lifted O'Malley's body onto it. The undertakers didn't have to remove any jewelry from the body, O'Malley never wore any, not even a wedding band.

Once O'Malley was lying on the stretcher, the undertakers straightened out his body and wrapped a crisp white sheet around him up to his neck, folding his hands across his chest under the sheet. Before zipping up the body bag, Rebecca escorted Donna out to the kitchen so that she could say farewell to her husband. This would be the last time she would see his human form again on the farm. She seemed to have aged in the last few hours, appearing very fragile as she stooped to kiss O'Malley's now cold and lifeless lips. She gave a cry of grief stricken pain and shuffled quickly back into the dining room, comforted by Rebecca.

The burgundy colored body bag with gold piping around the edges was zipped tightly closed. There was no need to linger and continue the stress any longer. Before leaving, the younger of the two men handed Mandy his business card. O'Malley's body left the farm for the last time with them, though his spirit remained behind.

* * *

The funeral took place at the small Catholic church in the village. Rachael and Duncan drove up to pay their last respects, stopping overnight with Rebecca. Rebecca e-mailed Julia with the sad news.

Emma held the leather reins, Rebecca and Donna sat on either side of her. The steady clip-clop, clip-clop of Maxwell and Minnie's hooves could be heard coming up the road towards the church, drawing the wagon that contained O'Malley's coffin. Men, women, and children lined both sides of the road, their heads bowed in respect.

Father O'Ryan presided over the funeral mass, a longtime friend of O'Malley. The church was packed from wall to wall and out into the small churchyard. The priest looked like Friar Tuck; larger than life, portly, with a ring of white hair around his bald head.

Addressing the congregation, Father O'Ryan began by saying, "Roger O'Malley was the finest man I have ever had the privilege of knowing, and I have met a lot of men throughout my worldly travels. He was a man who had the least Hail Mary's to say of any of us, including myself. He was a decent, honest, hardworking man who would rather do you a good turn than a bad one. And despite the terrible tragedy that befell Roger and Donna, when their daughter Rowena was so cruelly taken away from them many years ago, Roger remained true to his faith, when many of us would have wavered along the way. His love and knowledge of horses is unsurpassed, he was not one to stand idly by and watch another man beat such a beautiful creature. Personally, I am surprised God waited so long to take such a good man, I can only imagine that he needs a new head groom up there; he won't find better than Roger O'Malley. He will be sadly missed by us all, especially by his wonderful wife Donna, whom he loved so much. O'Malley would not want a congregation full of tearful souls, but a place of worship full of smiling faces. He brought joy and laughter to us all with his wicked Irish sense of humor. Many of you will recall how much O'Malley loved poetry. I am going to ask a very good friend of O'Malley's to come forward and read a poem the two of them wrote together before he died. Emma, will you step forward please."

Emma had practiced reading the poem in front of her mother and Donna. It had been easy then, now she was standing before hundreds of people. Rebecca, dressed all in black and looking more beautiful than ever, stood and gently held her daughter's hand, guiding her up to the pulpit, whispering softly into her ear.

Emma stood proudly on a wooden platform, so the congregation could see her, and waited until her mother returned to her seat. The congregation fell silent, except for the occasional cough that always forms part of these affairs. The small child seemed so tiny standing up there in the pulpit. Emma took a deep breath, closed her eyes briefly and spoke.

"To my best friend, ever. O'Malley, who taught me all about horses and how to ride. I love you and miss you."

Emma clenched her teeth until the muscles in her jaw

ached, her eyes full of tears. When she spoke again, her voice was loud and clear, echoing around the church.

"O'Malley's Lament, by Roger O'Malley and Emma Brown; that's me.

> I have toiled long and hard my whole life through
> Watched every season come anew.
> Cursed the black flies in the Spring
> But loved the flowers it did bring.
> Cursed the stinging insects that came in May.
> Until I smelled the sweetness of the hay.
> Ah, but the Fall's the season I love the best
> To gallop my horse through golden forest.
> Cursed the Winter with its cold and snow
> Until I harnessed up the sleigh
> And rode the Team again on Christmas Day."

The whole congregation stood and clapped as Emma walked back to her seat next to her proud mother. Rebecca hugged her daughter tightly telling her how well she had done and how proud O'Malley would have been.

O'Malley was buried under a flowering cherry tree in the small graveyard behind the church. The Belgians stood majestically by the wall, Brad and Julia with them. There were a lot of people there that day, the mark of a popular and much loved man.

* * *

It was raining heavily the morning Rebecca and Emma drove Donna to her new home in the town of Port Perry. The newly built rest home was on the shoreline of Lake Scugog. Donna's room was located at the rear of the building, the bay window looking out across the lake. The room was immaculately

O'Malley's Cottage

clean, with white walls, a small sitting area by the bay window, a bed and a washroom. Rebecca had helped Donna find it. They had visited the home a few times before Donna finally agreed to move there. Rebecca knew that when she and Emma left, Donna would feel like a child abandoned at school on her first day, that feeling of utter loneliness and despair.

Rebecca discovered that Jack, a lively old war veteran in his nineties occupied the room next door to Donna's. She liked him the first time she met him and knew O'Malley would have approved of him too and so decided to introduce him to Donna. Jack had been brought up on a farm in England by his grandparents and had spent many years working with horses. He'd led a very interesting and exciting life having seen action on the beaches of both Normandy and Dunkirk.

Rebecca had planned to show Donna around the quaint little town before leaving, but found that Donna and Jack were lost in lively conversation about the advantages and disadvantages of Belgians over Clydesdales. While the two of them chatted away, Rebecca and Emma hung some of Donna's favorite pictures. In pride of place they hung an old black and white photograph of Donna and O'Malley sitting on a rock, cuddled up together by a lake. Both Rebecca and Emma were sure it was the same lake where O'Malley had taken them for a picnic the first time they met.

It was dinnertime when Rebecca and Emma completed the finishing touches to Donna's room, with an occasional nod of approval from her. The time came for Rebecca and Emma to say goodbye and to make the long trip back up north. They hugged Donna tightly, promising to come and see her regularly and to phone her every day. Jack took Donna's arm in his and escorted her into the dining room to meet the other residents. At the entrance to the dining room, Donna stopped, turned around and waved, smiling happily.

O'Malley's Cottage

"I don't think we're going to have to worry about Donna after all, do you?"
"I don't think so, Mom," smiled Emma.
The drive home seemed to take for ever, not that the traffic was heavy, there just didn't seem to be anything to go home for, now that O'Malley and Donna were no longer there.
"I can't wait to get home to meet out new neighbors," said Emma.
"It'll be late when we get home, Emma, how about we both pop over in the morning and see how they're settling in. Perhaps they'll let you ride Toby? They promised Donna that wouldn't be a problem, besides, they might want a hand with the chores until they get the hang of things. I expect they'll be fine though. I don't really know much about them. Apparently, the real owners aren't yet ready to move and have rented out the farm."
"I hope they have a daughter my age."
"I hope they do too. It'll be fine, you wait and see. We better get a move on, Robby and Marmalade will be missing us."
"I'm missing them already, I just wish we could have taken Toby with us."
"I know, honey, but we just don't have anywhere to keep him. Perhaps one day we will, I'll work on it."

Chapter Seventeen

Rebecca awoke at 6 a.m. as she had been doing for the past few months. She would have got up and driven over to the farm to feed the animals and then given Donna a hand with O'Malley. Now they were both gone, there was no longer any need for her to get up so early on this Sunday morning. Unable to sleep she got up anyway and went down to the kitchen to make herself a drink.

She sat at the kitchen table sipping her coffee, looking out of the kitchen window at the woods behind her. It had begun to snow, the first snowfall of the impending winter. She pondered how everything around her was changing, like life itself. She already missed the O'Malley's terribly and began to think about moving back to Toronto. She decided she would stick it out until Robby had died, she felt the dog should see his last days out surrounded by the countryside he was familiar with. Rebecca didn't think he'd last a week in Toronto; she was beginning to wonder if she would either. She'd have to drag Emma away from here kicking and screaming, she had settled into school so well and had made lots of friends. Rebecca was torn between staying and leaving, but O'Malley's Cottage just didn't feel the same anymore, somehow its magic had disappeared with the O'Malleys.

Her mind returned to the present when she heard Emma walking down the stairs followed by the cat and dog. She let them out the back door and joined her mother at the kitchen table for breakfast. They decided they would head over to the farm to see their new neighbors at ten o'clock.

Rebecca and Emma got out of the Mercedes in the familiar driveway of O'Malley's Farm, to the sound of shouting and the back door to the farmhouse being slammed. They watched in disbelief as a lanky, pimply faced teenage boy with greasy black hair, highlighted with green and purple streaks jumped into

O'Malley's Cottage
Page 227

O'Malley's old pick-up truck and roared off across the farm, spinning up clods of soil, leaving two deep ruts across what had once been the well kept lawn that led out to the fields. A dumpy looking teenage girl ran past Rebecca and Emma, completely ignoring them. She was bare footed, wearing a pink tank top and hipster jeans. Her strawberry blonde hair was unkempt and in need of a good brushing.

"You asshole," she screamed after the truck. The teenage girl walked back past Rebecca and Emma and went inside the farmhouse without saying a word to them, other than to pass an unfriendly glance in their direction.

Rebecca decided that meeting the new neighbors after all might not be such a good idea today, or on any other day. These people were definitely not the business couple they were expecting. As she was about to get back in the Mercedes a short stocky man, with a shaved head and goatee and built like a bull appeared around the corner of the farmhouse wearing a string vest, jeans and boots. His arms and chest were heavily tattooed.

"What d'you two want? I don't want no bloody bible thumpers on my farm. Now git." Rebecca stood her ground, disgusted at the man's behavior.

"Actually, we're your neighbors. We came to see how you were settling in and to see if there was anything we could help you with," a look of suppressed anger in her brown eyes.

The man strode over to Rebecca looking her up and down from head to toe, his libidinous thoughts clearly obvious to Rebecca. She felt frightened and intimidated in the presence of the vulgar man. He smirked, almost salivating as he mentally undressed Rebecca and imagined having his way with her, the thought all the more exciting because he would be doing it against her will. Rebecca read his mind.

"You could give me a hand in the hay barn if you like," he smirked. "Could I ride Toby?" Emma asked innocently, not recognizing the lustful intentions of the man towards her mother, though she too felt intimidated by him.

"Sure you can. You can ride that pony any time you like, on one condition though. Your mom has to come over on her own and she and I are going on a wild ride together in the hay barn."

Further unpleasant conversation was halted when a bleached-blonde haired woman came out of the front door smoking a cigarette. She had been attractive at one time, but the stress of living with a thug like this for a husband had increased her smoking and drinking. She looked to be a hard woman and would have made a good barmaid at any dockside tavern.

"Garry," she shouted, in a voice that was immediately recognizable as uncultured from that one word. "What's going on?"

"These are our neighbors, Beth." He was staring coldly into Rebecca's eyes. "The lady wanted to know if she could help me in the hay barn." His wife couldn't see the evil smile that her husband presented to Rebecca.

"Hi, I'm Beth," she said presenting a hand to Rebecca. There was an awkward moment when Rebecca hesitated before shaking Beth's hand. "Don't mind Garry, he's just a big teddy bear really."

Rebecca recognized the man standing in front of her had no respect for women, seeing them as nothing more than objects to relieve his sexual frustrations and to be discarded when he had finished brutalizing them. Rebecca felt sorry for Beth, trapped in the same house as this monster.

Rebecca no longer wanted any further conversation with this awful family and wanted to get as far away from them as possible. She made some quick and pathetic excuse about having left something in the oven, grabbed Emma's hand and drove quickly away from the farm with a feeling as though she was escaping; a feeling that unnerved her. Neither she nor Emma spoke on the short ride back to the cottage.

Rebecca was furious and didn't even realize that she was looking up into the sky from the driveway of the cottage, inwardly cursing God and doubting her faith because he had allowed such terrible people a place on this earth.

By the time she walked into the kitchen she had tears of rage in her eyes and for a second she didn't care what Emma felt about moving, they were going and that was all there was to it. Toronto had its problems, but she would feel a lot safer there than living in the middle of nowhere with the likes of Garry as her next-door neighbor.

"Mom, I don't like it here now, it's not the same without O'Malley and Donna. I don't want to go there and ride Toby anymore; I just hope they take good care of him. I wish we had taken him away from there. Do you think they'll treat him all right?"

"Yes, I think so, sweetie," lied Rebecca. "I'll phone Rachael this evening. Duncan's offered us his house for a while should we ever need it, and now we need it. I'm going to miss it here, I really do love it here, well, did love it, but I'm afraid that we're just not going to get along with our new neighbors, I can see that and I think you can too. Tell you what, let's go into town and watch a movie together, we'll spend the whole day out, just you and me."

"Thanks, Mom, I'd like that."

"Come here, honey, don't cry, everything's going to be okay."

"No, it's not, Mommy, not now. I wish O'Malley was still alive."

* * *

One morning as Rebecca and Emma were driving into town to go shopping, Rebecca slowed down on seeing a police car parked at the side of the road with its emergency lights flashing. A uniform officer was standing by a pick-up truck crashed into a hydro pole; the truck was badly smashed-up, beyond repair. From the long skid marks on the road, the truck had blown the stop sign, skidded through the T intersection and on into the ditch on the other side of the road, smashing into the hydro pole on its way across the ditch.

"That's O'Malley's truck, Mom," exclaimed Emma.

"You're right, Emma, it is. I bet that boy we saw at the farm went flying down the road and lost control. I don't see anyone in the truck, I'm guessing it must have happened late last night. I'm going to miss O'Malley's old truck, and to think Donna offered it to me to take the garbage to the dump, I wish I'd taken it now."

"Do you think he killed himself?"

"Generally, only good people die in traffic accidents, bad people always seem to be the ones that survive with only cuts and bruises. That boy is at home licking his wounds. I bet his father has probably phoned the police to say the truck was stolen to try and keep his son out of trouble. He was probably drinking too much last night with his buddies, lucky they didn't hit anyone driving along the other road. We could have been driving along that road ourselves."

"O'Malley must be really mad about it, I bet," said Emma angrily. "I used to like going for rides in that truck. O'Malley used to let me drive it around the field and sometimes he'd let me drive it on my own. He used to make obstacle courses with straw bales for me to drive around and he taught me how to reverse in between them and how to park too."

"I know, I was watching you one day, don't you remember?"

"Oh, yes, I forgot, you and Donna came down to watch. Those were happy times weren't they, Mom? Since those horrible people moved into the farm I don't feel so happy anymore."

O'Malley's Cottage

"Neither do I, honey, that's why I'm anxious to move back to Toronto. If we reach a point where we can't stand it anymore, we'll just have to take Marmalade and Robby with us a little sooner that's all."

As it turned out, Rebecca was right in her deductions about the accident. It was in the local paper a couple of weeks later. *A youth has been arrested by the OPP and charged with leaving the scene of an accident after colliding with a hydro pole. They are unable to name the driver, who was unhurt, because he is a young offender. His father has been charged with public mischief after making a false report about the truck being stolen.* Rebecca caught herself gloating.

With Christmas fast approaching, Rebecca decided to take Rachael up on her offer of spending Christmas with her and Duncan at his house. Initially the plan was for Rachael and Duncan to spend Christmas up at O'Malley's Cottage, but the magic had gone out of the place, the thought of spending Christmas with her family in Toronto appealed to Rebecca, even Emma was looking forward to it.

* * *

The neighbor's daughter, Sarah, traveled on the same school bus as Emma and was forever taunting her about Toby, telling Emma that her father was making arrangements to have the pony sent to the slaughterhouse to be turned into pet food.

One afternoon Emma came home from school and burst into tears. The taunting from Sarah was getting worse and had reached a point where Emma no longer wanted to go to school, let alone travel on the same school bus as her.

"Wait here, Emma. I'm going over to see those bast'." Rebecca caught herself before finishing the word. "If I'm not back in twenty minutes, phone 9-1-1 for the police." She saw the worried look on her daughter's face. "Don't worry, honey, I'm sure

O'Malley's Cottage

everything will be fine."

Reluctantly Rebecca drove quickly over to the farm, clutching her cell phone, she had it programmed to dial 9-1-1 immediately. The likelihood of the signal going through was pretty remote, but she would use it as a prop to warn Garry. She turned the Mercedes around in the driveway of the farm and left the engine running for a quick getaway, should she need one.

With a sinking feeling in her stomach, Rebecca walked up to the front door of the farm and knocked heavily on the door. A pit bull slammed itself violently against the door, snarling furiously trying to burst through the door and savage her. Rebecca stepped back in shock and bumped into Garry who had come up behind her. He closed his powerful arms around her pinning her tightly. The air was squeezed from her chest, she couldn't even scream for all the good it would have done her anyway.

"Let go of me you bastard! My daughter has instructions to phone 9-1-1 if I'm not back in ten minutes."

"Oh, I thought you'd come round to take me up on my offer of a ride in the hay barn," he said, loosening his grip on Rebecca.

"I came to buy the Shetland pony off you. Just name your price."

"Oh, you can have the pony for free, a couple of afternoons in the sack with you should do it nicely. You probably haven't had the taste of a real man in ages, I'm surprised you haven't asked me over sooner, especially when your daughter's at school."

"You're disgusting, you're not a man, you're an animal."

Garry, as quick as lightening hooked a powerful finger over the top of Rebecca's belt and dragged her into him. With his other huge hand he grabbed Rebecca around the back of her head and pulled her face close against his, she could feel his stubbly face against her cheek as his lips searched for hers; she could feel his pelvis pressing against hers; he was becoming more and more aroused and more dangerous.

Rebecca slammed her knee hard into his groin and ran the short distance back to her Mercedes, jumped in behind the steering wheel, not even waiting to see his reaction. Tires spinning the Mercedes lurched out of the driveway. Glancing up at the rear view mirror she saw Garry's angry face bent over, shouting what she assumed were obscenities after her. She was still shaking when she walked into the kitchen. Emma was poised by the telephone, ready to phone the police.

In a frenzy, Rebecca locked and bolted the back door behind her, checked the front door was locked and all the windows secured. She was in such a state of shock her chest was heaving; she sat down on the stairs trying to catch her breath. In that split second she was prepared to forgive her husband and to go back to him, despite his cheating ways.

"Mom, what happened?" Emma put an arm around her mother.

"He won't sell me Toby, honey." She decided against telling her daughter the full details of what she would have to do to get the pony. "I'm sorry, sweetie, I tried, I know you're disappointed, but we're not dealing with nice people like the O'Malleys. I can't believe the O'Malley's allowed this to happen."

"They didn't know the new owners would rent the farm to these people, Mom."

"You're right, honey. If they only knew the type of people they'd rented it too. I daren't say anything to Donna, she'd be so upset. Tell you what, I'll drive you to and from school from now on so you won't have to travel on the bus with that awful girl, Sarah. The Christmas holidays will be here soon anyway. In the New Year I've decided we're going back to Toronto to live, we're going to stay at Duncan's for a while until we find a place of our own. He's going to move in with Rachael, which I think is actually a good idea, might make them get married after all. You can go back to your old school with all your friends again, how's that sound?"

"That sounds great, Mom. And Mom, thanks for trying for me." Emma gave her mother another big hug. "We'll get through this, Mom, you wait and see, everything will be okay."

"Emma, you are growing up so quickly. From now on we must make sure we keep everything locked-up, especially all the doors and windows. We must keep away from those people, never go there and never answer the door to any of them, especially him."

Chapter Eighteen

The following morning Emma let Robby and Marmalade out the back door before running back upstairs to get dressed for school. Not long afterwards Rebecca and Emma both heard the sound of Robby growling viciously outside. Emma ran to her bedroom window and looked out. In the garden below she could see the neighbors' pit bull with a limp Marmalade clutched tightly between its powerful jaws, shaking the cat savagely. She screamed hysterically. In her haste to get downstairs to save him, she tumbled down the stairs. She lay in a crumpled heap by the bottom step, choking on her words as she tried to tell her mother what had happened. Rebecca grabbed the broom and Robby's leash then ran out into the back garden, screaming at Emma to stay inside the house.

Emma dialed 9-1-1, but didn't have a chance to finish what she was saying. She dropped the phone and raced outside to save her mother. The shocked dispatcher could hear agonizing screams of real terror. She dispatched the entire emergency services; fire, police and ambulance.

The pit bull, having finished playing with the dead cat, charged at Robby just as Rebecca was leading him quickly towards the house. The old dog put up a gallant fight, intent on protecting Rebecca, who let go of his leash, but he was no match for the pit bull. It soon had him pinned to the ground by his neck.

Rebecca beat so hard on the pit bull with the broom that the handle broke leaving her with a shaft of splintered wood in her hand. The pit bull spun around and leapt at her throat. In terror Rebecca thrust the spear-like end of the broken handle deep into the animal's chest. The wooden dagger pierced its heart, but did not immediately stop the dog. The goal-oriented pit bull continued its attack. Her left arm shot up instinctively, the dog bit down hard onto her arm, protected only by the thin sleeve of her pajama top. The pretty white pajamas with their pink, yellow and blue flowers were quickly soaked in bright red blood.

Robby, panting and half dead on the blood-soaked snow heard Rebecca and Emma's screams. In a last desperate surge of energy, he tore at the underbelly of the pit bull, tearing it open. The whole episode only took seconds, but to Rebecca and Emma it seemed like an eternity. Finally the dog succumbed to its injuries and fell dead upon the snow.

Robby, covered in blood, limped triumphantly over to Rebecca. She bent down, affectionately stroking the dog's head. They were both in a state of severe shock. Emma helped her mother inside the cottage and began to administer some rudimentary first aid, trying desperately to stop the bleeding.

"Emma, honey, phone the vet and ask her to come straight over. Tell her that Robby's in really bad shape."

Rebecca was surprised at her calmness, she sat gritting her teeth in excruciating pain as she spoke, proud of her courageous daughter, who had charged out of the house brandishing a carving knife, intent on plunging it into the pit bull.

Robby collapsed on the kitchen floor. It was hard to tell if he was still breathing.

"The vet's on her way over right now, Mom," said Emma replacing the receiver.

When Madeline heard the desperation in Emma's voice, she rushed out of the house with her medical bag in one hand and stethoscope in the other driving furiously down the road in her Chevy Silverado pick-up truck.

Rebecca understood the look from her daughter and nodded. Emma, satisfied that her mother was as comfortable as she could make her, laid Robby's head carefully on a cushion, then walked out across the blood spattered snow towards the orange colored ball lying lifeless in the snow.

Emma stumbled across the back garden, saying a prayer to

herself, "God, if you let Marmalade live, I promise to be the best person in the whole world. I'll work in an animal shelter for free for the rest of my life, just please let my kitten be alive."

    Surprisingly there wasn't much blood. Marmalade's neck had been snapped like a twig, death had been quick and painless, that was why they hadn't heard the cat scream. Emma bent down and picked-up her beloved Marmalade, willing him to come back to life. The lump inside her chest felt as though it was going to burst out through her rib cage as she realized that her kitten was dead. Though it was a bitterly cold morning, she didn't feel the cold through her pajamas and slippers. She didn't even notice the large pick-up truck skidding into the driveway. The vet took in the scene instantly, running by the lifeless pit bull, across the snow to Emma, now kneeling in the deep snow sobbing, her kitten cradled in her arms.

    "Emma, it's me, Madeline. Come on, let's go inside and I'll take a look at your kitten." Madeline walked inside the warm cottage with Emma clutching her dead Marmalade.

    "My God, Rebecca. Let me take a look at you first." There was blood all over the kitchen floor, in the sink, down the cupboards. Blood soaked towels littered the table.

    "No. Please, Madeline, I beg you, please help Emma's kitten and the dog first. Emma's already called 9-1-1, they should be here any minute."

    "I'm sorry, Emma, the kitten's dead, there's nothing I can do for him now." The vet placed a comforting arm around the distraught child. "Emma, I need you to be a brave girl and help me with Robby. Let's try to save somebody here this morning."

    Rebecca knew Madeline didn't need Emma's help, but wanted to take the little girl's mind off the dead kitten, now lying on the kitchen counter by the sink.

    Robby was unconscious, his breathing labored. Madeline inspected the dog's wounds, which were deep and numerous. She had been Robby's vet from a puppy.

O'Malley's Cottage

"Okay, I'll be honest, this is pretty hopeless. I feel O'Malley telling me to try and save the dog. Ordinarily, with these injuries I'd put him down. I'll try and save him. Don't worry about the cost Rebecca. O'Malley was a wonderful man and helped me out many a time. This is my way of trying to say, *Thank you.* I'll stabilize Robby here and then take him straight to the surgery; I'm going to have to operate quickly if I have any chance of saving him. Now please, let me take a look at you."

Sirens could be heard coming up the road. Two police cruisers were first on scene. Two burly young officers leapt from them, guns drawn, heading towards the cottage. They had no sooner reached the back door, when an ambulance and fire truck arrived. The two officers saw the dead pit bull, then rushed over to help Madeline and Emma carry the unconscious Robby out to her truck. The paramedics insisted Rebecca come with them to the hospital in the ambulance, she certainly couldn't drive. Emma climbed into the back of the ambulance and sat beside her mother, holding her hand.

When the ambulance pulled away, the police officers drove over to the farm to speak to Garry about the dead pit bull, dropping the dog unceremoniously at his feet, the piece of broom handle still sticking out of the dog's chest.

Garry was furious. Quickly sizing up the two officers, he punched the smaller one in the face. The fight was on. The other officer grabbed Garry by the front of his collar, holding him like a brawling hockey player.

Garry squirmed and wriggled in the big man's grip, but try as he might he couldn't break the bigger man's hold. The officer liked to brawl on the ice anyway, and to him this was just another hockey fight. Repeatedly he punched Garry in the face, blow after blow. After the first punch Garry's nose was broken yet again, blood splattered across his face. His partner's nose on the other hand had been broken for the first time by Garry's punch. He wiped away the blood and tears streaming from his eyes then set about teaching Garry a lesson he had forgotten; *you don't touch the police.*

Had it not been for Beth running from the farmhouse screaming, they would have kicked her husband as near to death as they could manage. Hogtying him, they threw him into the rear of the cruiser and drove away.

When Rebecca and Emma returned to the cottage later that afternoon, there was a small animal coffin outside the front door with a note. *From your friends at the Fire Department. We are sorry for your loss.* An artistic firefighter had engraved, *Marmalade* on the lid.

"Oh, how sweet, Emma. Wasn't that thoughtful of them?"

"Now we can give Marmalade a proper burial. The ground's frozen though Mom, what are we going to do with Marmalade until the ground thaws?"

"He can stay in the coffin lying in state in the garage, then we'll take a drive down to Duncan's house and bury him in his garden, it'll be easier to dig the ground down there. The ground in Toronto will have thawed long before it does up here. Don't worry, Duncan won't mind."

Emma burst into tears. With her good arm Rebecca pulled her daughter close into her chest. "And then, honey," she said, fighting through her own tears, "we'll go to the nursery and buy the most beautiful flowering shrub to grow over his grave and every year it will brighten Duncan's garden with brightly colored flowers."

To their surprise the blood on the kitchen floor had been cleaned up. Emma, trying to be brave like her mother put the kettle on to make a cup of tea for the two of them. Sitting brokenhearted at the kitchen table together, they heard the faint sound of meowing coming from the hallway, somewhere near the back door. There was a stout looking cardboard box on the floor, where one hadn't been before, with small holes in it. An envelope was taped to the top. Rebecca opened the envelope and read aloud, *We hope you like your new kitten, Emma, if your mom doesn't, we have another good home for him so don't worry. All the best, your friends at the Fire Department. PS. He doesn't have a name yet.*

Emma opened the box as though she had just won a million dollars and carefully lifted out a jet-black kitten. "O'Malley," she cried, hugging the tiny kitten to her. Rebecca smiled and tickled the black fluffy ball under his chin as he lay contentedly in Emma's arms.

"Emma, honey, you make O'Malley feel at home. I'll find a nice piece of material to line Marmalade's coffin, then we'll go out to the garage together and put him to rest in the coffin. Don't worry, I'll find a place high on a shelf where he'll be safe before we take him down to Toronto."

When Rebecca and Emma walked out of the back door they fully expected to see bloodstained snow. To their surprise someone had even taken the trouble to dig away the offending snow from around the back door.

Out in the garage, Rebecca clutched the new kitten while Emma gently placed Marmalade in the coffin, lined with a piece of her mother's pajamas, a piece with lots of flowers on the material and no blood stains. She handled the dead kitten as though he was a piece of fragile china. Emma kissed Marmalade goodbye and began to cry as Rebecca tried to nail the tiny coffin lid in place. The firefighters had even left a small bag of tiny nails for the purpose. With her left arm full of stitches and bandaged Rebecca couldn't manage to do it. Every time she positioned a nail, sticking it partially in the wood and struck it with the hammer, the tiny nail shot across the garage. After numerous attempts she was beginning to get exasperated.

"Mom let me do it, O'Malley taught me how to use his

tools. We repaired a lot of things together. You hold onto O'Malley for me; is that name okay do you think? I don't want to upset you, it was the first name that came into my head when I saw him. He seems such a character, just like O'Malley was."

"That's a perfect name, Emma. I can hear O'Malley saying, *You named a cat after me.* They both laughed. "Okay, Miss Handywoman, let's see you in action."

Emma handed the kitten to her mother and picked up the hammer as though she was born with one in her hand. Expertly she nailed the lid onto the tiny coffin, all the nails went in straight. Rebecca was very impressed.

"Well, Emma, with you around the house we certainly don't need a man about the place, you're quite the little handywoman aren't you?" Emma smiled at her mother, delighted with the praise.

At Rebecca's suggestion Emma put the coffin inside an old plastic toolbox, placing it high up on a shelf where nothing could get at it.

"You know something, Emma, I don't blame that dog for what he did. It wasn't his fault, just look at who his owner is, that tells you it all right there. If that dog had lived with us it probably would have been as friendly as a kitten."

Chapter Nineteen

During the week Rebecca drove Emma to and from school. She tried to forget all about her unpleasant encounter with her neighbor and his vicious dog. Her left arm still hurt like hell. Unbeknown to Rebecca, her neighbor walked across the field each morning, and hid in the tree line, watching the comings and goings at O'Malley's Cottage through binoculars. From where he crouched he had a clear view of the cottage. Rebecca would never have seen him concealed in the thicket dressed in camouflage jacket and pants. For three days he timed Rebecca leaving the cottage to drive Emma to school, noting the time she returned. Give or take a few minutes, she was back at O'Malley's Cottage in forty-five minutes. Her dog was either dead or still at the vets, he didn't know. The main thing was it wasn't in the cottage.

Garry walked quickly around the back of the field, crouching low. He made a big detour so Rebecca wouldn't notice his footprints in the snow from an upstairs window, as he made his way to his hiding place.

As usual Rebecca closed the garage door manually behind her when she left, as she had done every morning that week. Garry knew the garage was not equipped with an automatic garage opener, and if Rebecca was true to form she would get out of her Mercedes and open the garage door, drive the Mercedes in, come out and close the garage door behind her before going into the cottage through the front door.

Garry secreted himself behind some bushes that hadn't been trimmed on the side of the garage furthest from the cottage. He checked his watch. In ten minutes time Rebecca would be pulling into the driveway. She was three minutes late this morning. He looked at the heavy snow falling and smiled. His tracks would soon be covered.

O'Malley's Cottage

Rebecca pulled into the driveway and got out of the Mercedes. The sound of her favorite Moose FM Country Station could be heard blaring out a popular country and western song, *I'm from the country and I like it that way*.Rebecca was unaware of the danger lurking only yards away from her. She parked the Mercedes inside the garage, as she did so, Garry pulled a black ski mask over his head. Rebecca walked out of the garage, the tune still in her head and closed the overhead door. She walked unhurriedly towards the front door, keys in hand.

She put the key in the lock, turned it and opened the door, as Garry slammed into her from behind, the full weight of his 240 lb body hitting her like an express train. She sprawled forward, face down on the granite-tiled floor. Garry, without looking round, grabbed the front door and slammed it behind him.

Rebecca felt herself being dragged around by her ankles, she began to scream and wriggled over onto her back, her legs were now twisted, held tightly in Garry's powerful grip. Even with his face covered by the ski mask, Rebecca knew exactly who her attacker was. She continued to kick out, screaming as loud as she could, terrified by the strength of the man. Garry grabbed her belt, hooking her off the ground like a rag doll.

Violently she kneed him in the groin, expecting, hoping for the same reaction as the last time, but he was expecting it and twisted his body, deflecting the blow, Rebecca's knee glanced off his thigh instead. He grabbed at her jacket with both hands, Rebecca wriggled out of it, lost her balance and fell backwards, slamming her head on the tiled floor and lay unconscious.

Rebecca had the vague sensation she was being dragged along the cold floor by her ankles, but powerless to do anything about it. Thoughts of Emma swirled around inside her bruised brain, she was no longer screaming, her cries came out in incoherent moans. She could hear, but was unable to interpret the sounds.

The monster dragged her limp body towards the living

room, never giving a passing thought that she was a mother, that she was someone's daughter or that she had a sister, a job and a life.

When Rebecca hurtled through the door, the floor mat slipped backwards, jamming in the bottom of the door.

* * *

Alison MacDonald and Brian decided to take a trip up north with the intention of killing two birds with one stone. They were going to drop in at the small garage they had recently purchased in the village and take the opportunity to visit Rebecca. Fortunately Alison won the toss as to where they were going first. Stepping out of the passenger side of Brian's truck she heard Rebecca's desperate screams.

Alison MacDonald charged through the front door of O'Malley's Cottage and raced down the short hallway, bouncing heavily off the walls as she slipped in the small pool of Rebecca's blood.

Big Mack raised her huge bear-sized right hand and slammed the edge of it across the left side of the rapist's bull neck, he was completely unaware that she had come through the front door behind him. The first blow stunned him. Big Mack wished she had struck the same blow again, but in anger she placed a huge arm under Garry's neck and dragged him semi-naked out into the snow. He staggered to his feet, his erection quickly disappearing in the subzero temperatures. Garry was a scrapper too; he delivered a punch to Big Mack's face that would have stunned a heavyweight boxer.

Big Mack shook her head from side to side, like a dog shedding water after a swim and spat out a bloodied tooth onto the snow, and grinned.

"Now you've made me really mad," she said spluttering her words through a mouthful of blood.

Brian was ordered into the cottage to help Rebecca. He rushed in, knowing that if Alison needed his help she would ask for it.

Garry swung another right fist, Big Mack did nothing more than raise her left shoulder and turned her head slightly to the right, but never taking her eyes off her opponent. The blow glanced off her shoulder, harmlessly sliding across the left side of her face. In a well rehearsed explosion of force, coupled with lightening speed she karate chopped him full in the throat with the side of her left hand. Instantly Garry's hands went to his throat. She immediately followed this with a right forearm-smash to his face, putting the weight of her whole body behind it, breaking his nose yet again. His knees buckled under him and he fell to the ground unconscious.

The fact that it was freezing outside and he was unconscious saved his life. His breathing dropped so much his body no longer needed the same amount of oxygen to stay alive. Had it been any other time of the year he might have died right there on the ground, not that Alison MacDonald was concerned.

Brian positioned Rebecca in the recovery position, dialed 9-1-1 and placed a warm blanket over her. She was groaning in pain, muttering incoherently. Brian pleaded with Alison to at least get a blanket for the body outside. She refused and wouldn't let him cover Rebecca's attacker; she was quite content to let him die. As it was, he had to restrain her from grabbing the unconscious man's head in her powerful arms, twisting it violently, breaking his neck.

"That bastard can die out there as far as I'm concerned, and don't you so much as go near him. If he makes it to trial those bloody stupid judges will have him out in no time so he can keep on attacking women. He stays right where he is."

You didn't argue with Big Mack. She was, however,

grateful for the warm salt water and paper towels he brought her. Before attending to herself, she pulled the laces out of Garry's boots and expertly bound his wrists and ankles, so that, pending a miracle he didn't get up and start fighting again. Then she went to comfort Rebecca, as she had done so many times before with other women who had suffered so brutally at the hands of a man that only Satan himself could have given life to.

Mandy Richards was the first police officer on scene, immediately followed by the paramedics. Lucy, the same paramedic that had been there when O'Malley died, ran into the cottage to attend to Rebecca, while her partner took care of Garry.

"Alison, what on earth are you doing here?" asked Mandy, shocked to see her old self-defense instructor, whom she hadn't seen since police college. When she saw Alison's bruised and bloodied face she gasped, "My God, what happened here?"

"Ask Brian, I'm having trouble speaking at the moment." She sounded like someone who had forgotten to put in their dentures, while chewing on a bread roll.

Mandy made some quick notes and asked for a sergeant to attend the scene. She requested the detective branch be informed and asked for scenes of crime to attend before the snow covered any more evidence. Because of the serious condition of both Rebecca and her attacker, the paramedics couldn't afford to wait for another ambulance to arrive.

"That's going to compromise the investigation," sputtered Alison.

"Then one of them will die if we wait for another ambulance," said Lucy calmly.

"Good, we know who that'll be."

Alison insisted on riding in the ambulance with Rebecca and *The Creature*, her new name for Garry. Lucy protested, but Big Mack told the paramedics and Constable Mandy Richards that the ambulance wasn't going anywhere without her in it. If they didn't like it, they could carry *The Creature*themselves and she would drive the ambulance with Rebecca in it to the hospital. When Alison swung open the driver's door and was about to climb into the driver's seat of the ambulance they readily agreed.

Mandy searched through Rebecca's purse for her cell phone and scrolled through the list of contact numbers, making note of any that pertained to her sister Rachael. Through her office in Toronto she was finally able to locate Rachael in her New York office. She told Rachael as much as she knew, while she waited for the investigative team to arrive. As Rachael listened she began to tremble uncontrollably, sinking into a chair. When the Officer told her that Rebecca was unconscious when the ambulance drove away from O'Malley's Cottage, tears streamed down Rachael's face.

Rachael immediately booked the next available flight back to Toronto then telephoned Duncan with the awful news, giving him instructions to collect her from the airport in the Bentley. They were driving straight to the hospital.

Rachael telephoned Emma's school from her office and advised the principal that Constable Mandy Richards of the Ontario Provincial Police would be arriving at the school to collect Emma, explaining briefly why. She asked to speak to her niece and waited for Emma to come on the phone.

"Hi, Aunt Rachael." Emma sounded excited.

"Emma. Mommy's had a bad fall at the cottage." She heard her niece inhale in shock. "Now don't worry, she's okay. She had to go to the hospital because she banged her head, it's just a precaution. Constable Mandy Richards is going to collect you from school. She's going to take you back to O'Malley's Cottage. Now don't cry, Emma, Duncan and I are making our way up, just as soon as I can get a flight out of New York. Do you remember Mommy talking about her policeman friend called Big Mack?"

"Yes," she sniffled.

"She and her fiancé Brian will be waiting for you at O'Malley's Cottage. They'll take care of you until I get there. Emma, don't worry, Mommy's going to be okay. I'm sorry, honey, I have to go, I have a taxi waiting to take me to the airport."

Rachael phoned the hospital. Rebecca had not regained consciousness. The hospital staff were monitoring her closely, but were very concerned about her. She remained in serious, but stable condition.

Rebecca's attacker had to have a tracheotomy to save his life. When Alison MacDonald heard this, she said the next time she saw him she would stick her finger in the hole and finish him off for good. She wasn't joking either.

It was nearly midnight when Rachael's Bentley pulled into the hospital parking lot.

Duncan had done all the driving, not because Rachael was tired, but because at the speed she would have driven, they likely wouldn't have arrived at all. She telephoned O'Malley's Cottage from the hospital to update Alison; Rebecca was still unconscious.

Rachael insisted Alison and Brian stay with them at the cottage, at least until Rebecca was well enough to come home. Emma was now asleep, totally exhausted emotionally. She had not yet been told how critical her mother's condition was.

"She knows it's bad, Rachael, that niece of yours has a sixth sense. She keeps saying, 'He hurt Mommy, didn't he? I know he did. I'm going to cast a black spell on him and his evil family." After that she ran up to her room and hasn't come down again. I've been checking on her regularly. The little black kitten is sleeping next to her."

"Black kitten? Where's Marmalade the ginger cat?"

"I don't know anything about that, Rachael. I haven't seen any ginger cat."

"Is the dog there?"

"There's no dog here either."

"I don't think my sister has told me everything that's been going on up there. I'm going to remain at the hospital. Duncan's coming back to O'Malley's Cottage for the night, what's left of it. He can bring Emma over later in the day. I wasn't really taking in everything Constable Richards was telling me on the phone. I want to know every little detail about what was going on at O'Malley's Cottage that resulted in my sister being in intensive care."

"I'm just going to check that Emma is really asleep. I don't want her to overhear what I'm going to tell you. Hang on a minute, I'll go and see." Alison tiptoed up the stairs to satisfy herself that Emma was sleeping and in case she wasn't, she made sure the bedroom door was closed before tiptoeing back downstairs to use the telephone in the kitchen, speaking in a low voice as she recounted what had taken place at the cottage. She made light of her part in the story, but Rachael wasn't having it and insisted on every detail, blow by blow. She was crying when she handed the phone to Duncan.

"Hi, Alison? … It's Duncan. Thank you so much for everything you've done. You saved Rebecca's life. Rachael and I will be forever in your debt, if there's anything we can do for you, anything, please, please let us know."

"Rebecca is my friend. You owe me nothing. Just see she gets home safely, otherwise I'm gonna have to kill some son-of-a-bitch. I'm sorry, I'm just so upset. Listen, tell Rachael, Brian and me have bought the garage in the village, the house comes with it, so we've got somewhere to stay and we'll be close by if we're needed. We're not going back to Toronto, this is our home now and I'm glad that I'm going to be near to keep an eye on Rebecca and Emma. Nobody will ever hurt that lady again or it'll be over my dead body, I promise you that."

"But what about the police force?"

"I quit. I couldn't put up with all the bullshit and petty politics any longer. Brian's a certified mechanic, we're both going to run the garage together and I'm going to be the new tow truck driver. I've got a pretty good pension, we'll be okay. For the first time in living memory, customers are going to be introduced to an honest auto mechanic."

After five days of living at the hospital, Rachael was exhausted, but she would not leave. She was fast asleep in the armchair when the nurse shook her gently.

"Rachael, Rebecca's asking for you," she said in a soothing voice, a big smile breaking across her face. Rachael covered her face in her hands and broke down.

Rebecca lay propped up in bed. She was in a private ward, paid for by her sister. Her head was bandaged, tubes and monitors connected to her body, a low *hum*permeated the room as the machines flashed incomprehensible information.

"Rachael, you look terrible, I think you should be the one in this bed, not me," croaked Rebecca weekly. Rachael couldn't speak, she knelt by the hospital bed close to her sister and wept into the blankets, her sobs masking the white noise in the room. Rebecca placed a gentle hand on the back of Rachael's head and gently caressed her sister.

Ten days later Rebecca arrived home, still looking swollen and very bruised. During the first afternoon back at the cottage, Rachael sat with Rebecca while she tried to recover in bed. She confided in Rachael that she was terrified Garry would come back and hurt her again or maybe Emma next time. She would never feel safe ever again. Rachael bent over the bed and gently kissed her on the forehead.

"Baby, he ain't never coming out of prison, honey, 'cept in a box. You must never speak of this again, and I will never mention it again. I've already made a phone call. It's all taken care of. Nobody hurts my family and gets away with it." She saw that Rebecca was going to speak and placed her finger gently against her sister's lips. "Shush, little sister, nothing left to say on that matter."

"Winston's taking care of business isn't he?"

"Rebecca, I told you he's not a nice man. I know he travels abroad as a hit man, he won't do it in his own backyard, but he has people that owe him big favors, and he's already called one in. When I told him what happened to you, he wanted to do the job himself, slow and painful over a week for free. Don't make me talk anymore about it, baby, I don't want anything to happen to my Winston, I've told you too much already."

"Don't worry, this is another one of *sisters' secrets*. Remember when we used to say that down at the cottage?"

"I sure do, honey, ain't nothing stronger than that bond."

"I'm sorry I can't work at the moment, I was planning to get so much reading done." Rebecca sounded weak.

"No worry on that score, you've already earned yourself a break after what I've seen coming back from you. How come you never told me about getting attacked by that dog, I never knew anything about Marmalade or Robby either until I got here."

"I didn't want to upset you. I knew you'd drop everything and come straight up. I'm sorry, I wish I'd told you now, you'd have taken me straight out of here and none of this would have happened. I didn't tell you, because part of me didn't really want to leave this place. I feel like I've been on a rollercoaster ever since O'Malley passed away. How do you think Emma's handling all this?"

"She's worried about her mom, but I got to tell you, Rebecca, that daughter of yours sure is growing up fast. Duncan's gone to collect her from school, I let him borrow my Bentley, it's all-wheel drive, good in the snow, especially with the tires I got on it."

When Duncan picked Emma up from school she was crying.

"What is it, Emma?" Emma handed him a crumpled note

that was childishly written. Duncan unfolded the note and read it.

Your preshus pony is going for dog food on 19th December. He leeves at 10 in the morning if you want to say goodbye. Happy Christmas! Luv Sarah XXX.

"Oh, Emma." He put a comforting arm around her shoulders. "That's all you need at the moment what with everything that's happened."

Emma buried her face against Duncan's shoulder, sobbing her heart out. He kept his arm around her all the way back to the cottage, thinking dark thoughts about the horrendous neighbors. The 19th was a Saturday, just two days away.

Rebecca insisted on giving Emma a sedative to calm the hysterical child. She cursed her ex-husband for being the cause of all her grief, she cursed the O'Malley's and their bloody cottage and hoped for a fitting and painful death for the man who had attacked her. In her anger she even cursed God. She clenched her fists in rage and looked up at the ceiling.

"How could you do this to me and my family. I'm a good person. What have I ever done to deserve this. I've gone to church, prayed to you and look how you've treated me and my family. You're as evil as the man that attacked me, do you hear me!"

Rebecca screamed in rage at her God, tears streaming down her face. Rachael rushed into the bedroom and hugged her tightly. She could feel the wetness of Rebecca's tears soaking through her blouse as she gently rocked her broken sister.

That night Rachael slept with an arm around Rebecca, silently saying her own prayers to a God that seemed to have forsaken them.

The following morning, the 18th Emma was very quiet, going about her business as though nothing had happened. She insisted on going to school. Rachael drove her in. She gave her aunt a kiss and walked off into the school as if everything was quite wonderful in the world. When Duncan picked her up that afternoon, Emma remained deceptively upbeat and never mentioned the Shetland pony.

Chapter Twenty

At 5 a.m. on the morning of the 19th Emma's alarm clock, hidden beneath her blankets, began ringing. She fumbled frantically trying to turn off the alarm, almost dropping the clock onto the wooden floor in her panic to shut off the piercing noise. She hoped she was the only one to hear it ringing.

She remained perfectly still for a few minutes to make absolutely sure that she was the only one awake, listening intently, aware of her own heart pounding in her chest. Nobody else in the cottage stirred. Though she missed Robby, who was still too sick to return home from the vets, it was better for her this morning that he wasn't home. He would have been sleeping by her bedside and would have started to whine when she got out of bed. Only the kitten lay on her bed and made no effort to move from his nice warm position. Emma got up and closed her bedroom door as quietly as she could, it only squeaked once.

She tiptoed over to her bedside lamp and switched it on, then pulled out her backpack from her closet. It had been a present from O'Malley, a good one too, along with a tent and winter sleeping bag he had bought for her. She had never done any winter camping before, but O'Malley insisted she knew all about survival, *just in case you ever find yourself lost in the wilderness.* He harped on about it every day, when he wasn't talking about horses. She had spent the previous evening packing it. Rachael had given her another sedative before bed, which Emma pretended to swallow, spitting it out after her aunt kissed her goodnight and left the room. She was grateful to O'Malley for getting her a good quality backpack because she was able to fit so much into it, lots of dried foods, frozen hamburgers, dried milk powder, bread, and a jar of peanut butter. Matches, lighter, newspaper, and kindling, plus a change of clothes should she get wet.

O'Malley's Cottage

Her most precious item, an old map of the back woods given to her by O'Malley, she stuffed inside her fleece-lined winter jacket. It was folded neatly and tucked inside a plastic lunch bag to keep it dry. The map was her lifeline, along with an old brass compass he had given her. Emma kissed the compass and silently asked O'Malley to guide her safely on her mission.

Before leaving her bedroom, she placed the letter she had written to her mother on top of her dressing table, explaining why she was taking the course of action she was taking, and then quietly stole out of her bedroom and went downstairs. She cringed every time a floorboard creaked, expecting at any minute to be caught out, and was thankful that Duncan was snoring in the spare bedroom, the noise helped conceal her movements through the cottage. She was finally ready, momentarily pausing on the threshold. The backdoor creaked open sending a blast of bitterly cold air into her face. She shivered and walked out into the snow.

Despite the heavy weight on her back, Emma's determination was so strong she hardly felt it. She walked boldly along the familiar road that led to the farm, turning right up the long driveway and then left towards the stables. The moon was shining brightly, illuminating the path that she and O'Malley had walked so many times before hand in hand. Emma felt his presence next to her, it was so strong that at times she looked around her, fully expecting to see him.

If it hadn't been for O'Malley's lectures, she would never have had the courage to do this. Emma looked up at the stars and felt joyful for the first time in ages. She didn't even feel afraid. She thought how upset her mother would be, and felt a pang of guilt, but when her mother read the letter, she would understand.

Emma walked through the stable that was now dirty and neglected, not like the way she and O'Malley had kept it. She opened the tack room door, closed it behind her and switched on the light, grateful that Toby's bridle was still hanging where she had left it. She found Toby's bareback blanket crumpled in a corner and opened it up, brushing off the dirt with a horse brush. She walked through the stable door at the other end, turned right and followed the fence line down to the gate.

    Cupping her gloved hands together she whispered Toby's name across the crisp morning air; and waited. She couldn't see the horses, but she could hear them thundering across the field towards her and opened the gate, walking quickly into the field, reassuring all the horses with her gentle voice. Toby immediately forced his way over to the little girl and nuzzled up close to her. Emma hadn't forgotten her training, she had Toby's bridle on him in no time and led him out through the gate, pushing back the other horses, eager to go with her.

    She wished she could have spent more time hugging each one of them and told them what she was doing, but she couldn't afford to waste time. Quickly, Emma returned to the stable with Toby, fed him a good size scoop of sweet feed, and brushed his back in the light coming from a crack in the tack room door and then picked his hooves, while he ate his grain.

    Emma purposely left the large side pockets of her backpack empty, filling them with feed. The next part of the plan didn't go quite as well as she had hoped. It took her many attempts to finally get the slices of hay to stay tied behind her pack using the orange bailer twine she always carried with her, just like O'Malley always did. It was he who had taught her many useful knots; the bowline, sheet bend, clove hitch, round turn and two half hitches and reef knot.

    Finally, she put Toby's bareback blanket on his back, secured the wide strap underneath his belly and led him out of the stable towards the open field and pulled herself up onto his back. By the time she reached the other side of the field and turned north on the track that led into the wilderness, it was almost seven o'clock.

O'Malley's Cottage

At eight o'clock, Rachael got up to make breakfast, glancing in on Emma sleeping in her bed. It didn't register that the hump in the bed was one of Emma's pillows, the blankets pulled up tight.

By ten o'clock all the adults were downstairs, including Rebecca, sitting around the woodstove in the kitchen drinking coffee. They figured the sedative had given Emma a good night's sleep. As ten o'clock was the time Toby was going to the slaughterhouse, they all decided to let Emma sleep in a little longer.

At eleven o'clock Rachael went upstairs to wake her niece. She opened the door wide and walked into the bedroom. The breeze created by the sudden movement of the door, was just enough to cause Emma's letter to topple backwards behind the dressing table and out of sight. Unfortunately Rachael neither saw it fall, nor heard it land.

"Oh, my God. Oh, my God," was all that could be heard by Rebecca and Duncan downstairs, followed by the sound of Rachael clambering down the narrow cottage steps, two at a time in a state of shock.

"She's gone!" cried Rachael as she burst into the kitchen, where Rebecca and Duncan were now standing.

Rebecca rushed past her without a word, hurrying upstairs to her daughter's bedroom, flinging back the blankets, revealing the pillow that Rachael had just seen herself. The alarm clock clattered across the floor. She opened Emma's closet; sure enough the backpack was gone.

"Phone 9-1-1, I can't speak," said Rebecca gasping for air and beginning to hyperventilate. She rushed into the bathroom and vomited. Duncan called the police while Rachael went to help her sister.

"The police got a call this morning from your neighbors, reporting the theft of a Shetland pony," announced Duncan. "You were right, Rebecca, Emma's gone to save Toby; where on earth would she take him?"

Rebecca remembered Emma's alarm clock and rushed back into the bedroom, grabbing the clock off the floor. Her heart sank when she saw what time it had been set for.

"This was set for five o'clock," announced Rebecca, holding up the alarm clock and trying hard to keep her composure and not fall to pieces, a sense of panic rising up inside her. "She's got at least a five hour start on us." She looked out of Emma's bedroom window, the snow was falling heavily, obliterating any tracks that Emma and Toby would have left in the snow. Rebecca closed her eyes. "Think. Think," she kept saying aloud as she paced around the bedroom. "Duncan, check the garage and shed, maybe she's hiding in there with Toby."

Duncan raced back downstairs and out the backdoor. He was back in no time with the bad news; Emma and the pony weren't in either of those places. Meanwhile Rebecca had been searching Emma's bedroom from top to bottom. Clothes were missing, she couldn't find the small brass compass O'Malley had given her daughter, and the old map that Emma had been studying the night before, another treasure from O'Malley was nowhere to be found. Most of all Rebecca was hoping to find a note from Emma.

Finally, she sat down on her daughter's bed clutching the little girl's pajamas to her face, sobbing into the soft material. "If I had known this was going to happen, I would have gone to the hay barn right from the beginning with that monster. It's all my fault," she wailed.

In the quiet of her daughter's bedroom she told Rachael how she felt, and the price she was asked to pay to get the pony for Emma. Now, no price was too high to get her daughter back; alive. Rachael grabbed Rebecca by the shoulders and shook her.

"Listen to me. It's not your fault. Say you'd gone to the hay barn and got the pony back, how proud of yourself would you be then? 'Oh, I just had to get raped in the hay barn to get the pony, Emma doesn't know, so don't tell her.' It wouldn't have ended there either Rebecca. Neither you, nor I or any other self-respecting woman would have done that, and if you had, I'd have disowned you. Give your head a shake, Rebecca, nobody could have foreseen this. Don't you ever blame yourself for this; you haven't done a thing wrong. You've been a wonderful mother. Had I been in your shoes I know there's not one thing I would have done differently. The only person that should be held accountable for all this is in jail, where he belongs. His real punishment is still yet to come; trust me. Now pull yourself together girl, Emma needs all of us to stay focused on finding her, and to be honest with you, I don't even think she's lost, we're the ones that are lost. She might be a scrap of a girl, but she has a plan all worked out and she knows exactly where she's going, the trouble is O'Malley has no doubt filled that child's head full of ideas and now she's acting on them. Come on, she could hardly have organized a horsebox to arrive in the middle of the night to whisk her and Toby away. On second thoughts, we're talking about Emma, anything's possible. Did you ever see that map O'Malley gave her?"

"Yes, not that I paid much attention to it. She would study it for hours, I don't even think she needs the map anymore, she probably has it memorized. I think it covers the area behind us up to and including Algonquin. I remember seeing Algonquin Provincial Park marked on it, Emma pointed out the lake where we all went for a picnic back in the summer. I remember that."

"Okay then, that's it, it makes sense. She's taken the pony deep into the woods to hide him somewhere, a place that O'Malley told her about."

"Do you think he had planned this with my daughter just in case the new people didn't look after Toby," Rebecca asked angrily.

"Not for one minute, Rebecca. O'Malley loved Emma, you

know that. He would never have put that child's life in danger. You told me yourself that he was always teaching her about what to do if she ever got lost in the woods. She's adapted what he taught her to find her way through the woods."

There was a knock on the door and Constable Mandy Richards arrived to take the report of the missing child. Rachael and Rebecca explained what they believed had happened. Mandy asked if they had done a full search of the whole house, including the loft space. That was the only place they hadn't looked. To satisfy the Officer, Duncan went up into the loft and confirmed what they already knew, wherever Toby was, Emma would be with him and there was no way even Emma could have got the pony up into the loft space, but they knew if there was even the slightest chance, she would have tried it.

"What about a helicopter or a plane flying over the area?" asked Duncan.

"I already asked on my way over here," said the Officer. "The weather's too bad for them to fly at the moment, I had enough trouble getting here myself. At least if it's snowing it means the weather is warmer, I checked the weather forecast before leaving the station, we're expecting heavy snow falls over the next few days. From what you tell me, it sounds as though Emma has thoroughly prepared herself for this trip, I'm sure she's fine, really, Rebecca. O'Malley was a good teacher."

They all knew that a ten-year old child lost in the wilderness in the summer was very real cause for concern. In the winter the outcome was not likely to be a good one.

"We've searched the house from top to bottom, all the cupboards, under all the beds, the garage, the shed, there's no trace of her," said Rachael. "Look, Officer, no disrespect, we're not going to find her with just the three of us and one police officer, we need more resources and we need them now."

O'Malley's Cottage

Constable Richards picked up the kitchen phone and dialed her station. Her sergeant answered. She immediately explained the seriousness of the situation. Mandy turned sheepishly towards Rachael, holding her palm over the mouthpiece.

"He wants me to go over to the farm and see what I can find out there first, before he organizes a command post.

"Give me the phone," shouted Rachael, practically snatching the phone out of the Officer's hand. "Listen to me." She was shouting into the phone. "Don't you dare tell me to calm down. You get a search party out here right now, instead of wasting precious time. Trust me, every second you waste, I promise you, I will see to it that you are accountable for it in the end. No, don't you argue with me, just do it. What's your name? Rebecca, write this down, Sergeant Webb, write the time and date next to it. I mean business and I expect a call back from you in ten minutes or the next call will be to the media and your bosses, you grandiloquent individual."

Rachael handed the phone back to Mandy, who was trying to hide the smirk on her face.

"Okay, we're going to turn this place into a command post ourselves," said Rachael, taking charge. "Mandy, you and Duncan head over to the farm and confirm the pony's missing. Try and find something that proves Emma was there. I bet if you look closely you'll see her footprints and the pony's hoof prints on that farm somewhere. If you do, confirm the direction she's headed and report back immediately."

Mandy and Duncan rushed out to the cruiser and headed over to the farm. Rachael telephoned the nearest airport, receiving confirmation the weather was too bad to fly. The woods at the end of the garden were no longer visible, the snow was so thick. The wind was getting stronger all the time. The thought of Emma lost somewhere out there in that blizzard was overwhelming.

Rachael was about to call her media and police connections, when the phone rang.

"Sergeant Webb here. We have a command post on its way to you, K9, sleds and extra officers and civilians on foot to help in the search. The helicopter is waiting to go airborne at a moment's notice as soon as the weather permits. We'll be fully operational in no time at all. We'll find her soon, ma'am."

"Thank you." Rachael exhaled deeply, letting go of some of the stress building up inside her. She turned to give Rebecca the news. Her sister had dressed in a thick overcoat, gloves and hat, pants and riding boots. "Rebecca, what are you doing?"

"I'm going after her, I should have gone straight away. She's gone into the woods, I know it, I'll find her, I have to find her. I'm taking Blazer, he's a powerful horse, I could catch up with her and bring her home."

"My God, Rebecca, you have no idea which way she went. At least she had the good sense to prepare herself before leaving. Look at you, you haven't even packed a damn thing to eat or drink. She's got a backpack, no doubt stuffed with provisions, a tent, her thick sleeping bag and knowing Emma, she would have packed food for the pony as well. Listen to me." Rachael grabbed her sister by the arms. Rebecca fought her off, prepared to sacrifice herself to try and save her daughter's life, like a lioness protecting her cub.

"I can't stand around waiting for others to help her, it's taking too long."

Rachael moved towards the back door.

"Don't try and stop me, Rachael," snarled Rebecca, a wild look in her tear filled eyes. "I'm warning you, don't even try."

"Rebecca, listen to me, honey, if the snow hadn't covered the tracks I would have ridden out there with you." The thought of Rachael riding a horse amused Rebecca.

"You can't even ride a horse, Rachael."

"I would have tried anything, I'd have run as far as I could

O'Malley's Cottage

go to find Emma. In my way I'm running to find her now. You go out there like that, Rebecca, you're definitely going to die. If you're going to go, at least have the sense to prepare for your journey like Emma did. We'll find her I know it, alive and well and you'll be nothing more than a frozen corpse in the snow. You want to go and look for her on horseback that's fine, never mind about stealing your neighbor's horse, I won't stop you, but at least get yourself properly prepared. You try and leave this house unprepared like you are now, I promise you it's going to get real ugly. I mean it Rebecca. We don't need to concentrate our efforts on looking for two people, a child that's probably snuggled up warmly in her down-filled sleeping bag inside her tent, with a chocolate bar and a juice box talking through the tent to her pony, and an adult slowing dying of hypothermia. No, Rebecca, I won't let you leave, but I will help you prepare to search for her if you must, to at least give you the best chance of survival. Listen to me, I really believe O'Malley is watching over Emma, let him concentrate on helping her instead of dividing his attention between trying to take care of her and trying to keep you alive."

"Damn O'Malley and damn this place. I wish we'd never come here."

Mandy and Duncan heard the sound of raised voices coming from inside O'Malley's Cottage. Opening the door they almost collided with Rachael, a blast of freezing air followed them through the back door, enveloping them in a shroud of swirling snow. Rebecca stood on the other side of the kitchen dressed ready to leave, a hostile atmosphere lingered uncomfortably in the room.

"The command post and reinforcements are on the way," said Rachael, looking at Mandy and Duncan and then across at Rebecca.

Duncan broke the uncomfortable silence. "You were right, Rachael. We found Emma's footprints leading out of the stable until they were obliterated by the snow. Toby's hoof prints were alongside Emma's. The lady there was actually very helpful, she came out and searched with us, she confirmed they weren't footprints belonging to anyone who lived there. Her son and daughter were as good as useless though; we won't talk about our conversation with them. I was surprised to hear the Officer use the *f*word when, Sarah isn't it? wanted to file a theft charge against Emma for taking Toby."

Mandy blushed. "It looks as though Emma took Toby into the stable, cleaned him up, because the brushes have been moved. You can still see the dust marks on the shelf. She must have taken grain for the pony, the lid was off the container. I found this on the ground inside the tack room."

Mandy pulled out a small clean white handkerchief from her pocket, with small yellow and red roses embroidered in one corner. Rachael took the handkerchief from the Officer and handed it across the table to Rebecca.

"Donna gave it to Emma. She always carried it with her, vowing she would never blow her nose on it." She looked up and smiled through her tears, remembering the moment Donna had given it to Emma in the kitchen at the farm. Rebecca carefully folded it into a neat square and pressed it against her cheek, her tears soaking into the delicate material.

Rachael stood next to Rebecca, placing a protective arm around her shoulder. "Look we're going to have an army of men and women here soon, most of whom probably don't want to be here. The best thing we can do for Emma is to see that these men and women have lots of hot drinks and plenty to eat, that way they'll be able to search longer and harder. Rebecca, make yourself useful and give me a hand to get a load of sandwiches made and endless supplies of tea and coffee."

"Rachael, why don't I drive down to the store and pickup some food, you'll never have enough here."

"Take my Mercedes, Duncan, it's four-wheel drive and very

good in the snow." Rachael was relieved Rebecca had finally come to her senses.

Rachael, Rebecca, and Mandy began to setup the kitchen so that the extra officers and volunteers would be taken care of. When Duncan drove back into the driveway, a huge mobile command post pulled up outside the cottage with the words, *Ontario Provincial Police Command Centre* emblazoned along both sides. OPP pick-up trucks pulling trailers containing snowmobiles and four wheelers followed behind, they were joined by two K9 units. Within an hour the road and driveway began to fill with all types of police vehicles and enough police officers and volunteers to police a demonstration. It didn't take long for the news media to get wind that something was going on somewhere near Algonquin Provincial Park.

A steady procession of police officers and volunteers made their way through the cottage, grabbing sandwiches, muffins and hot coffee, before braving the blizzard in search of Emma. Among the group were a few veteran die-hard search and rescue teams from the Ontario Volunteer Emergency Response Team, better known as OVERT. They had brought their own dogs, four wheelers and snowmobiles. They didn't hang around, a little girl was missing and every second counted. To find her dead because they had waited twenty minutes to warm themselves up with a coffee and a muffin at the cottage would be something they would never live down. Rachael, who was not often impressed by people, was very impressed by this small group of dedicated men and women.

* * *

Nightfall finally descended. There had been so much optimism in the air all the time there had been daylight. Floodlights blazed around the Command Post, illuminating the driveway and front garden of the cottage. The temperature slowly dropped further below freezing point and was now at -10 Celsius. In the early hours of the morning, the sound of snowmobiles could be heard returning. Rebecca sat by the woodstove in the armchair, wrapped in a blanket, Rachael sat on the other side, occasionally opening an eye to check that her sister hadn't stolen out of the cottage in a futile attempt to search for Emma on her own.

A very tired and weary looking police inspector walked into the kitchen. He had been in charge of the operation since the beginning and had kept Rebecca up to speed as to what progress was being made. The weather had not improved enough to launch the helicopter; they would now have to wait until the morning. The Rescue Team had just arrived back. The news wasn't good. There were huge snowdrifts blocking the trails, the snowmobiles sank into them. The riders spent most of the night digging themselves through them until finally the drifts were too overwhelming and they reluctantly had to turn back. The men and women stepped into the kitchen, every one of them looking tired, exhausted and dejected. Rebecca thanked them and would not hear of them leaving until they had sat down and had a bowl of hot soup, toast and a mug of coffee.

Duncan looked old and haggard. Rachael put a hand on his shoulder. "Enough, Duncan. I'll do this, you take a break, you've been going all day. There's another day to go yet and maybe many more ahead. Go put your feet up, please."

"I can't, Rachael, just let me take care of these guys, if I stop I'll fall to pieces, I'll take a catnap now and again. I need to do this; please, honey, don't get mad." She kissed him. "How's Rebecca holding up?"

"I don't think she is, Duncan, if we don't find Emma alive, this is going to kill her."

"Oh, my God," shouted Rebecca, clutching her face in her hands. "I haven't told George."

"I'll call him right now." Rachael walked into the dining room and telephoned Rebecca's ex-husband. She let the phone ring and ring, glad she had been the one to make the call. A young woman's sleepy voice answered the telephone.

"Yes?" said the woman. Rachael could hear the muffled sound of blankets being moved and George's drowsy voice asking the woman, "Who the hell's calling at this time of the night?" She guessed it was probably Suzanne, George's secretary. "Yes, he's right here, Rachael. Oh, my God, Rachael. George, wake up. It's Rachael, Emma's gone missing."

George was awake in a flash, he sat bolt upright in bed and grabbed the phone from Suzanne.

"When did this happen?" he barked into the phone. "Well, why the hell wasn't I told sooner? What happened? Have the police been called?"

Rachael felt her anger rising at being spoken to as though she was a child, but her feelings of guilt at not calling George sooner, kept her temper in check. She explained what had happened and what was being done, none of which satisfied George.

"I'm coming up to take charge right now," he shouted into the phone, before slamming down the receiver. Rachael closed her eyes and counted to ten, breathing deeply before returning to the kitchen.

With heavy hearts, the men and women who had been seated at the table left to get some well-earned rest. The temperature had now dropped to -15 C. The snow was so cold it squeaked as they walked across it to the Command Post to debrief.

* * *

Emma made the decision to keep going until about an hour before sunset. O'Malley had told her that it was no good trying to make a fire and get shelter in the dark. All that had to be done well before then. She tethered Toby to a small tree and set about erecting her tent, just like O'Malley had shown her. She unrolled her thick sleeping blanket inside the tent, placing it on top of a half inch thick foam mat. The snow had been falling heavily, initially Emma made good progress through the woods, following a trail that at times she could hardly see, but Toby seemed to find his way through without any real difficulty, almost as if he knew that this journey was a matter of life or death for himself. Sometimes he would veer off the path into the woods, as though he knew the drifts ahead were too deep to go through. He would find another way back onto the path. In places the path couldn't be seen from the air, tracking them through these dense woods would have been almost impossible.

    Having erected her tent, Emma began making a fire, remembering O'Malley's words. *You should always pretend that even though you have a full box of matches, you have only one match left and to treat that match as though it was the only thing between freezing to death and a warm fire.* O'Malley had even taught Emma how to make a fire from three pieces of wood, some string or even a shoelace would do, and some moss. The damp conditions prevailing at the moment were not ideal for that, let alone the amount of energy Emma would have to exert, burning up valuable calories just to make a little smoke.

    She removed the dry kindling and papers from her backpack, having found a suitable place to make the fire, opened her jacket to cut out the breeze and with great care struck a match. It burst into life and just as quickly it was extinguished by a sudden gust of bone chilling wind, despite her great care. *Oh, you're dead now Emma*, O'Malley would have teased when they were back at the farm and he had been teaching her how to light a fire. *Oh, look, you found one more match, this is it if you want to stay alive, try again*, he would have said.

Emma crouched over the newspaper and kindling, which she had set in the middle of a ring of medium sized rocks, some of which she had kicked out of the frozen ground, and struck the second match. This time she was luckier, the paper burst into flame and ignited the kindling, sending up puffs of white smoke, and then exploded into bright orange flame. Emma quickly applied small twigs to the fire and began to add larger ones the more the flames grew, until she had a raging fire. She smiled proudly to herself and looked up to thank O'Malley, feeling his presence with her every step of the way.

She melted snow in a pan and took care of Toby's needs before her own, as she knew O'Malley would have done. She gave the pony some sweet feed, which he ate quickly and a little hay. Toby was her best chance of survival; he seemed to know his way through the woods. She hugged him tightly, grateful for his company, saving his life made her forget about the enveloping darkness and the sound of the wolves that made Toby suddenly look up in alarm.

Emma stroked her hands over his body to calm him, aware the black bears would be hibernating. She knew it was too cold for them to be out foraging, and wouldn't worry about them, not unless it suddenly turned mild. She sat huddled by the fire, using the pan she had given Toby for water to cook some pasta. It took forever in the frigid conditions. When it was ready she added some cheddar cheese, cutting it into thin slices. She hoped her mom would forgive her for taking the tin of ham. She was careful to remember O'Malley's advice on not injuring herself by doing something stupid like cutting herself with her own knife or slicing a deep wound on a jagged can.

She rationed the ham, cutting it into thick chunks and dropped them into the hot pasta. Emma ate every mouthful as though it was her last, certain this was one of the best meals she had ever tasted, then scraped out every last morsel leaving little to clean afterwards. Before heading into the tent, she boiled herself some fresh water from the snow and made herself a cup of hot chocolate, savoring the taste of two Girl Guide vanilla cookies, remembering they were also her mother's favorite. She began to shed a few tears until she remembered what O'Malley had said. *Shedding tears uses energy and burns calories. In a survival situation you cannot afford to waste precious energy crying.*

Tucked inside her sleeping bag, still in her clothes, except for her boots, Emma slept uneasily through the night. She would awake at the slightest sound. Three times in the night she had to get up to comfort Toby, as the wolves circled their little camp. Sometimes the wolves would call out to one another, sending a chill down Emma's spine. She would pile the fire up even higher and shout out loudly at the unseen creatures that lurked deep in the dark woods, and in her imagination. She slept snuggled up to a small razor-sharp hatchet. In the event of a wolf attack she fully intended to fight them off with it, or any other attacker for that matter.

At first light Emma was up, reluctant to leave the warmth of her sleeping bag. The fire had burned out, but there were a few glowing embers left that she re-ignited, without having to waste another match. It was bitterly cold, Emma knew she couldn't afford to waste any time and moved quickly gathering more wood to get the fire blazing again. She could feel the cold right through her body, and for the first time since she had set out she began to feel afraid that she would freeze to death and never be found.

Toby's needs had to be attended to; she melted water for him, gave him more hay and a little sweet feed before crawling back into her sleeping bag and lay there shivering. The exterior of her sleeping bag was covered in a thin layer of frost caused by her own body's moisture condensing on the outside of the bag. She knew she would have to dry the bag off somehow before she slept in it again if she could.

O'Malley's Cottage
Page 271

    She couldn't get warm, knowing that she needed to warm the core of her body. She put another pan on the fire, and made herself a hot chocolate, keeping her body close to the fire, praying the sun would soon blaze through the trees. The hot drink warmed her spirits. By the time the porridge was ready, she felt a whole lot better. She didn't want to leave the camp, having got used to her new surroundings, but knew she had to get further into the woods to save Toby from the slaughterhouse. When he looked over at her as he ate his hay, she knew she was doing the right thing, all this discomfort was worth saving her best friend. She imagined O'Malley back with her again. He wouldn't have wasted any time, he would have cleared up the camp and been on his way in no time, only looking back once to make sure he wasn't leaving anything behind.
    Like an experienced wilderness traveler, Emma broke camp and finally threw a leg over the back of Toby once more. They continued their journey northwards through the woods. Occasionally they would enter a clearing where the sun shone through, blissfully soaking up its rays. It was still snowing, but not as hard as the day before, making the journey a little easier.

Chapter Twenty-One

George arrived at the cottage in his newest toy, a bright yellow Hummer H2 accompanied by a reluctant Suzanne. About the time they pulled up outside O'Malley's Cottage, Emma and Toby had set off from their campsite. George insisted Suzanne stay in the vehicle while he went into the cottage to take charge of operations.

As he was getting out of the Hummer, a procession of media vehicles arrived and pulled in behind his canary colored status symbol. Reporters jumped out of various vehicles, their engines running and heaters full on, dressed like celebrities arriving for the Genie Awards, briefed that a story was to be had, tucked away in this tiny community that would have the country glued to their television sets. Some advanced on the Command Post, others on O'Malley's Cottage. The more astute went to the farm next door; neighbors were always a good source of information. While all this was going on, larger vehicles arrived and setup huge antennae and satellite dishes to beam the story that was unfolding around the world.

A child has ridden off into the wilderness to save a pony from the slaughterhouse and is now feared dead, frozen to death somewhere in the endless miles of inhospitable forest. It is a race against time.

Alison MacDonald and her fiancé, Brian Carpenter sat up in bed to watch the morning news from the comfort of their new home. When they saw Emma's face fill the television screen they stared in disbelief. There in front of them was a reporter standing outside O'Malley's Cottage. They jumped out of bed and raced over to the cottage.

George entered O'Malley's Cottage without even knocking on the back door. He walked inside as though he owned the place and everyone inside shouldn't be in there without his permission. He was about to give Rebecca a piece of his mind, when he saw her badly bruised face, her bandaged left arm and her completely washed-out, dejected look.

"My God, Rebecca, what happened to you?"

Rebecca couldn't speak, she looked up in his direction with a faraway look on her face.

"What's happened to my daughter?" he demanded.

Rebecca continued to look in the direction of his voice, even the act of breathing seemed to be an effort for her. She was on the verge of a complete nervous breakdown.

There was a loud knock on the front door. "Not another bloody reporter," shouted Rachael, exasperated.

"I'll go, honey," said Duncan moving towards the front door. When he opened the door Alison and Brian were standing there filling the doorway, Duncan ushered them in quickly. Rebecca smiled faintly when she saw Alison. George immediately stopped his recriminations at the sight of Big Mack and fell silent. Like the seasoned police officer Alison had been, she surveyed the room before stepping in, locked eyes with George and strode quickly over to Rebecca. The two women hugged each other tenderly.

"We just saw the news this morning; we got here as quickly as we could. Brian and I are at your disposal for anything, even if it's just to take the garbage down to the dump, anything we can do to help."

"Thank you, former Constable Alison MacDonald. I've been in such a state of shock I haven't phoned anyone. I should have called you, especially you, I'm so sorry."

"There you go again, apologizing for being a good person, no apology necessary. I'm going to head over to the Command Post, see how things are going and if they've got something Brian and I can do to help."

"Suzanne's with you, isn't she?" Rebecca turned to look in

George's direction.
"I told her to wait in the car." His reply was curt, dismissing the woman in his car as a trivial matter.
"Tell her to come in, it's freezing out there." Rebecca rose to her feet unsteadily.
"The heaters on, she's fine."
In exasperation Rebecca stormed outside, through the line of reporters, without saying a word to any of them and led Suzanne back inside the comfort of the cottage. Rebecca found herself comforting the younger woman who kept sobbing and telling Rebecca how sorry she was; for everything. Rebecca made her feel welcome and sat her down by the woodstove and poured her a mug of coffee.
With Alison present, it was easier for Rebecca to explain to George what had happened to Emma, making a point of reminding him that she was, *their daughter*, not his. She was not about to waste her breath arguing over the fact that on almost every occasion Emma had telephoned him recently, he had been too busy to talk to her.
Rebecca looked around the kitchen, speaking softly. "Rachael and I are going to the little village church this morning, you're all welcome to come if you wish."
She walked up the small flight of stairs that led to Emma's bedroom, walked inside and breathed in the smell of the room that was filled with the scent of her daughter. She went over to the bookcase and rummaged through her daughter's CD's until she found Emma's favorite one and turned on the CD player at full volume. Beyonce's voice filled the cottage. Rebecca sat on the edge of Emma's bed and began to cry, her slender body heaving under the strain of each wave of grief. As the song played Rebecca collapsed to the floor and cried with an intensity that no one had ever heard before.

O'Malley's Cottage

Rachael took the stairs two at a time, closely followed by Alison, who scooped Rebecca up like a doll and under instruction from Rachael, carried Rebecca down the hall to her bedroom. The women put the grief stricken mother to bed and Alison did her best to comfort Rebecca while Rachael called Dr. Chalmers.

Later in the morning, Duncan took it upon himself to drive down to the church to speak to Father O'Ryan, who agreed after Mass to come to O'Malley's Cottage and hold a private service for Rebecca. That morning the congregation all said a prayer for the little girl lost in the wilderness.

"I should tell you, Father, Rebecca is not Catholic."

Father O'Ryan raised his eyebrows in surprise. "We're all praying to the same God Duncan, it's just that some of us have high speed access and others are using a slower server. The Vatican banished me here a long time ago for being too outspoken," he chuckled. "I've always maintained that Jesus would have been far happier if we all prayed in a barn instead of a multimillion dollar cathedral. All are welcome in my modest church. O'Malley and I were great friends, I miss his sharp intellect and quick wit terribly."

Dr. Chalmers arrived before morning surgery began and gave Rebecca a stronger sedative to help her endure the ordeal that she was going through.

"Rachael tells me you've stopped eating. If you don't start to eat I'll have you admitted to hospital." The doctor fixed his patient with a firm eye, "and don't look at me like that, I'm serious. You are not to give up hope. When they bring Emma home, alive, your daughter is going to need a strong mother to take care of her."

Stepping through the crowd of reporters, he shook his head and walked quickly out to his truck without speaking to any of them.

* * *

O'Malley's Cottage

Father O'Ryan arrived at the cottage carrying the troubles of the world on his shoulders as though they were as light as the air itself.

The small service took place in Emma's bedroom, where the Priest prayed for her safe return, afterwards family and friends went downstairs to the lounge. Rachael played the piano and began to sing, the melody and her voice echoing through the cottage. A female reporter who sang in a gospel choir opened the back door and began to sing along with Rachael. Soon the whole house was filled with reporters all singing together with the family, willing Emma to come home soon. At the end of the service, the reporters filed out of the cottage without a word. Duncan opened the front door and handed out sandwiches, cookies, and hot coffee to them.

Rebecca asked to speak with Father O'Ryan privately. They went back upstairs to Emma's bedroom and sat on the bed. He took her delicate hands in his huge paws and she poured out her heart to him, asking for forgiveness for past sins and for turning away from her faith. He told Rebecca, much to her surprise, that many times he had walked alone in the wilderness himself, his own faith sorely tested to breaking point.

Before leaving, Father O'Ryan stood at the front door and turned to Rebecca. "I don't believe God will bring harm to Emma, I trust in the Lord, but if I am wrong about that, I will not say it is God's work, or that the Lord works in mysterious ways or any of that claptrap. Like you, I will be lost in the wilderness once more, my faith once again tested to breaking point."

Despite the bad weather, the Armed Forces sent up a Chinook helicopter to comb the extensive forests north of the cottage. They searched for hours, but could find no trace of Emma or the Shetland pony. The thermal imager aboard the helicopter had picked up some hopeful signs, but they turned out to be deer and moose moving through the forest. Emma had now been missing for nearly two days.

Detectives back at the Command Post opened up another branch of the investigation, suspecting Emma may have been abducted and that was why they hadn't been able to locate her. They began checking the sex offender registry for all known offenders in the area, paying discreet visits to these creatures homes, checking their alibis.

* * *

Emma and Toby pushed on further northwards; the wind increased in strength, the heavy snowfall making the trek along the trail more and more difficult. Toby ploughed on through the snow, seeking out easier terrain whenever the necessity arose.

As the sun began to go down, Emma, chilled to the bone collapsed forward onto the pony's withers. She was barely conscious and perilously close to slipping off his back into the snow and certain death. The cold had sapped the last of the child's energy, only the warmth rising from Toby's back was keeping her alive.

The little girl was no longer conscious of her surroundings, and could only make out blurred shapes that were getting darker and darker. She began hallucinating and imagined herself tucked up in her cozy bed in the cottage, dreaming that she was riding Toby away through the woods to safety, now completely unaware that she was out in the middle of this vast expanse of forest, miles from anywhere.

It was now pitch dark. Clinging limply to the pony's neck she thought she heard the faint sound of a large dog barking in the distance. The pony continued its slow progress towards the sound.

O'Malley's Cottage was settling in for a second night without Emma. The wind was howling and huge snowdrifts were building up around the cottage and the vehicles parked outside. Rebecca was heavily sedated, sound asleep in her bed, while

Rachael and Duncan slept in the spare room. Rebecca had offered Emma's bedroom to her guests, but nobody would sleep in there, it just didn't feel right. George and Suzanne slept uncomfortably on the couch in the lounge and Alison and Brian slept on the floor in the dining room.

In five days time it was going to be Christmas Day and everybody dreaded its arrival. Except for Rebecca, nobody believed Emma could still be alive in these appalling weather conditions that would have tested the mettle of grown men, let alone a small child.

Chapter Twenty-Two

"What is it?" Inside a small log cabin an old man sat at a heavy wooden table writing by the light of a hurricane lamp. The glow casting long shadows across the room, where they disappeared into dark recesses. Papers and books littered the table. The old man removed his spectacles, carefully placing them on the page he was working on and rubbed his tired eyes with stubby fingers. A huge black Newfoundland began barking, pawing at the wooden door that led outside into the blizzard.

"Mordecai, what is it?" The old man turned to look at the dog. "All right, all right, hang on I'll get your leash." He downed the remains of the whiskey he had been sipping throughout the evening, and put on his thick winter coat, trapper's hat, mittens and boots. Then he grabbed the leash from a hook by the door and clipped it onto Mordecai's collar. He wasn't going to let Mordecai out on his own in case he got himself set upon by a pack of wolves. "Hold on there, boy, don't be so impatient, wait till I grab the lamp."

When the old man opened the door and stepped outside the cabin, he was almost knocked off his feet by the strength of the wind. The driving snow stung his face as it blasted against his body. It was so dark he could barely see where he was going. Without the dog to guide him and the lamp to see with, he would have perished. It was a whiteout. Ordinarily he'd never have ventured outside, but the dog kept pulling at the leash in a way he'd never done in all the years Leonard Rivers had owned him. There was something out there and Leonard judged by the way the dog wasn't snarling viciously, that whatever it was needed help and meant them no harm.

"Who's out there," he called. "Hello," he shouted into the howling wind. "Anybody out there!"

O'Malley's Cottage

Leonard had difficulty keeping his balance as the dog pulled him farther and farther away from the safety of the cabin. He prayed the leash wouldn't snap. His lamp was comforting, but without Mordecai he'd never get back to the cabin. Leonard thought he heard a horse neighing in the distance and Mordecai kept pulling him towards the sound. It seemed like the horse was calling to the dog, because every time Leonard heard it neigh, the dog barked. Then there would follow a period of silence and Mordecai would bark again. They went back and forth like that, the sound getting closer all the time, until Leonard Rivers was convinced beyond all reasonable doubt his mind wasn't playing tricks on him. In all the winters he had locked himself away in the woods to write, he had never seen a horse out here before.

It was hard to judge how far away the horse was, Leonard guessed it couldn't be more than fifty yards from them. The closer they got to the horse the louder Mordecai barked until finally Leonard caught a glimpse of a tiny pony. Leonard had his hands full, what with Mordecai getting over excited at the sight of his new-found friend, the lamp in his hand and the pony coming upon him out of the darkness. He couldn't afford to let Mordecai go so he tied the dog to a sapling, hung the lantern in the tree and moved closer to the pony.

The howling wind and driving snow compounded by the darkness made it a frightening experience for the old man. It struck him as funny the thoughts that came to him in this life or death situation. *I can't die out here. Who's going to finish my manuscript? I can't leave the story half finished.*

When Leonard finally reached the pony he nearly fell back in shock. There was a little girl collapsed across the pony's back. Immediately, the old man felt for a pulse on the child's frozen neck, but could find none. He had to get the pony and the frozen child back to his cabin, but she would have to stay on the pony's back. He couldn't carry her, he had enough trouble staying on his own feet.

Taking the reins, Leonard led the pony over to the tree and untied Mordecai. The dog barked excitedly and Leonard had to shout to calm him down. He held the dog's leash in one hand, and with the other he held the reins. "Let's go home, boy," he encouraged Mordecai to take them back to the cabin.

Leonard didn't know what on earth he was going to do with the tiny body of the dead girl. His cell phone didn't work near the cabin. To make a call he had to hike for miles to the big hill, climb to the top and hope for a signal. He cursed himself for not buying that satellite phone. Despite its huge expense in comparison with a cell phone, a satellite phone would have come in very handy right about now. It was yet another one of those things he had been meaning to get, but hadn't got around to. He promised himself he was definitely going to buy one now.

Leonard tripped, stumbled and cursed all the way back to the cabin. He felt the familiar ground beneath his feet, long before he actually saw the building. With the cabin now in sight, Leonard let Mordecai off his leash and tied Toby's reins to a wooden post that formed part of the veranda around the log cabin. Carefully he lifted the child off the pony's back and carried her lifeless form inside the cabin. Kicking the door back with his heel, he put his back against the heavy oak and shut it firmly against the force of the elements. Leonard Rivers sat down in his huge armchair in front of the fire, with the child across his lap. Mordecai came over and sat down by his master.

"Poor baby," he said gently stroking the frozen hair away from Emma's face. "Such a beautiful child; oh, how heartbroken your family is going to be and right before Christmas too. Poor baby," he said again, hugging the lifeless child to him. "Oh, Mordecai, this is a sad night," the old man said, his eyes glistening over with tears. "You've done well, Mordecai, you should be proud of yourself, it's not your fault."

O'Malley's Cottage

The old man wasn't ashamed to cry. His chest heaved with his sobs, causing the little girl's body to rise up and down against his chest.
The huge dog got up from the side of the armchair and began to lick the child's face. Leonard, physically and emotionally drained fell asleep with the girl in his arms. Mordecai pressed his massive head between the old man's arm and the child's face. Neither man nor child stirred. The wind continued to howl outside the cabin, there was the occasional loud crack as a dead tree snapped like a dry twig, its huge trunk collapsing against nearby trees, felling the smaller ones, sometimes snagging in the branches of the bigger and stronger, sometimes falling with a dull thud onto the snow covered ground. Inside the cabin, the fire crackled, the lamp hissed and Mordecai continued to whine.

* * *

Robby, now home from the vets was asleep by the side of Rebecca's bed. Suddenly he sat bolt upright and began barking. Rachael rushed into Rebecca's bedroom. When she entered the room Rebecca was groggily easing herself upright, pushing herself up against the pillows in a state of confusion. Then Robby began to howl, something she had never heard him do before.
Had they but known it, Mordecai stopped barking and broke into a howl at exactly the same time as Robby started howling. The two dogs were miles away, there was no way they could have heard each other, it was just not possible, the distance was far too great.
The old man stirred and woke with the child lying across his lap. The fire had died in the hearth. Stiffly Leonard eased the girl's body down in front of the fireplace and tossed a few more logs on the fire. Mordecai began to lick her face again. He

repeatedly pushed her head with his snout, barking and pawing at her chest.

"Easy, boy. I'm sorry, but we were just too late."

"O'Malley, am I in heaven?" The child spoke in a weak voice.

"God bless you, child," the old man exclaimed in wonder. "Mordecai here found you lost in the woods." He patted the Newfoundland on the head. "My name is Leonard Rivers, and this is Mordecai."

"You're not O'Malley?"

"No, my dear, I'm not."

"You're not going to hurt me are you?" A terrified look crossed her face.

"Good God, no. We need to get you warmed up, you're frozen right through to the core and those clothes are only keeping the cold in now and the heat out."

"Where's Toby?"

"Toby, is he the Shetland pony?"

"Yes."

"He's outside. Tell you what, I have a shed that's practically empty, why don't I put him in there for the night. I'll get him some fresh water." He stood unsteadily. "I left him with the rest of the hay you brought with you, he's probably eaten it all by now. Let me get you something warm to drink first, young lady."

"My name's Emma. O'Malley always took care of the horses before himself."

"Well, I think O'Malley would say that under the present circumstances I should attend to you first, you're in far worse shape than your Toby. Emma, you are not in the best of condition and if I don't get your temperature to rise, you might not be with us in the morning. You won't warm up enough on your own, you're suffering from hypothermia. You sit by the fire, while I fetch you a hot drink and then I'll sort Toby out, I'll only be a minute."

Thankfully, the water in the cast iron kettle by the fireplace was still hot enough to make Emma a cup of hot chocolate, into which Leonard added a huge dollop of honey, stirring it rapidly until it dissolved. He held Emma's limp body and helped her take small sips of the warm drink. When she had drunk it all, he made her as comfortable as he could in his armchair in front of the fire and rushed outside to attend to the pony, grabbing a bucket of water from beside the fireplace that he'd been topping up with fresh snow, then grabbed the lantern, leaving Mordecai with Emma by the fire.

Outside, Leonard threw open the shed door and like a man possessed, he grabbed boxes, tools, hoses and what most women would refer to as *junk* and piled it all up in a heap outside the shed, then he went back in to get his mountain bike, the old gas lawnmower and his ancient, temperamental chainsaw and piled them up next to the boxes.

Glancing quickly around the interior of the shed he satisfied himself that there was nothing left to hurt the pony. He untied Toby's reins from the post and grabbing an armful of loose hay, he led the pony into the shed. He then dumped the hay in the far left corner of the shed and left the bucket of water in the far right corner. Having been brought up with horses, it was no problem for him to remove Toby's bridle and his bareback blanket. The shed was big enough for a full-grown horse, so the Shetland pony had lots of room to move around. Leonard stroked Toby's neck and head and told him what a brave little pony he was. Then he left the shed, securing the door behind him. He walked briskly back to the cabin, lantern in one hand, bridle in the other with the blanket draped over his arm.

When Leonard entered the warm cabin he found Emma slumped in the armchair, shivering more violently than before. Quickly he pulled the bed closer to the fire, pushing the armchair out of the way and made up the bed for her. He draped a blanket near the fire to get warm, removed Emma's outer clothing and wrapped the little girl up in the warm blanket. She was far too weak to help him; he picked up her skinny little body and put her in his bed. Then he threw more logs on the fire and piled the remaining blankets over the sleeping girl.

The child's body was like ice. Leonard draped more heavy wool blankets near the fire and as they warmed he continually replaced the blankets that had cooled with the warmer ones. This went on throughout the night; Leonard dozing in his armchair, waking with a start, changing Emma's blanket, draping the old one by the fire to warm and then collapsing back into the armchair. He was terrified he would fall asleep in the armchair, only to awake and find the child dead in his bed. He didn't think he'd ever drunk so much coffee in his life and was sure he'd be wired for a week. The cabin soon became quite hot, too hot for Mordecai who moved away from the fire, preferring to sit by the door to cool down.

During the night Emma cried out in pain. Leonard knew this was a good sign. Her body was beginning to warm up and was at last sending warm blood to the extremities. The price to pay for fingers and toes warming up was excruciating pain. Leonard knew the child was frightened of the pain, and spoke to her gently, doing his best to reassure. Finally her sobs lessened and she fell into a deep sleep.

Periodically, Leonard would check that she was still breathing. Throughout the night he kept watch, and whenever he failed to detect the rise and fall of her chest he would press his fingers against her neck in search of a pulse. When daylight finally came, he was totally exhausted, but the child's body was no longer cold. The bed finally felt warm. Even for a devout atheist, Leonard Rivers raised his head and looked upwards, "Thank you," he mouthed. He became quite emotional, tears forming in his eyes.

Emma was very groggy when she finally awoke, but alert enough to remind Leonard that Toby needed to be attended to. She was going to do it herself, but the old man wouldn't hear of it. He

O'Malley's Cottage

went out to the shed to check on Toby, taking some of the sweet feed from Emma's backpack, Mordecai following behind him. There was precious little food left for the pony and Leonard knew that Toby was going to have to fend for himself during the daylight hours. He recalled that Shetland ponies were a hardy breed and no doubt this one was resourceful enough to find something under the snow to eat, but he didn't want to let the pony out on its own, just in case it ran off into the wilderness and was gone forever. Emma would never forgive him for that. He decided the best course of action at the moment was to convert the shed door into a stable door. Trying to work on the door with Toby attempting to barge his way out wasn't working very well. Leonard returned to the cabin to get the bridle, glad to see that Emma was still tucked up in his bed by the fire and had fallen fast asleep. Quietly, he crept back out to the shed with Toby's bridle.

     With Toby now hitched to the veranda, it didn't take the old man long to convert the shed door into a stable door. When completed, he led Toby back inside, closed the bottom half of the door and left the top half open, secured by a hook and eye. Toby seemed happy with the new arrangement when Leonard removed the bridle and went back inside the cabin to get some fresh water for the pony.

     When he entered the cabin he found Emma sitting up in bed with her hair all over the place.

     "Young lady, that is the worst case of morning hair I have ever seen," laughed the old man. "I'd get you a mirror but you'd faint at the sight of yourself."

     Emma smiled and attempted a faint laugh.

     "And how are you feeling this morning?"

     "Hungry and I need to use the washroom."

     "I'm afraid it's outside. You best get dressed warmly and take the toilet seat with you. I keep it inside, especially after the time my bottom froze to the seat. I had to stand with my backside towards the fire until the ice melted and the toilet seat dropped off."

Emma giggled and Leonard was relieved to see her feeling so much better. "It's to the left of the door," he said. "Porridge okay for breakfast?"

"Yes, please." Emma jumped out of bed and pulled on her clothes. She began patting Mordecai on the head affectionately. "How's Toby?"

"See for yourself. I turned the shed into a stable for him. At some point we're going to have to let him out to get his own food, I don't think he'll go too far away, not if he knows you're here and he has a nice stable to come back to. I'll rig up some kind of line so he can move about, but can't run off, just to be on the safe side."

"Thank you for saving my life, Mr. Rivers."

Leonard looked at the little girl clutching the wooden toilet seat under her arm and smiled. "You're very welcome, Emma. The real heroes are Mordecai and Toby, if Mordecai hadn't known you were out there and kicked up such a fuss, I'm afraid there wouldn't have been any saving for me to do."

When Emma walked back through the door, shaking off the snow she remarked, "That's one gross toilet, Mr. Rivers."

"I'm sorry, my dear," laughed the old man. "Had I known you were coming I would have had one installed with gold taps and a marble floor. What did you think of the stable by the way?"

"Beautiful. Toby told me to tell you that he really likes it and asked that we keep the door open so he can go in and out."

"I'll see what I can fix up for him."

"How's the porridge coming on, anything I can do to help you?" Emma was surprised at how much the old man reminded her of O'Malley.

"Sure, fetch some snow in that bucket to the right of the door and put it in that bucket by the fire, we need some more water for tea, and hand washing."

O'Malley's Cottage

"How do you take a bath here?"
"Oh, I break the ice on the lake nearby and take a polar plunge once a week." Leonard couldn't keep a straight face.
"You do not." Emma wasn't sure if she believed him or not.
"Damn right, I don't. I wash bit-by-bit using the bucket. Like you, there's not much of me to wash so it doesn't take much water and it doesn't take too long either. Okay, this porridge is ready." Leonard removed a cauldron from a hook inside the fireplace. "Grab a seat, there's brown sugar or real maple syrup. Try not to get anything on my papers please."
"What do you do here all winter?" Emma poured a generous helping of maple syrup over her porridge as she spoke.
"I'm a writer." Leonard added a spoonful of thick cut orange marmalade to his porridge.
Emma stared in disbelief. "O'Malley used to do the same thing with his porridge."
Over breakfast Emma told Leonard all about herself and her family, about coming to O'Malley's Cottage, all the good things that had happened and all the bad things since O'Malley had died. Leonard listened intently to her story, his writer's mind thinking how he could weave what she was telling him into a story.
"This has all the makings of a good novel, Emma, would you mind if I taped this? Perhaps this evening we could sit down together and go over it again, that's if you don't mind. I have an idea that might interest your mother. It's the strangest thing, your Aunt Rachael actually turned down one of my novels, can you believe that? I bet she kicked herself afterwards when it went on to become a best seller. She'll be shocked to think that you and I have become such good friends, which just goes to show what a small world it is after all. Perhaps you've read one of my children's books from the series, *The Amazing Adventures of Grandpa Ramsbottom*. Emma shook her head. "You haven't? What a shame. Well it just

so happens that I have a copy of the first one here somewhere. It's called, *The Flying Machine.*"

Leonard got up from the table and rummaged through his bookcase, pulling out books he had written and books that he had read and enjoyed. "Oh, this was a good story, I think I'll read that one again," he said, leaving a Lee Child crime novel out on the counter. He continued his search through the books, until he found what he was looking for. "Ah ha. Here it is," he said triumphantly, dropping a copy of the book down in front of Emma. "A gift from me too you, Emma, with love."

"Thank you, Mr. Rivers, that's very kind of you, I promise I'll treasure it for ever and always." Emma was absolutely thrilled to bits with her gift.

"Ah, before I forget, allow me to write something personal on the inside." Rummaging through the clutter of papers on the table he found a pen. "Here we are." He wrote, *To Emma and Toby. Welcome back to earth, Emma, after your short trip to heaven. With much love, your good friends Leonard Rivers and Mordecai the Newfoundland dog. May all your dreams come true.*

"Can I take this book home with me when we leave?"

"Absolutely, Emma. If we run out of paper we can always use some of the pages to light the fire. You know, Emma, you were very lucky not to have got frostbitten. I'm amazed at how quickly you've recovered. As soon as the weather clears and you're stronger we must head out and get you home. Your poor mother must be going out of her mind with worry. We'll make for the big hill that I told you about, it's about a day's hike from here. I'm going to have to climb to the top with my cell phone and see if I can get word out that you're okay, while you stay at the bottom of the hill with Mordecai and Toby."

"I can't take Toby back, they're going to have him killed." Emma sounded desperate.

"Emma, I give you my word that is not going to happen, in fact I am going to see to it that they sell me Toby and I'll give him to you afterwards."

"They won't do it, Mr. Rivers. My mother tried, I think that has something to do with her getting hurt by that horrible man, they won't do it."

"Emma, nothing and nobody is going to hurt Toby, I will not let it happen, and if they won't sell Toby to me, I'm damn well going to steal him myself and put him somewhere safe, where only you and I and your mom know where he is and where he'll be really happy. And that's a promise, okay?"

"Okay, Mr. Rivers, I believe you."

"Now, what would you like to know about me young lady?"

"Are you married?"

"Not anymore, she did the sensible thing and left me, I just wasn't any fun anymore I guess. Once I got my nose into writing, I would lock myself away in my study for days on end and never come out again. One morning I went downstairs to get myself a cup of coffee only to find she'd already left me. She'd been gone a week and I didn't even realize it!"

"I think you're funny, Mr. Rivers."

"Thank you, Emma, at least one person in the world thinks so. Next question."

"Do you have any children?"

"Yes, one son. He's a lawyer in Toronto, we love each other, but we're always busy."

"How old is he?"

"He's somewhere in his late thirties I think, I'd have to work that out."

"And how old are you?"

"Too old really to be spending my winters alone out here. I'm seventy something or other. I try not to remember my age anymore. Sometimes I feel like I'm in my twenties and other times

I feel like I'm a hundred and five. I'll clear up here, you go and check on Toby, take Mordecai with you, but do not, I repeat, do not wander off into the woods."

"I know, I know," replied Emma grabbing her hat, mittens, coat and boots.

"Don't tell me, let me guess. O'Malley told you the same thing."

"He did, Mr. Rivers, you could have been twins you know," she giggled and ran out of the cabin with Mordecai on her heels. Leonard felt so happy, the little waif of a girl had brought such pleasure to his lonely life.

During the nights that followed, Leonard insisted that Emma continued to sleep in his bed by the fire. He had aired out her sleeping bag and she was now able to use it. The old man slept on the old thread worn couch with Mordecai curled up on the rug next to him on the floor.

After the second night Emma closed her book, looked up at Leonard and said, "I really enjoyed the story, Mr. Rivers, it was very exciting and funny too. Do you have any more stories?"

Leonard Rivers sat on the edge of the bed. "Tell you what, Emma, I'll make one up from inside my head right now, in fact, let's make it up together. I'll start if you like and then you tell some of it and we'll go on like that, back and forth."

Emma finally fell asleep. Both she and Leonard had tears in their eyes, not from sorrow, but from sheer joy, they had both made each other laugh so much.

* * *

As Christmas approached the police decided to keep a skeleton crew on standby at the Command Post. At some point, someone was going to have the unenviable task of telling Rebecca that they were, *pulling the plug.* It was agreed by the powers that be, that if there were no developments by the day after Boxing

Day, the Command Post would be shutdown. Nothing would be said to Rebecca and her family until that day arrived.

Rebecca kept telling everyone that Emma was still alive, she could feel it deep inside her soul. If something had happened to Emma she knew she would have felt it. She didn't want to hear anyone say, *You have to prepare yourself for the worst, Rebecca.* Until someone brought her Emma's body she would never believe she was dead. She began to get a sense of how Donna and Roger must have felt when they lost their own daughter all those years ago and the lifetime of grief they had endured.

Chapter Twenty-Three

On December 23rd, there was a break in the weather. Emma had now been missing for five days. The police helicopter finally took off and began the relentless search of the forest that extended all the way into Algonquin Provincial Park.

At 10 a.m. Leonard and Emma stood outside the cabin, about to leave. Emma riding Toby, Mordecai on his leash held by Leonard.

"Emma, I'm an old man, in pretty good shape though, but still an old man. If God or the Devil claims me on this journey, you must keep going. I've done everything I can to prepare you, like O'Malley would have done. You've got to make it to the top of the big hill. Don't use my cell phone until you are at the top. It won't take long for you to be rescued after that."

"Mr. Rivers, we are going to make it out together, don't worry."

"Just in case we don't, I want you to take this envelope out of my pocket and give it to my son."

"I promise, but I won't need to."

"Okay then, let's get going."

Toby seemed anxious to be off. Mordecai began jumping around like a puppy, glad to be getting some outdoor exercise at last. Progress through the snow had been slow, Leonard only had one pair of snowshoes, they were far too big for a child anyway. For most of the way Emma rode Toby. Leonard had been hoping that by the end of the day, at least before it got dark, they would have reached the big hill. The going was much harder than he had anticipated. They didn't make the hill that day.

At 4 p.m. he checked his own map and soon found what he was looking for, an old hunting camp. They would make camp there for the night. Quickly he and Emma gathered wood and he allowed Emma to set the fire in the old woodstove inside the ramshackle cabin. There were a couple of old bunks inside, with damp, filthy looking mattresses on them. Leonard used the mattresses to block some of the draughts leaking through the cracks in the walls and door. Emma insisted on bringing Toby inside, after some negotiation Leonard finally agreed as long as she tethered him near the doorway at the other end of the small cabin. Mordecai seemed to be enjoying every minute of the adventure, and at times he was a bit of a nuisance.

Together Leonard and Emma prepared their evening meal of meatballs from a can, boiled potatoes and carrots, also from a can. Emma was in complete agreement that a glove of garlic should be sliced up and added to the meatballs together with some ginger and pepper. For dessert Leonard opened a can of rice pudding and boiled up some water for Jasmine tea to have with the ginger cookies he had brought along. That night they both slept soundly.

Toby was the first one to stir in the morning, anxious to be let out to find something to eat. Emma had given him the last of the sweet feed the night before and he was hungry. Mordecai bounded ahead of her as she led Toby out of the hut and tethered him to a tree.

After a breakfast of porridge, brown sugar and tea the adventurers set off again. By midmorning they had reached the foot of the big hill, the top of which crested the tree line. As agreed, Leonard climbed the hill, while Emma waited below with Toby. Mordecai took off after his Master; no amount of calling from Emma would bring him back. She didn't mind, she already had her best friend at her side and she knew Leonard would be a man of his word, he would not let anything happen to Toby.

Eventually Emma lost sight of the old man and began to worry. He told her not to get concerned about him until she hadn't seen him again for forty-five minutes. By then he would be standing on top of the hill, where she would be able to see him.

O'Malley's Cottage

His age now beginning to show; the old man had to make a few rest stops on the way up the hill, it was much steeper than he remembered. Finally he made it to the top, with a clear blue-sky overhead and the sun shining down on him. He pulled out his cell phone and dialed his son's cell phone.

"Dad, is everything all right?" came the response when Chuck Rivers answered his cell phone.

"No it isn't. Listen carefully and do not interrupt until I've finished. Have you been watching the news about the missing girl up here?"

"Yes, as a matter of fact I have. I'm pretty sure I bumped into the family at the Tim Hortons in Bancroft back in the summer, in fact I'm almost positive it was them, why?"

"Listen, my cell phone won't last long. I have her here with me and I'm bringing her out. Tell her mother she's fine and in good hands, hope to be out by Christmas Day."

Worried about the cell phone battery dying, the old man quickly told his son exactly what he wanted done. Before Chuck could answer, Leonard's cell phone went dead, that was his last call.

Emma was very relieved when she saw the old man walking slowly back down the hill accompanied by Mordecai at his side.

"Okay, that's done." He was puffing and panting. "Just let me get my breath back. I should have sent you up there with your young legs, or maybe ridden Toby up there, eh lad?" he patted the pony's neck.

"Do you know how to ride a horse, Mr. Rivers, because if you don't I could teach you?"

"It was a long, long time ago the last time I rode a horse Emma. My granddad kept horses on his farm, big Belgians, probably like the ones O'Malley has on the farm. I'd love to see them when I get you home."

O'Malley's Cottage

* * *

The telephone rang in the kitchen at O'Malley's Cottage. Rachael picked it up. She was furious with the television coverage of Emma's disappearance. They had made the whole affair into something that sounded like a soap opera, even going so far as to mention Rebecca's brutal attack at the hands of her neighbor. Rachael prayed to God that, *The Doctor* would be true to his word and make everything right again. *That bastard will never leave the walls of the prison except in a coffin,* she said to herself.

"Hello? Could I speak to Rebecca Brown please, it's very urgent."

"You another damn reporter? I already told you people, I will not allow you to interview my sister. How many times do you parasites have to be told."

"Ma'm, I'm not a reporter. My name's Chuck Rivers, I'm a lawyer, the good kind. I believe we've met. I need to talk to her about Emma."

"I don't think so, Mr. Rivers, have a nice day." Rachael slammed down the phone.

Rebecca stumbled sleepily into the kitchen. "Who was that?"

"Some nut, says we met. Said his name was Chuck Rivers. I don't know any Chuck Rivers," she said, and just as she said it recognition struck. *Oh, my God. Tim Hortons, Bancroft.*

"He said it was urgent, he said he needed to talk to you about Emma. I'm sorry, sis, I thought it was another reporter."

"My purse, my purse." Rebecca pointed to her dresser closet. "I still have his business card in my purse."

"Here it is." Rachael snatched up Rebecca's purse and handed it over. "I thought you said you'd thrown his card out."

Rebecca smiled like a teenage girl caught in a white lie.

She tipped her purse upside down on the kitchen table, rummaged through the pile of personal belongings until she found Chuck Rivers' business card.

Just as she held it up the phone rang again and Rebecca snatched up the receiver.

"Chuck is that you?"

"Yes, is that you, Rebecca?"

"Yes, yes it is, do you have some news about Emma? Please tell me you do."

"She's with my father and she's alive and well." He shouted into the phone.

Rachael was standing close to her sister in case the news was bad. When Rebecca cried out and dropped the phone, Rachael caught her in freefall. "She's alive. She's alive," Rebecca sobbed into Rachael's arms. "Oh, my God, my baby's alive."

"Hello. Hello. Is there somebody there?" Chuck was shouting into the phone, his faint voice coming from the floor of O'Malley's Cottage.

Everybody rushed into the kitchen, unsure what had happened and fearing that Emma had been found dead. That didn't make sense they were saying amongst themselves, the police would have told Rebecca that personally, not over the telephone.

Rachael picked up the phone. "This better not be some kind of sick joke, Mr. Rivers. My sister can't take any more, she's at breaking point all ready. I'll kill you with my bare hands if you're lying, I swear it."

"Just listen to me, damn it. My father spends his winters in the middle of the woods, he's a writer, he likes peace and quiet. You've probably heard of him; Leonard Rivers."

For a moment Rachael was speechless. "Leonard Rivers. The Leonard Rivers?"

"Yes, that's him, one and the same."

"Of course I've heard of him."

"Emma and my father kind of stumbled upon each other in

the middle of the woods. The weather was too bad to get her back and she was near death when he found her. He's on his way through the woods with her now and expects to be with you, he said, on Christmas Day, if the weather holds that is."

"Why didn't he just call us from his cabin, surely he has a phone?"

"Lady he lives in an old cabin with no electricity, no running water and an outside privy. The only phone he has is a cell phone that he keeps charged by a solar panel he got from Canadian Tire. The trouble is there's no signal where he is. He has to climb up a big hill that's about a day's hike from the cabin to make any calls. The old man is in his seventies, he's doing his best. Believe me, he'll get Emma home safe and sound of that I'm sure. By the way, he asks that you clear out your garage, get some straw on the ground, some clean hay and sweet feed; Emma's bringing home Toby. She wants to know if her mom got her letter, she left it on her dressing table and hopes you're not all mad at her. Oh, one last thing before I go. Would you ask Rebecca if my father and I can join your family for Christmas Dinner?"

"Why don't you ask her yourself. Hang on a minute. I'll fill everyone in on the details, and Mr. Rivers?"

"Call me Chuck, please."

"Chuck then. Thank you, thank you, thank you. Emma's alive. You'll have to excuse me a minute, Mr. Rivers, I'm sorry, Chuck, I'm so emotional. Please, please stay on the line, don't go anywhere."

"Rachael, I'm not going anywhere."

Everyone began squeezing into the kitchen to hear the news. Emma was alive.

"Rebecca, he wants to ask you something." Rachael handed the phone to her sister then ran upstairs to Emma's bedroom.

"Chuck, thank you, thank you so much for this wonderful

O'Malley's Cottage

news." Rebecca sobbed into the phone.

"It's okay, Rebecca. Everything's okay now." His voice was deep and soothing.

"I've kept your card in my purse like a good omen ever since you gave it to me. I just knew it was a good sign. My sister told me to throw it out, I'm so glad I didn't." Rebecca clutched his business card as though it was the winning lottery ticket. "I'm sure the police will send in a rescue team to get them, do you know where they are?"

"I'm sure they won't be too hard to find, but I doubt that Emma will leave Toby to the mercy of the forest and I don't think my dad can handle a pony and his Newfoundland dog. Are you still there?"

"I'm sorry, I'm just overwhelmed. Oh, before you go, Rachael said you wanted to ask me something?"

"Rebecca, my dad's bringing Emma home any day now. He wanted me to ask you if we could share Christmas with you? I know that's kinda short notice and we hardly know each other."

"Chuck, I would be so happy if you would, but what about your own family, you must have a wife and children of your own?"

"I'm not married, Rebecca. Okay, listen; give me a couple of cell phone numbers there as well, so I can be sure to reach you if I have any more updates. And you're not to worry, Leonard Rivers never let anyone down in his life and he won't let you down either."

Rebecca gave Chuck her cell phone number and Rachael's. She knew she was attracted to this man that she didn't even know and had only met fleetingly, and she knew he was attracted to her. The thought soon vanished when she thought of her daughter coming home to her.

"See you for Christmas," were his parting words.

Rachael came downstairs clutching Emma's letter. When she pulled out the dressing table she found the letter behind it, lodged in a crevice where the back panel joined the frame.

O'Malley's Cottage

"Emma wanted to know if we got her note, I just found it wedged behind her dressing table. I haven't looked at it." She handed the note to Rebecca.
All eyes were on Rebecca as she sat down at the kitchen table and silently read the note from her daughter.
It had a big pink love heart on the front, with the word MOM in red sprinkles across the heart.

Dear Mom, please don't be mad at me. If someone was going to kill someone you love I know you would do everything you could to save them, even if it meant risking your own life. Toby has been my best friend and I love him with all my heart. If I let those horrible people kill him I would never be happy again, knowing that I did nothing to try and save him. I'm truly sorry that this is going to hurt you, especially when you have been through so much hurt already. Every second of the day I will miss you and every second of the day I love you. I hope you will forgive me and not be cross with me when I come home again. If anything bad should happen to me I want to be buried next to O'Malley.
I love you always. Emma XXXOOOXXX

Rebecca clutched the letter to her heart and looked up, not at the ceiling, but far away to a distant place. "Thank you, God, thank you," she cried out through her tears. "Rachael, take me to church would you, sis, I have to see Father O'Ryan."
Chuck had told Rebecca where he thought Emma and his father were likely to be, having been to the big hill a few times with his father in the past. The police helicopter was quickly dispatched and found the hill with Leonard's snowshoe prints and Mordecai's huge paw prints in the snow leading up to the top of the hill. The woods were too dense to see exactly which path Leonard and Emma had taken from there.

O'Malley's Cottage

Emma heard the sound of the helicopter buzzing overhead before Leonard did. A few hours later they thought they could hear the sound of snowmobiles somewhere off in the distance. By nightfall Leonard found the next hunting camp he had been searching for. A light dusting of snow had covered their tracks, concealing them once more from their rescuers.

"Well, Emma, this is likely to be our last wilderness dinner together." They crouched around the woodstove, eating another can of meatballs with spaghetti this time. "You are the most remarkable young lady I have ever had the pleasure of meeting and I hope we will keep in touch and remain friends."

They chinked their plastic mugs together in a toast of friendship and were soon fast asleep on the floor by the woodstove.

Chapter Twenty-Four

"Merry Christmas, Emma." Leonard shook the little girl awake. "My present to you today is going to be giving you back to your mother, and you will be the best Christmas present ever. Come on, let's get cracking unless you want to spend another night in the wilderness eating meatballs again."

Despite their excitement, Leonard insisted they set off with a hearty breakfast. As he put it, "We're not out of the woods yet."

Eventually they came out by the lake. Leonard didn't want to risk taking a shortcut across it, they'd come this far without disaster. He didn't know this lake, there were possibly undercurrents where the ice was dangerously thin. To fall through the ice would likely mean they would both perish, including Toby and Mordecai.

Emma's surroundings became more familiar to her, she finally recognized the picnic spot where she and her mother had sat by the lake. She saw the shoreline where she had galloped on Star, watched by her teacher, O'Malley.

By midday they turned left onto the road and were now walking past O'Malley's old farm. Emma pointed out the horses to Leonard, all four of them were galloping around the field. She was surprised there were no vehicles parked in the long driveway leading up to the farmhouse, even O'Malley's smashed-up old pick-truck that had been dumped on the front lawn was now gone. The farm looked eerily deserted.

"That's O'Malley's farm, isn't it, Emma?"

"It used to be."

"It's a beautiful looking farm."

"The farm's beautiful, but not the people that moved into it."

When they came in sight of O'Malley's Cottage, Emma was

O'Malley's Cottage

confused by all the police vehicles, especially the large one that looked like a mobile home, parked next to the driveway. Suddenly the whole place erupted with activity, they could see police officers running in all directions.

"I think you'd better dismount and take a firm hold of Toby's reins if I were you, Emma. You're in for quite the homecoming that will likely spook Toby."

The police inspector looked through his binoculars and confirmed that it was Emma coming up the road towards the cottage. He lined all his men and women up on either side of the road to welcome her home and sent Constable Mandy Richards into O'Malley's Cottage to fetch Rebecca.

A huge cheer went up from all the men and women who had worked so hard and endured so much themselves to search for the missing child. In disbelief they watched Emma walking towards them. Convinced that she would be returning in a body bag, men and women openly wept. This was a wonderful Christmas gift for them too, as so often their days ended in tragedy, but not today. Those die-hard members of the media that had stuck it out were rewarded for their patience and filmed the approach of a miracle. Even the police inspector had tears of joy running down his cheeks.

Emma spotted a slight figure bursting through the crowd, running along the snow-covered road towards her. She recognized her mother and handed Toby's reins to Leonard. Then she ran as fast as she could to meet her mother. They fell into each other's arms, crying as they embraced. Rebecca pulled Emma to her and hugged her child as if she would never let her go again.

Leonard held Toby's reins in one hand and Mordecai's leash in the other. Through tears he said, "Merry Christmas, Rebecca."

Rebecca looked up at him, her eyes glistening. "Merry Christmas, Mr. Rivers. Thank you."

Those who had gathered at the bottom of the driveway, stayed where they were, allowing Rebecca and her daughter this most intimate and precious of moments. People all over the world were glued to their television screens watching this spectacle live. The picture of a mother embracing her daughter after such a terrible ordeal would be front-page news in the morning newspapers.

Rebecca, arm tightly around Emma's shoulders walked back to where Leonard was standing with Toby and Mordecai. As she did so, Robby raced up behind and began jumping up at Emma, she grabbed him around the neck hugging him tightly.

Rebecca wrapped her arms around the old man and hugged him to her while Emma played with the two dogs, as though nothing in the world was really any different because of her absence.

Together Rebecca walked arm in arm with Leonard on one side and Emma cuddled into her on the other. Leonard, with Toby's reins still in his other hand, stopped a hundred yards from the cottage and let mother and daughter go on ahead.

In a rare moment of human kindness, not one reporter stuck a microphone into the face of mother and child as they entered the sanctuary of O'Malley's Cottage.

Chuck Rivers emerged from the crowd and walked towards his father, embracing the tiny man in a huge bear hug. They shared a private conversation that seemed to please the old man immensely and headed back towards the cottage.

Leonard wasn't so lucky with the reporters. "There are only two heroes in all this," he told them. "One is a Shetland pony named Toby and the other a Newfoundland dog call Mordecai. Since neither of them can speak a word of English, there's not much to tell except Merry Christmas to all of you."

Chuck took Toby's reins and led the little pony into the garage. The light was on inside, with fresh hay in a small manger that Brian and Alison had built and a bucket of fresh water. In another bucket was a scoop of sweet feed. Chuck took the bridle and bareback blanket off the pony and then he and his father approached the front door of O'Malley's Cottage.

"I think I need a stiff drink of brandy, a hot shower and something good to eat," Leonard announced as they were welcomed inside.

Rebecca hugged him again and kissed him on his whiskery cheeks, thanking him over and over again for saving her daughter's life. George came up and shook the old man's hand, a look of deep gratitude in his eyes.

"Ah, you're the unlucky man," said Leonard, leaving George looking puzzled.

Pressed to tell his story, Leonard kept it short. "One of your heroes is probably lying down in the straw in the garage, totally exhausted like me and the other is sleeping by the woodstove in the kitchen. I merely did what my dog Mordecai told me to do. Your daughter's pony–by the way my son, Chuck, whom you've already had the pleasure of meeting has just confirmed to me that Toby now officially belongs to Emma." Loud cheers and clapping filled the room. "As I was saying, Emma's pony, led her to my cabin, my Newfoundland dog Mordecai heard them coming, and he merely dragged me to them and dragged me back with them to my cabin. The rest is now history. Rebecca, could I trouble you for a hot shower?"

Rachael took hold of the old man's arm and guided him up the stairs, with Duncan following behind carrying a large glass of brandy.

Rebecca turned to Chuck, placing a hand on his arm. "I must say thank you to all those police officers and volunteers that have been here every day looking for my daughter and manning the Command Post over Christmas. Would you mind coming with me?"

The huge man put a protective arm around Rebecca's shoulders and gently guided her towards the line of rescuers.

O'Malley's Cottage

Rebecca thanked the police inspector personally and shook the hand of every police officer and civilian who had been there trying to find Emma. Slowly the number of police and media vehicles disappeared along with the Command Post as everyone returned to their loved ones to celebrate their own Christmas, until finally only family and friends remained behind at O'Malley's Cottage.

* * *

After a wonderful dinner, Leonard Rivers stood up and requested everyone gather around him, and specifically asked Rebecca and Emma to join him at the far end of the dining room. On a signal from his father, Chuck Rivers stepped forward with a large manila envelope.

Leonard accepted the envelope and then turned to address the room. "Ladies and gentlemen. I have a very important announcement to make. Before I do, I want you to join with me in celebrating the safe return of a truly remarkable young lady. Ladies and gentleman, Emma Brown." A loud cheer filled the cottage accompanied by thunderous applause.

"And secondly, I would like you all to congratulate a most remarkable woman, who has endured much pain and suffering, but who never once doubted that her daughter Emma would return to O'Malley's Cottage, alive and well. Please raise a cheer to, Rebecca Brown." More loud cheering and applause. "On a personal note, I would like to thank the chef, Duncan Dashwood, and his wonderful assistant, Rachael, for a magnificent meal. Having now tasted the excellent cuisine produced by this man, I cannot wait to return to Toronto and feast at one of his restaurants. A little plug for you, Duncan." There was laughter and more applause.

"And now, the moment that is going to give me the second greatest sense of pleasure today, second only to the successful

O'Malley's Cottage

return of my good friend Emma." Leonard turned to his son Chuck. "I would like to say a personal thank you to my son for turning another impossibility into a miracle and at such short notice. I know he has worked non-stop on this project, which I gave to him when I was standing alone on top of that hill, with Emma below, waiting for my return. My dear, Rebecca. I have been blessed with the pleasure of having met your charming daughter, Emma, under the most terrible of circumstances and to hear from her first hand, the tragedies and evil actions that man has cast upon you. As an honorable man, as a decent old man whose remaining sunrises are likely few, I wish to try and repair the damage that has been done to you and your daughter. I sent my son, Charles, on a mission to buy O'Malley's Cottage on my behalf, with the intention of giving the cottage to you, with no strings attached. Alas, I was unable to do this. When my son went to see Donna O'Malley to see if this could be done, she refused absolutely point blank. She had seen the television reports of your terrible plight and was moved by them. She sends her love to you and as a Christmas present she has given me permission to hand over the deeds of O'Malley's Cottage to you, Rebecca, to do with whatever you wish."
    There were gasps from everyone. Rebecca placed her hands against her cheeks in disbelief as Leonard Rivers handed Rebecca the envelope containing the deeds to O'Malley's Cottage and a personal letter from Donna herself.
    "As I was unable to buy the cottage for you," continued Leonard Rivers. "I decided to buy O'Malley's Farm for you instead. I have taken over the rental agreement of the cottage, until the purchase paperwork is complete and the ink dry. Once you are the legal owner of O'Malley's Farm, I hope you will rent it to my son, Chuck, who has decided he'd like to live there and has told me that if you continue to live at O'Malley's Cottage he will reside at the farm and take a job locally in his profession. He has also requested the help of Emma to assist him with the horses and wants to know if you will allow him to raise horses on your farm. Secondly, I

O'Malley's Cottage

would like the pleasure of visiting the farm from time to time. I would like you and I to write, what I hope will become a best seller, the story about you and Emma and O'Malley's Cottage. Hopefully your delightful sister, Rachael, will publish it, I would hate to be rejected by her a second time."

Leonard stole a glance at Rachael, who smiled back at him. "Emma, you are now the proud owner of all the horses on O'Malley's Farm along with the champion of them all, Toby the incredible Shetland pony. Rebecca, you will be free to do whatever you wish with the two properties, whatever your heart desires and if you hadn't already noticed, the farm is now vacant, your demons have left; forever."

Rebecca was so overwhelmed with emotion she couldn't speak. Rachael rushed to her sister's side and hugged her tightly. "It's finally over, little sister, no one's ever going to hurt you again, not now there's a Rivers flowing through the farm."

Chuck Rivers crouched down on the other side of Rebecca, taking her hand in his. "Amen to that, Miss Rachael."

As the evening wore on Chuck asked Rebecca if she would mind if he and his father spent the night at the farmhouse. He told her to do whatever she liked with the two properties and if she wanted to sell them both and move away he quite understood.

"You know, Rebecca, this is probably very presumptuous of me, but I really would like to be your next door neighbor and to get to know you better if that's okay with you. You can evict me at your whim you know."

"Chuck, why don't we start right now."
"What, evicting me already. I haven't even moved in."
"No silly. Would you take me over to the farm?"
"What, right now?"
"Yes, right now. Please, if that's okay."
"Of course, I'll drive you over there."

O'Malley's Cottage

Rebecca turned and smiled at Rachael. Rachael nodded her approval and Chuck led Rebecca out into the crisp night air. Leonard smiled to himself, watching his son walk outside with Rebecca.

He whispered to Rachael. "He's a good son, a good man and would make the most wonderful husband for Rebecca and a good stepfather to Emma." He put his hand behind his back and crossed his fingers.

Rachael took hold of the old man's arm. "Now, about this new book proposal, Leonard. I like it. This time there won't be a rejection letter." They both laughed and Leonard told her he forgave her.

Chuck drove Rebecca over to the farmhouse in silence. As they got out of his truck, Rebecca handed Chuck the key to the front door and he unlocked it, swinging the door open and waiting for Rebecca to walk inside. She hesitated at the threshold, pleasant memories flooding into her mind. For a minute she stood there looking inside, imagining the sound of O'Malley's cheery voice calling her into the kitchen where she would find him sitting at the harvest table reading a copy of the Farmer's Journal. She could smell the pleasant odor of freshly baked bread wafting down the hallway, and then there would be Donna standing in the hallway, brushing her flour covered hands on her apron and beckoning her inside with a big welcoming smile.

Chuck remained standing just behind Rebecca, not wanting to disturb the moment by talking. Rebecca slowly walked inside, surprised to see how clean and neat everything was. She expected to find it in a mess. Just before Rebecca entered the kitchen, she glanced back behind her, expecting to see Chuck standing there, he was still waiting patiently by the front door.

"What are you doing, Chuck?"

"Rebecca, this is your house now, I'm just being polite and waiting to be invited in."

"Oh, Chuck, you are such a gentleman, please come on in

O'Malley's Cottage

and don't be so silly besides, I can't accept a gift like this from your father, it's not right, I just don't feel right about it."

"No, Rebecca, it would not be right for you not to accept it, especially once you get to know my father. You have no idea the immense pleasure he gets from doing this. It would be like a slap in the face to him for you not to accept it, he obviously thinks very highly of you and your daughter. Lord knows you deserve it after all you've gone through. It's what O'Malley would want you to do if you stop and think about it."

"I can't get over how clean they left it?"

"Believe me, they didn't. I had an army of cleaners in here sorting the mess out on strict instructions from my father. It was to be spic and span before you set foot inside it and restored as near as possible to the way Donna and Roger had it. Those were his instructions."

"I can't believe you would go to all this trouble for me, Chuck, I just can't. And how did you get them to leave so quickly?"

"Quite simple. Money."

Chuck followed Rebecca into the kitchen. The woodstove was still alight, making the room as cozy as Rebecca remembered it. The oil furnace had kicked in, taking the chill off the rest of the old farmhouse.

"Come and sit down here, Chuck." Rebecca patted the back of O'Malley's old armchair, still positioned where it had always been, by the side of the woodstove. Chuck eased his huge frame into the armchair.

"This was O'Malley's chair wasn't it?"

"Yes, it was. I want you to humor me, Chuck Rivers. Close your eyes and you are not to open them or to speak until I say so."

"Okay, Rebecca, but I have to tell you, I'm getting that tingling feeling on the back of my neck as though I'm about to

O'Malley's Cottage
Page 311

become part of an Alfred Hitchcock movie."

"Don't be so silly, we have to learn to trust each other, Mr. Rivers. I'm going to walk around this house from room to room and see if I can feel the presence of the great O'Malley himself. Maybe he will come to me and tell me what my destiny is, meanwhile you wait right here until I get back. Then I am going to tell you what my final decision is, Mr. Rivers."

"Just don't open the kitchen drawers, the carving knives are in one of them," Chuck joked, closing his eyes as she had requested.

Rebecca sat down at the harvest table and let her mind wander. She soon forgot that Chuck was sitting in the kitchen with her, it was as though it was O'Malley himself. She walked up behind O'Malley's chair and felt the back of it, rubbing her hands across the fabric. Then she placed her hands on Chuck's broad shoulders and closed her eyes, trying to open up her mind to whatever good feelings remained inside the farmhouse, or had they all disappeared with O'Malley and Donna, leaving behind a cold and empty shell.

She toured the house from the basement up to the attic, going into every room and lingering for a while in each one. All the time Chuck Rivers sat in O'Malley's armchair with his eyes closed, trusting his instincts that Rebecca was indeed a good person, wavering on occasion, but holding steadfast to the agreement.

As Rebecca began slowly to descend the stairs, feeling disappointed that the house no longer felt the same anymore and saddened that O'Malley had not come to her in her thoughts, she suddenly grabbed the staircase, almost losing her balance. She felt someone standing right next to her. For a moment she scared herself, thinking a spiritual presence was indeed beside her and then calmed herself with the more reasonable explanation that it was the warm air rising from downstairs that had wafted into her face.

O'Malley's Cottage

She turned around and walked back upstairs into Donna and Roger's bedroom. She poised at the door, drawn inside the room, but fearful to actually step into the bedroom. No matter how she tried to think rationally and logically, she felt O'Malley right there with her.

Rebecca didn't even remember entering the bedroom and sitting on what had been the O'Malley's bed, made up with the same duvet on it that she remembered. He was in the room with her, she could feel him, every nerve was on edge, her whole body tingling with a mixture of fear and excitement. He was guiding her through the house again, back into every room, down into the basement with its thick concrete walls and workbenches.

Suddenly the basement light flickered and went out. Rebecca stood alone in the darkness, the door swung shut behind her. She gasped, but the sense of panic that she was expecting to rise up within her, never came. She felt at peace. She could never adequately explain it to anyone afterwards. She had no recollection of how she had got from, one minute sitting on the bed in O'Malley's bedroom, to standing in the middle of the pitch black basement and then back into the kitchen, sitting at the harvest table in exactly the same spot she had just been in. When she glanced over at the clock, she was shocked to find an hour had passed. Chuck was still sitting in O'Malley's chair with his eyes closed.

"Chuck, wake up. It's Rebecca. Wake up."

"Wow, have I been out that long. I'm sorry, I must have dozed right off, I apologize. You look happy for someone that's just spent an hour listening to a guy snore. I'm embarrassed."

"Don't be, I've had a wonderful time. I hope you don't mind sharing your new home with some of my friends for a couple of days, the cottage is bursting at the seams."

"You mean you'll rent it to me?"

"For a small fee, payable to Donna, that's all."

"That's very generous of you, Rebecca, I appreciate it, thank you."
"I'd like to get back to the cottage now. I want to hug my daughter some more. Here, I'll help you out of the chair."
Chuck held Rebecca's hands, surprised at her strength as she pulled him up from the seat, only to lose his footing and fall backwards into the chair, pulling Rebecca down on top of him.
"I'm so sorry, Rebecca, my foot must have slipped out from under me."
"Sure, Chuck." Rebecca's head was over his right shoulder and her breasts against his face.
An awkward silence followed as Rebecca repositioned herself against him, staring into his blue eyes, the color of a bright winter sky on a cloudless day, with the sun blazing down. Chuck looked very worried, concerned that Rebecca would think he'd done it on purpose.
"No, really, Rebecca, I'm sorry, it was an accident I swear," he blurted out. "I would never do anything to hurt you, ever, I'm not like that. God, I'm so sorry. Let me drive you back to the cottage right now before I make any more blunders."
Rebecca already knew it was an accident, but she was enjoying the moment, watching the man squirm. He would do anything for her and she knew it. *This time*, she said to herself, *I've found the right one.*
She couldn't keep a straight face any longer and began to smile, and then she kissed him very gently on the lips. At first he did not respond, she kissed him again, this time more passionately and Chuck Rivers held the woman in his arms that he had waited a life time to find and kissed Rebecca tenderly, like she had never been kissed before.
Rebecca reluctantly pulled herself away. The only person she wanted to hold now, was her daughter and Chuck understood that.
"I see you didn't slip that time getting up, Mr. Rivers?"

joked Rebecca. Chuck blushed. "You promise you'll never hurt me, Chuck? I don't think I could take anymore unhappiness." Rebecca saw warmth and a kindness in his eyes that portrayed a decent human being.

"Rebecca, we have a lifetime to get to know one another and for you to find out that I am a good man. If you decide that I'm not, well you're my landlady and you can kick me out anytime. Let's just take one day at a time."

"Emma coming home today has been the best thing that's ever happened to me and I'm praying that you are another best thing, but I'm scared to start another relationship. I don't know, maybe you've got me fooled, but everything seems so right about being with you, Chuck, it's scary."

"That's because it is right, Rebecca, and with time you'll come to know that more and more. My only weaknesses are country music, my guitar and horses, well they were my only weaknesses until you came along, and I gotta tell ya, you top 'em all. That reminds me, I brought my guitar with me, maybe I could sing you an old country song around the woodstove in your cottage."

"I'd like that, Mr. Rivers. Can you sing like Allan Jackson?"

"I sure can, ma'am. Some folk even think I look like him. I'm gonna sing that song by him about, *when I look in your soft green eyes,* in your case soft brown eyes, kind of like the eyes of a deer caught in the headlights, *when I see your delicate body revealed to me as you slip off your dress."*

"I love that song, but he doesn't sing about deer in headlights," Rebecca laughed. "I presume that's supposed to be a compliment about the deer I mean?"

"Well you do have the most beautiful brown eyes, Miss Rebecca."

O'Malley's Cottage

"Maybe down the road I'll reveal my delicate body to you as I slip off my dress, Chuck Rivers, but that won't be for some time. Come on take me home, you've got to be up early anyway to attend to the horses."

The party was in full swing when Rebecca and Chuck walked arm in arm into O'Malley's Cottage. Emma ran over and hugged her mother.

"You look happy, Mom. I missed you, I thought about you every day."

"I thought about you every second of every day, my precious. I must ask your opinion on something Emma. Would you mind if we rented Mr. Chuck Rivers here, the farm?"

Emma looked up into the big man's eyes.

"Just because you dress like a cowboy, don't mean you can ride like one. O'Malley told me that one. Can you ride a horse?"

"Yes, ma'am, but I'm always willing to learn something new if you've got something to teach me."

"Well, as you're new, would you like me to come over in the morning to give you a hand with the horses?"

"I'd like that very much, Emma, in fact I was thinking about buying some more horses for the farm so I could breed them, but I sure could do with someone coming along with me who's got a good eye for a good horse at the right price. I was hoping maybe you and your mom would like to join me in that venture. How about you ride Toby over in the morning? I tell you what. How about, as we've got all these folks here for a few days, let's you and me hitch up those Belgians right now and take everyone for a Christmas sleigh ride?"

"You mean you know how to do that?" Emma couldn't believe it.

"Yes, ma'am, I certainly do. Are you up for it?"

"You bet I am, I'll just go and get changed, don't go without me. I may as well take Toby home this evening so he can be with his horse friends. I'll be down in a minute. Can Lindsay come?"

"Sure, if that's okay with her folks." Chuck then addressed the guests. "When we get back from the sleigh ride folks, I hope you all can sing." He lifted up his guitar. Everyone clapped and cheered.

Rebecca squeezed his hand. "My daughter adores you already, Chuck, don't break her heart either."

"No fear of that happening, Rebecca. Did you want to come? Heck, I didn't even ask if it was okay for Emma to come, it is, isn't it?"

"I'll wait here with our guests and of course Emma can go, it's the first time she has never asked my permission. I guess she's becoming Miss Independent, I'll have to keep an eye on that. With my daughter, horses come before anything else, rather like you I think."

"No, Rebecca, there's a pecking order. You will always, always, come first, no matter what, then Emma, my Dad and then the horses."

"You just want me to wear that dress don't you, Mr. Rivers."

Rebecca smiled and Chuck looked down at her with a big grin.

"What dress is that, Rebecca?" Rachael teased. "Mr. Rivers, I do believe you're blushing, yes, you're turning positively crimson."

"Rachael, leave the man alone, he said he was going to buy me a new dress for a very special occasion that's all, he's just shy about buying a woman clothes."

* * *

Chuck could not believe how professional Emma was at hitching up the Belgians to the sleigh. The only thing he provided was the muscle power to lift this and push that, as Emma commanded. Toby was happy to be back with his friends and was like his old self again.

Rebecca kept an eye out for the team that was hauling the sleigh. She could see them trotting across the field, Emma with the reins, Chuck and Lindsay on either side of her. When they arrived, Emma and Chuck took turns at taking everyone for a Christmas sleigh ride across the fields. Afterwards Chuck told Emma that he would take the team back and clean them up, she could stay with her mom. Emma wouldn't hear of it. "You and me and my mom are a team now, Chuck, so I'm helping you." He gave her a big smile. He'd never felt so happy in his whole life.

* * *

By the time the horses were put away and given sweet grain for their efforts, it was dark outside. Back in the kitchen at O'Malley's Cottage, Chuck got out his guitar and sang his repertoire of country songs. The whole household listened spellbound to his beautiful voice. When he finished singing Allan Jackson's song about the dress, Rachael couldn't help but shout out, "Oh, that dress, Mr. Rivers," making Chuck blush again.

Late in the evening, Chuck took his father aside and held the old man to him, enveloping the smaller man inside his massive body.

"Thank you, Dad, for everything. I want you to know how much I love and appreciate you, and now maybe you won't have to hide out in the middle of nowhere to write, you can do it at the farm."

"I intend to, son. This has been a rich and rewarding experience for me, but I'm sure glad I've come to the end of it now. Go on, enjoy yourself and you make sure you treat that woman like gold. Treasure her and bring sunshine into her life every single day. There's not a man on this planet that wouldn't want to be in your shoes right now and I'm not ashamed to say, I'm one of them."

Rebecca came over and whisked the old man away for a dance, her favorite Norah Jones song was playing, *Come away with me*.

A whole new atmosphere descended over O'Malley's Farm and O'Malley's Cottage, reuniting them as one happy place, just as they used to be when the O'Malleys owned the two properties. It was as if O'Malley himself had returned, but then, both Emma and Rebecca already knew that he had.

End

ABOUT THE AUTHOR

Ron was born in Brighton, England and has worked in the U.K. and Canada for over thirty years as a police officer. He has extensive international travel experience while working with the British Merchant Navy as a navigator, where he travelled extensively in the Middle East and throughout Europe.

He is an avid outdoorsman, enjoying wilderness camping throughout the year. With a love of nature, he also paints with watercolors.

Ron has always had a passion for writing which started in his early years. He enjoys writing in various genres, both adult and children's fiction. He continues to write from his home in Ontario, Canada.

NOTE FROM THE PUBLISHER:

Thank you for purchasing and reading this Books We Love eBook. We hope you have enjoyed your reading experience. Books We Love and the author would very much appreciate you returning to the online retailer where you purchased this book and leaving a review for the author.
Best Regards and Happy Reading, Jamie and Jude

Books We Love and Spice We Love
The Beverly Hills Boutique of eBook publishers.
Vintage and New from award winning authors.
Top quality books loved by readers,
Romance, Mystery, Fantasy, Young Adult

Made in the USA
Charleston, SC
25 April 2012